just like beauty

LISA LERNER

just like
beauty

picador
farrar, straus and giroux
new york

www.picadorusa.com

Picador ® is a U.S. registered trademark and is used by Farrar, Straus and Giroux under license from Pan Books Limited.

For information on Picador Reading Group Guides, as well as ordering, please contact the Trade Marketing department at St. Martin's Press.
Phone: 1-800-221-7945 extension 763
Fax: 212-677-7456
E-mail: trademarketing@stmartins.com

Library of Congress Cataloging-in-Publication Data

Lerner, Lisa
    Just like beauty / Lisa Lerner.
        p. cm.
    ISBN 0-312-42178-8
    1. Teenage girls—Fiction. 2. Suburban life—Fiction. 3. Dystopias—Fiction. I. Title.

PS3612.E39 J97 2002
813'.6—dc21   2001033479

First published in the United States by Farrar, Straus and Giroux

First Picador Edition: January 2003

10 9 8 7 6 5 4 3 2 1

To my mother, Marilyn Rubin Lerner,

my father, Harold Lerner,

and my sister, Jamie Lerner Gabriel

just like beauty

Prologue

"Pageant. P-A-G-E-A-N-T. Pageant."

You are on screen. Coughing. You are trying to spell the seven-letter word but you cough and cough until the word gets stuck in your throat, each letter a frozen square of poison. Cut to you as an X ray: what a mess. The letters are melting from your involuntary body heat; they are dripping slowly down into your stomach and intestines (large and small), swirling through the crinkly tube of your colon. Survival looks bad. It's a great screen moment, full of exquisite possibility: you, triumphantly shitting poison, beating the odds, a miraculous winner, your town's Feminine Woman of Conscience.

Or this: no more stomach, no more intestines, no more crinkly colon—no more you—nothing but a skull-sized mushroom cloud.

On this day of fickle weather, like so many others in quiet, security-patrolled neighborhoods just like mine all over the country, I am in training. Down in the family nook with my mother and the blow-up dummy, I am learning to make out. While I endure the fat shrieks of Maria Callas overreacting in *La Sonnambula* instead of my new Mystic Fangs release, my mother is teaching me how to use my tongue. The opera swoops to the family nook carpet like dying birds. But my mother's lips glow like ripe plums, her fresh manicure sparkles. When a palm checks my facial position, I want to fasten it there.

Inevitably, my failures and her agitation bring on the lecture: lick first along the upper and then the lower lip to a count of twenty, touch just the point of the tongue to the point of the dummy's, with flickers like the scarlet ribbon that darts out of the mouth of a snake. We go over and over the flicking part. I mash my mouth down on the dummy's surprised-looking lips, but my tongue is getting tired. My mother's hot, soft hand grabs me by the chin and I get the warning: a girl's tongue can never tire, it is her second most important muscle.

"Edie, how many times do I have to tell you to kiss with your head tilted?" she sighs. "Do you think all the other mothers have to go over and over something this basic?"

"Hell if I know," I mutter, although secretly I am afraid. I don't like to make her mad and I never mean to do it.

She smooths her hair with nervous fingers. "Edie," she says darkly.

"Yeah, yeah." It's during these sessions that I count the days until I am old enough to escape to submarine school in the Naval Academy, my eye tight against the cool metal of a periscope, my voice ringing with the command to *Fire!* again and again as torpedoes burst out and thrill through the deep blue sea. My mother's plummy lips open close enough to blast me with a whiff of the egg salad she had for lunch. Maria Callas trills out a final alarm.

I edge away from my mother's correcting touch, no hope of sweetness left today. Outside, the sun sinks below the rise of tired autumn grass as we move on to chest work. My mother nags me to tickle the dummy's stomach at the shore of his scratchy polyacrylic pubic hair, to squeeze his flat, pale nipples, to put some oomph into my strokes.

"Not everyone knows that men like to have some nipple play, too," she says, making her eyes wide with truth. "Lucky for you your father once had a libido way back when."

Any mother can teach her daughter how to get a penis to stand straight enough to hang a hat, but it is hints like this one, my mother assures me, that will earn me big points during the Electric Polyrubber Man event and help me beat the forty-nine other contestants to win that multimillion-dollar headdress when, in just seven and a half months, I am crowned Queen.

Of course, we don't know if I will be able to compete next spring, because while the average ten-year-old is already bikini waxing and having her C cups checked for breast cancer, I'm pushing fifteen and still haven't menstruated; but my mother is determined that I will bleed this year, cheerily shit-sure that I will compete at the age of fourteen just as she did in the Miss Deansville Pageant, thirty difficult and remorse-filled years ago.

When I was younger and openly longed to compete, I told her that if I ever got my period I was gonna lead my own parade right down the middle of our street, crazy with those huge jet-fueled balloons of Mr. Broccoli Face and grasshoppers that need about twenty muscled robots each to hold their strings and keep them from flying off, and a stream of pepped-up hatchet twirlers in mink bathing suits, smiling like hell and marching so hard their knees would practically crash into heaven. My mother sighed. "I wish you wouldn't say hell," she said. "It's grounds for instant disqualification if the judges hear you swear."

The different events in Pageant are posted in the family nook on a length of butcher paper the size of a hippo, next to the computerized blackboard my mother uses to diagram strategies for manipulating Electric Polyrubber Man's sexual organs. No one knows what he will look like. The robot is being made in a factory in Belgium and will be shipped over in a triple-locked crate; two guards will bring him by armored truck to Pageant's secret vault a week before. There was talk about using a real man instead of a machine, but the Rules Committee fought it on moral grounds—Rule #12, the Sexual Conduct Rule: Contestants may not have familiar relations with anybody except their blow-up dummies.

The secrecy surrounding Electric Polyrubber Man's body is critical, according to the Committee; they want to see how smoothly we girls can handle variants. Note the devastation during Preliminaries: Molly Finnigan, disqualified because she'd profaned her blow-up dummy's lacking testicle; Abigail Nesmith, unable to relax her throat enough during essential maneuvers, now spending her disqualified time in the Institute for Antidepressant Intolerants.

Besides Electric Polyrubber Man, the events in Pageant are: Freestyle Walking (flats allowed since a bad accident during Preliminaries in Elko, Nevada), Large Number Estimation, Needlework Odyssey (it's rumored that pom-pom trim will score highest), Poise and Cookery, Better Person Skills, Reflections on Hygiene, Mystery Powders (recently expanded to include liquids, and a controversial category because one Sally Monticello went temporarily blind during Preliminaries in Howardsville, Arkansas: she took off her safety goggles for a mascara check and got sodium fluoroacetate in her eyes), Drug-Addict Prevention Bee (a new event after overdosing hit summer camps), Juggling, Hair Construction, Double Dutch Jump Rope, Self-Expression through Memorization, Safety, Music and Dance, and Sacrificial Rabbit Raising.

Next to the blackboard on a special pedestal is the royal purple Feminine Woman of Conscience Pageant Handbook; its gold-embossed daisies greet me most every day, at three o'clock during the week after school and ten o'clock in the morning on weekends. The first thing my mother likes to do is read aloud from the rules. Besides Rule #2, the Rule of Menstruation, Rules #5 and #6, the Height and Weight rules, are making her crazy. I'm not five feet tall yet, and I still haven't reached 100 pounds, and while her finger traces along the type and her lips linger on each syllable, making her own exclamation marks where there's only a period, she glances up every other line, noting each swallow of my regulation eight-ounce protein milkshake with its three sawdusty tablespoons of Jimmy Dubois's bodybuilding powder, two raw eggs, and Just Like Heavy Cream instead of milk. We fight over the flavor because she says the chocolate will give me pimples, but I've been winning this one since I puked up the Just Like Strawberry syrup all over the new Just Like Sheepskin carpet.

After she reads a few hundred rules aloud to get us pumped, she starts in with the training guidelines. Today she wore out the section on exercise; I've lost a pound since yesterday and she's convinced that I am not doing my part to build muscle.

"Muscle weighs more than fat, as I have said umpteen times to deaf ears," she complains, and then reads aloud from the Handbook. "The ancient Egyptian water carrier was able to balance more than 100 pounds on her head and still keep her back straight and her chin tilted with elegant poise. It was daily practice and proper usage of the neck and spine that enabled her to go forth in her task without failure or humiliation. It is the daily practice of calisthenics that will bring health and energy to the blood circulating throughout your own developing body. Without a regular bodybuilding routine, your form will cease to attract positive attention, will in fact become an object of ridicule and revulsion in the eyes of the opposite sex." My mother closes the book. "Twenty-five push-ups."

"Right now? I'm not done with my milkshake."

"Please."

She's been ordering pamphlets from the government, subscribing to newsgroups on the Web. Several file cabinets in the family nook are filled with motivational literature: manuals of nutrient analysis, hints from retired Olympic athletes, top-secret army drills. I might be impressed by her drive if it wasn't kind of insulting. Has she forgotten how high I scored in Preliminaries? I ranked in the top ten percent of the whole country (and would have been even higher, if not for that stupid blow-up dummy). Yet ever since training began, it seems I can't do anything quite right. Once I was her adorable string bean. Now my brown hair is too limp, and I have a cowlick and an uneven hairline; she will never be able to make a decent construction without the use of hairpieces.

My mother's hair is thick as the blackstrap molasses she forces me to swallow to ward off anemia, and eighty-six times as shiny. With her zesty, overripe looks, she is unbeatably female. Her arms and legs curve in ways that make everyone around her look as if they've been put together by mistake. She walks in a planned, switching way, throwing in a dolphin-smooth undulation every fifteen steps. I tried imitating it a few weeks ago, watching myself in the full-length mirror in her bedroom when she was out, knowing that soon we will start training for Freestyle Walking and I'd better get the rhythm down. I started at the far wall and moved my reflection along her carpet. I held a bottle of her favorite cologne but I didn't open it, not even to smell it. I just wanted to be holding it. My body looked as if the top half was fighting everything below the waist, all stiff knobby hips and needle arms lost in space. It seemed like a good time to crawl under her bed and masturbate, and that's what I did until my hand got a cramp.

Of course I had to get corrective eye surgery, even though I want to wear glasses; she thinks they make me look like an insect. She'd like to get my nose fixed too, because it's blobby, but cosmetic surgery is against Pageant rules for some of us; after the malpractice suit of Girl Scout Troop 76—may they rest in peace—the limit is three procedures, girls over fifteen only. Unofficially, Feminine Woman of Conscience has to be a knockout. My mother coaxes me to accept her ministerings of Really Red

Karma Gel and honey-flavored Rebirth lipstick, and I try not to feel the futility of it all when I see my face in the mirror.

All over the nation, troubled girls are making it into the news: rich girls Buffy Ann Munson and Tanya Jones, the two wackos who tried to assassinate the president; that mystery girl, Lily Gates, who disguises herself as a nun and sets fire to Just Like Meat Planet restaurants; the white-faced comatose drug-overdose victim Penelope Samuels, whose parents want her to die with dignity. Here in our house, all heartbeats depend on whether I use liquid or solid Sin Concealer to hide the dark rings under my eyes. This is the story without an end; everyone else's problems go away as soon as my mother folds up the newspaper and puts it in the trash. I could take some comfort in the fact that all the other girls entered in Deansville's Pageant are squirming under six cubic tons of pressure, too, but I don't. I'm all smiles for the rest of the day when I see some mother slapping her normal-sized daughter's face in the cookie aisle at Grocery Town and shouting, "How did I ever give birth to such a fatso?" But it doesn't make me happy when my mother smirks at the ones who are worse than no competition: the pock-marked, pigeon-toed, frizzy-haired ones. I won't give her the satisfaction; and I'm as quiet as death about the fact that I'd like to spin seven china plates on sticks and identify the chemical elements that make up a smoking phosphorescent compound and watch the other contestants' faces fall down to their ankle socks. And sure, I'd like to estimate the square root of nineteen billion and five and see the judges' eyebrows rise toward the roof of Deansville's brand-new Franklin Echo Dome. I can memorize my ass off, too: give me the Hammurabi Code at noon and by dinner I'll know it upside down and backwards with my eyes shut and my feet in a vat of boiling potassium dichromate. I want to win. More than she knows, and I have my own reasons. It's Electric Polyrubber Man that's giving me dry heaves. I keep slapping my forehead, cursing my rotten luck: Why does this event have to be worth the mother-lode 100 points? Why is it that I'd rather crawl inside the mouth of *Tyrannosaurus rex* than touch my tongue to the blow-up dummy's upper lip? Why can't I make out?

I raise myself up off my knees and rub my sore pecs in time to see a flash of caramel-colored limbs through one of the family nook's high windows. I allow myself a tiny sigh of self-pity. If only those back-flipping knees had never appeared in our neighborhood, never graced my school, my mall, my town, the house across the street.

They belong to Lana Grimaldi, Italian gymnastics queen and professional floogie smoker from the Bronx, the most beautiful girl I have ever met. Lana Grimaldi: girl of long reedy hands that trail covetously across the hood of her father's prized Triumph TR3, that sweep the bangs off her forehead, pluck dandelions (the very ones that brighten and dishonor the perfect green of our front yards) for her Just Like Coke bottle bouquets. Those hands of hers rub summer rain on her bare tan arms, crumble sticky buds of mooch into a rolling paper, zip up her jeans after a secret pee in the topiary; the bones and fingernails of those hands are a wonder. One day those hands will rest against my face, my neck. They will slip down inside my shirt, glide effortlessly through skin and buzzing nerves, wiggle their way between my ribs and grab my heart.

I live off the scraps of her: Lana, slamming the screen door, roller-pole-vaulting at high speed down our street and out of sight; Lana, twirling cartwheels in the fields behind the convent and hollering obscenities at the top of her voice; Lana, face pale, smoking Bull's Eye cigars up at the reservoir, telling me what a sonofabitch her father is, underneath his restaurant smile. Best of all, Lana, alone on that Friday night, lying faceup on the roof of the Sweeneys' tool shed next door, staring at the black-leafed box elders and smiling when she saw me looking. That was the night she grabbed my hand to help me up, my heart knocking like hell in my chest. Later, after she'd actually taken me into the warm web of her confidences, she lit up another floogie and held my face to receive the smoke she blew straight into my rosy lungs. Her lips granted me the sweet, dirty air, and I took all of it.

Her hands were what made me finally see it. Those hands can corner the world, while I just stand by open-mouthed and dizzy. Those ten restless fingers waved at me one day and seemed to switch on an infinite number of stars inside my body, lighting me up like the dawn of the world, firing a torpedo message straight to my brain that said no way will you be one iota convincing as you try to raise Electric Polyrubber Man's penis, even though he is only a robot with cold, computerized responses, even though you are not required or even allowed to go all the way and pop your cherry, no way can you survive his synthetic beard burn on your cheeks as you perform your snaky tongue moves in his polystroob mouth. It's Lana Grimaldi's smart-aleck tongue you want to suck like your life depends on it, and bet your ass there's no multimillion-dollar headdress in the world you're going to win for wanting that.

1

A month after the Amazing Mister Fezundo willed himself to burst into flames, I have a headache and tell my mother maybe it's a brain tumor like Benny Gold's, but all she can say is, "Oh no, Edie. I'm expecting my period, and I'm not in the mood." Her sentence ends on a panicked note and I can feel the possibility of a good day collapsing inside her, how by mid-afternoon, even as she stands in the kitchen thermoconverting Just Like Beans, she will be wishing she could be traded in for her own improved substitute, a Just Like Lorraine. If only that were possible: just like her but not her at all.

The sound track at breakfast is one long, tight-lipped sigh. I crunch quietly, afraid to let my decibels blend in with hers. We are both on edge because Alice Jones, my sacrificial rabbit, is behaving strangely, might even be having a life-threatening reaction to her meds, and short of an emergency phone conversation with Mrs. Vrick, the rabbit expert, and administering two injections of Bun-Be-Calm, there is nothing more we can do but wait and see.

After the second injection, Alice Jones's floppy ears seemed to droop even longer; she's an English Lop and if I were to enter her in a professional rabbit raisers' rabbit show, her twenty-six-inch ears would be better than a hand job to those judges. I'm probably going to feel terrible when I have to skin her to make my fur muff at Pageant. It's the ultimate insult after all her hard hours of practicing the official routines, to be turned into a fashion accessory. But we girls are expected to know how to dominate and then kill animals, and the sacrifice is supposed to be a sign of maturity. Plus, a fur muff will last forever if you care for it right.

My father stares at his breakfast without eating. He has his own little problem. One of the topiary technicians at work gouged the throat of the company president with a pruning hook and then bombed a couple of greenhouses. Dad's rodent features are puffy today, and behind his glasses his blue eyes look like someone's airbrushed even more of the color out. He's got three gravy-colored moles on his cheek. Were they always there? Right now they are interfering with my digestion. I also notice his neck seems fatter, and as usual he has missed whole strips of stubble during his shave. If he were smiling, which he definitely is not, his teeth would appear too tiny for his face. Mouse teeth. Before I was born, he was so handsome no one noticed that his eyebrows were nearly nonexistent. His lips look exactly like a little girl's.

Dad and I. We've never had that much to say to each other. He's on the road a lot, peddling topiary. When I was smaller, he'd read the catalogue to me, teaching me the names of trees. When the Adventure Forest came to town, he'd volunteer to drive me there so he could stand motionless at the observation window as I bungeed down the redwoods, and even now sometimes he brings me things from his trips, like a V-release about the Amazing Mister Fezundo's paranormal childhood in Bakersville, California, or once a fist-sized ceramic frog for Valentine's Day. "Kiss it," he joked. "It'll turn into a prince." But his face looked like he'd just swallowed hexane, and later I found out that my mother had told him to say it. He seems happiest when he's wearing that awful vest with fifty pockets as he heads off to net some wings.

Battus philenor, Papilio troilus, Pieris rapae, Everes comyntas. He keeps his ever-growing collection on metal-lyte shelving next to his workbench, each butterfly and moth labeled and carefully arranged on black or white velveteenite, the names written in his girlish handwriting. What does he think about, on those summer days in the high grass, catching powdery wings in his net, with his wife at home glaring unfucked into her magazines, his daughter listening to the pages turn?

He looks at the clock, then raises his cup and sips. His little-girl lips come together in a prim line. "Cold."

"You want me to heat it?" My mother sighs again, and holds open the door to the thermurderator.

"I suppose." He hands her his cup, avoiding any skin-to-skin contact, although it seems to me that one touch would cheer them both up.

She sighs.

It drives her mad, but now he turns on the morning news. He has to hear the API, the Air Pollution Index.

"Great. Another breakfast ruined."

"I have to find out, Lorraine, because it affects the trees," he grouses, looking almost unhappy enough to cry.

"Why can't you just wait to read it after breakfast on your screen downstairs?"

"Because you know I like to hear it while I eat. And I've got to prepare for my Integrated Pest Management meeting at nine, so there won't be any after breakfast."

"Heaven forbid I should obstruct humanity's ongoing fight against pests."

"It's my job. Why do you have to give me a hard time about it?"

"I'm not," she says without looking at him. "Of course I'm thrilled having a basement full of dead butterflies."

"One thing has nothing to do with the other." Miserably, he clicks down the volume on the news.

"Untrue. Dead butterflies have everything to do with why a peaceful family breakfast around here is an impossible dream."

"I only want to hear the API, Lorraine," he sighs, fiddling with the moles on his cheek. "It's five minutes. Can you sacrifice five minutes?"

A forkful of eggs spears the air dangerously close to my father's head as she leans toward him over the table. "I can sacrifice a lifetime. I think I've made that clear." The fork's handle stays rigid between her beautiful fingers just long enough for my father to edge his chair away, then retreats back to her plate with a clang.

Outside, the streets are quiet except for the Insecticide Hut truck making its own pest-management rounds; the fish-faced guard inside his pale pink security patrol station at the entrance to our neighborhood is probably sleeping, dreaming about a better job than waiting for some hysterical nut to call him up and complain that alien grasshoppers have landed in the backyard birdbath. Which is what happened last week when creaky Mr. Pullings drank too much Mondo Surge. Everyone at the neighborhood association meeting had a good chuckle over it according to my mother, even Pullings was laughing until he lost control of his bladder.

The simfab Swiss chalet clock ticks without sound until the little Swiss boy pops out, the floor smells of sweet chemicals, the curtains my mother appliquéd hang stiffly at the windows, the hardware of the sink gleams from her religious polishing. Nobody says anything during the API report—very bad news for Rice County, but our county, Slerkimer, reports only mild increases in nitrogen oxides and sulfur compounds. A low API is always good for me, the allergic reaction queen. When it ends, my father switches it off, silently pushes away from the table, and exits. My mother tilts her head back and repeatedly rubs her cheeks, a shaky smile between her hands. "I knew he was going to do that. I had a premonition."

"Mom, please." When she talks like this, my heart grows soft for all the hatchet men locked up in Tenner State Prison. "I was born with an ESP," she is always whispering to people. "I wish it weren't so. It's stressful having all that extra power."

"I knew that technician was trouble, too," she says to his empty chair. "I dreamt those greenhouses would be destroyed, and when I woke up I told your father he should do something. Even after Petey, he still refuses to believe."

Way back before Alice Jones was in our lives, when I was just a kid, our cocker spaniel Petey got lost. By the second day, I cried so hard I threw up. Suddenly, my mother's ESP kicked in, and alone and coatless she drove out to the Mohawk Canal. It was dark and she forgot to take a flashlight, but she tramped bravely along the rocky paths in her heels, calling for Petey until she heard his yelp and he came limping toward her. He smelled like he'd been rolling in dead fish, but my mother scooped him right up, and when she walked through the kitchen door holding him in her arms, I hardly knew what surprised me more, the sight of Petey or the blood and dirt all over her dress. I practically knocked her down with my hug, and Petey had no luck getting his furry body between us.

I've been toying with my response time. "It was pretty amazing that you knew where to find him."

"Damn right I was amazing." Her voice is soft, melodic.

"Yeah."

"Your father thought I was pretty amazing once upon a time. Before he went into male menopause or wherever it is he's gone."

"Yeah."

"It's important for me to tell you these things, Edie, even though you don't like to hear them. You have to be prepared for what's to come."

"Yeah."

"Baby." Her lovely face flushes. I push away from the table and carry my dish to the sink. Behind me, I hear her say, "I want the best for you. More than the best. You know I love you more than anything in this world." I know that she means it. She works hard to train me; down in the family nook her antiperspirant struggles to do its job against her fluids every time she scissors the blow-up dummy's hips between her thighs. Everything she does is for my benefit, to insure my chance of ending up somewhere better than she did; with all her creative energy and intelligence, she could have been a force of great change in the world. She wanted to accomplish so much, but there was always some bad break: the prejudiced pageant judges, her near-death brush with breast cancer, the long struggle to stay pregnant, and then the postpartum depression; a thousand lottery tickets purchased, and all the numbers off by one.

Foolishly, I turn, and as her arms reach out to gather me in an embrace, a glass of Natural Prune-n-Low spills across my empty placemat.

"Sorry, hon. None got on your pj's, did it?"

"No, Mom. It's okay."

Now her fist crams my father's leftover breakfast into the trash pulverizer. "These new hormone meds are murdering my skin. Mark my words, a few years of Mymonolucoval and I'll have no face left whatsoever." She calls up to the ceiling, "Damned from the minute go! That's the real truth about women." Then she bumps into a kitchen chair, hard, and a phantom ache travels through my own leg.

"I wasn't done with that." My father reenters the kitchen.

"Well, next time say something instead of just storming out of a room."

"I went to the bathroom." His face is pale. Another emergency visit to the Gastroenterology Salon would just ice his cake.

She elbows him in the ribs and steps on his toe. Then she points her chin at both of us and we watch it tremble, the rims of her eyes reddening in their premenstrual focus on the life she's been denied, she of all that extra power, her inner eye once again ticking off the scenes of indignity and suffering. She's thinking perhaps of how different things might be if only she hadn't gotten stuck in a town where the height of fashion was a Christmas angel sweatshirt and the bells of Our Lady of Gentle Welcome dong the first eight bars of "Taking a Chance on Love" twenty-four times a day practically in her own backyard. It doesn't help either that several Virtue Club officials have quietly informed her that since she isn't currently observant of her faith, it might be a good idea to think about changing her last name to something less obviously ethnic; after all, there has been a resurgence of anti-Semitic incidents in some of the neighboring counties and she has me, a probable Pageant contestant, to consider.

Cabinets are slammed open and a loaf of sliced Just Like Bread is suddenly airborne. She whirls around to face us. "You want breakfast? Find me a blowtorch!"

In the Poise and Cookery event, fifty points go to the girl who can flip perfect pancakes while reciting protocol for entertaining international government officials. If she can do it while being attacked by a swarm of mosquitoes, she wins the event's medal.

The kitchen floor vibrates as my mother stamps out of the room.

"I had a dream you were wearing that orange dress from Palmer's," she calls out from her bedroom. "All the neighbors came over and gave you a standing ovation. You had the head-dress topping your hair construction and everyone was cheering. And sure enough, in the newspaper this morning there's an article about Franklin Echo's private art collection. That head-dress is over three thousand years old, and you know what it's worth. So I think you should put on the dress."

She claims padded shoulders are on the return and all the designer rage; the truth is this dress takes her right back to the year of the Slerkimer County Fertilizer Association Pageant when she was crowned Mulch Queen. Not exactly the prestige of being crowned Miss Deansville, but it was her one first-place win, and when she saw this dress on the rack at Palmer's she nearly wept for the memory of parading around a dung-scented pasture. Bubbeh had said she only won because Zadeh bribed the judges with free jugs of DDT, though, and so for two years my mother the Mulch Queen had refused to speak to either of her parents.

"It's a little big in the waist, but never mind about that. I'll get it tailored. That dream is an omen."

Dreams. Each night while I am standing on the blue and white seashell throw rug, squeezing an inch of intestinal red gel onto my toothbrush, like the Amazing Mister Fezundo I start willing myself; it's my private project, to will myself unconscious, so far gone I am certain not to dream. I've collected some theories about how it may be done, but so far I can't prove any. Some nights I will myself to be like Biggy, the fire-proof rag doll that I still keep in bed with me, even though I don't need her to protect me anymore—the smiling Just Like Meat Planet astronaut with burning chains and stale breath hasn't come through my wall at night to steal my soul in months. Sometimes it works; my arms and legs and eventually my stomach relax into the sheets, and deep down in my muscles my skeleton dissolves into white trails of baby powder. The octopus grip on my brain loosens and everything goes quiet for a while. I can forget how much the Sacrificial Rabbit event is worth in Pageant's point scheme, can stop mentally juggling a trio of kitchen chairs, and when I do sleep, my mind is a pure, deep-black blank.

On a lucky night, I'll manage to fall asleep despite Jupiter's dot of silver fire peeking through the gap in the curtains, but even then I may dream splashy, Vegas-like productions of fantastic gore. Last night I was a glamorous butcher, stashing my victims' breasts and thighs and livers in my mother's clothes flattener. Everything was lit up and sparkling. A twenty-piece orchestra was swinging. I wiped my bloody hands on the front of my silver evening gown and started to dance. Our basement laundry room was the Caesar's Palace of basement laundry rooms. My mother's heels tap-tapped down the stairs. A man signaled me to get off the stage. My mother had found out what I'd done and she was going to ground me. After dreams like this, the rotten air from Deansville Middle School doesn't wait for me to leave home, it has already blown out of the school and up the hill into my bedroom, ready to press against my clammy body as soon as I wake.

Down the hall my mother was dreaming too, her bat-shaped eye mask tight across her face, but I am not the star of her dreams anymore. "If only I'd tried to have another child after I managed to have you," she's gotten in the habit of saying, the faint lines around her mouth growing sharper. This morning she says, "If I'd had another girl, I think she'd be taller. All I could eat were tortillas, the whole time I was pregnant with you. I think that's why you turned out so small. Of course, after all those miscarriages, it's a miracle you turned out at all."

She lays the dress on my bed, a dress she herself would love to be able to squeeze into, her large curves held firm and eye-popping as she sweeps down some pageant runway. It is supposed to change everything, to make me taller, maybe even smarter; it is supposed to save my mother from turning into a tortilla under the eighteen wheels of an airbrushed semi, this dress that will make me look like a sawed-off carrot.

"I figured it out!" she says. "It's the color of my old boroonga contest dress! I was just thinking about Hector the other day. I saw a man at Grocery Town with the exact same eyelashes. God, Hector was sensitive." She was in Cancún on her honeymoon when she met Hector the bearded dance instructor at the Como Esta Hotel. "He was the first person to tell me what a fantastic mover I am, you know that? He looked at me through those long Latin eyelashes and told me that my body moved like silken wind, and suddenly all those years of modern dance lessons paid off. He got down on his hands and knees and literally begged with tears in his eyes for me to be his boroonga partner."

In my head I chime along with the rest of the story: even though she was very busy tanning she made time to practice, and they ended up winning first prize in the citywide boroonga contest. (My father, the other honeymooner, remembers nothing about it.) When she finishes talking, she strikes a boroonga pose and for a moment tears burn my sinuses. To see her dance is to know why music was invented. After I learned to walk, she taught me to be her boroonga partner, but we don't do it anymore because it's not appropriate Music and Dance material.

After she leaves I yell, "That orange is too bright. Bright colors don't look good on me." The truth is, I don't want Lana to see me wearing a dress. My calves are the same bony width as my ankles; my kneecaps are set wrong, turned in as if they've been slapped. Dresses make me nervous, like some horned insect will buzz up there; my body can't move right in a dress, or at least not this dress, with its fuss of ruffles down the front. I stand over my bed and feel the orange glare burn my face. Instinctively, my hand yanks the dress down to the carpet where Alice Jones huddles in her enigmatic misery. "Carrot," I joke lamely. "Come on, *eat the carrot*." The rabbit's nose twitches beneath her clouded eyes. This morning's freak behavior aside, Alice Jones is a genius; even Mrs. Vrick cannot believe how quickly she is learning the routines. If her current disorientation lasts and we have to start over with a brand-new rabbit, it will be a very serious disadvantage. I stroke her ears and whisper twenty-three healing suggestions, but the only thing Alice Jones seems to be responding to is a private behavior-modified hell.

After my shower, my mother taps for me to unlock the door, and I cover myself with a towel and let her in. I flush. I don't like my mother to see my skin with water on it. In fact, I don't care to have my mother see any of what I see in the mirror: my pointy, sallow-skinned face with eyes that show doubt too easily, the big teeth like hers just barely contained by my father's too-small lips.

"Make sure you use the head wringer to dry your hair. All I need is for you to trigger an allergic reaction by walking around with a wet head all day."

I'm about to argue that I don't have time for head wringers when from the window I see the Grimaldis' gigantic, eight-door miniwagon pull into their driveway. The sky is a creamy, dream-date blue. Immediately, I snap into high gear. She's back!

"Are you listening?"

"Yes! All right. Okay. All right." The sunlight breaks on the miniwagon as the doors are flung open and the Grimaldi family emerges—first Lana, then her dad, and finally Mrs. Grimaldi.

My mother follows my gaze. "Well, it looks like the Grimaldis are done with their funeral already. I guess he has to get over to the restaurant before someone steals him blind." My mother shakes her head and rubs her upper arms as if she's cold. "I feel sorry for that family. That man has one hot temper."

"You don't even know them."

"I know what I hear."

"Gossip."

"Don't criticize, Edie. Especially not this morning. I have to make forty-five turnip bouquets for my Virtue Club meeting. You know Bubbeh Esther is coming soon and I've got to get the house shined up. I only pray those renovations on her house don't take more than a month. Which reminds me, if she asks, you're only training an hour a day, all right? And don't get her started about Alice Jones. All those chickens she chopped up on the farm and she rides me about one measly rabbit."

I keep quiet. I am watching Lana's legs make contact with her driveway as she gets out of the car, watching her mouth talk fast into her phone as she lugs a sack the size of a pony. She's wearing an antique army jacket I've never seen before, and that skirt she made out of Amazing Mister Fezundo promotional neckties. I'd give anything to be wearing a silver sharkskin suit, standing outside on our front lawn lighting two Skull cigarettes with a silver lighter, my father's ancient CD player hooked up, playing one of my mother's old Latin CDs. Lana and I could do the boroonga after we smoked.

Her head is down, sun beaming her long hair into a strip of rippling light.

"She looks like a witch, with all that hair in her face." Automatically, my mother pushes my hair away from my forehead, but as she reaches for the head wringer, I wriggle away. "And that outfit! What kind of a skirt is that?"

It's the skirt of a girl people need to be careful around. When I asked Lana if she was going to compete in Pageant, she lit a Skull, took a long drag, and with smoke shooting out her nostrils pulled down the neck of her T-shirt and put out the lit end right where her breast swelled above her heart. "If I want pain, I'll make my own, thank you very much," she said. "That Pageant is crap." The smell of her burnt flesh stayed in my nose for weeks.

"I'm going to be late." I scoot out the door toward my bedroom but it doesn't matter how quick I am this morning. My mother follows, a comb in hand, ready for action. She nearly trips over Alice Jones. "What's this dress doing on the floor? Alice Jones could doody on it. Who knows what she'll do today?"

"She won't. Her elimination habits are regulated by the Bun-Be-Calm. She'll go in her cage. She's not that far gone," I add doubtfully, struggling into the dress before I dash back to the bathroom. My mother's words are eaten by the motor of the head wringer as I keep my eyes peeled for Lana. It's impossible to know the digital minute when she'll leave the house for school, and so far this fall she has managed to slip out of our neighborhood unseen by me; the only time we walked together was the day Bobby Lomer was killed by the bricks that fell off the school. I watched our feet the whole way. Now the closest I come to her in the morning is when I catch sight of her dark hair floating through the weapon detector. Other times, I walk by her homeroom and her seat is all cold empty metal-lyte, even after the last buzzer.

The head wringer growls away at my ears while I watch Lana help her mother unload the rest of the miniwagon. Mr. Grimaldi walks around them, waving his arms. Then he grabs a large box away from Mrs. Grimaldi and throws it on the ground; the box opens and a jumble of clothes spill out. When Mrs. Grimaldi kneels down to put them back in the box, Mr. Grimaldi pulls at her hair to make her stand up. Lana tries to stop him, but he shakes her off and stomps into the house. Lana's skirt blows around her knees as she stands over the spilled clothes with her arm around her mother; she's wearing black riding boots and the thought of her riding horseback quickens my pulse.

I plow into my mother on my way to the kitchen and we have to grab each other to keep from falling. As quick as I can, I get my hands off her, my nose registering for the fiftieth time this morning how no matter what perfume she wears, it never seems to mask her own peppery smell. I grab onto a straight-backed chair to steady myself.

"You nearly knocked me over." A hand presses against her heart. Her dress is red, shocking, like a fresh cut.

"I'm going to be late."

"What about saying excuse me? It wouldn't kill you to try practicing some Better Person Skills once in a while."

"Right."

My fingers shake as I reach for my jacket. Across from us, Lana is wheeling the Smell-Brite recycling cubbies up the slick blacktop to the garage, talking into her phone the whole time. She's always on the phone. I've seen her quietly speaking into it while leaning with her forehead pressed against her locker, her eyes staring intently at the place on the floor where the linoleum is missing. When her Fun Sports class goes outside, I know she'll be in the outfield with her glove up to her ear.

At the kitchen table, my mother's shoulders slump, and she holds her head with both hands like she's trying to keep the two sides from falling apart. She rubs her temples and massages her neck, her eyes closed.

"Come here. I want to look at you."

"I'm late, Mom. Please let me by." Lana is heading toward the street.

"Let me just see that dress on you one more time before you go. Unzip your jacket for a minute."

"I don't have time!"

She starts to hand me her lonely look, then catches herself. "You're right. I'm sorry, Edie. Sometimes I forget what's best, I get so wrapped up in my goals." She is sitting erect now, her voice young, truthful. "It must be hard for you, me getting so carried away about things. I know I overreact. I know I'm diffi-cult. It's no picnic for your father, either. I'm sorry you have to see us fight. I can understand why you'd be mad."

Her face is asking, not begging, for me to forgive her, and I know that I could leave right now and she would understand. My fingers play with the zipper pull. "I'm not mad."

"You're a sweetheart, you really are." The corners of her mouth turn down in one of those sad-chin smiles. "Go on, sweeties. Never mind about the dress. I don't want you to be late."

"It'll only take a second, I don't mind." I part the jacket with my hands on my hips and smile hopefully; maybe she does think I'm pretty.

She smiles then, too, an all-the-way genuine show of pleasure, and I'm about to slip the jacket off my shoulders and twirl when her green eyes go large. "Alice Jones is down here."

The jacket's sides flop back down.

"Oh, Edie, I wish you'd lock her up when you're not in there. Especially today, when she's so unpredictable." She gets up from the table, defeated. "Well, go, or you'll be late. I'll get her."

Beyond the windowpane, Lana moves out of sight. I turn to see Alice Jones, listless no more, scampering a bit hysterically down the hall. "That's all right. I have time to help."

We follow the flashing cottontail upstairs to my mother's bedroom. Alice Jones bounds from the corner, does a quick circle around my feet—a sign of love or sexual interest, Mrs. Vrick has told us—and races by my mother, who kicks out a foot, accidentally catching the rabbit in her side. Alice Jones keeps going, hopping away under the bed's dust ruffle, her butt raised in salute.

"I didn't mean to kick her. Do you think she's all right?"

I shrug. When she was younger, my mother worked one summer as a shoe model; her feet are a perfect size six. I won't deny that I have gotten down on all fours and circled them. As a joke, of course.

A terrible thought: maybe I will *enjoy* killing Alice Jones.

"Mom?"

"Yes, baby?"

"Would you do it? Would you kill Alice Jones and skin her?"

Seated in a beam of Li'l Stained Glass pansy light spilling over the bedspread, my mother adjusts the hem of her dress. When she tightens the strap of her shoe, the long muscles of her calf stretch. Between her slightly parted legs, darkness. "If I were entered in Pageant, and I had to make a muff for one of the events, well, then yes, I guess I could."

"Not *could—would*. *Would* you do it?"

My mother gives me a level gaze. "I know how you feel, Edie, and I know how you felt during the grasshopper dissection pretest for Sacrificial Rabbit at Preliminaries. And I was very proud of you, the way you held yourself together. None of the judges suspected a thing; you remember how high you scored."

"I remember."

"It's better not to overanalyze a simple task. Pageant is like a game, and every game has its rules. You play by the rules, you play well—presto—you win the game."

"I know."

I kneel then to peer under the bed where Alice Jones is barricaded among the shoe boxes filled with empty bottles of extra-high-dosage Psychozaryme my mother pretends nobody knows about; she's too paranoid to throw them in the trash. My thighs tense as I whisper, "Alice Jones, come on, baby. I swear I'll find a way to save you. Please, baby."

If she comes out now, I can be inhaling Lana's juniper-oiled skin in roughly two and a half minutes, but Alice Jones eyes me like the butcher I am pretending not to be. She makes a frantic scoot between my knees and escapes out the door. My mother moans, one hand fluttering to her throat.

"It's okay, Mom. I'll get her." I'm running downstairs before she can get up off the bed, and I quickly manage to corner Alice Jones under a low table in the living room. I gather all thirteen pounds of her into my arms. Her pulse is a bit fast, and I'll have to sit quietly with her for a little while. I pet her and feed her one of the Taffy Dots from my mother's hand-tinted candy dish; forget Mrs. Vrick and her rabbit meds, a good pat on the right set of neurons combined with a juicy reward are all anybody needs to get their point across.

The air in this room has turned into a solid block of polish. Being in here gives me a worse headache, and I think maybe I do have a brain tumor like Benny Gold's, a great black truffled tumor created cell by cell from my mother's love for Just Like Lemon Fresh Spray Wax, with its extra-strength shining and purifying powers. But right now a dead grasshopper is black against her cream-colored baseboard, and when she sees it, her face will rise up on its bones in indignation. I can just see her behind straining against her red dress as she bends to crush the grasshopper into her polishing rag. Her behind is shaped like an upside-down valentine, and when she leans over it reminds me of those cartoon hearts that pop out with each beat. My mom's got a nice ass.

With my toe, I gently push the grasshopper farther out of reach, but not out of view. I sit Alice Jones on the couch and stare out the window. The neighborhood is empty, the neighbors' drapes still drawn over their crusts of Toast Flipz. Across from me, the face of Lana's house is shut tight, too, the drawn window shades and closed doors like paintings of windows and doors, nothing anyone could ever open. The simfab Swiss chalet clock chimes out the time. Homeroom has started without me again, and I don't have a note. I strain my ears for sounds of life upstairs.

When I don't show up at Fernando's house at exactly twelve past eight, he leaves for school without me, forcing me to walk alone and risk an encounter with Alec Fogel and his Blow Torchers. In a recent unofficial development, the Virtue Club and Pageant Rules Committee have sanctioned their hijinks, and it's rumored that points will be awarded in Safety to girls who avoid trauma at the hands of the gang. Now that they have a focus, the gang has grown, and the only boys who aren't members are the weirdos, and the screen-game addicts who prefer to get all their violent kicks virtually. Unofficially, the judges will also deduct points in Safety from girls who have been "torcher-ed" too often, and any sort of permanent mutilation is grounds for official disqualification. Virtue Club members shrug it all off, saying boys will be boys so why fight it. When they become men (exact age still in dispute at club meetings), they will put away their acetylene torches forever.

I move Alice Jones from chair to chair and gently mime coronations, usually one of our favorite games, although today neither of us musters much enthusiasm. Craning my neck to look farther out the window, I am happy to see the back of Alec Fogel's big gray jacket moving fast in the direction opposite school. At least now I won't have to meet up with him. He's probably going to hitch a ride downtown, or maybe he'll go out to Blow Torcher headquarters at the Mohawk Canal to relax and get wasted, sit on the old locks and fry grasshoppers with his acetylene torch, spraypaint something profound like *Lick my scrotum* on the concrete.

"It's okay, baby. Everything's going to be okay." Alice Jones struggles on the ottoman and I have to squeeze to keep her from escaping again. She kicks and I watch more leaves drop off the chestnut tree in front of Lana's bedroom as my hands soothe Alice Jones's fur, praying for her recovery.

When we're both calm enough I head upstairs. I hear the sound of meds rattling out of their bottle from behind my mother's bedroom door. Her bedside water pitcher clinks. I shut

Alice Jones in her cage and go back downstairs, heavy with guilt. In six months, she will be a muff.

My mother's bedroom window scrapes open, and the pastel notepaper flutters down to the lawn: my tardiness excuse. The lines of her handwriting have a gloomy slant, the words so small they might have been written by a bee.

"Don't take the shortcut, it's not safe," she calls down, but without her usual conviction. The new meds work fast. I nod, but only a little, and feel her gaze until I'm out of view.

As soon as I'm positive she's left the window, I turn around and head for the shortcut. That means I'll be within eyesight again, but only for a few seconds. I count to sixty anyway before I pass our house, in case she's still looking, although she's probably already snaking an apron around her hips and making straight for the polish. Still, I risk big trouble by taking the shortcut through the fields behind Our Lady of Gentle Welcome. The fields are bordered by the woods leading to the reservoir, and trespassing at the reservoir is against the convent rules, so anyone found there has one foot already in Tenner, according to my mother. Of course, kids go there all the time. The water is pretty, and there's always a spooky, hollow sound in the air. True, the place has a bad reputation: rumors of some girl from another county raped and her chopped-off butt cheeks mounted on a trophy board in a Blow Torcher bedroom, somebody's sacrificial rabbit polka-dotted with airplane glue and torched, ghosts. Once in a while one of the nuns will be up there in her sky blue habit and pointy hat practicing her clarinet or trumpet; all the Gentle Welcome nuns are proficient jazz musicians, very popular with churchgoers for their hymns set to head-bopping and finger-tapping standards. I go up there to meditate on underwater maneuvers; I have my own secret bunk in the bushes.

And now it is Lana's hangout, too. Her shoulders hunched, red weatherbreaker soaked with rain or flaring in the bright sun, she often climbs through the dark woods up to the reservoir to smoke Skulls and trance out over the sooty buildings of downtown Deansville. Whenever possible, I follow her there, sometimes to spy from my bunk, sometimes to let her see me, pretending I am also struck by the urge to look out over the miseries of Deansville from a forbidden place. No time for that possibility, though, if I want my mother's note to save me, so I jog through the soggy fields, the orange dress bunching up between my thighs.

Unfortunately, my jacket doesn't quite cover the disgrace of the dress, and everyone who isn't sleeping turns big eyes to me when I inch open the door to homeroom. The drab walls are unusually bright and I am greeted by a stiff breeze; apparently some of the boarded-up windows have been relieved of their vinylwood, and of course the glass has not been replaced. Looking around at all the occupied seats, I see I'm the only latecomer today, and we all know that Mrs. Zimer likes nothing better than having a focus. Glee flickers around her penciled eyebrows as she looks up from her wide-body desk, tank face wreathed in mist from her morning tureen of Expressora. If I'm lucky, she hasn't finished drinking it yet; once all that high voltage has been consumed, my chances of getting the ultimate stretch on the leg rack are assured. The leg rack is the latest acquisition to Mrs. Geary's disciplinary equipment collection, "a little reminder of what two good legs are for—getting the rest of your body on time to where it's supposed to be."

Mrs. Zimer points to the time. The clock has been broken since the second day of school, but I don't see how it would benefit me to call this to her attention. "I see the last session on the leg rack made little impression. Maybe today you'd like to see how electric thumbscrews work"—she takes a giant slurp of Expressora—"or would the head drummer be more appropriate? It seems as though certain facts are too subtle for your grasp. Do you have any idea of how this world would be run without the benefit of a schedule?"

"I have a note." I shuffle over to the far corner of her desk. Overpowering fumes of Expressora threaten my sinuses. "In an actual court of law, an original handwritten parental note would be considered admissible evidence of—"

"Your mother's notes are starting to irritate me, Edie. One more time and we'll have to take the matter up at Personality Court to see if medication is necessary."

Behind me, Brittany Castle titters. What she has to laugh about is anyone's guess. Everyone knows that she's got meds running out her ears ever since she was disqualified during Preliminaries. Rumor has it that she slowed while turning rope for Sissy Duneen during the speed test in Double Dutch, the only team event in Pageant, because she'd heard that Sissy had given head to Brittany's boyfriend, Scotty Vincent, the night before. Mrs. Duneen vigorously squashed the rumor, so Sissy remains a qualified contestant. No one really has time for sex anyway; the boys are too busy comparing the blades of their compact scythes and contestant damage reports, and the girls are saving their romance for Electric Polyrubber Man.

I ignore the obvious delight of Brittany and several others at my predicament, as well as a stage-whispered "Jew-girl," and consider telling Mrs. Zimer about Alice Jones's escape; my status as a (nearly) bona fide Pageant contestant is worth a little something, after all, but do I really want people to think I don't have my rabbit under control? "Mrs. Zimer," I whisper, "my mother is coming down with leukemia. I'm not supposed to mention it, but I think you should know."

Harry York and Richard Robinson are chosen to get the equipment and bring it back to homeroom. Thankfully, there isn't a whole lot of time left in the period for a disciplinary session, but Mrs. Zimer is feisty enough to give me the leg rack, head drummer, thumbscrews, and a very long thirty seconds with the microtwisto capacitator.

First period, Food Science, has me feeling more nauseated than usual. I let my lab partner, gentle Cara Gainy, pour the test batch of Tender Dunk muffin mix into the bowl and whisk it around with the ultraGel while I shut my eyes. She pours it into the pan and puts it in the thermurderator, fills out all thirteen pages of the handout, and even brings me a glass of water because she thinks I need it.

"You got the microtwisto today, didn't you?" My mother can't believe Cara made it through Preliminaries because she has a screechy voice and zero sense of color psychology. It's true about the voice, but I kind of like the way her neon bright clothes make her complexion a little blue, and there is compassion in her small eyes.

I nod as much as the pain in my head will allow.

Bethany Prewitt breezes by us carrying a trayful of pointy muffins. Her Needlework creations are worthy of a spot in the National Feminine Woman Arts Gallery, her speed and form in Double Dutch have won trophies in half a dozen national tournaments, and it's whispered that she's an ace kisser. The way she moves tells me she is practicing for Freestyle Walking. Her legs and hips hug the counters as she keeps to a slow, quick, quick-quick, slow beat and the muffins slide back and forth on the tray. Cara and I grow quiet, and Mr. Mobley, the Food Science instructor, and Bethany's lab partner, Rod Sapp, watch through slanted eyes. Cara quietly places our jar of Crystal Fluff on the floor and gives it a little push, sending it rolling toward Bethany's freestyling feet.

"Oh!" Bethany's neosuede polymoccasins trip and the muffins fly up. Rod dives for the pastries as Mr. Mobley lunges toward Bethany's falling body. The whole class pauses, even Jack Undersol and Mark Billings look up from their not-so-secret game of Gothicathon; it's not often we get to see Mr. Mobley rise from his stool.

"Good work, Rod," Mr. Mobley says, with an arm around Bethany's waist. Rod holds a couple of muffins in his nail biter's hands. "Just put the rest of them back on the tray and give them a little spritz of Germ-Be-Gone. This floor's pretty clean."

Cara picks up the Crystal Fluff and lays sympathetic fingers on Bethany's wrist. "It fell off our table. I'm so sorry."

Bethany looks a little stunned as she squeezes out of Mr. Mobley's grip. "You should watch your supplies more carefully. Someone could break a leg, ya know." Her face is pink with embarrassment; Rod is already chatting up Justine Bender over by the sani-station.

"That's so, Cara." Mr. Mobley's hollow cheeks collapse further into his face as he reluctantly lets Bethany go free. "This is a room of science. Precision is God, sloppiness is the Devil."

"Right, Mr. Mobley," Cara says, dusting a small heap of dirt from a stray muffin that she's picked off the floor. Her little eyes shrink down into their sockets as she announces, "I keep telling Edie to be more precise, but I guess she's kind of out of it because of her disciplinary session last period."

So that's her game. I fix her with a glare, but, instead of acknowledging me, she tosses Bethany the muffin. Bethany's not ready for it, and this time when the muffin falls, it bounces around a bit before splitting open. The inside of the muffin is still pretty raw.

"Oops. Guess your test batch needs a little more time in the thermurderator. Here, Edie. Why don't you put this back in for Bethany?"

"Why don't you?" I snap.

"Give me that!" Bethany snatches the dripping muffin from Cara's hand.

Cara's gentle face colors as she stomps over to the sterilfrost-itron. Pageant can make even the nicest people a little edgy.

Near the end of class, Bethany accidentally spills a flask of hydrogenated oil blend onto Cara's lap. Mr. Mobley, having spent the last part of the period back on his stool scratching at his bald spot, gets up for a second unprecedented time to give us all a zap in the neck with the prickoscope right before the bell.

When I reach the reservoir that afternoon, I'm hot and out of breath. I yank off my jacket and toss it and my briefcase over the fence. The gate is locked, but it doesn't take me long to find a place where the wire is cut and bent back. I feel bold. Crisp October wind cools my sweaty neck as I squeeze through the fence and bushes and emerge into the high grass. Grasshoppers bounce out of my way. I'm still a little achy from the morning's discipline, but at least I'm not as bad off as Ginger Millman and John Frent, who were still tied up on the restraining block while everyone else plowed through the exits.

The old fire tower slices the skyline opposite me, and Lana's rock is on the other side of it, a little downhill and out of sight. My head bends back to look at the top of the tower, just in case she's sitting there on its small, peeling platform in her skirt of neckties. Not that it's likely. The fire tower is covered with barbed wire for the first ten of its seventy feet and nobody even tries to climb it until dark because the convent security will shoot at you until you're holier than fishnet. My gaze lowers to the sun spangling frantically on the ripples in the water and I catch my breath at all that glittering wetness. Any minute Lana will appear. Our eyes will lock for an instant and then we'll be tit to tit, glued together by the force of our own gravitational field, clothes torn off and our bodies warmed by another special law of physics.

I am struck by something hard. The force shoves me off balance and I fall, a sharp pain in my side.

"Torrrrrrcheeeerrrrr!" The gang's rolled-*r* yell of triumph echoes in the still air, and I scramble to my knees just in time to see Alec Fogel disappear through the bushes on the opposite side of the water. My hipbone throbs and there's a creeping wet stain on my dress. A Just Like Meat Planet astronaut doll has landed in the grass beside me, naked and streaked with black grease, half its red curls plucked out to leave pinpricked bald patches. I pick it up and see that someone has gouged a hole in its smooth polystroob crotch and stuffed it with weeds. A few drops of dirty liquid trickle out onto my hand, and then the strong smell of urine hits. I feel sick, knowing without even checking that my dress is not wet from the dewy grass. Quickly, I drop-kick the doll away. Around me now: explosions. Alec Fogel is hurling his specially decorated M-80s—he likes to tape finishing nails on them to better the chance of flesh wounds. Most of the nails bite the water, but two of them hit my shoe and it doesn't take any more to get me sprinting out of there. This year I've been lucky—so far the worst the gang has inflicted on me has been a little pounding with a ha-ha groan hammer and a lit firecracker glued to my sweater. Only a small firecracker, more noise than burn.

As I run back down through the woods, I'm not sure where it's smart to go. If it weren't so cold out, I might hide in the underbush until Alec is gone and then dive into the reservoir, maybe stay in there, my body a living submarine, subsisting on algae until I'm old enough to leave Deansville forever, or at least until my years of Pageants and sacrificial rabbits are over.

2

"Urine!"

My mother's neck looks tight enough for something in there to snap. I told her that I'd slipped on some wet leaves and then hurried upstairs, but as soon as I took the dress off, she had it against her nose. "How could this have happened?"

I change into a plaid jumper, profoundly hideous and one of her favorites, but she's not looking at what I'm wearing. She's clutching the orange dress to her and sliding down the stairs, crying with a weak sound I've never heard before. The pit of my stomach is ice.

"Mom." I can't seem to get any volume in my voice and she keeps sliding, bumping from one carpeted step to the next, her red dress riding up under her yellow apron and giving me an eyeful of her slip and part of her girdle. Her legs really are spectacular. An uncapped can of Just Like Lemon Fresh Spray Wax is in her apron pocket, lipstick marks around the nozzle. I stand at the top of the stairs, holding on to the banister. The hexagonal window in the front door shows a white sky threatening another freak snowfall. "Mom." My own legs shake. *"Mom."*

"They give you a nice bust." She brushes the ruffles up with her palm, then lets one ruffle remain between two fingers so she can rub the pads of her fingers back and forth over its weave.

Her mouth grows soft and slack. "The workmanship is excellent," she whispers, more to herself than to me.

She stops sliding before she hits the floor. She stays on the bottom step rocking over the dress, rubbing it back and forth over her thighs, then sprawls back against the stairs and throws the dress up, yelling, "Just fuck it all, the whole thing!" The dress lands on her face but she doesn't move it away, just lies there in Alec Fogel's cold pee.

Clots of snow dump out of the sky. I watch for a while, and when I finally take my hand from the banister, both my legs are prickly with sleep. "Mommy?" I pick up a safe corner of the dress and look at her face. Expecting to see . . . what? The bones of her skull? Her skin and tissue burned away by the acid in Alec's pee? But no, the makeup she applied earlier is still artful. Her eyes are wide and staring, a squish of Temptation Eyeliner and mucus caught in the corner of each. "Mom?"

She is asleep. Her face is too still, eyes unblinking. I've seen this before. Her "pretend dead," we used to say and laugh. Carefully, I take the dress away and creep back up the stairs to soak it in the bathroom sink, my pulse hammering out a song of revenge on Alec Fogel, a familiar song, each note its own bloodthirsty opera.

I leave the dress in a stew of orange water, go back down to where she is lying, and debate whether I should wake her. Maybe I should kiss her cheek, gently pluck the stray hairs from the glistening saliva of her open mouth. I could whisper that I love her, that I will toe the line from now on, and we'll beat the Just Like Cotton underpants off those other girls.

I look down upon my mother's magnificent cheekbones. And then I put one hand on the wall and one on the banister and hoist myself over her. My Clickies dangle inches from where her dress and apron are tossed up over her stomach, one good stomp is all it would take, I could fake my way into submarine school with nothing but a smile. Instead, I jump to the floor and run for it, not even bothering to close the front door as I leave, my feet chilled and skidding in the already melting snow.

The shuttle to the Identity Mall is actually at our neighborhood stop for a change, so I get on it. My stomach growling, I head straight for the mall parking lot Just Like Meat Planet as soon as the shuttle's doors whine open, even though there is a better Just Like Meat Planet with screen games just a half hour's walk away on the Identity Mall's maze of moving sidewalks; I've got the whole afternoon to get there.

The Just Like Meat Planet is mostly empty; there's only a small group of mental patients and their wardens out on a field trip. Already, though, there's trouble. One of the mentals has ripped down a No Happy Endings sign off the wall and is giddily shredding it onto his plate of Krispee Stix. Ever since Judge Rawling's wife, Meryl, did a Happy Ending, the signs are all over the place, in all the store windows, on-screen after every commercial break.

"Happy Endings! Happy Endings!" the mental crows, while a Just Like Meat Planet manager accosts a warden.

"We don't allow people to talk about that sort of thing in here," says the manager.

"He's not talking about it," says the warden. "He's ripping it up."

"We don't allow that, either. Especially if he's going to keep talking about it."

"He's not talking about it. He's mentally retarded. He doesn't know what he's saying."

"I'm sorry, but your group is going to have to leave. We can't allow any of that sort of thing in here. This is a family restaurant."

I buy my own bag of Krispee Stix and douse them with Just Like Ketchup from the Just Like Meat Planet astronaut condiment bust. Somebody is always vandalizing those No Happy Endings signs, although you hardly ever see anyone doing it.

One of the Just Like Meat Planet fryer-boys sweeps up the shredded sign. While he coaxes the curls of paper into his dirt dominator, a strange, private smile appears on his face. As he wheels his cleaning equipment back behind the counter, I notice how the part of his neck showing between his Just Like Meat Planet cap and his Just Like Meat Planet shirt looks obscenely naked, and suddenly I imagine him doing his own Happy Ending. It's as if he'd pulled down his pants and showed me the crack of his ass.

I am startled to think I could be three feet away from a person who won't be alive in a few months to see the Just Like Meat Planet astronaut dolls ride their holiday rockets down from the ceiling this Christmas, who will wake up one morning soon and decide that doing something so creepy and wild is better than putting up with one more minute of crap.

His guilty eyes meet mine, and immediately his expression becomes indignant.

The manager claps him on the back. "Mental jerk-off," he says. "Crazy nutbags don't give a shit about what's decent."

"Hunh?" Fryer-boy shakes the dominator's contents into the portable trash pulverizer, watching as it vibrates with destruction. "Sure. Guy was a mental for sure."

The vibe inside the Identity Mall is no improvement on the mood in the restaurant, with only mothers and babies and old retired men ambling forlornly through the maze of vinylchrome pillars decked with creepers of reglupolate ivy; Thursday is two-for-one at Drive-By Sausage Adventure Forest, so everybody who isn't training has rushed off there after school. The towering caged neon store signs blink at every corner, desperate for shoppers to follow the arrows and surrender their credit cards at every air-freshened counter. As I walk past Dent's, sample people charge at me with spray atomizers, their faces hard and decorative, anxious for me to try Blessing, Atonement, and Howitzer ("A fragrance for the oppressed," one sample woman wearing howitzer-shaped earrings tells me). A woman in fur squeezes past, putting a hand up to the spray atomizers, spitting at the sample people, "Don't you dare. This is Sable-Mastr, are you an idiot?" I am afraid if I try to run I will stumble.

Shivering in the chill Identity Mall air, I browse through At Last Music and treat myself to the brand-new Mystic Fangs release, vandalizing the bar code and slipping it into my bag. As soon as I'm clear of the store's window I run all the way to the Just Like Meat Planet at the other end of the mall, blood slamming in my head. I play screen games until all I can see are red blinking dots and it's time for Fernando's after-school Carnivorous Plant Lovers Club meeting to end. If I can catch the next shuttle, I'll get to his house just in time for snack.

Homemade blueberry muffins with real blueberries from the U-Pick in Lafayette that Mrs. Popoff froze back in August. Fernando and I sit at his kitchen table while Mrs. Popoff places real fruit preserves and soft butter in front of our plates.

"*Es muy rico, no?*" Mrs. Popoff teaches Spanish at the high school and likes to imagine that she is still twenty-two years old and backpacking through Spain. My mother thinks she's "a little too woolsy-folksy," but to me just the sight of cheery, disheveled Mrs. Popoff is a relief.

"*Claro que sí*, Mrs. Popoff," I say through a mouthful of juicy berries.

Fernando picks at his muffin, smiling because he loves my accent. Mrs. Popoff says I sound a little more German than Spanish, but Fernando has told me privately that he thinks I sound neat. "You sound like a high-ranking foreign diplomat," he said once. "You've got international flair." He doesn't say a lot, but when he comes out with one of his observations, it's usually pretty perceptive. Most people don't know what he's really like, just that he's tall and skinny and quiet. He's very patient, too. He reminds me of a walking stick, the bug that looks like a twig and hangs around forever on the bark of a tree. He's the biggest sissy in the Western world—goes limp as an overdrugged bunny if you try to give him a judo flip—but for some reason the Blow Torchers won't attack when he's around. Just the sight of his weird aquamarine curls puts the deep freeze on all their evil.

Fernando says he learned how to be quiet from his mostly mute father, who surprised everyone after Fernando's mother divorced him by taking up the accordion. Fernando feels sorry for his dad, playing all those bad tango chords in his studio apartment downtown. But if you ask him what he's been thinking when he's been quiet for so long, he'll show you the two spots that form a brown barracuda shape on his front teeth and say, "Hey, what's up, doc?" like he had only just noticed you. He's practically a professional corpse. If you take his food away in the middle of a bite, he'll just drop his fork and sit there watching you eat it or dump it with the same thrilling expression. You can turn the screen to static and he'll stare at it with the exact interest he gave to the program he'd supposedly been watching. He hears everything, though. His eardrums are abnormally large because of the Diet-ora Nips Mrs. Popoff ate when she was pregnant; although probably it's because he's pale and keeps so still that people forget to whisper when he's around. And he's not retarded. He does all our math. He can draw perfect feet, too; he's got this thing about drawing feet, on account of having toes all in the wrong places, another casualty of Mrs. Popoff's Nips. Even blindfolded he won't make any mistakes.

"My room," he says when Mrs. Popoff goes into her garden to pick her last tomatoes of the season.

I climb up on his bed as Fernando loads our favorite Amazing Mister Fezundo V-release into the screen. When he settles down beside me to watch, I nudge his foot with my own as the opening credits flash: *The Amazing Mister Fezundo! Mental Artist!*

"Probably the Amazing Mister Fezundo got a lot of his mental training from being a sonar operator." Again my foot taps the side of Fernando's, but he doesn't tap back. "It's all about knowing vibrations. He must be a vibration expert."

Still Fernando doesn't say anything, just fiddles with one of his Venus flytraps and obediently glues his eyes to the opening explosion. I get the feeling that he's not really watching, which is odd because the Amazing Mister Fezundo can usually hold his attention. The Amazing Mister Fezundo is such a great actor that even though we both know that the feats are just optical illusions, we still get chills when he wills a twenty-story hotel to detonate while he is inside, and walks from the ruins unscathed, brushing invisible dust specks from the jacket of his gold suit. And we love it when he wills the hotel into a perfectly restored state, and walks into the lounge to order a perfectly mixed martini. He may have his critics, but everyone agrees he's got style.

"We should drink martinis," I say when the show ends. The last shot is a close-up of the Amazing Mister Fezundo's powerful dark eyes staring right into the camera over the rim of his cocktail glass.

Automatically, Fernando hits rewind so we can watch it again. We always watch it twice.

"I wouldn't mind having that gold suit, either. Do you think it would look good on me?"

"You look good all the time."

"I do?" I twist my body around to face him, but now Fernando's eyes are closed.

"Sure."

Under a final blaze of sun, the snow disappears without a
single wet trace and Fernando offers to walk me home. We take
the long way. He stops when I stop, does nothing but watch as
I scratch the word *Love* on Mr. Powell's driveway with a rock. I
add some lines around it to look like sparks are flying out. Mr.
Powell has never married, and he sits in a wheelchair all day until a freelance Controlled Healing nurse comes to cook him dinner, change his diaper, and give him an antibacterial sponge
bath. On another part of the driveway I write *psych your mind*
with my left hand so it looks like someone else's writing, then
bend my body over the smooth wooden fence that separates Mr.
Powell's driveway from his yard, my stomach pressing against
the top rail as I hold my legs and arms out from my body like
I'm flying. I can almost touch Howard McKay in the Stillwells'
presidential topiary display next door.

I don't fall.

I grab the fence post and jump backwards, do a handstand
and stay up for a count of thirty-three. When I finish there are
tiny black stones stuck to my palms. I pick them off one by one
and throw them at the grasshoppers as they fly over the Insecticide Huts. I don't hit anything, which is a little weird considering those grasshoppers are almost as big as monkey wrenches,
and I don't mean the subcompact kind the Blow Torchers hide
in their jacket pockets to bloody some girl's new manicure.
Maybe creaky Pullings wasn't as cooked on Mondo Surge as
everyone thought. I'd like to mention it to Fernando, but he's in
a trance, staring at nothing and not saying a word, his blue-
white curls shining in the hazy light. The API is high now, and
Fernando's nose runs like a faucet.

Across the street, Rodney Spivey sits hunched over the han-
dlebars on his action chopper, looking our way, and even from
here I can see that he doesn't look happy.

"How long has he been over there?" I ask, steering toward
home.

Fernando shrugs; he blinks, squints, then smiles his bar-racuda smile.

". . . and let me tell you something else: if you don't start men-struating soon, Edie, we're going to have to use the Just Like Leeches." My mother's eyes are hard, burning jade. I am grounded.

In the morning, she's hungover from the new meds and wants me close to her, so I don't go to school and she doesn't go to her part-time job in the Better Dress department at Merry's ("Extra drills with the blow-up dummy, though, so the day isn't a total waste"). She makes my father call Mrs. Geary and use his head-of-household tone to convince the principal that a le-gitimate family crisis is preventing my education. Then he heads for the basement, but she blocks the stairs.

"Off to play with your bugs?"

"Lorraine, relax."

"Please don't patronize. You know what Dr. Plow said about that." She worries an imaginary dirt streak on the wall with the corner of a dish towel.

"What do you want, Lorraine?"

A look is held between them, and even from my challenged vantage point, it seems as though they both have gone suddenly shy, until my mother reaches out a hand and my father bends forward. It looks like she is going to touch his cheek just as he is going to give her a peck, but instead she knocks his glasses off.

Silence. I hold my breath, waiting to see if this will be the time he'll pull her hair or give her arm an Indian burn, but he just stoops down to pick up his glasses. Then he stands and puts them back on his face, and lifts his chin as if he is trying to re-member something—a joke maybe, just maybe he will surprise us all and tell a really great joke.

But no.

The bones in my mother's hands are clearly defined as she bunches up the dish towel. It's a deep pink, with green piping, and the way she's got it smooshed cuplike in her hands makes it look like she's offering my father a beautiful flower.

"That was an accident," she says. "It really was."

My father places one hand on the wall, as if he needs to hold himself up. "Apparently."

She reaches for his arm, but fails to make contact as his body goes stiff. Her hand retracts back into the dish towel's folds. "I *need* things, Neil. You know that."

"I just want to relax," he says, sighing. "I've had a hard week."

"It's no picnic for anyone around here." Her voice starts to thin. "There's a lot of pressure on me to help her get it right, and I'm doing the best I can. But every day I have to pray I have the strength for it."

"No one says she has to be in that contest. The world will continue to spin."

"Why can't you just be a little more supportive is all I'm saying."

"That dummy is not something I . . ." He steps back and clears his throat. "I'm going downstairs, Lorraine."

"Just fine," she calls as his graying head disappears into the basement. "Be that way." She throws the dish towel after him, but it doesn't get very far, so she goes and picks it up. I park myself on the living room couch with a book just before she comes huffing past.

There were happier times. My mother tells the stories. My favorite is a butterfly-hunting story. They had only been dating about a month. A hot June morning. She wore a white ruched one-piece bathing suit, the same one she'd seen some princess wearing on a yacht in *Look Rich* magazine. While my father stalked through a field of bluebells and buttercups, my mother spread a blanket and sunned herself. All of a sudden, she had an ESP feeling that something out of the ordinary was going on behind her, and sure enough, she turned her head to see a magnificent orange and black butterfly swoop down and perch on the sole of her foot. She hardly dared breathe.

The butterfly stayed on her foot like that for twenty minutes, licking her toes with its long black proboscis. My mother and father held hands and watched. And just to prove to my father that she knew a little something, she said it must be a Monarch (the one butterfly whose name she knew), but my father had said no, it's a Viceroy, which is a very lucky butterfly since it looks like a Monarch, and, since most birds know that Monarchs are poisonous, it doesn't get eaten by birds very often. And my mother was overjoyed to find out that she had such a clever, sneaky little butterfly lapping away at her toes.

That night she dreamt she rose from her bed, naked, and floated out her window into the deep blue sky. At first she worried that she couldn't fly, and that she might get ill because she had no clothes on and the night was cool, but then a thick fur coat came down from above and covered her. And then she saw that the coat was moving, flickering and undulating all along her skin. Her whole body felt tingly and a little wet, but in a nice way. Of course, this was no ordinary fur coat. This coat was made of hundreds of butterflies, all busily licking her with their wondrous tongues, and in her dream, she moaned from happiness. Never had she felt anything so delightful, and when she looked around for someone to tell, she saw that the sky was full of women, all floating just like her, but all of them were dressed badly. And then she woke up, and she knew that one day my father would ask her to be his bride, and that her answer would be yes.

When I hear her go into her bedroom, I tiptoe upstairs to listen outside her door for more of that weak crying she did yesterday. Or the sickening hiss of a spray can. Maybe I will hear Thorserhazil or Prixoforgasol rattle happily as they are shaken from bottle to hand, and the gentle trickle of water poured from the bedside pitcher to a glass. Instead, she whips open the door, surprising me with her cheery "Oh! I was just coming to find you. Let's try to forget our worries and play a game of Bloodsucker, whattaya say? We can play it in here, on my screen. Or in your room, if you want. Whichever you want."

Never one to trust a good thing, I hesitate.

"I know I said no screen while you're grounded. But if you do it with me, it doesn't count. We'll have some Cheese Links and Bac'n Dip and make a dinner party before I go to Dr. Plow's. How 'bout that?"

"I don't know. I want to sit with Alice Jones. I don't think she should be left alone too much right now." Why is my mother seeing Dr. Plow on a Friday night? I met him once, and found his soft handshake repulsive. His dark blue eyes fixed on mine like a spy's, unreadable, ready to deny that they ever actually saw anything. My mother claims he's the best-dressed male she's ever met, with his buttery suits (always in shades of blue to intensify his eyes) and expensive black pillproof Woolie sweaters. He also has both ears double-pierced and a braid.

"Oh Edie, you can sit with her all night." She does a little bellydance step, her face mock sexy. "Honey. Lighten up."

Who can resist her? My father must have rocks in his head. We pile Cheese Links and Bac'n Dip on her bed tray and turn on the screen in her room. She sings along with the Bloodsucker theme song, "One, two, three, four, who's that knocking at the trailer door? It's the Bloodsucker, ooh ooh, come to suck your life away," swinging her arms up and down and tossing her hair back and forth like a go-go dancer.

"Say," her eyes are filled with secret meaning, "how about some you-know-what for old times' sake? Before we play." She puts the game on hold and switches on our favorite Candy Cupsby release, then crooks a finger and gives me her widest smile.

There is nothing, *nothing*, so joyous as standing on my parents' beds with my mother, jumping and wriggling like two-year-olds to the great big funky gospel of Candy Cupsby. Our Candy dance: it fills us with private, hilarious relief, and its very inception was built on the kind of perfect coincidence that makes you certain you exist for a high purpose.

One day my mother put on the Candy Cupsby song "Things Are Lookin' Up" while she was cleaning her bedroom, and I happened to pass by in the hall and catch her eye; something flashed between us as Candy's rich contralto stretched out the *uh* in *up,* and suddenly my mother let the dirt dominator fall out of her hand, I raced into the room, and we were both sucked up onto the beds and compelled to dance. We lost our balance and fell in a giggly sprawl to the mattresses; we rose, we fell, again and again as we thrashed our way through the entire release, while I marveled at my mother's hair sailing up to the ceiling, her grunts of noisy pleasure, the happy mounds of her breasts bouncing over her rib cage beneath her silky green housedress, our bare toes occasionally making bumpy contact. When it was over, we flopped down onto our backs, wordlessly side by side on the beds with our abdomens heaving, our breath like the breath of running dogs, and the front of my mother's housedress dark with sweat. We went back to our respective business without saying a word or even glancing at one another. But ever since, once in a while, one or the other of us sends out the signal by playing that Candy Cupsby song, and no matter what we are doing, we find our way to the beds to dance.

The polyacrylic birds of paradise growing from the headboards tremble behind us as we work the mattresses, and I feel my spirits rise, but they don't rise quite high enough, and after a couple of minutes I find myself doing the unthinkable: stopping

Candy Cupsby in the middle of a note and switching Blood-sucker back on.

"Let's just play."

"What the—why did you do that?" She has to grip a head-board to keep from falling.

"The game's gonna start in a minute, Mom. Pick up your re-mote."

"Okay, okay." Her legs fold with a snap as she plops down on the bed, making the Cheese Links jump in their container on the night table. "Pooper." Dip churns as she twists a Cheese Link into it; she takes a huge bite. A tiny piece of Bac'n sticks on her upper lip and she licks it off. "I don't get you sometimes. But this," she waves a Cheese Link, "this I get. Heaven. How many calories do you think? Oh, who cares. I'll wear my fat dress tonight to hide the bloat."

Usually, I can get through the door and suck all the blood from the little kids in my mother's trailer before her blood-sucker even gets to the gate of my trailer park, but right away, my bloodsucker falls off the highway and gets sprayed with the anti-bloodsucker power spray.

"Gotcha! Three hundred bonus points!"

"Two hundred."

"Whatever. That was smooth, hunh? Gotcha right in the kitchenette and the foldout bed. I've never done *that* before. Bloodsucked two kids at once!"

"It's not that hard to do."

"Well, I've never done it. So it feels pretty good."

"It's just not that hard. If you know what you're doing."

"Gotcha again!" Her lips shut around another Cheese Link while her finger sends a king bloodsucker scuttling around a barbeque pit.

"Wow. I'm hot tonight, aren't I? Are you sure you're really trying?"

"I'm trying."

"Well try to enjoy yourself. It's only a game."

"You're getting Bac'n Dip all over the remote."

"What? Oh." She puts the game on pause and frowns. "Are you picking on me on purpose? Because you'd better watch it."

"I'm not picking on you. I just thought you'd want to know that there was Bac'n Dip on the remote. Why do you always have to be so paranoid?"

"Okay. That's it." She punches the off button and picks up the bed tray. "You've been riding me long enough. This party is over. After all I've been through today I certainly do not need any more criticism."

"It's not like you really wanted to play with me anyway. You're just using me because Dad wouldn't—"

"Halt. You are treading on very thin ice. Remember, you are grounded and I still have not forgotten why."

"I know what I am."

"I wonder about that sometimes. I really do." She brushes a few stray Bac'n crumbs off the bedspread with a quick, fierce hand. One of her needlepoint sonnet pillows rolls off onto the carpet. "Go take the tray downstairs and clean up. I would like some privacy while I dress for Dr. Plow." Her cheeks have pinked the way they do when she feels the injustice of everything.

"Mom, I'm sorry. I didn't mean to spoil things." I stand there with the tray, digging my bare toes into my ankle. If she's not already thinking about doing a Happy Ending, I will surely drive her to it. My eyes swim with tears, and I wipe them onto the back of my hand.

She has already turned away, her face in the closet, sorting fashion.

The backyard is off-limits when I'm grounded. So is the Identity Mall, the Screenplex, and the Drive-By Sausage Adventure Forest. If my mother could install an invisible fence that would shrill in my ears every time I even thought about going anywhere, she would pay good money to do it. This afternoon it's Fernando Popoff's house that I am thinking about, too far to escape to, three yards up from mine at the top of a long horseshoe driveway, and all of the windows blocked by Mrs. Popoff's forsythia and fruit-shaped topiary. I can see part of his front yard from mine, but he won't be in it. He doesn't like to be outside much because of his allergies. Since the phone and screen are also forbidden, I have to wait in my front yard for him to pass on his way home from Social Hop.

Just before noon, they drive up our street. The day is warm and the windows are open; Mrs. Popoff says Chemfresh Air Coolant is a major cause of allergic reactions. And this is why Fernando's pale curls swirl around his head like frantic doves. He's sitting in the far backseat of Mrs. Popoff's lime-colored miniwagon even though she's up front alone. He won't ride in the middle or front seats, ever since he nearly choked on a Snuggle Pep once when Mr. Popoff stopped short at a yellow light. Fernando says he saw an exact copy of himself burst through the windshield, that the copy took the best part of him and dove into a galaxy where one long invisible fence surrounded nothing. Mrs. Popoff hauled him to a specialist after that, but with Fernando's lips sealed shut for eight sessions not covered by Controlled Healing, the cure was nixed and Fernando now rides in the backseat without a peep about it from anybody.

A little later, he comes over in his bowtie and orthopedic fancy shoes. He always wears orthopedics, but on Saturday afternoons he wears the fancy ones because he goes to dancing school. My heart sinks every time he wears them; they're too desperate—shiny, with little tassels that are supposed to distract people from noticing that the cripple who's wearing them is dancing like a spaz.

"I'm grounded," I say, and shove him into the lilac bushes where my mother can't see us.

He knows the drill. "I can't stay too long," he says, wiping at his streaming nose with his sleeve. "My mom's making tacos and then we're driving to Lafayette to pick real apples. She said you could come, too."

Just looking at the wet part in Fernando's glowing hair and the way the two tiny buttons hold his shirt collar in place depresses me. Mrs. Popoff is always stroking Fernando's hair and calling him Milkweed-head. If one of his shirt buttons were to come loose, she would sew it back on tight without complaining that her talents were going down the drain. Even if I could go to his house and eat tacos and then get in the miniwagon with them to go to Lafayette, I wouldn't.

"Forget it. I don't want to go. I've got stuff to do. My mom's setting up some Mystery Powder specimens for me to identify. She found out some brand-new procedures, stuff only government research scientists know."

"You heard about Lily Gates, right?"

I steal a glance around the yard, in the unlikely event that my mother is walking toward us, but the only thing moving is a group of scarlet pin oak leaves blowing gaily across our lawn on their way next door. "What about her?"

"You didn't see it on the screen?"

"How could I? I'm grounded, remember?"

"She blew up the Just Like Meat Planet at the Identity Mall."

"She *what*?"

"Last night, actually around 0300 hours. Naturally, they didn't catch her—"

"Wait. Which one did she bomb?"

"The one in the parking—"

"I was just there two days ago!"

"She did it when it was closed—"

"I know that!" She only firebombs them when they're closed so nobody gets hurt.

"This makes nine so far, if you don't count the one in Fishkill since that bomb was defective."

Above us, a V of Canadian geese head south, *ka-ronking* an off-key farewell. The wind starts up.

Fernando sneezes. "I think I'm cold." Again, he wipes at his nose but only succeeds in moving snot from one facial area to another.

"Look, just go home then."

"What's up, doc?" His blue eyes are red-rimmed and watering.

"Nothing." I practically hurl him out of our yard. He eats real apples and he still gets sick.

I watch him all the way back to his house, his heels lifting up from the squishy ground in that tiptoe step of his, his pants sagging around his walking-stick legs. I know I hurt his feelings. To Fernando, Lily Gates's bombs are more excellent than even the biggest Amazing Mister Fezundo detonation, and usually we both do a dramatization of the crime, taking turns playing the star role of Lily Gates when she gets away with it. But right now I just want to be by myself. Fernando's inability to manage his own mucus can really bring me down, and I certainly don't need that. Lily Gates was in Deansville! She could have been in the restaurant the same time as I was! Was she there in disguise, casing the joint? If she can dress like one of the Gentle Welcome nuns, she could just as well dress like a man. Of course, she could actually *be* one of the Gentle Welcome nuns, although they've all denied it in the investigations. And if she is really one of them, so much the better to be that obvious and not get caught. I marvel at her ingenuity, proud to be connected to her geographically, if only for a few unknown moments.

I sit on our freezing steps and watch someone's newspaper

come loose from an opened Smell-Brite recycling cubby. The wind tosses the sheets of news up and around; the stories deny gravity, flirt with satellite dishes and the tips of topiary. Is the story of Lily Gates flying above me? I am practically in that story—so what if Fernando heard about it first? I picture him eating his taco, his barracuda-spotted teeth breaking through the real corn tortilla, ground beef and shreds of lettuce squirting back onto his plate. In their poppy-colored kitchen, his mother will be pouring him a glass of real milk, standing near him in her beaded suede house moccasins. She'll be looking at him, not talking because she'll be respecting Fernando's love of silence, and her puppy eyes will be saying how nothing is better than this, not even maybe being in the same restaurant as Lily Gates, not even that one great year before she met Mr. Popoff when she was screwing her ass off in Spain.

3

As the sun drops out of Deansville's sky, my mother and I are still down in the family nook. Alice Jones has finally returned to normal, and today's training has gone exceptionally well; that hush-hush government research my mother got hold of will definitely give me the edge in Mystery Powders. Not that I need it. I spin the microdiorometer's dials like I am chief of staff at the National Nucleatorium; I identify every chemical in the Little Miss Scientist Home Lab, as well as my mother's improvised mixtures of cleaning solvents, bath salts, and Massacre-o-Lux flea and tick killer left over from the days of Petey. I fillibrate the jelioscope without breaking any needles and remember to put petrolubie on the synchropacitron; my usual trouble differentiating barium compounds just disappears. My mother holds up beakers of barium chloride and barium sulfate and it takes me less than a minute to tell which is insoluble in water and which can be used to make a murderous cocktail.

"This is fantastic, darling," she gushes. "You're unstoppable. That Prewitt girl will be pea green with envy. And when you work in those tips about antineutrinial calibration, you're going to make the judges' heads spin." She leans over a row of beakers to give me a peck on the forehead. Quick and a little stingy, but it's the sign I've been waiting for: she's over her mood and has forgiven me at last.

She brushes a few crumbs of sodium carbonate into a dish and empties it into the trash. "Now, how about we pack it in for today after you name the allotropes of sulfur."

"Okay." I am not eager to stop, but I recite the list and finish with an extra recitation of a bunch of sulfur compounds and their uses.

She's more than pleased. "Let's celebrate with a little sweet-and-sour takeout from Wong's, whattaya say?"

"Sure. If you want."

"Technically, you're still grounded. But you can drive down to Wong's with me. You know I don't see so well at night." She pulls back and pins me with a look. I lower my eyes; it's useless, though, I'm back under her spell.

"You're a good girl, Edie. My Edie." She comes around to my side of the table and presses her lips to the top of my head, gives me a real hug. That peppery smell of hers wraps itself around me like an extra set of arms, and I sink into her curves with relief. Who could not have seen her as the true winner of the Miss Deansville Pageant?

"Mommy," I turn and whisper against her abdomen. "I'm sorry I made you mad."

"Oh, my baby. What am I going to do with you? My only treasure."

I squeeze her harder.

"Ouch, Edie. Not so hard."

She loosens herself from my grip. "The woman at Habibi Cleaners says the dress will be okay. But I was so embarrassed. I just don't see how you managed to fall in urine." At this, her back straightens and she looks to her framed tropical beach embroidery scene, where her own face stares fuzzily back in the glass. Then her green eyes return to me and she cups my chin in her hand. "You're telling me the whole truth about that, aren't you?"

"Of course."

"Well. Just remember that life will not get easier unless you learn to play by the rules." She speaks quietly, as if the room might be bugged, and I take this to mean that she still harbors a suspicion that she has not heard the entire story but is not all that keen to know the truth. "I think you understand what I'm trying to say." I put on an expression of sorrow, her face shows satisfaction, and she drops her hand from my chin and moves to the chemoflagellator, one finger inspecting its hairspring for dust. "Just remember that saying *I'm sorry* does not go very far in excusing bad behavior. Especially when you nearly destroy a Better Dress." She sighs, and I sigh too. I am her only treasure. Without me in this world, she would be all alone, pouring all her artistry into crafts, unable to realize the one thing she ever truly longed to create.

I load the intraligniates back into their case, careful not to jam them between the spikes like I usually do; several have broken, and she's made it clear that the next time it happens I can shell out the nineteen bucks to replace one myself. I swipe at each anticipator, switch, and indicator before laying them inside their separate trays. When I am finished packing up our supplies, and my mother has called in our order to Wong's, she asks me to rub her back. She slips off her sweater and sits with arms crossed and head down on the kitchen table; I squirt a cookie's worth of hand lotion in my palm and rub my hands together to warm it the way she has taught me. My hands press down on her tiny, flower-shaped freckles, and she moans gratefully.

"Ahhh. Ooh, that feels so good. Oh, Edie, what would I do without you?"

"You've got Daddy. And Bubbeh."

"Right. *Them*." She shifts on the table. "Ohh, that's the spot. Just a little harder. Go under the strap."

I slide my fingers under the tight elastic of her bra strap and feel for the evil eyeballs.

"That's it. There. Poke that evil eyeball right out. Oooh, too hard. Not so hard!"

I ease up uncertainly. My mother's body is a tricky landscape. I know all about the asteroidal moles we keep an eye on, the stretch marks delicate as petals yet so obstinately reappearing despite the collagen injections, the fine black mustache that grows back even after the laser removal session every six months. Some days, she's as easy to read as a well-worn map that falls open at a touch; I know just where to use my thumbs to knead with pressure and when to send all ten fingers lightly tripping. But then, without any warning, a volcano of pain will erupt. When this happens, I am flummoxed; she really is a stranger after all.

"Ow, Edie. Stop. It's no use." Her gleaming bra disappears under her sweater. "I've got a bad case tonight. But you tried."

Above the driveway, bleary night clouds smudge the sky as we back out into the street. At the light, my mother stops the miniwagon short. "I nearly forgot. I have to stop at Mrs. Vrick's."

"What for?"

"She's got some new literature I want to borrow. Don't look at me like that. If we put in a little extra elbow grease now, the road is going to be that much smoother later on."

"Well, I just don't want to overwork Alice Jones."

"Don't be so concerned about overworking a dumb animal. As long as she's fed, she's happy."

"She's not dumb."

"You know what I mean." With the yellow traffic light on her face, she is suddenly sunken and old. I don't care to see it.

"Alice Jones knows how to unlock her cage and open the door. Maybe we can get a new rabbit, one that's smart, but not *so* smart, because it just seems like Alice Jones is kind of special, and maybe we—I mean *I*—shouldn't . . . you know." Even as the words come out, I know it's useless.

She doesn't say anything.

"The light's red. You can't go."

"Don't tell me how to drive."

"I'm just saying."

"Well don't *just say* anymore."

The Amazing Mister Fezundo would will the steering wheel to spin. He would make the miniwagon do twenty donuts right in the middle of the intersection, right under her powerless hands. His mastery over the stupid, the ordinary, the boring, even the fantastic is undisputed. He can destroy and resurrect as casually as most people pull on their socks. Next to him, my mother is limp as parboiled Wiggelini.

"Buckle," she says, as she hits the gas. Her own seat belt dangles untouched above her shoulder.

I hover in the hall while my mother and Mrs. Vrick, chesty in her tight pale green scrub dress, confab importantly in the living room over some pamphlets. Mrs. Vrick hulas through the room, a half-smoked cigarette clenched between her teeth.

"You're not smoking again." My mother tries to smile from her perch on a low chair. Her hands snake around her body to squeeze her waist, secretly checking for fat.

Mrs. Vrick plucks the cigarette from her mouth and shakes it in front of my mother before scooping up another stack of pamphlets and dropping them in my mother's lap. "Darn right I'm smoking again. These little honeys are saving my nerves."

No way will I enter that room. The hallway is bad enough, with its taxidermy squirrels and display of dried roses on the table next to the coatrack. Even my mother questions Mrs. Vrick's decorating scheme. Who could relax in front of the fireplace with those jars of preserved bats on the mantel? Would anyone feel comfortable sitting on her stiff, genuine zebra-skin couch? She's a real bone fanatic, too, and I'll just bet some of the ones on those end tables are human. There's something a little werewolfish about Mrs. Vrick—could be her enormous, pawlike hands and the black down that mars the white of her cheeks and back of her neck—despite her perfect bone structure and wide eyes, her movie star lips and teeth. And her voice is rough, as if she spends the better part of each day gargling with hydrochloric acid.

Now she says, "The chemicals should do most of it, but remind Edie to get all the large clumps of fat off the pelt and to be careful not to tear it. Sometimes the pinbone area can be a real problem. By next week I'll have some extra rabbits in stock for her to practice on."

"You want her to rehearse the sacrifice? That's against the rules." My mother lowers her voice. "I wouldn't want to—you know. And if she looks too efficient during the actual event, the judges will suspect. Of course I appreciate the offer, and I'll think about it, but, well, what do you think? I mean, really."

What kind of nightmare is this? During Sacrificial Rabbit Raising we are supposed to respond to the commands given by the state animal husbandry expert to slaughter our rabbits and sew them into muffs. No girl is expected to know how to do this before the event. Rule #97: No killing of animals for rehearsal.

"I think we should think about it. It's true that I'll receive a fair amount of attention from the National Association of Rabbit Experts if her form in the event is what I think it will be, but remember, Edie is my star. And the association will be looking at her, too, so there could be some extra scholarship money in it for her. Wait'll I get my shipment in next week. All righty?"

"I guess so." My mother's tone is doubtful. "You know Edie's grandmother is coming to stay for a month and she's giving me a lot of grief about the sacrifice. Not that she didn't do her fair share of butchering on the farm." Her voice trails off, then comes back with a little self-congratulatory pep. "But I'm making a special glitter club for Edie to use when she delivers the deathblow. Nowhere in the rules does it say they can't be decorated, and I just bet nobody else has even thought about it."

Mrs. Vrick gives a sigh of disgust. "Those Rules Committee people are stressing my last nerve with their regulation this and regulation that. It's been crazy around here."

I can just picture the look of sympathy on my mother's face.

I take a determined stand in the hallway, as far from the frolicking stuffed squirrels as possible, until finally my mother shrugs back into her coat, and we escape Mrs. Vrick's shiny-gummed laughter.

In Wong's parking lot, she hands me a hundred because she doesn't have anything smaller and tells me to go in without her. Her nails graze my palm. "I look like hell and I'm not in the mood to run into anybody. Plus, I'm sweating like a pig. Where's my Automatic Handy Ice?"

I push my way into the restaurant, smacking right into the back of Bethany Prewitt's baby blue skater jacket.

"Hey, you don't have to shove people." She turns slightly in the packed waiting area, just enough to show me her kittenish profile with its new, shimmery silver Just Like Eyebrow Piercing.

"Sorry. I didn't know you were standing there. It's really crowded."

Bethany shrugs and turns her back to me once more, then takes a blue comb out of her pocket and slowly runs it through her glossy hair. The fragrance of Holy Spirit Shampoo (my mother's brand of choice) challenges Wong's special Five-Spice

Chicken, his signature dish. Everything here has the smell of it, even the fortune cookies and orange slices.

Wong has no neck and about forty chins. My mother says that he has some neurological disorder, the way his tiny hands are always fluttering around his hippo cheeks, but she listens to his advice same as everyone else: Chinese people are supposed to be wise. The restaurant looks like a temple; Wong says it is full of ancient Chinese spirits—warriors, emperors, concubines—and I believe him. It's dim, except for the dusty antique lanterns that hang high overhead, and on the walls battle scenes mix with color blowups of bright, fake-looking food. None of Wong's dishes look like the food in these pictures; that's the thing about Wong's food—it's real, made of fresh vegetables and choice cuts, but it looks like pig slop. The battle scenes are fantastic, lots of guys in robes and ponytails with spears jutting from their bodies. I like the warriors' delicate faces, with their trim facial hair and pale skin; their violence is so polite.

The waiting area is close with heavy winter coats and steam, trapping me between Bethany and the door. Her jacket gleams in the thin light and her hair reeks. She boasts that she is one-hundred-percent natural—no surgeon's blade has been within a mile of her—and I believe her. I can already see how her Holy Spirited locks will be squashed by the golden headdress as she sashays down the Dome's runway, making those forty-five-degree-angle turns as she waves. Will my expertise in Mystery Powders give me enough of an edge to beat her?

Being right next to the door, I feel the inevitable smack.

"Oops! Sorry, Chumly."

I stiffen at the sound of Lana's voice.

"What are you, the new bouncer or something?" She wriggles inside, clutching an unopened pack of Skulls. "Sorry if the door got you."

"That's okay, I've got another one," I try to joke, but it comes out wrong and Lana gives me a confused look. "I mean,

I've got another backside. It's my frontside. Which would technically be my backside if my head was rotated one hundred and eighty degrees." I jam my hands in my pockets and give Bethany a look that says mind your own business.

Lana raises one thick eyebrow toward her widow's peak. A scar from a stroller accident when she was three cuts the eyebrow in half, and when she raises it like that it makes my knees shake. Her unzipped jacket reveals a shimmering button-down shirt printed with photos of snow-capped mountains; the caramel skin of her chest and neck is reddened and moist from the cold; her shoulders are right angles of dignity, and I've never seen eyes that huge in anyone's face, eyes the color of the eggplants in Bubbeh's garden. The juniper oil she wears brings me a forest, blending perfectly with Wong's Five-Spice Chicken.

"That brain of yours never stops, does it, Chumly?"

Before I can answer, Lana cuts through the crowd and goes right behind the counter to give Wong a kiss on his plump cheek. They whisper together, laughing. Then she comes back near the door, her phone ringing. She presses it to her ear, listening. When it seems like whoever has called has put her on hold, I tap her on the shoulder.

"After the Cold War ended, Swedish sonar operators thought they detected Russian submarines in their territory. But what they actually heard were minks mating near the coast. Minks do a lot of squeaking and stuff when they mate."

Lana tilts her head to the side and crinkles the skin between her eyebrows. She snaps her phone shut. "Uh . . . wow."

"Yup." I would tell her more, but having this much of her attention suddenly makes me shy.

"Oh my God." Bethany puts a hand to her cheek and rolls her eyes.

Lana lights a Skull, even though smoking is not allowed, while I study the hundred my mother gave me. Benjamin Franklin's face looks away, as if he can't wait to leave my sweating hand. Bethany opens her purse and fishes out a lipstick. She glides the color along her ace-kisser lips and I recognize the brand as one my mother tried for me: Salvation, too pink against my sallow skin. When Bethany arranges her face into a screen-girl look, I sneer, but she pretends not to see. Fine. I grab secret glances of Lana's profile, at the way her nose gently rises from her face like the prow of a sub. She catches me staring but is distracted by another phone call, so I look down and concentrate on folding Benjamin Franklin into an airplane. At least I have one consolation: Mrs. Vrick told my mother that Bethany Prewitt is lousy at handling her rabbit. And I know for a fact that she couldn't identify a beaker of milk. She probably thinks diethyl carbinol is the name of an Algerian fashion designer.

"Mr. Anderson! Shrimp Lo Mein, small! Special Five-Spice Chicken, big! You remember no need big hook to catch excellent fishy!"

Lana laughs into her phone and turns away, cupping her hand over her mouth as Mr. Anderson inches past, licking his lips, the take-out bag gripped limply in front of him like a lady's purse.

"Miss Hill! Special Five-Spice Chicken, small! Shrimp Roll, one! Here extra shrimp piece for your cat no run away to New Jersey!"

I nudge Lana and she turns around, still on the phone. Her eyes are bloodshot. Mooch's okay this year, old-fashioned, but cool.

"Hang on a second." Lana covers the phone and plucks at my hand. "Hey, what's this?"

"I'm sending Benjamin Franklin on a long day's journey into outer space."

"Hunh?"

"Benjamin Franklin, his face is on the hundred." I take back the bill and unfold it to show her.

"A hundred bucks? How much Chinese food can you eat?"

Bethany sniffs, running her blue comb through her hair again.

Quickly, I fold the bill back into an airplane and pretend to launch it, my body managing an action hero swagger. Before I can stop myself, the bill sails out of my hand and over the heads of the crowd. I watch my mother's money fly up against Wong's high red smoke-stained ceiling in a smooth arc, the kind of balletic, looping arc you only see in cartoons of paper airplanes, gracefully dodging lanterns and ceiling molding until it crashes out of sight.

Lana's red-veined eyes are full of admiration. I will die a real action hero, lots of hard-driving guitars in the background, and even if the entire state hears about what Alec did to me, it won't matter now.

"That was beautiful, Chumly." Once again, she snaps her phone closed.

Bethany's eyes search the room. "You'd better get over there before somebody pockets it."

"*Beautiful*. Man! That *was* beauty." Lana tilts her head back, the smile on her full lips growing wider, dreamier.

"It's a cinch if you know what you're doing. I can sometimes make one stay up for ten minutes, or twenty."

"Oh, *please*." Bethany folds her arms across her chest.

Lana's gaze shifts to look behind me. The dreamy smile vanishes.

"What's going on?" My mother's hand grips my arm. Her fingers are frozen sticks from clutching her Automatic Handy Ice in the miniwagon. "I called over an hour ago. Our food has to be ready."

I pull back.

"I—uh, it's really busy."

Both Lana and Bethany grow quiet and turn away as my mother scans the crowd. Bodies form a solid wall between me and the fallen hundred.

"Mom, why don't you go back in the miniwagon so you can sit down? I don't mind waiting." I talk fast, my voice low.

"What? I can't hear you." Her own voice drops as she spies the mother of another Pageant contestant. "Oh God, there's Helene. I knew I'd run into somebody."

"Lorraine! Hi!" Helene waves and my mother returns her greeting with a smile. Helene's gloved hand beckons, forcing my mother to move toward it. I grab the opportunity and squeeze my way into the wall of bodies.

"Excuse me, sorry. I dropped my money." Murmuring apologies, I push over to where I think the hundred landed. My hand blindly gropes shoes and dead grasshopper husks and wood gummy with sauce. "Ow! Sorry, I'm looking for something."

"Mrs. Stein! Sweet and Sour Soup, small! Special Five-Spice Chicken, big! Egg Roll, two!" Wong's voice rings out and my hand stops dead. "Mrs. Stein! Order ready!"

Hunched among the legs, I pray.

"Edie! Where are you? Edie, where did you go?"

My mother's voice cuts through the chatter and the fast chop of cleavers. I stagger empty-handed to the counter, where Wong is smiling his fat smile and my mother is rummaging through her purse. The Chinese lanterns sway dizzily above me as I make my way to her side. In an opening between the bodies, I see Lana staring at me. It might be the weak light, but it looks like she is mouthing the command: *Run, Chumly, run.*

"There you are. What happened to you?" My mother is signing the bottom of a credit card slip.

As he tears off her copy, Wong turns to me, his voice like a loudspeaker positioned right above Lana and Bethany. "You eat Wong's food, you be so smart and pretty girl. One day you make surprise for everybody and win Pageant. Wong say so and you make bet he never wrong." He throws a couple of extra fortune cookies in our bag and hands it to my mother. "Your mother one looking-good lady. Lucky husband for have such sexy wife to come home to every night."

She's actually blushing. "Oh, well. Well, now." But she thanks him and gives me a sharp nudge with her foot so I have to thank him, too. Then she hustles me out the door, but not before I hear Bethany drawling *Bye, Queeeeeen,* and see her flawless face broadcasting pity, her baby blue skater jacket blocking Lana from view.

"Where did you disappear to?" My mother revs the engine and backs out fast.

"Please slow down." I buckle my seat belt without her telling me. "You saw how busy it was."

"And I had to run into Helene Adams."

The dashboard lights up with information. While I strain my eyes to see the speedometer, she strains to see her face in the rearview mirror. "Oh my God, I don't have a speck of lipstick left on my lips. Why didn't you tell me?"

"You look fine." The needle of the speedometer kicks up.

"A lot you care." Her right hand rustles wildly in her purse. "Damn. I've got so much junk in here I can't even *find* my lipstick."

"You don't need your lipstick now."

"Don't editorialize, Edie. Dr. Plow doesn't want my blood pressure to rise. And where's the hundred dollars I gave you to pay for our food?"

My lungs snap shut inside my chest. "I—I think I dropped it by mistake." The lies fall off my tongue like black stones. "Some lady lost her wedding ring on the floor and I was helping her look for it and the money must've slipped out of my hand—"

"Since when does a hundred dollars just slip away from a person!"

The miniwagon swerves crookedly, and I press my back tight against the seat, willing us like ten Amazing Mister Fezundos to stay in the middle of the road. What good is being able to differentiate barium compounds now?

My mother yanks her hand out of her purse and it falls off the seat, spilling Just Like Breath Mints, tinkling silver change, Mrs. Vrick's pamphlets, and thirty tubes of Creation Lipstick around her shoes. Her shoes are barely visible in this crowd. "Cripes!" She tries to brake, but something from her purse has wedged itself between the brake pedal and the floor. Is that a picture of us smiling at the Identity Mall Fashion Expo? The photo slides down her ankle as her body twists and she leans down, trying to loosen whatever it is that is stuck while struggling to keep control of the wheel. The miniwagon weaves from one side of the road to the other, but I just keep pushing my back into the seat so hard my head feels like it will pop, and by the time my mother's freed the bottle of Zantickasolubazil from underneath the brake, someone's front steps have come rushing up under the wheels.

The back of the security guard's head seems unnaturally still—a huge polystroob security guard action figure. To punish myself, I imagine taking off his uniform and massaging him, suffering the cold hunk of his neck, his back bristly with hair. Sliding my hands underneath my butt, I shrink down into the backseat of the patrol cart, making sure my face is never visible through the window; the crime show crews that roam the streets would just love to get a Pageant contestant in their lenses. Unfortunately, these carts can't go more than twenty miles an hour, and we poke along the streets like an old, sniffing dog. Since I insisted I was fine and the Controlled Healing ambulance workers aren't supposed to waste a ride on anyone who isn't almost dead or likely to start trouble, the security guard from the neighborhood next to ours has done my mother the favor of giving me a ride home; of course, with one look she had all the men falling over themselves to escort her into the ambulance.

At the entrance to our neighborhood, we have to stop and explain my humiliation to the night security guard. At least it isn't Fish-Face, always looking to catch someone's pain in his camera. Inside the patrol station, a woman's voice comes over the police radio in a staticky whine. Someone is having a domestic dispute on South Green Street. The Projects. The police will have to go over there and break it up; the Projects are under public security. I wonder whether Fish-Face would ever have to come to our house to settle a domestic dispute— whether he'd have to arrest my father for kicking my mother in the shin instead of taking her to the Screenplex, or arrest my mother for spraying all the Shaver's Helper down the toilet on the morning of the annual Topiary Salesmen's Breakfast at the Airport Inn?

When at last we pull into our driveway, the headlights from the patrol cart light up my father like a discovered thief. The security guard jerks the cart to a stop and gets out. I note his flat, square-shaped butt.

My father folds his arms across his chest and when the security guard speaks, small phantoms of breath fly at his face, his eyes invisible behind the reflected glare of the headlights on his glasses. It's the security guard who does all the talking. My father just nods his head, and when he points at me still in the cart, the security guard trudges back and opens the door.

"Come on now, your Daddy wants to make sure you're all right."

I have no choice except to drag my ass up the driveway, head down. My mind is crowded with images: our miniwagon's puckered hood, the owners of the house we hit—a grim, silver-haired couple who took us in and called the police—my mother's face, frightened and distant as the ambulance workers helped her and her Automatic Handy Ice onto a stretcher. The old woman had wrinkled her lips and clasped her arms in front of her thin breasts while her husband kept whining, *Why didn't that Jewish woman take her foot off the gas?*

My father pulls me to him before I can sneak into the house. "You're all right." He bends down and stares.

"I was wearing my seat belt."

"And what about Mommy? Was she wearing hers?"

I look at the security guard, his bulging gun.

"Yeah," I lie.

"Like I said, Mr. Stein, your wife is going to be all right. They just took her to General Memorial General for observation. You know how women can be when they get shook. I'll be glad to give you a lift over to the hospital, though. If you don't mind taking the scenic route. Ha, ha." He ruffles my hair with his heavy hand. "This one's a trooper. Came through the whole thing just like a real . . . *scout*, didn't you?"

"Thanks for all your help." My father steers me toward the house. "But I've got another vehicle parked in the garage."

As far as I know, my father has never in his life called a mini-wagon a *vehicle*.

After the men shake hands, I bolt upstairs. I don't want to answer any questions. My mother's given me the bottle of meds to hide at home. The floor groans under my father's step.

"Edie."

I turn to face him, looking down from the top of the stairs.

"Are you . . . sure . . . you're . . . all right?"

"I told you. I'm fine. Just go and get Mom." I kick at the baseboard with my sport shoe.

He moves up one step.

"Your mother . . . ?" The staircase light isn't on, and in the weak spillover from the upstairs hall, it looks as if my father is just a leaning column of fuzz. He stops talking and rubs his eyes behind his glasses and I don't say anything. I've learned that if

I'm quiet long enough, he'll usually give up and go away, especially if, like now, he isn't totally sure what it is he is asking. But when his foot moves back down, and his body starts to turn, I want to jump to him, yelling *catch*, like a little girl.

I run into the bathroom and lock the door. When I hear my father's miniwagon back down the driveway, I slip to the floor and rest my forehead against the perfectly folded towels hanging on the rack. Even the towels smell of her. I picture Mrs. Popoff driving, with her competent, Spanish-teacher smile. When she drives she plays bossa novas and sings along. An open tube of Creation Lipstick on the counter mocks me, its flattened, waxy shape the same rich color as the scratch on my mother's hand when she tucked the Zantickasolubazil into my coat. I dig into my pocket for the bottle. Whenever she got a new prescription, I used to try to guess what color the meds would be. Even then it was as if I was training for Pageant, trying to identify a mysterious element. Sometimes the meds were a brilliant, shocking mix of colors; sometimes they were just teeny white dots; always, they sparkled.

I set the bottle on the counter next to the lipstick and turn on the water, let it get cold while I take off my clothes. From underneath the extra towels in the cupboard, I feel for my polystroob bag. Then I wet my arms and chest with the frigid water and put the bag over my head. I tighten it snugly around my neck. The thin polystroob follows my breaths, sinking against my face and then away in a familiar rhythm as the air inside the bag gets cozy and stale. Outside the bag, my nipples are freezing hard enough to break off, but I keep the bag over my head until it hurts, make myself count a slow seven before I tear it off, gasping.

She'll be all right now.

I lie on her bed and stare at the blank screen. I try to picture Lana's face smiling at the beautiful loop-di-loop of my money airplane, but here in my mother's bedroom, that image has a lot of competition. On the nightstand, her bedside water pitcher is half full, and a greasy jar of Confession Makeup Remover sits on secret web site printouts smudged with black. On top of the bureau, her bed tray waits for her to finish the half-eaten sandwich lying forgotten on a styroplated plate.

4

The day dawns overcast, but turns into one of those heart-breaker afternoons—a bright diamond of sun, sky blue and plush as the velvet lining inside a wedding ring box, everything smelling like God. The yellow warblers are chirping and hopping around in the unmowed grass. Good weather scares me if I'm feeling unlucky, like an all-smiles neighbor who turns out to be an ax murderer. Which has happened. And there's no escaping it either, since, with Pageant training suspended today because of my mother's injury, I've got strict orders to clean the yard until it whistles.

Just as I'm rounding a corner with the last full wheelbarrow, something knocks the naval officer's cap off my head and I lose my grip, dumping a heap of leaves on the whistle-clean lawn.

"Whoops! *Excusez-moi.*" Lana jumps down from the willow at the side of our house, wearing my cap. She rights the wheelbarrow, motioning for me to get in. The cap topples to the ground and neither one of us makes a move to pick it up. Her hair is parted strangely, hiding her expression. "Let's go for a ride," she says.

In a bottom drawer of my dresser, there are nine strands of this very hair hidden in a pocket of a shirt I never wear anymore because my mother thinks it makes me look like an Insecticide Hut deliveryman. I've collected these strands with more care than my father maneuvers his arcing net, and believe me, no butterfly can match their rarity. It's almost as if Lana's hair is supernaturally rooted to her scalp; where it is natural for everyone else to lose (according to my mother's fallout statistics) between fifty and sixty strands a day, as far as I can tell, Lana sheds only one or two a month. I would doubt that the dirt-dominator pouches or trash-pulverizer bin in Lana's house hold more than the little group gathered in the pocket of my old shirt. One day I will have collected enough to present her with a freestanding hair construction.

My mother will ground me for another month if she wakes up from her nap and finds me gone, but I fold myself inside the wheelbarrow's cold, rusting basin. Lana pushes me, her long fingers half-covered by those fingerless gloves that poor heroic kids in old movies wear. As we bump across the grass, she switches to a one-handed steer so she can pull something out of her pocket. "My mom says she saw a patrol cart in front of your house the other night," she says, dangling a hundred dollar bill over my head. "I figured you probably got in trouble for defacing government property. It's illegal to fold money into airplanes you know."

"Oh really?" I give her what I think is a knowing smirk, my gloved hands gripping the sides of the wheelbarrow. Did she really hunt through the feet in Wong's to find my hundred for me? All day I looked for her in the halls at school, and although I saw Bethany combing her hair in the off-limits computer center and combing her hair by a frisking station and combing her hair with a group of other girls by her locker, I didn't see Lana once. Now she is in front of me, close enough for me to smell the garlic on her breath. Coming from her, it is the scent of proposition, fueled by garlicky spaghetti; right here in full daylight, Lana Grimaldi might jump my bones.

Lana's face pinks as she steers the wheelbarrow through the obstacle course of topiary, polystroob hammocks, Insecticide Huts, and Just Like Farmers Squares full of withered brown cornstalks in the backyards of our neighbors. I think I see people moving on the treeless grounds of the Springfield Gardens Disciplinary Camp for Girls, no doubt the girls in their convicts' uniforms lined up for bondage by some cross-eyed superintendent. Several of these girls have been featured on true crime shows; one girl assaulted over seventy cripples in an Emmy-winning episode of *Sins of the Pretty.*

"Yup," Lana says, panting as she steers clear of a compost heap bright with Just Like Tomatoes and their gleaming yellow seeds. "Folding money'll get you twenty to life in most states. And in Deansville, they don't even let you apply for parole."

"Yeah, right. Like I care." My small attempt at acting cool is spoiled by the squeals popping out of me as we bounce over the uneven yards. I love being given rides (the Drive-By Sausage Adventure Forest, despite the meat theme, is still my favorite motion experience), but I try to keep my face tough.

Lana's forehead is beginning to sweat, and as she lifts one hand to wipe, the hundred falls. I reach out to save it just as Lana is turning a sharp left to avoid Mrs. Vrick's topiary. The movement rocks our balance; we pitch too far, and the wheelbarrow's front stabs into the badly pruned legs of a leprechaun. Lana and I tumble after it sideways, heads knocking, limbs tangled, branches breaking with vicious cracks, the metal-lyte lip of the wheelbarrow pressing painfully into my side.

But we laugh.

Lana's phone rings inside her jacket, but she doesn't answer. Locating and pocketing the crumpled hundred, she springs to her feet. "Come on," she says, grabbing the wheelbarrow and taking off into the fields beyond the yards. For one long moment, the whole neighborhood seems to fall away, leaving nothing but me and a jumbo Insecticide Hut.

I hear shouts from the field. A noise escapes my throat and I fly from the yard, my legs whirling me out toward Lana, who is bent low, driving the wheelbarrow in S shapes through the field. I run to meet her in the middle of all that wide green space, and we ditch the wheelbarrow in the woods below the reservoir. I pray it's still there when we come back.

As we climb through the woods, Lana tells me about her dead cousin, Rita Domino. I know from my mother's list of previous Pageant winners that when Rita Domino was younger, she was once crowned queen in Buffalo.

"She was a great individual. People just didn't understand her. My father for one. He thought she was a mental, but she had more sanity than you and me put together."

"That sucks." I have a charley horse in my side, and on the pretext of tying my sport shoe, I bend down and discreetly massage my cramping flesh.

"Rita Domino used to babysit me while my parents worked at my father's old restaurant in the Bronx. We'd hang out downstairs in the storeroom and play swashbucklers with toothpicks shaped like swords."

"Cool."

"It was more than cool, it was life-saving." Lana's long leg restlessly kicks a tree stump. "One day while we were playing, my mother ran downstairs with my father right behind her, swearing. He kicked her in the ass and when she fell, the plate she was carrying broke. A piece of it went into her cheek and blood poured all over her striped dress. I can still see those blue and yellow stripes getting all bloody. Anyway, just as my father was about to sock my mother for breaking his plate and bleeding on his floor, Rita jumped in and jabbed two of our swords into my father's neck, like this," Lana demonstrates on the stump with a couple of sticks, "giving my mother enough time to grab me and run home."

"Wow. What happened then?" I sit back on my heels, still fighting the cramp.

"She didn't cry or anything. She fed me a slice of lemon pie and held me on her lap and told me that nothing could ever stop her from loving me. And I realized right then that a person's most important duty is to honor their mother. I vowed that somehow, someday, I would get her away from him."

I turn over a rock and watch two grasshoppers jump away. Lana looks at me expectantly; I should either walk or talk.

"Your cousin sounds brave," I say. "What happened to her?"

A shade is drawn over Lana's features. "She killed herself."

I turn over another rock, but there is nothing beneath it. "Because, um, she was part of that . . . group?" Fernando, who hears everything, has heard that the Happy Endings headquarters is a broom closet with an illegal phone line in the basement of some empty building. They have secret meetings and people called Consolers who you can call up if you're considering joining. They believe that as soon as enough people do a Happy Ending, the dead are going to come back and change the world, eliminate all evil from life—eliminate death itself. The world will be guaranteed beautiful.

A very delicate, whitish grasshopper bounces up on Lana's knee. She tickles the fine hairs on its back legs with her thumb, but it doesn't move away. We both watch its antennae gracefully furl and unfurl. I know she thinks it is beautiful, and suddenly I want to slap the bug from Lana's knee. I could almost slap Lana's face, too, with its worrisome expression.

"How could she have killed herself," I say, "if she was so sane and nice enough to save your mother?"

Lana doesn't take her eyes from the bug. "Don't be so quick to think you know the score. Facts have a way of twisting themselves to fit more easily into the small brains of our society. Sometimes people get stuck in the wrong place at the wrong time. Which I can fucking relate to." She stands then, and the grasshopper falls into a tangle of weeds. "Besides, people have to act on their beliefs. Even if you don't agree with them, you have to admire a person for following through."

"Sure, sure. You're right about that," I say, trying to sound enthusiastic, like I am not one of the small brains of society. My side is still in a spasm as I struggle to follow Lana's perfect posture up the trail.

The sun bounces off the crystal water of the reservoir, smashing our eyes like the flash of a camera snapping a picture of Lana and me making it to the top of Deansville. Maybe we are going to climb up the fire tower to hawk gobs of spit down on all the feebles of the world. The maple leaves bow in the slight wind, their burnt candy colors dancing. There are no Gentle Welcome nuns around, but the air feels pleasantly disturbed, as if one of their fluttery, whirligigging saxophone solos had recently displaced some molecules.

"Domino!" Both of us yell it at the same time and Lana tags me, saying, "Jinx, owe me a beer." Then she's spitting out her gum in an arc like her mouth is a gun and tying her jacket around her waist, running, turning cartwheels, backflip after backflip, the star of Deansville Middle School tumbling. I watch her, wondering how it would be to have muscles that could move like that, leaving the ground with such grace. When she reaches the other end of the reservoir, she walks around on her hands and sings from the new Mystic Fangs release, mixing up the lyrics of three different songs. Beside her, the water is a bright and dark sheet. When I catch up, we settle ourselves on Lana's rock. "These cracks make the outline of a TR3, see?" she'd said to me the first time I met her up here, showing me with her amazing fingers.

There's a rustling in the bushes, and my lower back prickles, but it's not Alec Fogel's dirty Turbine-Spike sport shoes that emerge, it's the brown-furred feet of a wild rabbit, hopping

across the grass toward the edge of the water like a pulse freed
from a body.

"You're training a rabbit for Pageant, yes?"

"Yeah." I sigh dramatically so she'll think that the whole
Pageant thing is making me weary. The wild rabbit lifts its head
and listens, its nose searching the air for the scent of danger. Its
ears are not floppy like Alice Jones's. Would Alice Jones be able
to survive up here?

Lana's hand emerges from a pocket and she points at me
with a lumpy floogie, smiling. "Care for a taste of honey?" She
lights up, then passes the floogie to me.

This is the first time since summer that we've smoked mooch
together. I tell myself that I'm doing research for the Drug-
Addict Prevention Bee and take a small hit.

Lana takes the floogie between her lips and sucks until it
crackles. "I've seen that rabbit before," she says, again using the
floogie as a pointer. "I'm gonna name her Domino. What do
you think?"

I drum my fingers on the rock, my anxiety—is it the subject
of Pageant or Happy Endings that has me so worked up?—
giving way to mooch-induced cheerfulness. "My rabbit's name
is Alice Jones, like that girl in the story who got acid thrown
on her face."

"Yeah, is that a true story?" She leans in closer, interested.

"No, it's a book. A whole novel."

"Oh. I was hoping it was a true story. It sounds juicy."

"Well, actually it might be true. Yeah, I forgot, it is a true
story."

Domino hops closer to us and then away, as if someone was
whispering directions into her ears.

"Who threw the acid at her?"

Pleasure glows inside me, and I let the slight accent of a foreign diplomat flavor my speech. "Well, this girl Alice Jones was
really smart but she had no legs. And she was too poor to buy

fake ones. Everyone in her town pretended to be nice about it but they actually hated her. She only had one friend, Franco, this really skinny Spanish guy, and he didn't even live in her town. He was one of those prison pen pals."

"What was he in for?"

"He accidentally poisoned a few people to death. It was gruesome, but he was really sorry. They put him in prison for life anyway because it happened in Germany and they're very strict about making mistakes over there."

"So how'd Alice Jones get hooked up with him?"

"She saw an ad he wrote in the classifieds of *Invent It!* magazine. See, Alice Jones was into inventing things. For example, she built her own nuclear submarine."

The asymmetrical eyebrow rises again.

"Just a small one. She kept it in her swimming pool."

"Indeed."

"I told you she was smart. Anyway. One day Alice had a vision that everyone in her town, except her, was going to get a terminal disease. And so Alice got all worried for the people. She was a very compassionate person."

"I don't follow. Here, suck hard."

I take the floogie again and do as I'm told. I try not to cough. "Well. Since Alice had no legs she was extra nice. But of course everybody hated her more because of that. And then a bunch of girls who really despised Alice snuck into her house when she was sleeping and poured acid onto her face. Alice nearly died and while she was at the hospital recovering, all the feebles in town actually did get a terminal disease. Then one of the doctors who really liked Alice donated some fake legs and gave her money so she could move away and finally have a decent life." As I speak, the sky is getting brighter. My tongue is dry and burning but it feels good, like when you think you've said the wrong thing but instead made a great joke.

"And what, I'm supposed to believe this shit?"

"No! Of course not."

"But you just said it was true."

"Only sort of true. It's one of those urban myths that took place in France. So it's not guaranteed fact. I mean, it's hard to say."

"Whatever."

Is it the mooch or am I an idiot? But now Lana is smiling at me in a very friendly way, so I smile back and we pass the floogie some more. Again, her phone rings, and again, she doesn't answer.

"I like your story," she says then. "It doesn't matter if it's true or not."

"If Alice Jones had a friend like Rita Domino," I say, "she probably would have gone after all the feebles with a shotgun and blown their faces off."

Lana's neck arches back and she snorts. "That brain of yours never stops, does it, Chumly?"

But she's pleased, I can tell.

"Hey. Here's your money. Some fat guy was just about to snarf it when I told him to drop it or he'd never see his family again." Again, the hundred appears from the tight pocket of Lana's cords and I reach for it, but her fingerless glove holds it captive.

"I know what you could do with it." In the trees above us, a solitary squirrel quacks angrily at a blue jay. Other than that, the only sound is the blood pulsing round and round inside of me.

"What?"

"Ever done Jiffy? I know where we can get some. It's quite mellow. You'll like it."

"Um, I think I tried it once." My brain is starting to glide down and out my ears like poured honey. Diagonal threads glimmer in all the bushes and branches, silky spider poop turning colors in the sun, and the flannel shirt Lana is wearing looks incredibly soft. Her phone rings but she doesn't answer, because there is no one she'd rather talk to right now than me.

"Suck up for round two." She relights the floogie, which she'd snuffed on the rock, and brings it to my lips. As I inhale, the fuzz of her glove tickles my nose and the smoke bursts from me in a cough. I stumble off our perch, gasping, and Domino shoots off into the woods.

"Hey, easy. Take it easy, just breathe easy."

"It—must've gone down the wrong pipe," I manage to rasp. "Wow, this is good stuff." Suddenly, a fit of giggles overtakes me, and I start hacking again, "Your cousin Domino is excellent!"

"Oh yeah?"

"Happy Endings is mellow," I shriek, and spin around in a fit of hysterical wheezing. "Domino!" My voice cracks weirdly as I tear leaves from branches with a terrible need to destroy. "Domino! Domino, Domino, Domino!"

"Yo, Chumly. Calm down, you wild thing. If you don't stop it, you'll have a heart attack and croak. And then I'll have to dump your body in the reservoir to hide the evidence that you're a moochhead."

"Yeah, and then when I decompose, little bits of me will get into the water supply. And everybody will be drinking me, they'll be drinking the molecules of a moochhead, and everybody in Deansville will get stoned and freak out!" I collapse on the ground, gurgling. "Hey, how come you didn't just keep the money and buy the Jiffy yourself?"

My question hangs naked in the sunlight. Lana stands up on her rock and stretches, offering the wide V of her arms to the far-off heavens, her head flung back, long hair dripping down below her thighs. I feel a quaking sensation in my bowels. "I didn't mean—you wouldn't *steal*." My mouth is dry, gummy beads of spit catching in the corners of my lips. I swallow.

Lana turns and leaps off the rock in one fluid twist. She

drops to her knees and pushes me flat on the grass, hands pinning my shoulders. "You've got lyccra-gauze mouth, don't you, Chumly? From all that mooch you've been smoking." Through the curtain of her hair, I watch as she licks her lips, sucking each one quickly in and out until they are both gleaming wet, her tongue skittering over them, and then her face drops, soaking my mouth with a rushed but generous kiss. The world feels like it is being played at a too-fast speed as she rolls off me, taking the strands of her hair that got caught between us. She lies next to me, squinting up at the cloudless sky through two impenetrable slits, and says, "So, what about that Jiffy?"

"Every girl should kiss another girl at least once a day. It evens out the world's power balance," Lana says as we wait for the downtown shuttle. My insides are still reeling from the unexpectedness of her mouth on mine.

"Only kidding," she says, spinning away from me on the sidewalk. The light is leaving the sky, my mother will wake and roar, Lana's sudden urge to go view the headdress on display at the Franklin Echo Museum is not something to which I should nod like a mental.

"Well," I blurt out, confused, "diethylstilbestrol is $C_{18}H_{20}O_2$. Calcium fluoride is the main source of fluorine. Potassium nitrate is used in fertilizers and gunpowder, whereas potassium permanganate is—"

"Okay, okay. Take it easy. I don't know a potassium whatsit from a pound cake." She gives me a strange, enigmatic look. "Although I'd like to." Her mouth is working like she's about to say something else, but instead she digs a mangled pack of Skulls out of her weatherbreaker and starts to hum.

"You would?" I sit up straighter on the shuttle stop bench, trying to stop the shivers by forcing my knees against my chest.

"Sure. Who wouldn't? Knowledge is power," Lana says,

blowing a long stream of perfect, smoky Os. She doesn't offer me a drag. "Only very scientific minds are going to make it into Pageant finals." She taps the side of my head, giving me a wry smile. "Word on the street is that brain of yours is going places."

"People are talking about me?"

"You bet."

She rises then to look down the street, so I don't say any more. I'm not exactly sure how to respond—is she making fun or expressing respect?—so in case she looks back at me, I keep my face still.

The gray and white shuttle pulls over and beeps as it stops. I don't have my shuttle card, so Lana tosses hers out the window after she gets on. I almost don't make it in time to board and have to knock on the closing doors. As I pass Lana's card over the scanner, the driver gives me a suspicious look, and I wonder how my being caught might affect my points, but Lana waves from the back of the shuttle and I scurry down the aisle before there's trouble.

The streets have a claustrophobic layout that I have never noticed before. Everything is right angles; there is nothing graceful or inviting about any of the pale pink security patrol stations jutting out from the concrete entrances to the neighborhoods. I get a feeling of nausea, but it's not in my stomach, it's behind my eyes, in my brain, and when I turn away from the window to look at Lana, there's no relief.

"Pageant Committee's changing the point scheme," she says, bringing her face closer to mine so we won't be overheard. I can still smell the mooch on her breath. "It hasn't been officially announced, but Mystery Powders is swapping places with Better Person Skills."

I pull back to stare at her. "I thought you didn't . . . How do you know?"

She gives me a lopsided grin, cigarette hanging, its tip glowing on her inhale like an agreeable little friend. Only Lana would dare to smoke on a shuttle. "I have my sources." Her nostrils suck up the smoke coming from her mouth. "So Mystery Powders is going to be worth almost as much as Electric Polyrubber Man. Good news for you, right? The president's been all over the screen lately, yakking about patriotic duty and biowarfare. The chairman of the National Toxic Death Prevention Society was in the news just the other day blabbing how girls in training for Mystery Powders could provide an invaluable service to humanity if they take their research seriously. Little Miss Scientists like you are pretty hot property these days."

A few people board and give us nasty looks. It's because of the smoke, I guess, but I wonder whether it's obvious that Lana kissed me. I think of Shirley Hurley, who had to move out of town after she was caught taking a bath with the receptionist from the Gastroenterology Salon.

Lana's eyes glow with dark fire. "Remember Benny Gold? The boy who died? Do you know how he got that brain tumor?"

"I think I heard . . . it was from . . . " Those eyes of hers are the most amazing things I've ever seen; winged beasts are swimming in there, galaxies are popping open.

"I'll tell you. Benny Gold's tumor was caused by the synergistic effect of breathing the vapor from his new Just Like Polyvinyl wallpaper, wearing clothes washed with Missus Pretty Hands laundry soap, and playing ball near an Insecticide Hut, which is full of Just Like Organochlorines. The NOEL dose of that laundry soap was about one grain in the lab tests and they still—"

"I don't think they sell Missus Pretty Hands laundry soap anymore."

Lana pounds the window with her fist. Her voice is low, but passionate. "That's not the point! The point is that there are three thousand new chemicals on the market for household use each year. Did you know that? And nobody has time to check out what happens when certain compounds are in the vicinity of other compounds. Forget other countries blowing us away with their bioweapons, we're blowing ourselves away! We're talking herds of unknown carcinogens. We're talking mutagens, scads of aeropathogens. The Just Like That Conglomerate is shitting their pants from all the fatality lawsuits. It's all political, Chumly. You should know it."

I watch her lips shape the syllables, but it doesn't matter to me what she is saying. Lana Grimaldi kissed me! The truth rises like a fish leaping from a lake. She wanted to kiss me from the time she roller-pole-vaulted past the Insecticide Huts on our front lawn, that day she grinned at me and said, "Hey Chumly, how long's that Vrick witch had a pole up her ass?"

Of course I know that is no way to win Pageant, no matter how many points I score in Mystery Powders. It's official grounds for disqualification, in fact worse than being caught with an aerosol nozzle in your mouth and a collapsible hatchet under your mattress. It hits me hard and fast: I have to stay away from Lana Grimaldi.

The sudden ring of the phone startles me. My knee falls away from hers.

"You've got a damn good chance to win Pageant, but you should definitely think about whether it's worth it to take up with bad politics," Lana says. Then she presses the talk button, says, "I'll talk to you later," and turns back to me, her lips peeled back from her teeth and canines sparkling. "Capeesh?"

In front of the headdress's hushed gold, I wonder what Lana means, but it's a little difficult to talk about it now, with the usual gaggle of Pageant contestants and mothers lighting the shrine candles or dropping notes into the prayer bucket in front of the display case. The headdress recently made it out of Franklin Echo's private collection to take up residence here at his museum; he's decided to have a public showing because it will be the first ancient relic to adorn a Feminine Woman of Conscience's head; all other cities use the standard white-gold-plate and cubic zirconia tiaras; Deansville's defection from the norm sent the Rules Committee into a minor tizzy until it was decided that the headdress was a significant historical artifact, thereby justifying our city's individualistic deviation. Also, there's been a serious amount of news coverage regarding Queen Ankameretikia, who owned the headdress, and it was an easy leap for reporters to suggest that the headdress itself was responsible for her success as a ruler. Hence the shrine and the organized busloads of Pageant hopefuls coming from as far away as Idaho to make their offerings.

"The cobra ornament alone could finance you well into senility," Lana whispers into my ear. "With proper portfolio management, of course."

"Rita Domino won Pageant one year, didn't she?"

Lana snorts. "She regretted *that* move."

"Why?"

"Chumly. She didn't even get to keep a *quarter* of the money. What with taxes and hidden fees and Rules Committee bullshit."

"But she won. She must have been at least, uh, kind of . . . proud of herself." A pair of twins get down on their knees in front of the display case, while their mother presses a clenched fist against her mouth.

"Don't be ridiculous. She entered because of the money." Lana lights a Skull with one of the shrine candles. No Smoking signs are everywhere, and mothers click their tongues disapprovingly. "Money buys freedom. You can dig that, right? At least Rita got enough money to leave godforsaken Buffalo and start a real life."

"Is it the cigarettes?" A mother in a crisp Silk-Mastr suit puts her hand on Lana's arm. The woman's voice is gentle and she has on a shade of dark red lipstick that makes her look like she's been shot in the mouth. "I'm sorry to bother you, but you have a very nice body." The woman gestures toward a chubby girl ill-advisedly wearing Stretch-Tightees. "We tried Sniff-to-be-Slim, and Dr. Mort's thirty-day plan, but nothing works. I'm at my wit's end with her. She can't take Stimeralax or Dexitroxitrate. She was tolerating Amphetanuts for a while, but then she got the hair loss and the breakouts."

"Yeah. Give her cigarettes. It'll work out." Lana drops her half-smoked Skull to the floor and steps on it.

"Thanks." The woman's face is grateful.

Lana is staring at the headdress, so still that she might be part of the display, an ancient queen gazing upon her hat. "If I had the money, I'd get us the hell out of here."

Immediately, I brighten. It's not that I should stay away from her; I should stay away from wherever she is *not*. "Where would we go?"

Lana turns to look at me, as if surprised to find me standing next to her. "Not *us*. My mother and me. I've got to get her out of here before it's too late."

"Where would you take her?" I keep my eyes fixed on the lapis lazuli vulture's head poking from the brow of the headdress.

"It depends. Anyway, I'm leaving town tomorrow for a few days. Gotta go help my cousin Maxine and her kids get settled in their new house."

I don't say anything. The chime of recorded bells plays above our heads and Lana fishes inside her jacket for her phone. Before she finishes dialing, a security guard taps my shoulder. "Gotta move it along now, ladies. Next busload's waiting."

Posters of the ocean line my bedroom walls; I buy them at the Identity Mall: corny shots of sailboats at sunset, surfers catching the wave, toddlers building sand castles at the beach. Each one has been altered to include a hidden destroyer, drawn by me in invisible ink, sometimes so large that the outlines run off the poster and onto my wall. Sometimes I draw it with periscope up, sometimes the entire sub has surfaced. Inside the subs are the mysterious submariners, the naval elite; only the smartest brains can make it into submarine school, because a sub operates deep in enemy territory, unaided and alone. This is what makes the crew of a submarine so different from the rest of the military—they have to be emotionally supportive. Submerged for months at a time with no outside contact, they become more of a family to one another than any blood relative, and there's no room for secrets: each crew member gets a sled-sized cubicle, and that's it. The only privacy you have is between your ears. That's the best part. Submarine duty teaches you how to keep people from parking themselves in your thoughts. Every day I look at my posters and think about what lurks there, unseen and deadly.

Two messages from Fernando are on my screen; he's sorry about my mom's accident, and heard something about Lily Gates planning to firebomb the next Just Like Meat Planet somewhere downstate. I consider writing back to get details, but after a couple words my fingers wilt on the keyboard. Surrounded by my hidden subs, polystroob plugs stuffed in my ears, I watch Alice Jones hop soundlessly around my room like some toy come alive under a spell. She nibbles a chair, then leaps. She thumps a leg, sniffs the air, rubs her chin's scent glands on one of my Clickies to mark territory. The mooch is still swirling through me, and I am overwhelmed suddenly with the burden of responsibility. Did I let her out of the cage? I don't remember doing it, and I *know* I checked her lock before I went out to clean the yard. I won't think about it. When I catch her, I can feel the blood running beneath her warm fur, and I get a strange little thrill to think how I can make it stop, just like that, forever. A Happy Ending, of sorts.

Lana doesn't know the whole story about Pageant; unless you're actually in training, you can't understand the true point of it. I'm not killing Alice Jones because of bad politics, I'm killing her to prove I can sacrifice something I love. It's not until just this minute that I realize how clever the Rules Committee really is: they don't come right out and say it, but they are expecting us to bond with our rabbits—to grow to love them as they grow to obey us—which will make the killing that much more meaningful as a rite of passage. What rite of passage will Lana go through in her life? Without Pageant, what do you have to mark the difference between one day and the next?

I understand now why my mother has been too busy to nag me about the yard: down the hall, my parents' voices are sniping at each other behind their bedroom door. Since she popped her jaw in the accident, my mother's been in there even more than usual, like after a visit to Bubbeh's house in Waterburgh or when she can't get dressed. If I knock to be let in, I know I'll find the curtains drawn, and she'll say she's sick to death. One time when I sobbed at her blanketed knees that I was afraid she would die, she pushed aside her bed tray with the thermometer, nasal spray, and Just Like Profiterole and gathered me into her arms. "You don't ever have to worry, baby," she said. "Whatever happens, it's going to be all right. Because you're a survivor. You got your Bubbeh's fearless nature."

"But what about you?" I said. "What did you get?"

My mother pressed me right up against her. "I got you," she said. "My strong girl."

I take the plugs from my ears and creep down the hall to listen, a true member of the stealthy elite.

"Touch it. Please Neil, just once. I need you to. Day after day I'm down there showing her things with that dummy . . . It's just acting, but . . . Look, I'll do it myself. Only, please give me your hand. Doesn't this excite you at all anymore?"

I don't wait around for his answer. Behind my own bedroom door, with the curtains shut to all the light of the day, my fingers involuntarily reach inside my own pants. I revisit the aching surprise of Lana's mouth, her garlicky breath. Lana. Keep the focus on Lana. Quickly, I get off the floor, cut the fingertips from one of my woolly gloves, and put it on. Eyes closed, I feel her hand on me and the sweet trembling rush between my legs. Lana's mouth finds mine and then she is exclaiming in surprised delight: I am wearing the headdress, the petals of my bouquet blow around us—I am the Queen! My breath leaves my lungs in high gasps.

I am fearless.

My mother said.

5

"*Mamaleh,*" she cries, and her fur coat squashes into every pore of my face. "Look at this *punim*!" The gnarled, man-sized hands grasp me to her bosom while she pecks my head with kisses. Bubbeh learned Yiddish through a home-study course when she was first married, determined to keep her new family in touch with its ancestral roots; and nowadays, if she gets a whiff that someone holds her ethnicity against her, she'll brandish her acquired Yiddish accent like a razor. My mother gnashes her teeth and warns her repeatedly to tone it down, but Bubbeh'd sooner drink Just Like Organochlorines.

"*Oy, mamaleh,* you're such a beauty!" *Mamaleh*: little mother. I blush with pleasure despite myself. There's something irresistible to me about my grandmother, everything about her, from her dragon nose to the star-shaped birthmark with two hairs pricking out on her cheek, announcing her enthusiasm for life. Unfortunately for my mother, her tongue can cripple anything in its path.

"*Oy,* Lorraine. What happened to your chin? All this because somebody gave your car a little bump in the parking lot? I don't believe it for one second."

"Ma, it's a *miniwagon*, not a *car*, and that's what happened."

Bubbeh Esther hasn't been in the house five minutes of her month with us and already my mother looks as though someone has removed all her bones.

My father brings Bubbeh Esther's things in from his miniwagon. The kitchen is suddenly too crowded with luggage, boxes of baked goods and jars of homemade borscht, thick garment bags draped over chairs, and my big, furry Bubbeh. She may be eighty-five years old, but she exercises and swims three miles a day, and I'd bet good money that those big hands could still turn my mother's ass purple. Of Bubbeh's children, six total, five deceased (cancer: breast for the girls, prostate for the boys), my mother has always been known as difficult. Maybe because she was the youngest, born ten years after Bubbeh decided she wanted no more *kinder*: a mistake. My mother always resented her siblings, always felt estranged. Now she is wedged between the sink and a cooler full of frozen kreplach. "Watch it, Neil. You're going to break something, the way you're rushing around."

"Lorraine, what's wrong? Always there's something wrong." My grandmother motions for me to help her off with her coat. I know that the mink cost as much as a small country, but she shakes it from her arms like it's crawling with grasshoppers. She wears the mink because it was a gift, but she gives money to the Fur Stinks people. "Don't make such a big *tsimmis*. Every time I come here, you're yelling at him about something." Her eyes, still sharp under their wrinkled lids, fix on mine like two green barnacles. The skin on her hand is warm silk against my cheek. "That's no way to keep a husband, right, *mamaleh*?"

My mother's cheeks are flaming under her makeup, and I stand uncertainly between the two of them, clutching the pungent fur, as my father's feet clump back down the stairs. Bubbeh Esther has managed to outlive three adoring husbands, the last of whom left her with a big fat investment portfolio. As far as Bubbeh's concerned, this makes her an expert on married life.

She came to America when she was one year old, but to my mother she's always been foreign and backwards. To me, she is a miracle of optimism. "Make sure you get a good laugh every day," she'll tell me. "I've got three husbands and five children gone already! My parents are gone, my brothers and sisters and aunts and uncles, everybody. How can I spend my time worrying when I've been the one chosen to do all the living?"

"Edie," my mother says now, controlled. "Go hang up Bubbeh's coat like a good girl, and don't drag it on the floor. Neil, could you please just take it easy with those boxes? There's glass in there."

"I made borscht, and I made kreplach, blintzes, strudel, all your favorites. The real thing! Vegetarian, but still real!" The excitement in my grandmother's voice follows me out of the kitchen and down the hall. I know that my mother is thinking about the stacks of Just Like Gourmet dinners in the sterilfrostitron. She forgot to throw them out, and if Bubbeh Esther finds them, even my mother's cleverest lies won't be able to cover that frozen tower of shame.

The Great Food Debate: who cooks from scratch, who uses store-bought; who eats everything on their plate, who's a picky eater. Bubbeh won't touch meat since she got chummy with the Rights for Chickens people. My mother thinks Just Like Gourmet Filet Mignon with Green Peppercorn Sauce is the answer to her prayers.

Later, after Bubbeh's things are safely transported to the guest room, I'm in the upstairs bathroom mixing the different shades of my mother's liquid makeup; I'm the only one in the world who can get the right color to match her skin, she says.

There's a tap at the door.

"*Mamaleh*, it's Bubbeh."

"Just a minute," I say, putting away the bottles. When I open the door, she squeezes me in a hug.

"Come. I want to show you something." She lifts my chin and lodges a kiss in the middle of my forehead. "Oh, how I love you."

I wrap my arms around the waist of her rhinestoned sweatpants.

We go to the guest room, where she lowers her bulk to sit on the neatly made bed, patting a spot next to her travel case for me. She turns off the light and points to the sky outside the window.

"Look. The first crescent moon."

When my eyes adjust, I see the thinnest sliver of white just visible in an opening between the upper branches of the large maple tree in our backyard. Even in the dark, I can tell that she is enthralled.

"Here, you light it," she says, handing me a box of matches. I scrape the sulfur tip along the rough edge of the box, and put the flame up to the candle she holds. The thick pancake on her face glows.

"Last week was the *yahrtzeit* of your Zadeh Sid. Remember Zadeh Sid? Oh, he was my maharaja." Zadeh Sid, her last husband, was the one who bought her the mink. I liked him because he'd do things like give me ten dollars for every meal I finished without complaining. He used to say that he got rich by guessing the sex of pigeons back when he lived in a barrel in Detroit. He was ugly, with cooked cabbage breath, but he was always in a good mood, and around him, Bubbeh would wiggle her hips and do striptease pantomimes while she sang from *Gypsy*—guaranteed to make my mother exit and head straight for the meds.

Now she's rummaging in her travel case, rooting through herbal remedies, horoscope books, and crystals wrapped with silver wire.

"Ah. Here. Pretty, no?" She shakes a half dozen dried beans

from an otherwise empty vitamin bottle. It's a type of bean that's new to me, dark red with white speckles. "Think a prayer for new life," she says.

I take three beans from her and put them under my tongue and she does the same with the rest, pinching them one at a time in her big fingers. The pink root of her tongue strains as she lifts it toward the roof of her mouth. Her caps sparkle. The beans feel important under my tongue; I try not to make too many annoying clicks with them against my teeth as we sit.

This is our ritual. After we are finished, Bubbeh will pour precious caraway seeds into two saucers, one for under each of our beds to ward off bad luck. She will do more, too, throughout her visit, with sprinkles of essential oils, patterns traced in the air, backwards steps on staircases. She's been doing these things since I was very small, and for some reason that I don't remember, we hide it from my mother. Sometimes my mother catches her hopping backwards and muttering, and Bubbeh will lie and say it's part of her yogaerobics. Even with all her ESP and omens and dreams, the cords in my mother's neck will tighten. I'd always thought that Bubbeh's rituals were just Jewish customs. It was very surprising to me to discover last year that Bubbeh's "other prayers" were learned from a certain Ada Benitez, long dead and buried, previously a pest exterminator, and a goy.

Bubbeh Esther stares at the moon, hypnotized, her lips twitching with silent wishes, her tongue held carefully over the beans. I sit beside her, staring at its glowing curve and wondering what we would do if we ever got up there. Maybe we'd just lounge around in craters all day like unapprehended criminals, feeling lucky.

I try to concentrate on my prayer. Usually, the prayer for new life means that we pray for the health of all the things that are being born: flowers, animals, little boys and girls. But this time I am saying the prayer for all the little boys and girls I wish would die: all those potential Blow Torchers and Pageant contestants. It's a variation I don't think I'll regret later; I'm sure Bubbeh would understand. As for God, well, I'll answer to that authority when the time comes.

"She how thin tha moon isth?" Bubbeh sounds drunk, her words sloppy because of the beans still under her tongue. "Owah prayahs rill be answerth."

Outside, the maple leaves wave back and forth in the wind, sometimes hiding the moon entirely, and just in case, I add the usual prayer for the health of new babies, in case I ever do menstruate and get to have one of my own.

We spit the beans into our hands and blow out the candle together.

"Bubbeh?"

"*Mamaleh.*" I feel her eyes on me. "What is it, *mamaleh*?"

"Nothing."

The inch of space between us closes as something in me bursts and my head falls on her lap, tears wetting the soft fabric of her sweatpants. A large rhinestone digs into my nose.

"*Mamaleh, mamaleh.* Shhh, don't cry. Everything's going to be all right. Your mommy's going to be fine." Above me, her voice circles around my head like a big-winged bird. "Don't be depressed, *mamaleh. Oy,* ever since you were a baby, how you loved your mommy. Everywhere she went, your little eyes followed. And when Zadeh Mort died, do you remember? What a fit you pitched when you saw your mommy cry. Just four years old, but it took the three of us to hold you down. You wanted to take her sadness. You loved her that much."

In the hall, my mother's voice shakes. "Edie? Where are you? I need you to do something for me. Edie?! I can't yell!"

Gently, Bubbeh pushes me off her lap and wipes my nose

with one of her batik hankies. If only I could explain. "Go, *ma-maleh*. Go and see what she wants."

One Fourth of July, Bubbeh joined us for the annual Independence Day picnic at Hiawatha Lake. It was the summer I had three prime scabs in a trail from knee to ankle, perfect for endless hours of picking, and my mother generously allowed me to keep fourteen jars of grasshoppers in the garage. (This was before the plague of grasshoppers, well before the Insecticide Hut Act.) My mother was smiling and relaxed in her flowered sunhat and new sunglasses, my father clowned for her as he masterminded the real chicken sizzling on the grill. Bubbeh was full of compliments for the weather and my mother and her color-coordinated picnic. Petey was still alive back then, and together we tramped along the banks of the muddy water with my empty jelly jars, hunting for the sparkles of mica, and more grasshoppers. Every so often, I'd call to my mother to tell her what I'd found and she'd call back how wonderful it was and everyone would wave and no one said look out be careful don't let her play so close to the water you won't be happy until they're dragging the lake for her body; they just let the day roll on as if danger was for aliens and not the slogan of our lives. I was so gleeful, I was foaming at the mouth. Later on, everyone was full; even I, the famed picky eater of the family, had managed to pack away a drumstick *and* a wing, an entire ear of real sweet corn, half a dozen gherkins, and a whole deviled egg before racing back down to the canal with a handful of my grandmother's special poppyseed cookies. My mother pronounced it a miracle of eating, and everyone beamed. Even Petey wagged his tail and received some chicken skin straight off a plate.

It was quite a day. My father showed me how to float a ship made from a cracker box while my mother and Bubbeh talked quietly in the fading light. Of course, our cracker-box ship was not seaworthy for long, but, uncharacteristically, Dad rallied. He told me that our sunken cracker box was now a tiny submarine cruising the bottom of the lake, patrolling Fish Town, keeping peace in that wild land of snapping turtles, toads, eels, and snakes. He told of the beautiful Angel Fish who needed protection from all these foes and how our cracker-box submarine was captained by a brave little sailor named Mike. Mike was down there right now blasting frogs with torpedoes and saving the Angel Fish from harm. It was nonsense and I loved it.

It was a day when the battles over eating and cooking and everything else seemed as distant and meaningless to me as the prehistoric roughhousing of mastodons. But later, as the fireworks sprouted over us huge and close enough to taste the gunpowder, my mother shouted in my ear that it was just like the *Amazing Mister Fezundo Show*, just like on screen, and I felt like crying then because I knew that the pyrotechnics of the Amazing Mister Fezundo were nothing compared to this day.

When I see Lana coming around the back of school, my impulse is to fly right to her, except that one of her arms is stretched out behind her as if it is caught in a trap. A second later, Alec Fogel's body stumbles around the corner, still tugging unsuccessfully on Lana. He's wearing one of the gang's welder helmets with the dark glass face protector pushed up; black gauntlet gloves cover his hands. I can see the gang's logo painted on Alec's helmet: a male stick figure shooting a long flame out of his fist, a female stick figure with her head blown off. I hear them laughing, and even from thirty yards I know they are wasted. Like the stick girl's, my own head floats somewhere high above my body, the MiteyPop Gum in my mouth stops dead on my tongue. Alec Fogel's black-gloved hand is clasping Lana's, and even though her expression says he's a big pest she'd like to slap, they are still connected as they disappear behind the bullet-holed glass doors of Deansville Middle School.

The torture continues: a slide show. While the class sleeps in the dimmed classroom, Ms. Cranston the art teacher clicks the remote, her sweat stains blooming in the old projector's beam. In the front row, I have a prime view of those stains; every time her arm reaches with the pointer to fixate on some detail of ancient Yoruban sculpture, the big wet one under her right arm grows legs. Next to me, Fernando's curls are bent over his notebook as he pretends to take notes; he's drawing feet. Somewhere in another room of the school, Lana's hand is contaminated with the heat of Alec Fogel.

". . . shows you how African art is very exaggerated."

"How do you spell *exaggerated*?" Melissa Hammer's coo breaks out of the silence behind me. Leave it to Melissa Hammer, simplest form of bacteria masquerading as a human being, author of the grammatically incoherent Reflections on Hygiene essay in Preliminaries ("It is my reflection to think that hygiene is an internationally important fact of life for all people of all races and religions no matter what culture they live in around the world or what hygiene they do or do not practice on a daily basis"), and owner of café au lait and butterscotch striped hair that falls in a dramatic plunge over her C cups.

Ms. Cranston spells *exaggerated* and her voice drones on, ". . . the reproductive organs are especially exaggerated. These Bamana figures appear in the celebration of Jo and the rituals of Gwan, which are concerned with the fertility of women. You may also notice the finely incised marks on their faces, necks, and torsos. These are tribal scars, cut during sacred rites of initiation."

"What comes after the *g*?" Rodney Spivey's loud whisper.

"It's e-x-a, then I lost it—"

"g-g-e—"

"There's like three *g*'s—"

"Is not."

"Doofus! I heard her say g-g-*G*—"

"She said *E*, asshole!"

"Ladies. Please try and focus. Now, what else do you notice? Can anyone point out any unusual characteristics in this next slide?"

"Big hooters." Rodney again.

"All right. Class. Please try to quiet down. Rodney has pointed out that this sculpture has very large breasts. Gentlemen, please. When you don't focus, you disrupt those around you." Ms. Cranston is one of the few teachers who won't keep disciplinary restraints or pepper spray in the classroom. She's an artist who believes in old-fashioned classroom control. "Now. What do you think these very large breasts might symbolize?"

Melissa pipes up. "Love."

More people wake up to snicker.

"Okay. Love. But love of what? Fernando?"

Fernando raises his head and looks at me, dazed. "Well, it could be a number of different things. Could I get back to you on this?"

Ms. Cranston sighs. I roll my eyes.

"Class?"

"Love of big hooters!"

"Sex!"

"Happy Endings?"

Speech and action quit like a held breath. No one is sure who spoke. Was it Fernando? I try to catch his eye, but his head is bent over his drawings.

Ms. Cranston clicks the remote and as the carousel spins, slides flick on and off the tattered screen at an alarming rate. From the windowsill, someone's lumpy ceramic vase crashes to the floor. The classroom No Happy Endings sign is dim against the chalkboard.

"Whoops, can someone get the lights? I seem to have pushed something I wasn't supposed to, and—"

Blank-faced as usual, Fernando gets up to hit the light, and as if on cue, the rest of the class resumes commentary.

"Where did *you* hear about Happy Endings, freak? From your *mama*?"

"No, I heard it from *your* mama, the last time she sucked your dick!"

The overhead lights have blown, but the slide carousel stops then to show a sculpture of a child straddling its mother's belly, clinging to her like a parasite; the mother is frowning. On the craft counter, the face falls off someone's papier-mâché Buddha.

Ms. Cranston struggles to be heard, "I believe *maternal* love is the love that Rodney was referring to when he pointed out the large breasts on the previous sculpture. Never mind about the lights, Fernando. Can you get the shades?"

"Ms. Cranston? Oh, Ms. Cranston?" Rodney's voice rises over the din. "Isn't it true that African women were forced to hide supernatural tokens in their buttock cracks? As part of a voodoo initiation rite?"

Someone stage-whispers, "Happy Endings!" Laughter.

Rodney tries to keep a straight face. "Or was that a Happy Endings initiation rite?"

Someone's desk tips over. Two of the patched window shades fly up at the same time; a harsh sun turns Fernando's hair into a blaze of white fire.

"Well," Ms. Cranston's entire shirt is sopped, "I really couldn't say for sure about that, Rodney. But you know how Mrs. Geary and the school board feel about mentioning . . ." She surveys the current damage even as several more clods of plaster fall down from the ceiling and the first period lunch buzzer blasts through the PA.

By the time I get to the lunchroom, it is roaring. Polystroob forks and spoons hum in sweaty hands. By the windows, away from the louder kids swallowing meds with their cans of Mondo Surge, Fernando holds a spoonful of his mother's homemade chili to his lips. He waves me over.

"What's up, doc?" His teeth are coated with orange sauce.

I slump into the cold metal-lyte chair, clutching at my thighs. "Ohhh."

"What's wrong?"

"I'm sick," I say. "Listen, here's money. Go get me an ice sucker. I don't want lunch."

"Sure."

The cafeteria smells of canned Corn Bits. Turning away from Fernando's tray, I put my cheek down on the destroyed surface of the table; it's covered with melted black pockmarks from hundreds of Skulls. I feel disordered, fluish, pre-allergic. There's an annoying thrum a few inches below my navel, and my feet are beginning to sweat. Through the window, dark weather-copters chop by. Then a hand is covering my eye, someone's body weight on my back; the edge of the table jabs me in the chest.

"Happy Hollow-weenie."

I lift myself up and turn to see Lana in a slinky black dress and matching beret, phone dangling from a leatherite cord around her neck like a giant gem. She gives a little hop to sit on the table next to Fernando's lunch.

"What are you doing here?" I push the bowl away. "I thought you ate second."

"I'm just here for the hors d'oeuvres." She gives me a bloodshot wink. "Actually I was thinking of sauntering over to have a chat with the wise Miss Flood. It seems certain bureaucrats think I am in need of a little guidance." Wink, wink. "But I thought I'd stop in and confer with my fond aquaintance Chumly first." She leans down, hair dripping into Fernando's chili, phone swinging on its cord. "I'm meeting with someone tonight who might be able to obtain a certain item. What we discussed."

The Jiffy!

"What about you? Going to stroll around the neighborhood and scare the pants off Mrs. Sweeney?" More winks.

"Uh, ah, um—I'm not sure what I'm doing later."

Beads of spicy sauce dangle from her hair, a tiny dark crumb of something is stuck to her lip. Her fingers splay out on her thighs and drum absently and she is quiet a moment. Then, "I've got something special in mind for when we get it. You don't do Jiffy just to cop a buzz, it's a spiritual experience. Dig?"

"Yeah, of course. I dig completely." I swivel around, wincing.

Lana's eyebrow lifts.

"What's wrong? You're not chickening out, are you?"

"No. I'm . . . not feeling that great is all. Too much learning." I shrug, give her a look. Off to the side, I see Fernando tiptoeing his way along the windows sticky with spoiled food, holding my ice sucker up high.

"Oh. Tough luck. Well, pretty soon you'll have a taste of some excellent medicine." Legs spring out, black fabric grabs against her, and instantly the eighth grade boys at the next table stop their fooling around and look at Lana with a concentration that is positively chilling. She cocks her hip at them, bends down toward me again and whispers *Ciao bella*, and then, sailing through the cafeteria doors, she brings the phone up to her ear.

"What are you looking at?" I say, grabbing the sucker from Fernando and wolfing down the coldness.

Ethics with stroke victim Mr. Seegerton. He insists on holding the chalk in his palsied right hand even though whenever he tries to write, it pops out of his grip and falls on the floor. He always gets some Pageant contestant to bend over and retrieve it with the same tired joke, "Here's a great opportunity to practice Better Person Skills and help the handicapped." Maybe he doesn't remember that I'm in training; he's never asked me.

No chalk dropping for Mr. Seegerton today, though—a pop quiz gives him the chance to drag his bad leg up and down the aisles while we scratch out wrong answers to his trick questions ("A mother is being sued by her child, to whom she gave birth by artificial reproduction techniques, because the child developed genetic defects due to medication the mother took to relieve migraines during her first trimester. During the legal procedures, the mother suffers a stroke. Is it ethical for the child to continue with his lawsuit?" "A butcher knowingly sells dubious meat to a couple who serve it to their small child in the form of a hamburger. The child dies. The butcher suffers a mild stroke when he hears of the tragedy. Is it ethical to sue?"). The cracked clock over the blackboard looks out of focus and something drips into my underpants. War alert! Moisture situation in panties! Mr. Seegerton hauls his deadened limb past as the thick, hot drops fall. I shift around on my seat. My mouth opens and shuts, the pen in my hand moves across my notebook, forming a long line of zeros. I'm afraid to look around, afraid who might be smelling my sticky crotch through the school's mildew. *Discharge.* I may now be officially eligible. Of course, if I don't bleed, she'll be sticking Just Like Leeches on my pubes. And if that doesn't do it, in a matter of weeks she'll be reaching in there to milk it out of me herself.

The bell! In the corridor, I jump potholes and hurry to the second-floor bathroom that nobody uses because the toilets don't have seats and it's next to the teacher's lounge. Inside the stall, I check for blood. A brown leaf shape shocks the white of my underpants; a cooked meaty smell, strangely sweet, fills my nose.

It looks as if I've stopped bleeding. I'd thought it would be like a waterfall, a powerful red scream, not this muddy drip. I try to remember what I wrote about menstruation in my Reflections on Hygiene essay, but draw a blank. Still, here it is: this drip is the entrance ticket I've been waiting for. It's here. I'm in.

It's business as usual in the infirmary: Nurse Fogg bellowing at the patients to keep it down, her chapped hands full of catheters, feeding tubes, and surgical clamps and saws. Graffitied bags of blood line three walls. The Just Like Leeches poster and interactive display (broken) loom at the back of the room. A good third of the school limps in and out of the infirmary each day, and at least half that number should be in a real hospital, but our penny-wise principal, Mrs. Geary, doesn't want the bad publicity to screw up funding; too many injuries or deaths means an automatic county audit. Nurse Fogg's death rate is excellent, though. No one has croaked since way before Bobby Lomer. Benny Gold did his dying off school property.

It really stinks in here. Two grasshoppers the size of model cars chase each other around a black polystroob garbage bag; there's a hole in the bottom of the bag and a tail of yellow petrolubie leaks out onto the filthy linoleum. Someone in the corner is making choking sounds. I weave precariously through fallen syringes and the students overflowing the few cots onto the floor. The ones who get cots are the regulars; you don't want to mess with a regular's territory no matter how deep your wound—they're a righteous lot, mostly diabetics and asthmatics. A very fat girl lying center floor opens her eyes as I step lightly over her gut. "Watch it with those Clickies," she snaps. "I have a fucking baby in here."

"Caitlin!" Across the room, Nurse Fogg growls from between teeth clenched around tubing. Both her hands are busy stitching up some kid's head wound and the tubing drops from her mouth. "That type of language is not allowed in my infirmary and you know it."

She jerks her head in my direction. "What's the matter with you?"

I hesitate, before bending to whisper into her ear.

"Ugh," Nurse Fogg grunts as she gives a final tug on the kid's skull with her threaded needle. "We might be out. I ordered six more cases, but I don't think the bill has been paid. I'm a registered nurse, not a magician. But you don't want to mention priorities around you know who."

A couple of boys near us look up. One has his head bandaged, and the other has a split lip and a mouth packed with lyccra-gauze, so whatever they say is too garbled to understand. I fix my gaze on a girl vomiting onto a mop. Across the room, a sterilization kit clatters to the floor. "Just leave it." Nurse Fogg eyes me wearily. "Go look in the supply closet though, maybe there's something hidden away in the back."

A stack of musty hospital gowns spills out of the supply closet. Behind a row of warped containers marked with red crosses is a solitary box of Jumbo Glide-Ins. One plug left. I heave the stack of hospital gowns back into the closet and slam the door, hiding the Glide-In up my sleeve and maneuvering toward the exit just before the supply closet's latch gives and everything tumbles out.

I rush upstairs and dive under the covers of my bed. All the way home the Jumbo Glide-In hung half in and half out of my vagina. I saw Lana go off in somebody's miniwagon right after the last buzzer and felt my head detach from my body again. But we have a plan: Lana and I will do Jiffy and get spiritual. A warm trickle escapes my underpants, the Glide-In is useless; I will have to ransack my mother's cupboards for her private stash.

A knock at the door. "Come in."

Bubbeh's capped smile falls when she sees me huddling in the bed.

"What's wrong?"

"Nothing, Bubbeh." I hesitate. "I got it. My—period."

She slaps my face. It's a light, playful slap, but the unexpectedness of it makes me cry out.

"Ouch! Bubbeh!"

"It's an old custom, *mamaleh*. Don't be offended," she says, smooching my head loudly. "It's to make sure you don't get into trouble. Now that you're a woman."

"I'm not going to get in any trouble."

"Of course you're not," she says. "You're my good girl. My best girl."

I lap up her affection guiltily as I trace the sea green petals in my bedspread. Outside, I hear the calls of boys raking in the next yard. Tonight maybe I will smell leaves burning. "I'm not going to win. Mom's going to be so disappointed."

A knobby finger polishes the giant diamond from Zadeh Sid. "Pageants are supposed to be fun. This one is a terrible game."

My feet snuggle against Bubbeh's warm thigh and she rubs my calves through the bedspread, staring out the window, remembering perhaps how it was when she competed in the Miss Deansville Pageant so long ago, the only contestant born on foreign soil. Her profile is strong against my bedroom walls, nose jutting out like a dare, star-shaped birthmark an elegant tattoo. Her eyebrow is an arch of triumph. The back of my throat tightens to think of her dead someday.

"I want to win," I croak.

"Do you? You sure you're not saying that because she's making you?"

"Yes. I want to win. I want to be a feminine woman of conscience." Only a partial lie.

She lifts her proud nose but doesn't question me more.

"I feel bad about the sacrifice." I focus my eyes on the edge of the bed.

She leans to kiss the hump of my bent knees. "Sshhh. If you want to win, I don't care what you do or why. I want what you want. Now rest. I'm going to take a shower. Be a good girl and help me unzip."

As the zipper splits to reveal the hump of Bubbeh's back, permanently bent in planting mode from all those years on the farm, I feel a twinge of guilt. Bubbeh, my mother, Lana—all three believe a different truth about me, all three would probably dump me like a bowl of wormy Squeezie-Jax if they knew the secret of the real Edie. I barely allow myself to know it, but in that private slop known as one's heart of hearts, I do admit why I want to be queen. It practically strangles me to admit it, but I do; it's not the headdress or the money or even the fun of showing off. I want that power. I want to reek of superiority over everyone, even Lana, even Bubbeh. And even though it could burn me alive like the hottest fever, I'll never tell a soul.

6

Free at last. The joyous news of my menstruation has brought an end to my punishment, and now I glide my liberated way over to Lana's. As Fish-Face chugs by in his pink patrol cart on the after-dinner neighborhood disturbance patrol, I wave right into the sights of his camera. Hey, Feeble! I'm about to take Jiffy and commit a crime! He peels his face away from the viewer and blinks, surprised. When he's not napping, he's dreaming of submitting footage to the crime shows, but as far as I know, the only crime he's ever managed to film was Mrs. Fitz's dog taking a crap on Mrs. Sliminsky's lawn.

Then, Mrs. Grimaldi. I don't see her at first. She's crouching on the front porch with her back up against the house, flanked by two soldier topiaries, a human topiary wearing a white Woolie my mother would call *better schlock*.

The porch sensors beam on as something rustles in the dead leaves next to the porch; Mrs. Grimaldi's hip jerks awkwardly. I hesitate behind a bucking stallion topiary at the side of their driveway. Inside the house, lights are being turned off in one room and on in another. Mr. Grimaldi's mighty chest comes to the front window in a sleeveless undershirt and his chin snaps left, then right as he surveys his property. Then he looks down at Mrs. Grimaldi huddled on the front porch and points. She rises to go inside and the drapes snap closed.

Yelling. Mrs. Grimaldi didn't close the door all the way, and I inch farther up the driveway, sneak up against the porch rail to listen. Lana giving it all she's got, Mr. Grimaldi's booming response—Mrs. Grimaldi's Italian is weakly audible in between. The autumn air is tart in my lungs, my muscles are charged and ready. My new platform Clickies make my feet look huge, and I've got on the perfect pants. Another minute of Mr. Grimaldi's bellowing and I'll break through all that Just Like Aluminum Siding. I walk up the porch steps.

Mr. Grimaldi's voice assaults the air: ". . . and if I say there's too much goddamn pepper, there's too much goddamn pepper!"

"Te l'ho gia' detto, ne faro' ancora. Non mangiarle," Mrs. Grimaldi pleads.

I slide down the metal-lyte railing.

"You know I don't like so much pepper! Are you trying to poison my stomach?!"

"She didn't make it. I made it. And I put too much pepper in on purpose!"

"Lana, ti prego non parlare cosi."

Tiptoeing back up onto the porch, I press one eye against the window to peek through a slit in the drapes and see Mr. Grimaldi toss first one and then another plate of something red and white against a wall. Lana holds her plate aloft, out of his reach.

"Keep your hands away from my food."

Mrs. Grimaldi goes to step between them and Mr. Grimaldi shoves her out of the way. Lana moves out of my line of sight.

Mr. Grimaldi's face is dark and he could use a shave. "YOU DON'T TURN YOUR BACK ON ME WHEN I AM SPEAKING!"

"You're not speaking—you're . . . *SCREAMING!*"

And then the sight of her hurrying through the house, a scowl on her face, still carrying dinner, and now wearing some long, belted coat I've never seen before, turns my spine cold. I move away from the window just as she bursts onto the porch to hurl a plate of lasagna over the side and into the topiary. I would kill for her.

"God *damn* him."

"Uh . . . Lana?"

She whirls around, sees me, and grabs my wrist. We hustle off the porch and onto the sidewalk even as Mr. Grimaldi throws open the door and hollers for Lana to get the hell back inside.

Lana is striding so fast I almost have to break into a gallop. We cross the road and hike up the hill away from the reservoir, to the fields on the other side of Our Lady of Gentle Welcome. Lana throws herself on the ground and lies there, arms stretching up against the night-clouded sky. It looks like even her nose is yelling. Yes, I think. Yell. Any minute, my own throat will open to join you.

"He's a FEEBLE!" She raises her head just enough to look at the surrounding topiary. I wait, transfixed. "Now let me tell you what I really think."

I wait.

And then, "FEEBLE, FEEBLE, FEEBLE—oh, fuck it." She sticks a Skull in her mouth and lights it and then her hands drop at last to the grass, empty, fingers curved like she's waiting to make a catch. Smoke streams out her nostrils as she works the cigarette between her lips for several inhales. Finally she really looks at me, and everything inside my chest tumbles like puppies. Lying on the grass, she might be an exotic tree hit by lightning, fallen and smoking.

"Chumly. Hey."

"Hey."

"You want a smoke?" She raises herself up to hold the pack out to me, one thin cylinder stuck up in the air, waiting.

"Thanks," I mumble, taking the cigarette and its dirt flavor into my mouth.

"I didn't know you smoked. Well, I know you smoke *mooch*." Lana's broken eyebrow rises. "Here, you can catch a light off mine." She takes a big drag as if to prove how much fiery heat she has to share, and for a moment, I'm taken aback. Should I bend down and put my unlit end to her lit one? Or should I take it from her mouth with my fingers? What if I touch her lips? If I touch her lips, I might touch her tongue, the very tongue that dashed across the bumpy surface of my own only days ago. There is tingling in my crotch. Lana works herself around to sit Indian style. I've never smoked a whole cigarette before.

Gingerly, precisely, I take Lana's cigarette without touching her flesh, noticing how the wet filter shines invitingly under the convent lights. Lana's spit.

"Can you wish a heart attack on someone?"

"Maybe you could call the cops."

"Fuck that. I want to *murder* his feeble ass! I'm so sick of his shit. He treats my mother like she's a piece of garbage." It feels like the night has a hundred ears, but Lana is oblivious to everything, she pounds the grass with her gorgeous fists and stands, grinding out the last of her cigarette on the sole of her steel-toed boot.

The tobacco tears my throat as I inhale, but I don't cough. "Well, you can't kill him."

Lana throws the back of her arm across her eyes and grimaces. "Can't I?"

I tap my ashes and hope she doesn't notice that no ashes fall.

"I've gotta make a call." Lana fumbles in her coat pockets and frowns. "Shit. I left my phone in the house. Shit, shit. You see what he does to me?" She lights another Skull and then shields her eyes from the oncoming headlights of a miniwagon. "Feebles! They've got their brights on."

The miniwagon zooms past us, honking. Bethany Prewitt's laughing profile is a flashing white demon in the passenger window. Lana and I stare at the twin red eyes of the taillights as the miniwagon makes a skidding turn to race back past us. In the driver's seat is Judd DeMoan, a senior Blow Torcher and the only ninth-grader with his own miniwagon—but then, he's the only ninth-grader who's eighteen years old.

"DeMoan." Lana spits. "What's up with that feeble Bethany? She's gotta be using him to get immunity from the gang."

I'd like to ask Lana what *she* was doing with a gang member yesterday, but instead a guilty flush fills my cheeks as she adds, "Pageant makes people do some freaky shit."

I stand and brush twigs off the knees of my pants, nearly falling on my face as Rodney Spivey comes rushing out of the pines on his action chopper to smack my ass with a steel-pinned vampire glove. The steel pricks right through my underpants; this will give me a handprint of bloody dots on my left butt cheek. I haven't been vampire-branded in more than a year, but there's still the question regarding publicity of the urine incident. I can just see my Safety record now, blighted with unofficial commentary.

"*Torrrrrcherrrrrrr!*" His skinny body lifts his chopper up to pop a wheelie in front of us, strings of black hair flying over his flat, acne-crusted face. The colorless jacket that streams out behind him is the same one he has been wearing since the third grade. "*Peeeyewww.* Is that piss I smell on your clothes, Frankenstein?"

"Fuck off."

"Fuck you too, Jew-girl."

"Rodney, you fungus. Get a life." Lana throws her arm around my shoulders.

"Fuck you, Grimaldi, you wop. Pizza pussy."

I freeze, feeling Lana's arm tense. Usually, the Blow Torchers don't even verbally molest noncontestants, especially Lana. I shift my eyes to see what her face is doing, but she's already moving, holding out something thin and white to Rodney.

"Hey Spivey. Ever taste a wop floogie? Homegrown in the old country. All the way from Rome. The fucking pope blessed it himself."

"You shouldn't say that shit about the pope, bitch. Those nuns'll beat your ass with their freakin' drumsticks." But he's interested, circling closer to her on his chopper.

And then she's on top of him, belted coat flying open behind her like a pair of wings as both of them go down, the chopper between them and Rodney howling.

I let out a gaspy shriek and move back.

Rodney's on top, fastened to Lana like a buckle. She kicks at the backs of his calves with her boots, her hands grasping his wrists, the vampire glove still dangerously close to her face. I try to get close enough to grab at him, but one wrong move would be very unwise, and it's still a Pageant rule that permanent mutilation means you're out of the game. When one of Rodney's Turbine-Spikes grazes my ankle, I jump back again. Lana bucks underneath his stained jacket and they roll together, hands locked, elbows tense.

"You shit-sucking douche bag!" One of her hands breaks free and gives him a wet-sounding slap in the head. With astonishing quickness, she unsnaps the vampire glove and tosses it out of reach.

"Fuck off, dago bitch!" He tries to bite, but without the glove he's lost his one real advantage.

She flips him, lands a wicked knee to his groin, and is upright. Her boots stomp full force to mangle the front spokes of his chopper.

"Whore!" Rodney yells, his voice squeaking.

Lana watches while he lies there, turned on his side, thighs clutched together to shield his testicles. She's not laughing, but an angry smile is on her face and breath leaves her mouth in loud exhales; her coat hangs open around her heaving body. "Better watch your mouth, Spivey. Bigots live short lives. Capeesh?"

Tears run down his grimacing cheeks. "You . . . b . . . itch . . ."

Lana's boot jabs him in the balls once more. "I mean it, freak."

Rodney moans. Lana retrieves the vampire glove and uses her lighter to set it on fire. The krapylon burns quickly in the grass.

"I've got a call to make." She dismisses us and heads toward the street.

A dot of elation bounces inside me as I stand there and stare at the writhing boy. She fought for me. I look up at the Gentle Welcome dormitory to see if any of the nuns are watching, but all the shades are drawn.

"See," I say, cocking my chin at Rodney. He nurses his aching balls while I hawk up a goober onto the ground near his knees. And then I race home.

Our backyard blinks in the moonlight. It's the wings of grasshoppers reflecting the light as they take off and land. I'm not supposed to be out here, I should be tucked under my DuoWeaveRite comforter and dreaming at this still hour of the night, but when I woke and looked out the window, I had to be where I could smell the air, feel all the movement.

I can't count them all, but it seems like there are a couple of dozen plump hoppers. The Sweeneys' yard has them, too, and the Rileys'. I vaguely remember the last invasion: a family of grasshoppers whacking you on the cheek and getting caught in your hair every time you left the house; I didn't mind it though,

I was just a kid and all that jumping around the neighborhoods gave Deansville a liveliness it never had otherwise. Slowly, I creep along the grass in my Clickies, my pajama bottoms absorbing several inches of dew, and make my way out to the closest Insecticide Hut. A hand on its humming warm cover tells me it's on. But is it working?

One of the bugs leaps up and attaches itself to my pajama leg. Quickly, I catch it in my hand and its strong little legs scrabble and kick against my palm. I feel pricks and guess that it is biting. It's only a very small grasshopper, like the ones I used to catch before the Insecticide Hut Act. Now I pry open the lid of the Insecticide Hut with my free hand and drop the bug inside, right into the swimming pool of Just Like Organochlorines. Normally, the grasshoppers do not have direct contact with the chemicals; the Hut pumps its poison through tubes under the ground.

My little grasshopper is instantly destroyed. Its body bloats up and turns a light neon blue, then collapses in on itself as an ever-shrinking dot until it's nothing, a vapor rising off the chemical liquid and flying back into the night.

The next day, I use the dirt dominator to suck at the carpet, prowling for crumbs and the shed molecules of my family that have found their way into the guest room even though my mother has cleaned in here at least twenty times since Bubbeh arrived. My mother held up a can of polish when I got home from school and chanted, "Always strive for perfection." She's still sporting a polystroob chin buttress because of the accident, so I didn't say anything too smart back. When I reach up with the prongs to get a dainty cobweb, I see Alec Fogel zooming through my backyard on his action chopper. Pressing my face against the windowpane, I watch as he crosses the next couple of yards, in the direction of Springfield. How long do I have before my mother finds out about the vampire branding? And then the truth about the dress? When I can't see Alec anymore, I turn off the machine and lie back on the bed without taking my shoes off, my body fitting into the shallow valley where my parents used to spoon together in the center of the mattress. This was their bed when they were first married. The day my mother brought me home from the hospital to live with them was also the day this bed moved into the guest room and the twin beds were installed.

I only mean to lie down for a few minutes, but it's like I am stuck in warm, toxic adhesive; above me, the ceiling could buckle and collapse and I would be unable to get off the bed in time. I close my eyes and see the black tires of Alec's chopper spinning, leaving deep trails in our grass. I can already feel his grip on my throat.

My guts are clenched with the newfound bliss of menstrual cramps.

When I finally do manage to get up, I am almost too tired to stand. But I make sure that my shoes don't leave marks on the bedspread. I even use the high-powered attachment to get rid of any atoms my body may have left behind.

A couple of hours later, I'm wheeling our Smell-Brite recycling cubbies to the curb. The streetlights are buzzing into a warm glow while inside my mother heats up the Just Like Gourmet dinners. Bubbeh's dining out with some of her Rights for Chickens pals. The clock up in the sky plays eight bars of "Taking a Chance on Love," and in his patrol station, Fish-Face dreams of winning an Emmy. Alec Fogel comes whizzing up onto the driveway, his acetylene torch poking up out of the knapsack on his back.

"Frankenstein. Good job for you. Garbageman." He skids in front of me so I have to walk around him on my way back to the house. I try not to run. His hand catches my arm, hard, and the skin on his knuckles is cracked and white, his cuticles raw from chewing. A light breeze blows a few strands of ponytail onto his cheek, but I try to keep my eyes away from his face so I won't have to see how the upper lip of his cupid mouth thins to nothing, or how his eyes have narrowed to dark slits. A bad smell hangs off his clothes like a chemistry experiment gone wrong, and there's a muddy red ski cap rolled low on his forehead.

"Let go, please."

"Let go, please."

My arm burns in his grip. "What do you want?"

"Nothing. Your body. Same thing." He tightens his grip. Then, "I heard you were there when Grimaldi kicked Spivey's ass. My boy Spivey's not too happy about that."

"So what? He deserved it."

"That's not what his balls say. He said you put Lana up to it. Cause you couldn't take a joke." I move to go. "You're not very good at taking a joke. Are you, Frankenstein?"

"I have to go in." Above me, the first star of the night shines down.

"What are you going to do? Call Lana to come and beat me up? She thinks she's a real pro wrestler." He twists my flesh a little harder. "You like that about her, right? Makes you hot, hunh?"

"I have to go in. My mother needs me."

"For what? Breast-feeding? Those big Jew-tits of hers are just bursting with all that vitamin double D."

"Fuck you."

His hand squeezes my forearm till I cry out. Like escapees from a Hollywood cartoon, bluebirds swoop across our lawn to perch on the Insecticide Huts. It is strange to see them at this hour, particularly in November, but they make the neighborhood look pretty. To the naive eye, Alec and I might be two cartoon sweethearts, our connection as snug as that of an arrow in its crossbow.

Cars swing into the driveways around us as parents return home from work. I hear a child laugh. Mrs. Sweeney looks out her front window, sees us, and waves.

"Want to get married?" he whispers. A wistful look crosses his face; I'm surprised to see that underneath his stubble of beard he is baby smooth. Around us, a few soft drops of rain fall. It might be summer, everything smells so sweet and fresh. "Why waste time with a dummy when you can have flesh and blood?" His black eyes brighten, his cupid mouth purses into a kiss and gently plants itself on my cheek.

I feel the grip on my arm relax a little.

But then: "Lana's deluxe joints, you know that? How'd Frankenstein get such a babe for a girlfriend? Hunh? You like munching her spicy little rug?" With a quick tug, he brings my arm behind my back. The pain in my arm is so bad it's hard to breathe. "I could eat Lana's ass while you lick my balls. Jews can eat meat, can't they?" His voice is sounding faraway, like there are double panes of glass between us. The rain falls into my eyes, washing them, and I lift my face into the warm, clean air. There is a movement in the Sweeneys' front window again. A telephone is pressed to Mrs. Sweeney's head.

"I asked you a question, Stein."

Rules Committee spies are everywhere these days. Mrs. Sweeney may be my next-door neighbor, but her Pageant allegiance is no doubt with her niece Sarah Tetter, three neighborhoods away.

"Maybe you're not answering because you'd like to know what happened to the last female who crossed me and Spivey." He fishes out a subminiature cleaver from his jacket, and when he pops the blade, I see that it needs a good cleaning. Then my father's headlights swing into the driveway, and the cleaver disappears into a pocket. Alec's grasp on me lifts.

"Daddy to the rescue," he whispers.

I take a breath, catch a glimpse of Mrs. Sweeney's crestfallen mouth paused over the phone.

"*Torrrrrcherrrrr*," he adds, and rides back into the gloom.

"You've been *torcher-ed*."

My mother and I are in the kitchen and my palms are prickling as I fold them under my arms and against my chest. "It was hardly worth mentioning," I say.

"It's terrible. It's just so . . . *heinous*." She sits at the table across from me, giving her throat and chest and the tops of her shoulders a quick, nervous rubbing. Fiercely, she twirls the lazy Susan she hand-painted at Kitchen Creations in the Identity Mall last year. Through the window, I see the Insecticide Hut delivery truck pull into our driveway, but she doesn't seem to hear the van door slam. Instead, she plucks up a Kizzerba jar and a bottle of Just Like Balsamic Wine Vinegar from the lazy Susan and rubs them against her cheeks.

"I just didn't want to worry you." Circulation is stopping in my hands and feet.

Deliberately, she lowers the condiments and places them on the table in front of her, as if they are dolls, a Just Like Balsamic Wine Vinegar mother and a chubby little Kizzerba daughter. "Well, I am worried." Her voice is soft, concern fills her eyes. "I know that you lied to me about what happened to the dress. I know that Rodney Spivey vampire-branded you the other night. I know why you didn't want to tell me these things, but I'm telling you it's not going to happen again." She spins the Kizzerba jar like a top. "It's not worth it, to have you in danger. I won't have my only child risk bodily harm, or *worse*, for the sake of a headdress. I just will not do it."

"You're pulling me out of Pageant?" Every hair on my head feels like it's a burning wick.

"I'm thinking about it."

"But you knew about the Blow Torchers. You always knew that something might happen."

"But nothing ever did. That I *know* about." She puts the condiments back into the lazy Susan. "Anyway, I don't want to know. I know too much already. To *urinate* on a *dress*—"

"He didn't urinate on it, he—"

She holds up her hand to silence me. "However it happened, it's not important. What is important is that you, my only daughter, are a target for these very dangerous, very disturbed boys, and with six long months between now and Pageant, I do not want you to be hurt. That is all."

"Fine."

"And another thing. Mrs. Vrick had an idea, not kosher with the rules." Her green eyes become greener. "She thought that it might give you a slight edge to practice skinning some of her rabbits." She registers the terror on my face and leans forward. "Not to worry, sweeties. I knew that my sensitive little girl wouldn't like to do it. I told her no thank you." She sits back in her chair, her mouth wide and satisfied. "You see? I was already wondering if things weren't going too far."

I get up from the table and wander around the kitchen, stroke her Just Like Fur oven mitts and straighten stacks of paper doilies. With my face to the wall, I flick the elf-shaped light switch she made out of eggshells and pom-pom balls. The elf's wiggle eyes gleam beneath their polystroob lenses.

"Don't you have anything to say?"

What can be said?

"Thanks a lot," I say, flicking the switch back off.

"Watch that tone. And quit playing with the lights. I'm only trying to do what's best for you." Her eyes arrange into a new, cool stare. "I've always said that your well-being is the most important thing."

"You probably don't even believe I could win."

"What? If anyone in this house thinks you could win, it certainly is not you. Sometimes I wonder whose efforts are really holding this operation together."

"I do stuff."

"After I nag myself hoarse."

"So I'll drop out of Pageant. I'm only doing it for you, anyway."

"Oh, Edie." She looks like she feels sad for the both of us, two people who can't love without causing an accident. "Let's not argue about this right now. I only said I was *thinking* about taking you out of Pageant. Naturally I'm upset, having just found out about . . . what happened." She reaches for me, but can only get her fingers to graze the side of my pants. "Honey. Don't be mad. Let's let things settle and see what's what then, okay?"

In the night I am lucky and fall asleep right away. I dream that my mother and I are holding hands, spinning around in a big circle of dirt. Bubbeh is there, watching us and calling out warnings from her window. My mother has a long braid like Dr. Plow's and we are wearing matching artist's smocks. Bubbeh leans farther out the window, but I can't understand what she is saying. My mother's hands slip from mine and now she is just holding my wrists. I wriggle in her grip, helpless. We keep spinning and she is so happy. If she gets mad, she will let go of my wrists and I will tumble back and be swallowed up by the dirt. Bubbeh leans far out the window, her big thighs and behind poking up from the sill, her triceps flapping as she yells. When I see her cushioned sandals slide off the window ledge, I break free of my mother's grasp to stop Bubbeh's fall, and the last thing I see is my mother zipping backwards like a balloon with all its air let out. I wake up on the floor just as dawn hits the world, my legs pinned in a twist of flowered sheets.

When morning comes I am so tired I screw up the command sequence for Alice Jones's Sacrificial Rabbit routines. She does everything backwards and then I can't get her to do one simple twirl on the monkey bars. I am afraid. My mother says very little. We're continuing to train, although my mother still hasn't said whether she'll allow me to compete. I know she's anxious, though, I've heard the rattling of her meds behind her bedroom door. Every time Alice Jones fails a routine, my mother's eyelids close over her eyes and her cheek muscles go slack. By the time practice is over, she is totally blissed, if barely breathing. I put away the equipment and return Alice Jones to her cage.

Suddenly, she straightens up like she's onstage, breaking the silence. "I had such an interesting dream last night." Her tone is light but sure. "I woke up with a clarity I haven't felt in years."

"The cage is locked, Mom," I say, keeping my voice steady. "Do you want to check it?"

"No. That's all right, sweeties. I trust you." She closes her eyes in that deliberate way again, and her lips part in a long, delicate exhale. "Last night, in my dream, you and I were spinning around on a huge circle of earth. We were both wearing artist's smocks, blue ones with empire bodices, and I had my hair done in a long braid. We were so happy, spinning around like two kids. Bubbeh was there, yelling at us from a window. We didn't care though, we just kept spinning and spinning. Then I felt you slipping, somehow your hands slipped out of mine."

I back against the Feminine Woman of Conscience Pageant Handbook on its pedestal. A corner of the book jabs my spine. "No—"

My mother opens her eyes and smiles sadly. "Yes. You were

in danger, but fortunately I managed to grab your wrists so you didn't fall. Meanwhile, Bubbeh kept leaning farther out the window and yelling. I knew she was asking for trouble, but common sense told me it was more important that I save you."

For the first time, Lana has invited me to cross the threshold of her house. Her parents are at the restaurant, and she wants to show me the Jiffy she bought with my hundred. She had to pitch in a hundred big ones of her own, too. We're not going to do it yet, we're only going to talk about doing it. I nod, keep nodding, yes let's talk about it, let's just sit and stare at it and not talk, let's just sit in your bedroom alone together, breathing, with both our asses touching the same floor. I keep licking at my lips to get rid of the dryness.

"Your house is so . . . decorative," I say.

"My mother's always cleaning it. My father goes wacko around dirt."

Most impressive are the mile-long white crushed velveteenite couch with a clear polystroob slipcover and a five-foot bronze-tique statue of some big-shot army feeb in the living room. When the Sliminskys used to live here, there were damp baby clothes and Mr. Sliminsky's handknit yarmulkes all over the place. Trouble-wanters, my mother called them. She could not understand why in this day and age they'd flaunt their difference.

"It looks a lot better than when the Sliminskys used to live here," I say. "They were big Jews."

Lana raises one eyebrow. "You're Jewish, aren't you?"

My face boils. I swallow and lick my lips.

"Chumly. That's nothing to feel bad about. It's cool."

"Well, I just don't feel like I have that much in common with other . . . people. I mean, the Sliminskys were . . ."

"Look." Lana takes my hand and leads us over to the statue.

Her hand is warm and firm; it's a great disappointment when she lets go. "Mussolini. Believe me, I used to hate this statue. Now, every time I walk past it, I forgive Mussolini for being a Fascist. He was wrong, but now he's dead. Not the nicest Italian that ever lived, but hey. Same thing with my father; he's a feeble who just happens to be Italian. What I'm trying to say is not to let the feebles spoil things for everyone else, capeesh?"

Anyone else talking this way would be embarrassing as hell, but Lana knows how to word things, she's really quite a wordsmith. And she has very strong fingers.

"Yeah. Capeesh."

"Hey, are you embarrassed? Fuck those prejudiced feebles. It's cool that you're Jewish. Jews have done some wild stuff. For instance: all those people who committed suicide on top of Masada. Which as you know is not allowed according to Torah, but they were saying fuck you to all the feebles who wouldn't let them do their thing. You've got to honor something like that. That's big."

How does she know these things? Has she read the Torah? Not even Bubbeh's done that. Lana seems to know an awful lot about dead people. It makes me very uncomfortable, but then I just look at her, standing there with her hand draped casually over Mussolini's head, smelling like a whole forest of juniper. She hooks a finger up inside his nose and wiggles it around, then she winks, and I suddenly feel like I could throw my arms around her and old Fascist Mussolini.

"My grandmother was born in Poland. Her grandparents died in the Holocaust, so now we do a lot of Jewish things together. She makes all kinds of Jewish food. Really Jewish stuff."

"Oh yeah? You like to eat Jewish stuff?"

"Yeah, I eat it. All the time. You know, for my grandmother's sake. But, she's—I just meant that our family is different from certain kinds of Jews. We're more modern."

"You're a modern miracle," she says, and pulls me with her toward the kitchen.

As we pass the couch, the polystroob slipcover reflects like a cloud in heaven.

Joy in the Grimaldis' kitchen: Lana's making us a snack of submarine sandwiches (hearing her say it gives me chills). Every time she pulls something out of the sterilfrostitron or a cupboard she exclaims, "Oh yeah! Wait'll your tongue gets a load of this action, Chumly!" I sit on the bar stool with my thighs pressed together. The Grimaldis' food is dangerous, exciting. There are tins of headless anchovies and sardines and jars of slimy black pellets, fat bulbs of something called fennel (Lana eats it raw), fishy red peppers, long crooked hot green peppers, miniature wrinkled peppers the color of toads. Lana opens small, oil-filled jars to show me what look like lab specimens; she says they are artichoke hearts and hearts of palm. I like that she is showing me all these hearts. Another nice thing: one whole cupboard is devoted to crackers, my favorite snack. I see crackers I have never seen before, crackers that are shaped like stars, thick, donut-sized crackers that look like they've been sprayed with Shellack-it. Even as Lana hauls out box after bag after box, the cupboard still seems full to bursting.

Lana thrusts a bowl of marinated onion salad into my arms. She sticks a glob of dates in my mouth. Grinning obscenely, she tosses me sticks of hard, wrinkled meat. "Electric Polyrubber Man in about a hundred years, hunh Chumly?" Carcasses of cooked birds are removed from a second sterilfrostitron I hadn't noticed before. Out come pickled beets, bumpy-skinned gherkins, frowns of cut carrots floating in water. Prunes. The cheese, if that's really what it is, smells a little spoiled and doesn't come in individually wrapped slices.

Sicilian cuisine. The food of organized criminals.

"Just make me a small one," I say. "I had a late lunch."

"My mother made olives." She brings out a jar of drab green

balls in greasy liquid swirling with red flecks. "Here, eat one."

When Lana talks, I can see the unchewed food in her mouth. I take the olive she offers between my teeth and bite down, hardly noticing the bitterness.

"How's that rate? Right up there with blintzes, right?"

I nod, trying to raise one eyebrow like she does, but both of them go up.

Lana's room is nothing like I thought it would be. There is a bed and a desk and a chair and a ruffled vanity with a mirror and a bookcase and two lamps. This is where Lana sleeps, where she undresses each night for bed and stands and sits and bends and yawns and looks at herself in the mirror with the same eyes that first opened in that wild land known as the Bronx. Those are the tissues she uses to blow her nose.

Lana reaches under her bed and pulls out a briefcase. Wrapped inside a pair of regulation Fun Sports shorts is a big spray can of Jiffy. "Now, here's a mystery compound that can only be identified by direct ingestion." She gives the top of it a loud kiss.

Seeing her kiss something makes me both relieved and nervous. "Hey, it's the Jiffy." Her fingers slide up and down the sides of the can, and I'd like to stop them with my own. The Jiffy wobbles on the rug and nearly falls.

"This was my mother's vanity table when she was growing up," Lana says, smiling now. "It's the one really nice thing she ever owned." She pulls the vanity bench out from the table's ruffled skirt to sit, her smile dissolving into seriousness. "She had a pretty rough childhood."

I put a fingertip to the top of the Jiffy where Lana kissed it.

"Oh," I say.

"And this," Lana says, lifting something that seemed to be stuck to the back of the mirror, "is Lily Gates." She is holding a framed photograph. "Autographed."

The photo shows someone dressed in a Gentle Welcome

nun's habit with a ski mask hiding the person's face. The picture is signed: *To Lana—Victory over Feebles. With Respect and Love, Lily Gates.*

"Wow," I breathe. "You met Lily Gates?"

"Once." Lana lets me hold the photo. "She used to be a stuntwoman, did you know that? Remember that scene in *Dogcatcher*? The one where the Chihuahua gets raised up out of the pit of bubbling sludge? You only get to see Lily's arm, because the rest of her is down under the pit, but it's so cool the way the Chihuahua comes up all wet and shivering in the palm of her hand."

I'm careful not to smudge the photo's glass as I hand back the picture.

Lana shines the glass with the hem of her shirt, revealing several inches of stomach muscle.

"How'd you meet her?"

"My cousin Rita knew her. They were buds."

"Oh."

Lana lays the photo in her lap and leans forward. "I need you, Chumly. I need some help. Will you help me?"

I gulp, my eyes wide. "Sure."

She leans down to touch me on the arm, her lips wet with pepperoni grease. "I want to use the Jiffy to do a Contacting."

"Wh-what's a Contacting?" I stammer.

"It's a little help from the dead. I want to ask them to help me save my mother's life. The ultimate Happy Ending—the end of this crappy world—is a ways down the road, but you're supposed to be able to contact the Happy Endings dead for some help vaporizing the negativity in your personal world now. You make an offering—like Jiffy—and ask them to remove bad stuff from people, like the need my father has to treat my mother like a piece of shit." Lana's fingers are warm on my skin. "I want to do it next Saturday night up at Hiawatha Lake. Will you help me?"

"Well . . ." She keeps plucking at my sleeve to get me to look at her, but I won't.

"To tell the truth, I'm not a hundred percent sure if I'll be free that night," I say. "I might be busy galvanominimizing neutrons. My mother's pretty strict about my training schedule and all of that."

"I have to do it soon. I'm asking you because I need someone I can trust."

"Why don't you ask one of your relatives?" The Grimaldis have family in every state, Lana has told me, and she's visited them all.

"Believe me, Chumly, if I could, I would."

"Why don't you ask Alec Fogel?"

"*What?*"

"Don't look so surprised. I saw you two together. In back of school." Let her get Alec fucking Fogel to help her contact dead people. I don't need Lana, and I don't need my mother, either; I can strain beakers of sulfuric acid into the umbradecimatoraton and get the full range of connective carbon-hydrogen bonds to pop out. I'm no fool.

"Chumly, Chumly, Chumly. Sometimes you are such a little girl." Lana laughs, and it's such a delightful sound I almost laugh with her. "He's in love with me, the feeble." She waves a dismissive hand and makes a face. "But he knew the freak who got us the Jiffy so I let him drool over me. Alec's got some pretty decent mooch, too."

"Oh."

Lana eyes me like I'm a little baby whose chin she's about to chuck. "I'm asking *you*, Chumly." She puts the photo of Lily Gates behind the vanity mirror and sits back down beside me on the rug. She takes one of my hands between both of hers.

"I'm not helping you." I waggle my hand out from between the warm sandwich of her palms. "I can't. I don't believe in Happy Endings."

"Edie. Chumly." Gently, she pulls my neck toward her and puts her mouth right up to my ear, crooning against the side of my head. "I'm not asking you to do a Happy Ending. I'm not asking you to believe in anything that you don't want to. But you believe that my father shouldn't be hurting my mother, right?"

I nod, feeling her chin rub against my ear. I try to resist, but then she shoves her face under my nose and crosses her eyes in a really beautiful way and soon we are both cracking up and the feel of her fist knocking gently at my shoulder makes me melt with such happiness, I give her a little kick with my Amazing Mister Fezundo sock; and we are wrestling, a gorgeous slow wrestle because somehow our limbs have turned to ribbons. Of course, she pins me in two seconds anyway. But her hair is dripping down on me like it did that day at the reservoir, and her laughing cheeks are so nice that I don't struggle to get up. Her weight on me is fantastic.

Abruptly, she falls backwards and rolls off onto the braided rug.

"Let me show you something." Her body bumps mine again as she twists around to pull a magazine out of her briefcase.

The magazine is black and the gold title is written so it looks sinister and fun: *Grenade: Special Happy Endings Issue*. There's a psychedelic painting of a bat on the cover. Lana winks and opens her mouth wide, like a vampire about to sink its fangs into somebody's neck, and my own neck gets a funny cramp, anticipating her bite, but she doesn't do it. Instead she flips the pages of the magazine excitedly, crinkling some of the pictures. "Look at this! Actual unretouched photographs of the dead beating the crap out of feebles." She flips to a painting that takes up a whole page. "And this is *Beauty*." Her face fills with solemn admiration. "You have to admit, it's damned inspiring."

At first glance, it's just a color copy of a painting that looks as though it's probably in a museum somewhere. It seems like a religious painting, except there's no guys in robes with long beards, or sad-eyed women pressing their palms together, just a beautiful girl standing in the dusky bright light of heaven. She's on tiptoe at the edge of a cliff. Her long hair is the color of sunset and she is wearing a dress white as a wedding gown. Even though her mouth is closed, she looks like she is about to burst into song, and there are three luminous stars in the sky right above her.

But then: "This picture reminds me of something," I say, leaning in to get a closer look. The girl's arms in their rippling white sleeves are my mother's arms, all strong curved muscle. Her toes are ready to fly.

"There's a really gorgeous poem that goes with it." Lana's voice is slow, remembering. "It's about this girl who can tell the future but only if she stays inside her house. Then one day she sees a man walk by her window and she falls in love, so she goes outside. But then she loses her power to tell the future and the guy has disappeared and she doesn't know where he went. All of a sudden she knows she will never have the life she wants. And she goes up to the cliff and jumps off. As the girl is falling, she has a feeling of awe, a feeling like she's never had in her life, and she knows then that she is doing the right thing. And after, when she is dead, she is even happier."

I feel a heaviness in my lungs. I look at her looking at the magazine.

"I don't really think I can help you. I'm sorry."

Her voice turns harsh. "Wake up, Edie. There are tons of people who are into it. Lily Gates is into it."

Around me, walls press in and steal all the air from the room. *Lily Gates*.

"I don't see how you could be against people taking control of their own lives, wanting to end their pain and move on to something better, when you are going to kill something that doesn't want to die and never did you any harm."

Alice Jones.

"It seems a little hypocritical."

I clasp my hands in my lap and focus on the rug until I feel her arm go around my shoulders.

"I'm doing it for my mother," I say.

"I know," she says, and I don't meet her eyes.

"What about you? Are you going to do a Happy Ending?"

"Oh, Chumly," she pats my cheek. "There's a whole process you have to go through before you can do a Happy Ending. You have to be over twenty-one and you have to fully comprehend the world's pain. By that time, who knows what I'll be doing?" Again she picks up the Jiffy and gives it a kiss. "Lots of this baby, I can tell you that. And I've got a few billion dozen floogies to smoke. With my good pal Chumly," she adds.

When she laughs, grateful relief pours through me, and I bring my head up to face her.

I sigh.

Lana hugs me against her. "You're in, right? You'll help me do the Contacting. Oh, great, that's so great of you." She looks at me with narrowed eyes. "Alec might be able to get me some Quilotodinol. You ever do downs?"

I hesitate. "Sure. Not a lot, just what I can steal from my mother." I know enough about drugs from my Drug-Addict Prevention Bee pamphlets to fake my way. "She doesn't do Quilotodinol anymore, uh, but I can get Vacnodorofixal."

"Vacnodorofixal! Deluxe!" She lets the magazine drop to her lap. "Can you get some for next Saturday? What else has she got? My father won't even let us keep Just Like Aspirin in the house."

I take a large bite of my sandwich and start chewing it up fast. "Oh, she's got a lot of different stuff. Ups, downs. Weird tranquilizer stuff I can't even pronounce."

She hugs me again and puts on some Mystic Fangs. She teaches me the cramp, leading, her hand long in mine—not as warm as before, but her fingers still feel strong and they grip mine tight. I'm not sure how hard to put my hand on her shoulder, but she says do it harder, hold on, and so I do. And then I don't want to let go ever; it feels like I might get caught in a freak indoor wind and fly like a paper scrap.

I follow her all around the bedroom, sweating, but I don't mess up. I know how to concentrate and give in to a partner's rhythm from doing the boroonga with my mother. But then I catch a glimpse of my face in the vanity mirror and see that my hair is stringy from dancing and my skin is an uneasy mix of green and white.

I wish we could get in the Triumph and leave this minute, drive to some other state, find a quiet motel in the woods and lie down and rest on the cool, Just Like Cotton sheets, with the flowered bedspread pushed to the floor. We'd keep the lights off, and watch the late afternoon sun slipping between the polystroob blinds. We would touch then, slowly, with our eyes closed, listening to the lip-smacking sounds of our kiss.

After Lana closes the front door behind me, I don't go home. I need to walk around for a little while. I walk through the fields, skirting my neighbors' backyards, Lana's magazine tucked under my arm in a grocery bag. As I pass the Spiveys' place, I catch a glimpse of Rodney through the hedge, helping his baby brother learn to walk as he checks squirrel traps. Rodney halts every few feet to point, and the baby claps and laughs as Rodney loads their furry catch into a bag. I duck under the skirt of a large topiary nun until they take the bag inside the house.

I run home, clutching the grocery bag tighter under my arm. I wish I could throw the magazine in someone's trash, get it out of my life, and Lana's life.

Bubbeh runs naked from the bath. "Come and look at this. Something funny's going on."

I follow her great wrinkled butt cheeks into the bathroom. Immediately, a strongly buzzing object attacks my head.

"*Ack!* Get away! What is it?!"

"Look, down there." Bubbeh slaps at the grasshopper until it flies out the door and into the hall. "They've been coming up from the drain. A whole parade of them, right after I finished my bath. I've been shooing them out the window, but they're still coming." Even as she talks, a line of five grasshoppers emerges from the plumbing.

"Should we plug it up? Maybe that would stop them."

"They look strange," she says, catching one in her big fingers. "See how big they are? Their eyes aren't normal. That scarlet color. And look at it trying to bite me. See those teeth? Those aren't the teeth of an ordinary garden pest."

In the mirror, I watch the reflection of the insect struggling in my grandmother's grip. It doesn't quite seem to match its live self, but I can't say exactly what is off about it.

"I'm going to plug the drain," I say. "Throw those others out the window."

First thing Monday after school I am spread-eagle flat on my back, a speculum clamping me open in front of my mother while Thickee Wig–wearing Dr. Kent swabs around in there as if he thinks he might stumble across the long-lost Eighth Wonder of the World.

"Oh, thank God!" My mother claps as he holds the bloody swab aloft. "I thought maybe she'd stopped bleeding." She burbles like a fountain. "You made us wait so long for an appointment, after all."

"I'm a busy man, Mrs. Stein. Lots of girls getting their periods these days, lots of menstrual samples to take and send. The paperwork is endless."

My mother's eyes go wide. "*Mrs. Stein!* I almost didn't know who you were talking to! Everyone calls me Lorraine." She looks at me and winks, her laugh echoing in the sterile air. Suddenly, today, she is back on Pageant trail, full steam ahead.

"This feel okay? Doesn't hurt?" He's stabbing me hard enough to split flesh, but I nod that everything's great. Except for the fact that he can't take his eyes off my mother's cleavage poking up out of her magenta scoop neck. Her face is made up in the special tubercular look she says doctors find so attractive: pale and feverish, with Holy Water Droplets glistening along the hairline. She twists her polystroob chin buttress seductively.

"Relax," he grunts. "Just try and relax and it won't hurt so much."

"It just makes it worse if you tense up." Her eyes with their carefully blackened under-eye circles bore into Dr. Kent's. "I remember my first time. I sobbed for a week."

"Well." Dr. Kent stands and snaps off the latex gloves slick with jellied lubricant and my piteous blood. "She's an official Pageant contestant." He looks at me, his eyes focusing somewhere near my chin. "So now you've got years of Pageants ahead of you." The corners of his mouth lift halfheartedly. "Unless of course you get lucky and win your first."

"I don't think luck is going to have anything to do with it." My mother's soft voice has just a hint of frost. "She's beautiful and talented and smart. There's a lot of girls that scored the minimum in Preliminaries and are just trying to scrape by. Edie scored very high." Here she takes a modest pause, long enough for Dr. Kent to give her an appreciative leer. "And she inherited my drive. Look out for her during Mystery Powders; you should see her with that chromatography business. You can put any electrolyte in front of her—any electrolyte at all—and before you've said boo hoo she's telling you whether it's an acid or an alkali. Isn't that right, Edie?"

I squirm beneath Dr. Kent's lubed paws massaging what

there is of my breasts to check for lumps; breast cancer is one in two these days. He burps in some kind of acknowledgment, the thinnest layer of sweat beginning to show at the fringe of his Thickee Wig. No sweating for me: I am speeding through black waters two thousand feet below the gleaming white examination room.

". . . which is small potatoes compared to her juggling. She can keep anything up in the air. It's practically witchcraft the way she can make things fly!"

"Really?" Dr. Kent pushes back from me and signals that he has done all he can do. As soon as my feet hit the floor, my mother hoists herself up on the examination table and swings her legs like she's at the playground. Her hands rub the tops of her thighs. "Say, Edie, why don't you juggle a few of those speculums over there for Dr. Kent?"

Dr. Kent slips a hand inside his pocket and sucks in his gut.

"I don't feel like it. Can I get dressed?" The floor is freezing under my bare feet, but my clothes are piled on a chair behind my mother.

"Oh Edie, lighten up. Just juggle for a few minutes. Dr. Kent probably doesn't get a chance to have any fun while he's working. Do you, Dr. Kent?"

"No, not much. Things are usually pretty dull around here." He looks at us sadly.

"Come on." She nudges my thigh under the hospital gown with her toe. "Give Dr. Kent a little break. Show him how a future queen does it."

Dr. Kent hands me three shiny speculums.

"Oh, give her a few more. And some of those glass jars." She giggles mischievously. "Don't worry, she won't drop too many!"

The sound of Dr. Kent's smug chortle is almost more than I can stand, but my mother's eyes are beautiful and pleading, and so I stand there with my enormous hospital gown flapping open at the back and juggle. The metal-lyte speculums make clanking noises and the yellow liquid inside the jars gets frothy as I toss them up and around my head. I would kill for some socks.

Dr. Kent is visibly impressed; he pats my mother's knee in appreciation. "That's some daughter you've got there. Lorraine."

My mother leans into him ever so slightly, "I am just very lucky."

"Her vaginal cavity is a uniform pink color and has a healthy amount of moisture."

"She's a good girl, what can I say?"

I keep up a perfectly alternating rotation. But it's possible that I might have to scratch, or reach over to restore the neckline of my mother's shirt to a more discreet position. That shirt definitely seems a little small for her, maybe it shrank in the clothes flattener and she was too preoccupied with Virtue Club business to notice. If I'd been at home when she was dressing, I could've told her. I could've pointed out any number of suitable outfits for her to wear.

One jar falls, but I keep juggling.

"Edie!"

"Oh, here, that's all right. I'll have my nurse clean it up, don't worry about it." Dr. Kent leaps back from the glass and the splattered liquid and lays a hand on my mother's hip as she turns toward the towel dispenser. "No, no. You're not to lift a finger. My nurse can take care of it."

"If you insist."

"I do, madam. I do insist," he drawls, reaching around the small of my mother's back to push the intercom, causing her to giggle.

Two more jars drop, and a speculum hits Dr. Kent in the head.

"My God! Oh, doctor, are you all right? Edie! What are you doing?"

"I don't know, I got itchy."

"Oh Dr. Kent, she is so sorry. Edie, apologize right now."

"Please, don't even think about it." Dr. Kent is slapping at his shoes and trouser legs with a mountain of towels. I look at my mother and shrug, helplessly continuing to toss and catch a lone speculum.

"Stop playing with that and get dressed. Watch out that you don't step in the glass." She swivels around on the table and hurls my clothes at me. I duck, and the incoming nurse takes a Clickie to the gut. *"Oof!"* she cries, clasping a dripping sponge to her chest.

"Oh! I'm so sorry! Edie, you were supposed to catch that. *What is wrong with you?"*

I back into a metal-lyte tray of instruments and they go clattering to the ground. A bottle of something sticky tips and leaks onto Dr. Kent's phone. While my shoed feet wrestle with the leg holes of my underpants, Dr. Kent lifts my mother off the table so she won't have to walk in the glass and spilled specimens. She wraps her arms around his neck and leans her head on his shoulder. Struggling to get out myself, I can't avoid wet glass crunching under my Clickies as I squeeze by the hump of the nurse's uniformed back. She curses me, and I emerge from the examination room just in time to see Dr. Kent's foot pushing the door to his private office shut. I hear some shuffling, a thud, and both of them laughing. I feel sick to my stomach, I can't even bear to eavesdrop.

In the waiting room, the only place to sit is between two hugely pregnant women. When my mother finally comes out of Dr. Kent's office, she announces that I am out of Pageant whether I like it or not.

7

"I feel just like that woman in the Squeezie-Jax commercial."
Carrying two bowls of real popcorn, my mother enters the family nook, where Bubbeh, my father, Alice Jones, and I are awaiting the start of what all the newspapers are calling the screen
event of the year—an offbeat musical comedy thriller adventure
romance with none other than chic Ava Frenette, my mother's
idol, as the female lead. "My feet actually feel like they are
walking on a cloud." She bends down and offers a bowl to my
father, her face coquettishly tilted. Since her decision two weeks
ago to take me out of Pageant, she's been acting kind of silly.

I study her covertly. On a submarine, the crew takes it for
granted that the enemy is always lurking and listening. During a
war alert, personnel must be silent all the time. They speak only
when necessary, into one another's ears. They wear soft slippers
and take care not to drop one naval pin. The only advantage a
submarine has is its stealth. Silence is power, sound is death. If
located, a 20,000-ton destroyer becomes a wee, vulnerable target. I stroke Alice Jones's ears; my mother has allowed that I
may keep her as a pet since she's so smart, but I'm taking it as a
sign that she isn't really convinced that pulling me from Pageant
is the best thing.

It's been a while since any of us has watched screen down

here in the family nook, not since my training began in earnest, but now that the blow-up dummy, computerized blackboard, and pedestal for the Feminine Woman of Conscience Handbook have been banished to a closet, my mother has dusted off the screen and declared a family movie night. Surprisingly, my father has left his dead butterflies to join us.

"Great popcorn," he says now, crunching. "I haven't had popcorn that tastes like this since I don't know when. Did you put something special on it?"

"I got real butter for the occasion," my mother smiles. "To heck with the cholesterol for one night, you know?"

My father pats her arm, then lets his hand rest on hers.

"We used to make it in the winter, and have hot cocoa, remember, Lorraine? After you'd come in from ice-skating on Hyde Lake." Bubbeh passes me a bowl, and I scoop up a big handful. It *is* good. Even Alice Jones enjoys a nibble, and lord knows what a finicky eater she is since she's been on the meds.

"Ice-skating! God. Remember how we went down there that first winter we were dating, and we thought the lake was frozen and were just going to get on the ice when you threw that big rock on it to check. And sure enough—kerplunk! The rock went right through." My mother squeezes my father's biceps playfully. "Of course, it could just have been all that rowing you were doing back then."

"Good thing." My father chuckles, half bashful, half proud. "It would've been a long, cold swim to shore."

"I went skating on the lake last winter," Bubbeh says. "You should come up this year after the house is done and we could all go. Edie hasn't ever gone, has she?"

"We pulled her on a sled when she was little. But since then the lake hasn't always been frozen, with the winters so mild." My mother settles deeper into the couch, looking relaxed and more beautiful than ever between her husband and her mother. No one mentions that the reason I've never gone ice-skating at Hyde Lake is that my mother will only take the family to her old house in Waterburgh for two days every other August, when she visits her father's grave. "But maybe this winter. They're predicting a cold one."

"I'd like to ice-skate," I say carefully. "If we all go."

"That *would* be fun," my father says. His arm is resting behind my mother, one hand on her shoulder. I'm lying on the carpet in front of their feet.

"Oop, movie's starting. Turn around Edie, or you're gonna miss it." My mother's slippered foot gently pokes my knee, but I don't want to move, I'd much rather watch the three of them.

It would be like one of those snow globes: all of us together on the ice, snowflakes fluffing down, forever holding hands while skating a perfect figure eight.

My father kisses the side of my mother's head, and she gives him a sidelong glance of contentment. As the screen flickers with Ava Frenette's tears, everyone is quiet. During the commercials my mother asks if anyone needs anything. I scarf down the popcorn, cramming huge handfuls as fast as I can into my mouth. It tastes like meat, like meat filled with air.

"For once the papers didn't exaggerate," my mother announces during the end credits. "That was really something."

Bubbeh gets up to do some of her stretches. "I'm surprised, but it was actually worth watching. Did you enjoy it, Edie? You've been so quiet all night."

"Yeah, it was pretty good."

"You mean not as good as your Amazing Mister Fezundo, but 'pretty good' is right. Even Alice Jones liked it. I couldn't believe it, she sat still for the whole thing, even the commercials. I swear to God, that rabbit is part people." My mother's still leaning against my father, her fingers in the popcorn bowl hunting the burnt kernels that didn't quite pop, her favorite.

"Say," my father says, "remember the scene when they were

in that nightclub? Did you see the guy on the bongos? Where are my old drums? Aren't they down here somewhere?"

My mother sits up, giggly. "Why? Are you going to give us a concert?"

"I might." My father stands then and brushes the top of his hair with his hand. "I think I know where they are."

"That's right, Neil," says Bubbeh. "Give us a show. And you too, Lorraine. Remember how the two of you used to do those routines?"

"Well, it's been a while." My mother sets the popcorn bowl down on the carpet and wipes her hands on a napkin. Her hair is slightly mussed from leaning against my father, and her eyes are bright as she watches him go off in search of his drums. "But I think I can still remember a few boroonga steps. You remember the boroonga, Edie, don't you?"

"Maybe." I would dance with her if she asks, but I'd much rather watch her and my father.

"Or I could do the swindy-bendy. Remember that one, Ma? That was my signature dance, my ace in the hole. Without the swindy-bendy, I don't think Neil would ever have got up the guts to propose, but once he saw me in action"—here my mother performs a very complicated set of hip and stomach gyrations—"he couldn't keep his tongue in his head. Lost in swindy-bendy land." Her laugh is bubbly, and both Bubbeh and I watch her admiringly. On my lap, Alice Jones is a warm bundle.

"Lookee here," my father bursts back in the room, lugging a conga drum with one hand and carrying a suitcase in the other, a set of small bongos hooked on his shoulder. "I found all my old percussion instruments, too. I tell you, it brings back a lot of memories, seeing this stuff."

"You should keep it in here, Neil." My mother taps the drumhead with her manicure. "Why keep it locked away?"

"You're right, I should." He brings over a small table and starts setting up his instruments. "Boy, I hope my hands still know what to do."

"Oh, I'm sure your hands know what to do." My mother's voice is sly.

Bubbeh laughs, and bends to smooch my head before settling back down on the couch with her feet tucked up beneath her. "Your parents are quite the good-looking pair, aren't they, *mamaleh*?"

"Yeah." I'm a little dazed by the number of warm feelings kicking up all over the room, and nervous that it will soon end in someone's anger or tears.

Sleeves rolled up along his forearms, my father beats out a brisk rhythm on the conga with the heels of his hands, pauses to give us a grin, then resumes playing in earnest. He nods some private signal to my mother, who begins to execute vivacious swindy-bendy twists and twirls. I clasp Alice Jones to my chest and edge back toward the couch to give my mother as much room as possible to dance. The family nook rings with the deep, bouncy sound of my father's drums. His eyes are closed as his hands fly from the conga to the bongos to the maracas, shakers, wooden blocks and sticks and bells, and my mother keeps up with every switch, every change in the beat: it's like they were born to do this and nothing else, a natural function and a miracle all at once. Once, when a stick flies out of my father's hand, she catches it and whips it back to him as if they'd planned the whole thing, and he goes right back to beating his wooden block while Bubbeh and I clap and hoot them on. Normally, this amount of noise and movement would send Alice Jones running, but she's calm as sleep on my lap.

"*Heyah—ah—ah,*" my mother calls out.

"*Ho—ey—hoy—ho!*" my father answers.

Her body snakes around him as he pounds out ever-more-fevered rhythms. Who would have guessed that my dad had so much soul? A few strands of his hair fall across his forehead and I have to admit he looks a little like the new drummer for the Mystic Fangs.

"Go, Neil," Bubbeh crows. "Shake it, Lorraine!"

It's better than the screen event of the year, more amazing than the sight of the Amazing Mister Fezundo detonating (and then miraculously resurrecting) a turkey farm at the start of every holiday season. The family nook is no more; we are all exquisitely lost in swindy-bendy land until, beating faster and faster, my father's hands create a powerful blur and suddenly disappear from the drumhead; the routine is done. Underneath his raised palms, my mother bends backwards over the conga and his face falls onto hers in a passionate kiss.

"*Brava! Mazel tov!*" Bubbeh whistles and claps as their kiss goes on and on.

I'm so stunned I can hardly feel my hands clapping when my parents finally rise to take a bow.

"I want to invite you to something."

My mother looks up at me from the wicker swan magazine holder she is painting, her face alight with interest. The kitchen table is spread with newspapers and painting supplies, opera warbles from the entertainment module in the living room, and she is wearing her artist's smock: all good signs.

"An invitation, hunh? Are you throwing a party?"

"Not exactly, although there will be hors d'oeuvres."

"Really?"

"Yes. And it's happening pretty much now."

"Okey-dokey." She points her paintbrush at me and feigns drawing a mustache under my nose. "Just let me put the finishing touches on our new magazine holder, and I'll be right with you. I'm going to put it in the family nook. Thought I'd spruce the place up a bit down there now that Dad is going to be using it to practice his drums. I think this color combination is going to work out nicely with the sofa print. I just have to figure out if I should paint the base Poppy-Ochre or use the New Black. What do you think?"

"I think either color would be nice. It's going to look great." If she wants to build a Greek amphitheater down there, it's fine by me. "In fact, the family nook is where I'm inviting you, so you can bring it along and check out the colors right away. If it's dry enough to handle."

"I can carry it by the throat, that part is dry." She brushes the swan's tail feathers with a final dab of Kiwi-Green and then swishes the brush in a cup of black water. "Okay. I'm ready. Or do I need to change?"

"Nope. You're dressed just fine."

"Anyone else coming?"

"Nope. Just Y-O-U."

She follows me down the stairs, humming, swan throat in hand.

"Oooh! What's that?" She deposits the swan near the couch and then, as planned, her eyes light on the tray of miniature treats: seafood blintzes, mushroom-olive pies, chocolate and vanilla cannoli, bite-sized pastrami in a blanket. I got the recipes from Bubbeh and Lana and stayed up all night cooking with Bubbeh's help; my mother'd taken Sonambutussit before bed, so I knew the smells and the noise wouldn't wake her. "Who made all this stuff?"

"Please." Gallantly, I guide her to a seat. Then, demonstrating kick-ass Poise and Cookery skills, I walk backwards on tiptoe, hoist the tray over my head, do several twirls, whip a brilliantly folded napkin from a plate into her lap, and serve, reciting laws of etiquette all the while.

"Did *you* make this stuff?" Her teeth sink into a mushroom-olive pie, one of Mrs. Grimaldi's secret recipes. "It's fantastic! I can't believe you made all this. Did Bubbeh help you? This is real lobster! When did you make all this? The kitchen was spotless when I woke up this morning."

I just smile mysteriously as I continue my recitation. Then I segue into a medley of snippets from the emotional thermostat survey in Better Person Skills, a short segment of innovative choreography accompanying my sung version of Franklin Echo Sr.'s manifesto on the use of bibliomancy in community decision making from my brand-new Self-Expression through Memorization routine, and several lightning-quick Large Number Estimation drills. Before she has time to collect her jaw from the floor, I whip off the Just Like Satin coverlet that has been hiding Alice Jones's cage and announce the beginning of Sacrificial Rabbit routines.

"Wait, wait. When the heck did you learn all this?" She helps herself to another cannoli.

Again I hand her my Sphinx grin and rake my fingers through my hair stylishly.

"Just watch." Opening the cage, I clap out the call for Alice Jones to come, then whistle the command for Alice Jones to hop onto the chair, stand on her hind legs, and move her ears in the official introduction routine: together, apart, left, shift right, alternate forward and back, three quick flaps, wriggle, flick, bow. Despite the rabbit's near-perfect memory and physical agility, this routine has always given her trouble, but now she executes the correct sequence five times in a row without goofing once; that stuff from the hypnosis book I borrowed from Bubbeh last year never worked on anybody until I got the bright idea to try it on Alice Jones.

"What do you think of that? And check this out."

Alice Jones's steps are perfectly coordinated during Log Roll, not one drop of water spills out of the basin.

"God! Did you give her more meds? No? My God, Edie, it's magnificent. It's perfection."

"It's eighty points, that's what it is." I give the three-fingered signal for Alice Jones to get a running start for Monkey Bars. There is a look on her face, my mother's face, that I haven't seen since the day the president of Merry's came down to the Better Dress department and told her she looked ravishing.

Alice Jones is turning somersaults in a figure-eight pattern. I snap my fingers twice and the rabbit stops mid-somersault. For a moment she looks bewildered, then she flips herself back onto all four paws and jumps up into her cage to hide inside the small nesting box, so far back I can't even see her nose twitching.

I stand there, my hands limp. My mother shakes her head in disbelief; even I am not totally sure I didn't imagine what just happened.

"Well, well." My mother licks cannoli cream from her fingers and gives me a sidelong glance. "Mrs. Vrick would fall over if she saw this."

"Sacrificial Rabbit is a very important event, it's a sacred act. You've always told me that without sacrifices, nothing would mean anything."

Her eyes narrow. "Unh-hunh."

"It would be a great shame to let this amazing opportunity go to waste."

"Unh-hunh."

Together we listen to the sound of heat traveling through the ducts until at last my mother sighs. "I just don't get you."

"What's not to get? Why waste all the time and energy we've spent? Not to mention the money."

"Boy, you're a real piece of work, you know that? A real objet d'art. But, okay. Point taken." She stands and surveys the room, the newly painted wicker swan gliding next to my father's conga. "We'll see. I'm going to give it some thought. Remember, I am still concerned about your safety. If you *are* going to compete, you'll need to be extra careful from now on."

"Right. I will."

"And I'm not making any promises." Her heels click on the stairs. I flick off the lights and stand there in the dark, waiting for the sound of Alice Jones hopping out from her hiding place, but the only thing I hear is my mother upstairs in the kitchen, chattering into the phone to Mrs. Vrick with Pageant-gassed conviction.

The facsimile rabbit just happens to be an English Lop, with great sad blue eyes and a fluffy pink coat. Its ears aren't as long as Alice Jones's, though, and for this small detail I am thankful. All fifty contestants are gathered in our neighborhood association clubhouse for Mrs. Vrick's Sacrificial Rabbit Workshop, and right now Mrs. Vrick, wearing green aviator glasses that match her scrub dress, is demonstrating proper handling of the knockout club. Bethany Prewitt takes several pages of notes.

"There's a right way to deliver the deathblow, and there's a wrong way," Mrs. Vrick tells us. "The first step is getting the correct grip." She picks up her knockout club and points it at our heads. "Who just saw what I did wrong?"

Cara Gainy tentatively raises her hand. "You're holding it too close to Melissa's face?"

"Negative!" Mrs. Vrick slaps the knockout club into her open palm. "What I did was pick up the club by the wrong end. Never, and I do mean *not ever*, should any contestant handle their club by the killing point. The proper grip is clearly marked by the finger grooves in the handle. I cannot emphasize this fact enough: the judges will deduct *twenty* points for mishandling."

From mothers' seating, my mother raises her eyebrows at me significantly. We spend the next thirty minutes practicing our swing.

"Lift your elbow, don't let it sag! Keep your fingers together—you're not sipping champagne, you're bludgeoning a head! Think *arc*, Justine, think *follow-through*!" Her coaching voice bordering on fury, Mrs. Vrick adjusts spines, shoulders, and chins as she ducks clubs throughout the room. The mothers just barely restrain themselves from shouting advice; several arms twitch uncontrollably as the limp wrists of their daughters flail at the air. It's less than six months to Pageant. I'm glad to see that Bethany is especially inept at keeping her spine straight during follow-through.

"What is wrong with you ladies?" Mrs. Vrick is practically screaming. "Are you all shrinking violets, fanning yourselves at a garden party? Is there anyone here who can swing a death-blow like she means it?" She takes off her aviator glasses and shakes them at us. "You were born with a consciousness higher than any other form of life. You have the brains and the power to do this." We stare at her, muscles aching. "Doesn't this mean anything to you?"

When it's my go, I focus on the facsimile's ears, shorter than Alice Jones's by at least two inches, and this fills me with a sudden urgency. I haul back from the top of my shoulder, chin raised to a perfect ninety-degree angle, and let my mind envision the invisible arcing line. I even give it a color—vermilion—as Mrs. Vrick suggested, and let it heat up to a boiling glow from which my club will gather superior forces. Joints and tendons synchronize as my energy flows with higher consciousness, every inch of skin radiating power power power, club contacting air with the pure focus of purpose unleashed, my arm swings with style, flourish, and—whomp! The facsimile falls; tufts of polyfill fart gently from its busted seams.

For a moment, the room is on pause, and then Mrs. Vrick re-hooks her glasses around her ears and regards me solemnly from behind their lenses. Her two hands rise. "Way to go, Edie," she says, clapping. "Let's give it up for the one person in this room who didn't recoil from duty." Reluctantly, the others join in her applause. My mother beams like a weather-copter searchlight.

Afterward, she buys us both Hot Tutti-Frutti Banana Busters at the Sugar-Free Palace of Sin.

"You're a natural," she says, licking a drop of Fudgey Sauce from her thumb. "You've got the killer instinct, which by the way is the hallmark of royal competence. Believe it or not, I don't have it. At the crucial moment, I cave. Too sensitive, I guess."

"Are you saying I'm insensitive?" I poke my spoon into the rapidly melting treat.

My mother puts a hand on my hair. "Hardly. You're the precise embodiment of sensitivity. I'm always saying so. But you're growing up, Edie, becoming a woman, and the woman you're becoming is a realist."

"So?" I can still feel the weight of the knockout club hitting the facsimile's skull; I felt the blow strike my own head even as I was delivering it elsewhere, and for an instant, I too knew a facsimile death.

"So, those other girls are too captivated by fantasy. They waste their mental energy conjuring up images of themselves looking pretty under a headdress. They see only the end result, instead of focusing on the cold hard facts of the process." She swallows a marshmallow-coated Cherry Butz and gives me a tender smile. "Looks aren't everything. That's all I'm saying."

8

Saturday. It's probably ten miles to Hiawatha Lake, so we are going to hitchhike, an idea that is tearing me apart with excitement and dread; naturally, hitchhiking is a Safety offense. The windchill has dipped into the minus zone, and I'm shivering in my naval officer's cap and the wrong coat over the orange dress from Palmer's, because Lana said that's the color for a Contacting. She's got on an orange beret and her long plaid coat. Neither one of us is wearing gloves. Lana seems angry. She's walking ostrich fast, searching her pockets and her briefcase for something.

"Damn. I must've left my smokes in the house. That's great."

At the street, miniwagons whip by us, a few horns blare. I keep my cap pulled down low in case of Rules Committee spies.

"We could go back and get them."

"Chumly. Use your head." Lana sticks out her thumb and starts walking backwards.

I copy her stance, but hold my thumb close to my side so it looks like I might only be about to put my hand in my pocket.

"Did you see that? That guy just gave us the finger." Icy clouds burst from her mouth as she complains; the miniwagons keep passing us by.

My feet and legs are so numb with cold it hurts to walk. I

consider telling her that I've got to run home to get my gloves, and then never coming back. If anyone finds out what we are about to do, I could get kicked out of Pageant, maybe sent to Springfield Gardens Disciplinary Camp for Girls.

"Hey! He's stopping." Brake lights flash as a miniwagon finally pulls over. Lana runs to the passenger's side, taps on the glass. As I come up behind her, a chinless man wearing yellow nightglasses reaches over and opens the door from inside to let us in. The back is full of big boxes marked *Handle with Care: Sulfuric Acid Gaverterator*, and I'm about to say that we can't fit, but Lana shoves me in the front and climbs in after me.

"Where you girls headed?" His hands are slim, like a woman's. I gather the sides of my coat around me even though now suddenly it is stifling hot; I don't want any part of my clothes to touch any part of his. I inch toward Lana and she shifts irritably, trying to get comfortable. Our bags are on my feet.

"We're going to my Auntie Carmen's house," Lana says. "She lives over on East Lake."

"Pretty far. Cold night to walk, hunh?"

"We're desperate." Lana leans forward to give the man a sweetheart of a smile, "Can I bum a cigarette?"

Quickly, the man reaches inside his jacket, takes out a pack of Braves, and tightens one hand on the wheel as he offers them first to her and then to me, even though I am sitting closest. His dry lips are grinning, his thin hair shining like faux chrome under his old man's hat. I start to refuse the cigarette, but Lana nudges me to take it. "For later," she mouths. I notice that she has taken three, stuck one in her mouth and the other two under her beret. Chinless is talking, doesn't notice, wants to know if we're from the college. Lana says yeah, we're Civil War majors, her father's the ex-mayor of Buffalo, we're going to visit his sister, her aunt, who has multiple sclerosis and a hernia and might die any minute while Chinless takes it all in, his grin widening and shrinking. The miniwagon turns corners I don't remember. Is this the way to Hiawatha Lake or someplace completely opposite? We are in a cigarette mist—characters in a crystal ball. Lana and Chinless gab on and on, none of it seems real; it's as if we are acting out our future before it actually happens. When Lana says how my fiancé is a security guard for the secret vault of Electric Polyrubber Man, I have to stare hard at the dirty butts in the ashtray.

"It's sure cold enough out tonight, hey? I found clumps of grasshoppers all huddled together trying to stay warm in my garage." Behind his yellow glasses, his eyes slide over to Lana. "I stamped them to death with my foot. Should have put them in a gaverterator, hunh? That'd be something, hunh? Fry their heads off. I bet you girls would like to see something like that, hunh? Watch their wings sizzle up like Bac'n Stripsies in a pan. Now that would be some fun."

"Here's good." Lana motions for him to stop the miniwagon, but Chinless doesn't want to end our little trip.

"If you want, we can stop somewhere and get a drink. I know where we can sit and relax and nobody will bother us. The owner's a friend of mine. He's serving up those grasshopper cocktails now like everybody's into. You girls ever try a grasshopper? It's sweet and green with a refreshing minty taste. I bet you'd like a sip of that right about now, hunh?"

"All's well that ends well," says Lana, casually tracing an X on the dashboard with a compact scythe. She must've had it folded away in her pocket. The scythe tears the dashboard's coating, leaving bright white veins, and Chinless jerks the miniwagon to the shoulder. After we crawl out, he leans over with a womanly hand outstretched and shaky to present his business card.

"Any time you girls need a ride."

"Thanks . . ." Lana snatches the card from him, squints, "*Bill*. We sure *will*. *Bill*."

"That's my direct line." He grins uneasily. "You won't get the receptionist."

"Cyclo-Cyan Industries: Top-grade Nutrients," Lana reads. "I guess you make artificial additives. How very useful." She tucks the card into her pocket with elaborate care and then lifts out her phone to waggle it in front of him. "I'll make sure to call." She waves good-bye with the scythe so heartily he has no choice but to reluctantly pull back into the street.

"And fuck off forever, you poisonmonger!" She rips the card into tiny pieces that flutter to the ground, then stomps up the hill toward the old farmhouse. Midway up the hill, she stops at two flat rocks.

"Cheers." A bottle of Summer Storm emerges from Lana's bag and we both choose a seat, brushing away grasshoppers as Lana unscrews the cap. As she tilts her head back, her throat is exposed in my tecknolight and I stare at the skin pulsing as she swallows. She pulls the bottle away with a noisy suck and lets out a loud belch. "Vacnodorofixal."

"Okay," I say, reaching for my bag. Stealing the pills was not one of my smarter moves; they had to be popped from a foil containing twelve; the two ragged gaps I made were as alarming as bullet holes.

"Down the hatch," Lana says, downing hers. She lets me gulp some Summer Storm to get mine down, then I watch as she finishes the last of it.

We drop our bags in front of the boarded-up farmhouse. I don't know what would be worse: to see the house lit, farmer and family enjoying a cozy old-time evening of fresh-baked cookies and songs around the piano, or to find them all dead in their beds, a family of dusty corpses in moldy long johns, spiderwebs in their smiles instead of teeth. I shine my tecknolight on the grassy two-track road that leads out to South Lake Drive.

"What if somebody comes?" I whisper.

Lana is busy unfolding a compact shovel and clicking its joints into place. "Don't worry. Nobody comes here." She unfolds a piece of paper and motions for me to come closer. "These are the instructions. We've got to follow them to the letter. No matter what. It might seem at some point that things are not going to work, but they will, and you can't chicken out. Do you understand?"

"I'm not sure I feel ready to see a ghost."

"There won't be any ghosts. Only dead people. There's a big difference." Lana's leg bounces uneasily beneath her coat. "Remember the whole picture, Chumly. Think if it was your mother that was in trouble. Can you wrap your mind around that?"

"Yes."

"Okay, then. The Contacting shall begin." Lana embraces me and bends to kiss my cheek, and I shut my eyes and try to get my arms up to embrace her, but I'm too slow. The spot where her lips touched my face is the only place on my body with any feeling, like a little hole drilled to let the air in.

Lana reads the instructions. "Choose one to be the gravedigger, and one to be the body."

"This is bad," I croak. "We should do this someplace else. I've got a bad feeling about this place."

"We're here." She hands me the shovel. "You will be the gravedigger. You'll also be making the offering after I'm buried. Can you do that?" She takes off her coat, unveiling a tight orange dress.

Slowly, I take off my coat. "Yow, the wind is peeling my skin off."

"This will get you warm." Lana shakes the handle of my shovel.

"Here's the Jiffy for the offering. You're going to spray it right after the grave is all filled in. But you should only spray half the can. We have to do the rest after I'm back so we can fully accept the new reality."

"But—"

"Shh."

What else can I do but start digging? We don't talk, suffering in our thin orange dresses. All is silent, except for the sound of metal hitting earth, and a distant hum on the wind: grasshoppers somewhere—flying, searching, never sleeping.

"Lana," I barely sound the word. The field is dry, and among the pebbles and rocks, there are only lifeless brown weeds that emit an acid, bad-tempered smell. I pause in my digging and lean on the shovel, willing it to bury itself straight down into the center of the earth.

She moves closer to me, takes one hand from the shovel, and squeezes. Her face is eerie in the moonlight. She's breathing hard, grunting, readying herself for her contact with the dead. I want to grip her hand tighter, but the muscles in my fingers have gone numb from digging in the cold. I know I shouldn't say anything; it's stated in the instructions that no one is to speak until the body is in the grave. Once she's buried, Lana is supposed to be a contact point for the Happy Endings dead to reenter the world. It's not clear to me how Lana will know when the dead people have gone off to get rid of Mr. Grimaldi's bad attitude, but the instructions say that she will feel the presence of the dead leave her body and then she should dig herself out of the grave. If she makes it without any help from me, the Contacting is supposed to be a success.

When the grave is large enough, I drop the shovel, heaving. I'm actually sweating in this frigid air. Then, while I shine my beam on the freshly dug pit, Lana climbs in and lies down. I flick off my tecknolight as per the instructions, and Lana's disembodied voice speaks up at me from the dirt, "Come to us. We are alive. But we are ready to meet the dead."

As my eyes adjust more to the moonlight, I follow the instructions and scoop up armloads of the soil to hurl it over Lana's body in the grave. Lana keeps repeating her invitation, her voice quavering only the smallest bit on the word *ready*. The dead have nothing more to lose, nothing to gain except to bring about more death. I accidentally kick the Jiffy into the grave.

"Sorry. Mistake. Oops, I didn't mean to talk." I reach into the grave for the can and feel Lana's hot breath on my hand. Her face is in my shadow.

It's time to plug Lana's nostrils with the polystroob plugs. She stops chanting and lets me place the soda straw into her mouth. I sit on my knees. Lana shuts her eyes. It's time to cover her face with dirt and then fill up the rest of the grave. I feel the bile rise at the back of my throat. After Lana's head is buried, I am supposed to call for the dead until the grave is full and the earth over it is smooth and neat.

Hesitantly, I remove the straw from the earth—a sterile stem plucked from barrenness—and Lana's last breath is held fast in her lungs. This is what she wants, I remind myself; if it were my mother, I would be down there holding my breath too.

I force myself to keep my pace steady as I walk, spraying Jiffy around the spot where Lana lies buried. My eyes narrow against the growing wind, and pieces of dry dirt blow against my face. With so little feeling in my fingers, it's a struggle to push the can's nozzle, and the spray comes out unevenly, most of it blowing back onto my dress. Grasshoppers dive-bomb into the woods at the edge of the field. In the distant trees, bare branches whip back and forth and break with violent snaps. The sharp, unhappy smell of the field grows stronger.

How long has she been under there? I stop spraying, cover my eyes, and wait. It's been too long, Lana is dead, she can't possibly still be holding her breath, we should never have taken the Vacnodorofixal. Blood is roaring in my ears. Lana is under-ground—*buried alive!*—with dead people's thoughts taking over her mind, stopping her blood in its tracks. It must be over a minute, maybe even three minutes, since her last strawful of air—my sessions with the polystroob bag have given me a keen sense of timing. I stare at the grave. She was here and now she has disappeared; the world is too empty without her; I scoop a handful of dirt from the grave.

All around me is the smell of diseased soil, and I take it into my nose and mouth as I scoop more and more earth from on top of Lana. Underneath me, dead people fight to claim Lana's soul, and the earth bucks.

It's both terrible and a relief to see the earth break apart and scatter as Lana's hands and knees and orange beret rise out of the ground. Turning to the side, she spits and gasps, expelling the plugs from her nose, retching, and then puking, propped halfway out of the hole on her forearms. I shine the tecknolight on her bobbing head, see the shine of her vomit, click off the light, and walk away in the direction of the woods. What a mistake this was. What's the point of her nearly dying and leaving me behind?

The wind has died, and the air is almost hot compared with before. I trip over a fallen limb and cry out, feeling the scrape of a branch digging through my tights into my thigh. Suddenly a hand is prying my mouth open, spraying an inky taste into the back of my throat.

I struggle to get away.

"Don't fight it!" Lana pants. She holds my arms and then the Jiffy can is half-swallowed by Lana's own hungry mouth. We're some distance from the grave now; the black woods loom close.

In a burst, I am coughing and gasping, tears pouring from my eyes. The aftermath of the Jiffy is so hot I hear the skin inside my mouth sizzle. I spit and spit, fanning at my tongue. Lana is still taking the spray into her mouth, her eyes welded shut.

She swallows, then opens her empty mouth wide. "Haaa,"

she says, looking right at me. Her eyeballs are extra bright, enormous burning holes in her face, her features are askew, tweaked from the inside to accommodate a new personality—a dead one! I back away from her, but cannot tear my eyes away from this unfamiliar girl.

I am a flounder. The skin on my face floats away from my bones. Not unpleasant. No memory of how I have changed location: my beached body is prone on the ground, eyes rolling in my head on a high mountain of stone. The air is gentle, it is music trembling up my skin, then entering each pore. Lana lies beside me, quiet. Our orange dresses rise and fall with our breath, and the sideways sight of Lana breathing easily inspires me to stand, my arms twisting over my head. She raises her head to look at me swaying in the buttery moonlight, and I know that I am a wonder. My face tilts upward, and I feel a deep tenderness wrapping around me under an ocean of stars.

We have made contact with the afterlife, and everything Happy Endings says is true: the new world will be guaranteed beautiful. I spin around and around, knowing with all my heart that now there is a way to stop all the crap. Why couldn't I see it before? Lana is staring at me, and without a single word spoken, I know what it is she wants me to do. I start running, leaping over rocks and dry weeds toward the overlook.

"Beauty," I call out. "My name is Beauty!" Above me, the moon swells to the tenth power to better light my path, each magnified star blazes a hole through our black galaxy to guide me straight into the next waiting world. I can feel it so clearly, the exhilaration of the Happy Endings people when they took that final plunge, no net waiting to catch them, just the soft lap of death; when I reach the cliff, I will call out to them and dance right over the edge.

Grasshoppers leap out of my way, fly in waves over my running head. In my ruffled orange dress I too am a winged creature, never have I felt so light, so much a part of the sky, and when I make the leap from solid ground into empty space, the fall will be awesome, just like Lana said, it will be slow and floaty and glorious.

I scramble down the little path to the overlook and perch on the big rock at the edge. Below me the glossy surface of the lake calls its song: *plash, plash, plash* against the rocks. Giggling, I imagine the surprise of all the sleeping sunfish and trout when they hear the smack of my watery landing. I will leave life with all senses open, my eyes, nose, mouth, and ears will gobble the lake's soft, clear coolness as I slide into the beautiful future. I pause, look all around, amazed at how certain I really feel for the first time in my life. It's not the Jiffy or the Vacnodorofixal or the Summer Storm or even Lana that has given me this clarity. It's the realization that all my life I've been carrying a mini-wagon full of crap on my shoulders and now I've finally got the chance to set it down. Standing here with the wind whipping my dress and hair, I am Beauty, the only thing I wish is for Lana to be here to see it, and turning, I actually do see her, running toward me, her arms stretched out; yes, we will have a final embrace in this ugly world before we meet again in heaven on earth.

"What do you think you're doing?!" She pulls me by the front of my dress down off the boulder, falling with me and covering my body with hers.

"Ouch!" We cut ourselves on sharp rocks, grasshoppers buzz around our heads.

Lana hauls me to my feet, slaps my face hard. "Dead girls cannot compete. Rule #23. Remember?"

Shaken, my head falls away from her and sour liquid spills from my mouth. I heave and heave, expelling the Jiffy and half my guts. Lana's grip loosens when I finish, and with a hand pulling my hair back into a ponytail, her voice is unexpectedly tender as she tells me it's time to go.

On the way back through the field, there is a crackling sound underneath our feet. All around us on the ground are piles of twisted wings, claws, hard unseeing eyes. The whole field is littered with grasshoppers. Shock flutters in my stomach. I have never seen so many dead things.

9

The moon is fat tonight, waxed to fullness, a hazy yellow beach ball. In the space between it and our house are perfect miles of blackness, upside-down leagues of sea. Moving up through the sky, or down through the sea, always gives a sense of accomplishment; each mile contains its own clear destination. It's random sideways terrestrial motion that is so feeble: we think we are making progress, but we're always stuck on the same flat plane, one sorry earthbound situation displacing the next.

I feel sick, tainted with germs that will never disappear. The day was one long headache, but I didn't nap, went through my chores and training speaking as little as I could get away with. My mother seemed preoccupied as well; a Saturday night session with Dr. Plow gave her plenty to chew over, and for once I didn't wonder what she wore to see him. I tried calling Lana but only got her voice mail, and when I called the family number, her father sounded like he was about to punch somebody when he said she'd gone away for a few days. He hung up on me without even saying good-bye.

So the Contacting failed.

Standing on the precipice, ready to swan-dive onto the scaly back of a trout, I fell in love with death. When you die, all your problems are gone, and if that isn't guaranteed beauty, what is?

My mind feels sucked dry, as if everything I've ever known has faded away and been replaced by half-thoughts that squirm and escape when I try to pin them down. I still want to be in Pageant, don't I? But then what about Lana? She pulled me back from the precipice last night, but will she pull me back today? Am I going to lose her for good if I compete? Am I going to lose my chance—or my will—to compete if I continue to want her?

Wouldn't dying solve everything?

Can I trust my brain anymore? After all, there are facts in this world, statements that can be checked and proven. All night I stand facing away from my bed, listing, willing myself to stay awake in the world of objectivity.

I start with A.

Aldrin: $C_{12}H_8Cl_6$: tremors, convulsions, foaming at the mouth. Allyl sulfide: $C_6H_{10}S$: irritation of eyes and respiratory tract, unconsciousness at high levels.

B. Benzene: C_6H_6: mild poisoning causes confusion, hysteria, cursing, stubbornness; persistent symptoms include nervous irritability and unsteady gait; acute poisoning occurs in minutes, causing headache, coma, and death.

On the top shelf of the vinyl-wood bookcase in the family nook lives my father's oversized antique dictionary. I steal glances at it during training for Large Number Estimation.

"Is anything wrong, honey? You just multiplied those googols. I thought we said we were going to move on to Buchberger's algorithm for computing Gröbner Bases." My mother nibbles Fried Onion-Bits and looks at me worriedly.

"Right. I was just . . . double-checking." I give my calculations a stare of great concentration. "It never hurts to be sure." She doesn't know it, but my numbers are way off. During Preliminaries I aced this stuff; now basic addition is giving me hives. I cover the page with my hand, glance up at her and smile. "Let's move on, then. I'm ready." In her cage, Alice Jones burrows noisily.

My computation of Gröbner Bases goes awry, as does my polynomial factorization. I cover up with a few cinchy Quantum Lie Algebra equations, but she's not fooled.

"What is it, darling? You don't seem yourself today. Do you want to take a break? It's New Member Tuesday at Virtue Club tonight and I've got to finish glueing the wiggle eyes on all the name tags anyway. You want to help?"

Sighing, I close my notebook. What has happened to my brain? "I guess I'm a little tired. But I can help you out with the name tags. I just want to look up something in the dictionary. For school."

She puts the back of her hand against my forehead. "Sure you're not sick?"

I nod. "I'm sure."

After she goes up to the kitchen, I check a bunch of other words first, just in case someone dusts for prints—*superciliary, glissando, clubfoot.*

When I turn to the correct page, I see that the definition spills over onto the following page. Actually, there are a lot of definitions, and after, there is a list of synonyms: *affection, devotion, fondness, infatuation.* The dictionary says that *love* is different from these because it is the most intense and you are the most out of control when you feel it. *Infatuation* is pretty out of control, but it is indicative of folly. *Devotion* is intense, but it is more old-lady-like. *Affection* and *fondness* really just show up in greeting cards.

God loves everyone, Bubbeh says. Does that mean God is out of control? It seems like it. Maybe in the beginning of time God loved the world, and all those intense feelings made God mixed up, and by mistake, God made people.

While I think it over, I flip through the pages and look at the little illustrations. There are crocuses and crosses, a juggler, glockenspiel, ladder, igloo, and idol. The picture of the human heart is disgusting, crammed into the outline of a body between the person's lungs and liver. The veins and valves of it are obscene. Is this the organ that causes someone to risk her life and all her plans?

No pictures of *love*, only one picture of an ugly, uncomfortable-looking *love seat* and one of *love-lies-bleeding*, a plant with red flowers. If I had jumped off the overlook and landed on a rock, would anyone have made the connection between my smashed and bloodied body and these stalks with their drooping blossoms? Maybe to feel love is to always be seconds away from that sorry state: a fallen body whose life fluid pours out in a waste. So long as you can love, you can avoid lying there bleeding, but the very act of loving brings you ever closer to risking it. I shut the dictionary, fatigued. Who's the qualified brain who writes these definitions? I feel sorry for whoever had to concoct the definition for *love*. It's probably the most disappointing bunch of words that feeb ever had to write.

We are in my bedroom, watching screen, Fernando lying on his belly, knees swinging his deformed feet in their socks backwards and forwards in front of my face. I ignore them, relieved that he came right over when I called. Dazed from some new meds, my mother couldn't deflect Bubbeh's insistence that they attend Thursday Night Yoga at the Airport Inn, and my father's on the road. Usually I would be glad to have the privacy, but tonight I didn't trust myself to be alone. I seem to be losing physical control: if I'm sitting, my legs turn crooked and twitch and I have to get up; if I'm standing, my balance goes, and if there's nothing to brace myself with, I fall. When I talk, words come out in the wrong order; diphthongs and vowels warp my tongue.

Right now it's just me, Fernando, the honey-toned narrator

of *The Just Like Nature Show*, and the pelicans busy doing their slanted dives for food. "What big mouths you have," I say over and over to them in my head. "The better to eat you with." I slide my butt down in my chair and contemplate the repulsiveness of digestion. The pelicans skim low over the brown water. It scares me to see their large jaws scoop up fish; they are ugly, awkward-looking creatures, and when they dive they hit their mark.

After *The Just Like Nature Show*, the Amazing Mister Fezundo wills a whale to leap out of its tank at Grandpa Lou's Marine Park World and land on his nearly naked body stretched out in a beach chair (strange to see no bulge in his silver thong). He disappears under the whale's enormous flubber, all except for his pointy slippers. I can't watch, actually turn my head away although I have never not watched his magic all the way through, and even though I know he will survive I don't want to see the Amazing Mister Fezundo's struggling feet under all that weight, don't want to know that he is almost nude under that ton of rubbery flesh. I can hear the whispered narration, but even when Fernando breathes a *yeah* of admiration as the whale leaps back into its tank, even as the Amazing Mister Fezundo is said to be revealed intact on the lounge chair drinking a tropical fruit drink out of a coconut shell—I keep my eyes averted.

Sins of the Pretty is on next. During the opening credits, I tickle Fernando's heel; I'm the only person except his mom who he will let touch his feet. The screen light flickers on his blue-white hair: a halo. The cop hosts all have spray-on suntans and hair that wouldn't move in a hurricane. Right now they are cruising down the coastal highway in St. Augustine, Florida, on their way to arrest this girl and her drunk boyfriend driving a souped-up miniwagon on the beach; the miniwagon's huge tires smash a lot of sea turtle eggs and kill a few big female turtles trying to squeeze out some more. I've seen this episode already and it's lame. The girl is excellent, with teckno glasses and hair like Cleopatra, but her boyfriend looks inbred and has no eyelashes. You can't believe a girl like that would be with a feeb like him, except at the end. Her forehead wrinkles and she says she really never thought about endangered turtles before while the boyfriend's copping a feel. After you see her let him do that while she's trying to think, you could believe anything.

"Change it," I say. "I've seen this one."

A public service announcement for No Happy Endings flashes on.

"Choose life," a crying woman says to a man slumped against a wall.

"Change it," I say again, my voice sharp.

"Okay." Fernando's thumb presses the remote and the screen goes all squiggly. Then the squiggles give way to hissing static and a girl in a sky blue nun's habit. Actually, the reception is so bad it looks as though the top and bottom halves of her habit are being yanked to opposite sides of the picture, and her masked face is going in and out of focus, but it could be—yes, it is.

"Is that a channel? What channel is that?" I grab at the remote, pushing all the buttons, always getting the same staticky picture: it's Lily Gates. I'm sure of it. I turn the volume up full. That is her masked face in the electronic snow, her voice I hear through the crackling roar.

"Do not eat the meat at Just Like Meat Planets!" Lily Gates cries. "It is rabbit meat! All the rabbits killed at Pageant will become Just Like Meat Planet food! Don't eat the meat!"

Abruptly, a miniwagon commercial takes her place. I stand on my chair, blinking. "That was Lily Gates! Did you see that? It was Lily Gates!"

Fernando rubs his ears and wriggles around until he is sitting up. "It's loud, Edie."

"Well," I demand, pushing the mute, "did you see her or didn't you?"

"I don't think so. There was a lot of dots . . . you know . . . screen snow . . ."

I feel like slapping his soft, ignorant cheeks. He doesn't even have any hair on his face yet. He's a boy, not a man, probably he'll always be a boy. He wouldn't know Lily Gates if she fell on him. "What's wrong with you? Weren't you paying attention? She was right there, in her nun's outfit, saying that the meat at Just Like Meat Planet is rabbit meat. She must've pirated the lines. Weren't you listening?"

"Gee, Edie. It was just static." He starts putting his orthopedics on the wrong feet. "But if you say she was there—"

"No! Not if I say it! She was right there on SCREEN! Lily fucking *Gates*." I kick his left shoe away from his right foot as he strains to shove it in.

He doesn't retrieve the shoe from under my bed, just quietly goes downstairs and lets himself out.

There is so much I need to know: how the Amazing Mister Fezundo survives all those disasters, whether winning Pageant is better than doing a Happy Ending, why everyone I know seems to need a med or a shot or a spray can, if it is possible that I am going to kill the one clearly innocent being in my life just so she will end up as a shish kebab dressed in a squirt of Just Like Ketchup?

I reach for the phone.

Lana's sleepy, but at least she doesn't sound mad. She says she got back in town late last night and has been taking a nap. She also says that it's possible that Lily Gates was on screen, but that the meat at Just Like Meat Planet is a combo of pork and turkey refuse parts. It isn't rabbit meat: she knows because she's actually tasted real rabbit meat, and it's not something she'd ever do again, but Italians eat, tasting stuff is their adventure.

So don't worry, she says, but she's got to go, she's got business to attend to, and we'll be in touch.

"About that thing," I begin.

"Forget it," she says.

"But I have a couple of questions. Because I'm feeling a little strange . . ."

It's so quiet then I think she has gone away. "Lana?"

I start as her voice comes back on, louder than before, full of sudden energy. "Don't worry. You probably just have a Jiffy hangover."

"But—"

But then she's off the line, without once calling me Chumly. The heartless dial tone settles in my ear before I can ask why both living and dying now seem like poor options, and I'm left without one hint that her adventurous Italian mouth might plant itself on mine ever again.

The Amazing Mister Fezundo would suggest that I persevere. I can hear his confident magician's voice telling me to concentrate my will on being tiny, that if I really focus and concentrate, I will actually become small enough to travel down Lana's throat, to slide to a stop among her lungs and liver and heart with all its jagged blue veins and tubes. Her torpedo tubes. I can hear his voice telling me to crank the wheel and close those tubes. All the risk and the loss will be worth it: I will be rocked safe behind her ribs, lulled by the melodious thumpings and gurglings of her blood.

Her face still radiating concern, my mother tells me she thinks I'm under too much stress, gives me thirty bucks, and says go have a good time with Fernando at the Drive-By Sausage Adventure Forest. She reminds me to watch out for any suspicious kids, and then, almost before Fernando's mom has a chance to honk, I pocket the money and am out the door.

After California auctioned its redwoods to balance its budget (Franklin Echo's millions to the rescue!), I could not get enough of the Adventure Forest for a while. But after the Just Like Meat Planet people came up with the idea of a merger and the sausage theme was born, I lost a little enthusiasm for pleading with my mother to let me bungee in peace. Now you have to wear a Sausage Suit when you bungee down. And there are Sausage Cars, too, with sensors that cause them to stop before they crash into a bungee-er or any of the redwoods. I still get to feel that great combo of terror and thrill, but now it's minus the dignity, and mostly I just go to get a whiff of something rare.

My mother's take on the Drive-By Sausage Adventure Forest has always been that the whole place is a disaster waiting to happen. There have been some minor accidents, all pretty tame stuff: once a sensor malfunctioned and one of the Sausage Cars dented a redwood, and once, before the new safety precautions, some feeble broke the security lock on his Sausage Suit during a jump and crashed the whole system. But risking my life here seems oddly comforting now—if death is what I'm after, at least it will be among the giant old redwoods, and not be a part of Happy Endings, just the regular accidental kind of thing. I'm not looking for torture, though. I want a clean break: the cord breaks just as I bungee down from the top of a redwood—instant impact. Or the preprogrammed speed of my Sausage Car goes whacko and I ram straight through one of the thick, rust-colored trunks.

We allow the Adventure Forest technicians to strap us into our protective Sausage Suits; we're going to start out with the bungees. On the escalator to the treehouse launching pad, I look down to see Bethany Prewitt pay one of the trolls at the cash registers, then disappear through the knothole to Suit rentals. I'll have to be extra discreet with her around; she'd just love to report me to the Rules Committee and watch my points drip down the drain.

"This is excellent. I'm really glad we came." It must be the talk button that distorts my speech.

"Yeah, but—" Fernando lifts his finger off the talk button too early, so the rest of his sentence stays with him inside his Suit. It's hard to see his face inside the helmet, but it seems that when he looks at me, the usual adoration is gone.

At the launching pad, another technician hooks on our bungee cords. The music, some of that annoying polka, is loudest up here in the tops of the trees, but at least it's not smarmy nightclub music, or opera. While I wait for my turn to fall, I let the odor of the old trees calm me. That smell is the best part as far as I'm concerned, even better than falling one hundred feet and ricocheting off tree trunks for seven minutes, but today my polystroob Sausage Suit itches, and I'm having trouble breathing through the nose holes. Far below, other kids and a few parents in Sausage Cars zigzag through the trees.

The upper tracks jerk my bungee over to the edge of the launching pad, and with a blare of polka, I am whipped off my feet and shooting down past the longest tree trunks in the world. Just as the bungee stretches to its full length, the sensor on a Sausage Car activates its brakes, and I am yanked away from a collision with a little kid, maybe the littlest kid I've ever seen in her own Sausage. She's screaming bloody murder. Her face fills me with doubt. I reach up to feel my bungee and will myself to have a good time. Guided by gravity, my body bounces off one ancient tree after another, polkaing through the high leaves as I narrowly avoid smashup after smashup with the other Sausages in the forest.

Fernando is tired of falling. It's time for the carnivorous plants in the museum to feed, and he wants to go into the gift shop and buy another Venus flytrap for his ever-dying collection.

"Look at this." He holds up a pot containing some kind of

genetically modified shrub that tries to chomp down on his fingers. "Excellent, hunh?"

I murmur some words of admiration and then linger over the smooth amber jewelry filled with grasshoppers, thinking how swell the largest grasshopper ring would look on Lana's hand. Then Bethany Prewitt pops up next to us and asks the clerk if she can see one of the amber grasshopper chokers. Abruptly, I drag Fernando through the exit. Outside the door, a small orange card catches my eye and I bend to pick it up while Fernando wanders over to the observation window. While he stares at the Sausages zooming around in the forest, I read the card. *Happy Endings.* A phone number. I snap my head around to make sure no one sees, and the whole Adventure Forest looks rough, like someone sandpapered everything. The few people who pass by are preoccupied with their own business, their faces an unhappy aluminum color in the utili-light. Fernando turns then, and I give him my most exciting smile as, skin crackling with heat, I tuck the card into the pocket of my jeans.

It is not another sub that is a submarine's worst enemy. The real enemy is the marvelous sea itself—always there, fighting to get in, exerting a crushing force on every millimeter of a sub's surface.

"Edie! Yo!" Lana's arm beckons from the middle window of Judd's miniwagon, Alec and Judd are up front. When Lana yells for me to get in the miniwagon next to her, I hesitate. Is she trying to get me torcher-ed? She flashes her knock-'em-dead smile and waves me over, every finger a magic wand. I crawl in beside her, wishing I could keep going right onto her lap; she's wearing silver pants.

Judd and Alec are drinking something out of a mixology bottle and trying to get Judd's release player to work. They don't

look at me or say anything, and as soon as I get in and shut the
door, Judd shoves the stick into first gear and squeals off in the
direction of the Mohawk Canal.

"Yo, mama, you look like you need a friend." Lana winks
and raises one thick eyebrow as we hurtle through every stop
sign and red light on the way. She squeezes my hand and whispers in my ear, "Don't worry about them. I told them about all
the great meds you can get from your mom."

I stiffen and pull away, horrified.

She pats my arm. "Believe me, they're too intrigued to do
anything."

"No secrets. Any secrets, we're dumping you right here right
now." Alec sounds different when Lana's around, smaller.

"Don't be such a baby. We're not talking about you." Lana's
eyes are darker than usual, but maybe it's because the skin underneath has a new, grayish tint. She looks like she may have a
cold.

Alec swivels around to give Lana a sexy face. It's like I'm
not even there. Judd doesn't say anything; he's a schizophrenic
talker: sometimes he says nothing, just sticks his fingers under
his armpit and sniffs them quick, other times you can't get him
to shut up. Lana rolls her eyes.

The release player is finally working and the Mystic Fangs
sing loud enough to pop blood vessels. The name of the song
just happens to be "Contact" and I can feel my neck get hot
when Lana sings along; she doesn't know the right words, but
her voice is husky and it's obvious from our silence that everyone would rather listen to her mistakes than be invited by the
Mystic Fangs themselves to hang out backstage at their next
gig.

At the canal, everybody gets out of the miniwagon, and immediately, Judd and Alec start throwing snowballs at the de-
faced sign that used to say HISTORICAL LANDMARK. Judd smashes
snowballs against trees, picnic tables, and trash cans. He lobs a

few over the canal, throwing fast and hard—doesn't even wait to see one snowball explode before he starts packing another.

"C'mere." Lana drags me over to look at the water, dark and still as tar against pure, undisturbed snow, a weird steam rising. "A shitload of weapons are sunk deep within its depths. Blow Torcher paraphernalia I managed to confiscate from headquarters when Alec wasn't looking. Do you think they're disintegrating? You're the underwater expert, what do you think?"

"Uh . . ."

From her pocket: ringing, and without removing the phone, Lana cuts off the sound. "Do not disturb," she says, lighting up a floogie. She sucks on it until her lungs fill to bursting, then pokes it under my nose. I shake my head no, but she gives me one of her darling looks so I take a small puff.

"At first he said it wasn't cool for me to be at headquarters, but then I just gave him the old one-two-skiddoo and he saw the light."

Something tells me I don't want to know the exact details of this. I exhale, struck by the juxtaposition of snow, water, and steam. "H_2O in three forms. Pretty wild, hunh? One solid, one liquid, and one gas, and yet they're all made up of exactly the same elements."

"Little Miss Scientist tells it how it is all day all night." A joke, but there is admiration in it, I can hear it clear as the sound of dolphin chuckling in a shallow bay. Smoke pours from between her lips.

"Life is pretty amazing," I say carefully. "I really dig it."

Her neck bends back and sideways to look all around her. "Ditto to that."

"It would suck to miss out on all of this," I say, gesturing.

"Did you ever notice trees?" She points to an eastern hemlock. "Whichever way a tree grows, it always looks great. It's always the right color, always the right shape—" She smiles, sheepish. "No offense to your father."

"That's his problem."

"I know what you mean."

"Listen!" She cocks her head, eyes closed tight in concentration.

I hear the sounds of distant weather-copters and the thuds of shattering snowballs.

"The trees are speaking to us. They're telling us to watch out for feebles." Her eyes flash open, and then she winks, but she's not mocking. "You know I really appreciate what you did for me the other night. I hope you know that."

I stare down into the canal, straining to catch sight of a rusting blade, or perhaps an entire row of destroyed Blow Torcher arsenal. Did she really dump those weapons? "The Contacting didn't work."

"It sure didn't. And you know what I say to that? Fuck Happy Endings. It's the biggest load of crap ever imagined."

"Ditto to that." I don't meet her eyes. Grasshoppers skim across the canal in a V formation. The toe of Lana's riding boot digs at the snow to uncover a hooked vein of black mud.

"I'm sorry I got you involved," she says. "Of course you didn't tell anyone about what happened."

"Of course not!"

"Easy. I trust you." She wipes mud from her boot on a snowy rock and her bloodshot eyes look at me with the concentration of a headphone-wearing sonar operator pulsing with the sounds of whales and destroyers. "More than anyone else I know." Her elbow knocks against my side, tender and deliberate. "Not counting my mother." She sighs. "If only I had the money to get her out of here." Her hands sag at her sides.

"How much do you need?"

"More than I've got."

A snowball whizzes by my ear. Another one lands just short of my toes.

"Leave her alone," Lana calls. To me she says, "What I really need is a new plan."

Alec and Judd shoot a few more snowballs at each other and the head of one unfortunate squirrel desperate to bury a nut as they make their way over to us. I shrink down as far as possible inside my naval officer parka. Alec throws his arm around Lana's shoulders and she shrugs out from beneath it.

"Not now," she says, holding in smoke. She passes what's left of the floogie to me. "You got any more mooch? We're going to sit in the miniwagon. It's colder than Franklin Echo's ass out here. Judd! Toss me the keys so we can hear some tunes."

In the miniwagon she's quiet, and she keeps the music low. "Life is complicated right now," she finally says. "Ultimately, I think disaster and stupidity are always gonna take the cake."

I shove my hands inside my pockets.

Alec is looking at us. Judd's climbing one of the leafless trees, stomping branches with his boot so they break, showering snow on the ground, but Alec isn't moving, doesn't even have his hands in his pockets, and he's not wearing gloves so I know they must be cold. He's just staring at us, at the top of Lana's head pressed down on the wheel.

"Alec's looking."

Slowly, Lana raises her face to peer through the windshield. She stares at Alec, and then, still staring and only moving one finger, she pushes the power button to lower all the windows. Another finger glides over to push the plus sign on the volume button till the bass distorts. I don't cover my ears and try not to shiver. She turns to me, now wearing a hard expression, and yells over the music, "Do you know what he is?"

I shake my head.

"An amateur." Her mouth opens wide to scream at the glass in front of us, "Amateur!" Then she whips around and grabs me to her, planting a big wet one on my mouth. Her nose bumps over mine as she twists her face to give my lips a rough kiss from a bunch of angles. When she lets me go, the cold air hits my lips like a slap. "Let's see how the amateur likes that."

I've been kissed publicly. There are witnesses. I could be worried about losing points, but somehow I feel safe. Still, I steal a look at Alec; only his head moves, nodding, his mouth open like he's laughing except he's too above it all to make the sound.

10

After the Blow Torchers' nonstop bonanza during Christmas vacation (Cindy Blicker's tooth loss during a group rectal, Mindy Swann's all-night session chained to the angel of death protecting Hank Gaskin's grave, Nina Turner's marathon nipple-twist, et cetera), girls in training have become totally homebound, avoiding all public spaces other than school. Some of the girls get pit bulls and rottweilers; Marsha Brandt gets one of each, and on their first night they charge into her family nook and chow down her sacrificial rabbit, Harry. The Identity Mall is a virtual ghost town.

I couldn't be happier. These days with Lana near me, everything makes sense. She's invited me over every evening and weekend since the kiss so I can help her think up a new plan to save her mother, and although it's tricky to escape my mother's worried surveillance, I feel that nothing can harm me—Lana's protective aura envelopes us both.

I'm lying on my side. The ground up at the reservoir is a little soggy, but it smells fresh, enchanted, like all the old dirt was washed away when the snow melted and then replaced by special, clean dirt sprung from Earth's center. Even the old fire tower looks new, showing a glimpse of its past importance, recalling the legions of dangers scouted and wiped out. Every blade of grass stands proud and tall, the minuscule legs of ants and spiders and potato bugs purr through the green, grasshoppers thrum by, up and down, up and down. Locusts and maples and white, peeling birch all have little knobby buds on their branches; they are speaking to us, to Lana and me. Bluebells, my favorite wildflower, are sprinkled around us like a little flower army, their fluttering petals the blue of muscles in the human anatomy poster that hangs untorn in Hygiene. It's springtime in January, a new season for a new year. For once, the weather makes sense.

"I've got an infection! Spring fever!" I turn a couple of somersaults and bound over to where Lana's sitting cross-legged. "There's no weather on a submarine. No rain, no wind, no sun. The only way you know when the sun sets is when the lights are turned down." I like standing over her. She looks up at me like I could tell her something no one's ever said to her before. "Giant tube worms live in hydrothermal vents in the ocean floor. They can live there even though the vents are completely dark and boiling hot and full of extrapoisonous chemicals. Amazing, hunh?" Her mouth drops open a little and so I add a few more facts I'm not completely sure about. "Scientists have been studying the communication system of the giant tube worms for clues about how they survive all that stuff, and after I graduate from submarine school and become a sonar operator, I'm going down to listen and crack the code. The worms are really talkative, they mumble and mutter all night long."

The deep purple of her eyes is hidden under delicate lids fringing her cheeks with eyelashes sparkling dark in the sun. Look at that skin, I want to cry. I turn my head to no one and wink. We're together all the time now. She's mine, this darling beauty with her hands in the grass, and I'm not letting her go without a fight. Her belly button is an inviting tunnel. Below her, the earth's layers are her private cake; she's the crunchy sugar rose on top that everyone hopes will grace their slice.

"Hey." I poke her foot with mine. She might be asleep. Maybe she can do that thing that my mother does, that falling asleep in two seconds thing. If she's asleep, she won't even know if I kiss her. The wind blows slightly. The voices of history that have spoken on this very spot are now calling to me; in unison, they tell of their loves and wishes, their trials and defeats, cautioning me not to fail, something easy to do. "Don't be a timid tippy," they intone windily. Back then, people were often afraid. They didn't have the benefit of modern thinking to guide them.

There's no one to see us. I lean over, let my breath warm her cheek, marveling at all the colors the light finds in her brown hair, and when she doesn't move or say anything, I place my mouth on hers.

"Jesus!" Lana jerks up, and I tumble away from her. "What was that?" She's squinting at me with the same look I've seen her give Blow Torchers.

My whole body feels like it's been pounded by a ha-ha groan hammer.

"Nothing—I was just kidding around—"

"Jesus!" Her fingers start pulling up clumps of grass, tiny thin roots and all. The dirt she uncovers looks naked and raw, it stains her hands brown, gets in under her nails.

The back of my throat swells and the tears just flow.

"Oh, Edie. Don't start trouble." She slaps dirt off on her pants, but her hands don't come clean.

Later, when the sun's nearly set and the ground has frozen onto the seat of my pants with real January vengeance, I walk home alone. Gray snowflakes are coming down fast.

A week later I follow her all the way to the reservoir. If she knows I am only a stone's throw away in the bushes, she makes no sign of it; she is one hundred percent intent on something else besides me. Through the bramble, I see her crouch down and whistle. Her knapsack is off and opened wide on the grass in front of her, and within moments, Domino is hopping toward it, hopping into it, like she's come home to the rabbit warren of her birth. I am dumbstruck. Lana is standing, carefully swinging the knapsack around on her shoulders to rest against her spine, and it hardly seems real when I see her pull on a pair of thick gloves and begin climbing the barbed-wire base of the fire tower.

Nothing exists in the world but this: Lana's yellow knapsack shifting along her back under her dark hair, Domino's head and ears poking out of the top, Lana's long thighs stretching toward the next toehold, the card-table-sized platform seventy feet in the air. Brambles poke the inner and outer helices of my ears as her feet ascend the fire tower. A bubble of anxiety rises in my chest, a Gentle Welcome nun's drumroll would not be out of place.

At the top, Lana lets Domino out of the knapsack and motions for her to stay up on the platform while she herself climbs back down. Her body moves smoothly, skipping toeholds with a reckless confidence, and I know I am not supposed to see this.

Domino huddles up there against the clouds.

When Lana stands at the base of the fire tower and claps her hands, I know that she means for Domino the wild rabbit to jump, and I am riveted as surely as if my whole body was screwed tight into the earth. Has Lana given Domino meds? Not that this type of thing is anything like the Sacrificial Rabbit routines, but if Lana's planning to enter Pageant, it's too late. Isn't it?

Domino sails down from the sky.

Gentle Welcome cymbals crash in my head and I shut my eyes right before the animal hits, for once wishing I had stayed home and done something harmless like emptying the dish flagellator as my mother had asked.

Of course the urge is all-powerful, my eyes open, and I shrink my body farther down into the brush as Lana turns, grinning ear to ear, Domino cradled in her arms. If I want the answer to what the hell she is doing risking Domino's life, I can forget it; even if I could ask her, I might not, considering what she could say about me and Alice Jones. When she bends to put Domino back onto the grass, I wait for a moment to make sure that Domino has not lost her ability to hop freely before my Clickies hightail it out of that place; and I don't stop running until I reach my backyard, my body bent over an Insecticide Hut, panting.

Pageant mania. Two months to go. Cold sweats, heartburn, drowsiness, personality changes, stiff necks—the female population of Deansville empties the shelves in the pharmacy, wears out the nibs of doctors' pens in search of relief. In our house, training continues with renewed vigor.

School is closed: some kid put a virus in the school's screen system and all the bookkeeping got erased; the teachers haven't been paid in over a month, so they're on strike. There's a rumor going around that Mrs. Geary paid the kid to do it; when she heard about the strike she went on holiday to Brazil. Lana has vanished. When her father finally answers the line, he grumbles that she's gone to visit a cousin in Texas, then as usual he hangs up without saying good-bye.

This afternoon in a fit of lonely frustration, and aided by the new meds that have carried my mother into a lengthy nap, I am able to sneak out and drag Fernando to the Identity Mall. Two Blow Torchers eye us on the shuttle: rubber-lipped Ritchie Wagner, who gives tattoos in his basement, and super-short Daniel Dedabber, stepson of a congressman. Fernando stares out the window, oblivious, his nose running buckets.

"The Amazing Mister Fezundo is going to blow up China," I

whisper, keeping my eyes trained on Fernando and not on the Blow Torchers sitting across the aisle. "Some people think he won't be able to put it back together. They're picketing his screen channel."

"Yeah?" Fernando's tongue creeps up to lick at a line of snot while he fishes around in his jacket pockets for one of the many bandannas his mother has started buying him because they remind her of Spain. Drawings of feet spill out. He doesn't bother to pick them up. I reach down to collect them; after all, things haven't seemed quite right with us ever since that day I thought I saw Lily Gates on screen and yelled at him.

"Hey. This isn't one of yours." I let Fernando's drawings fall back to the floor and pick up a magazine photograph folded into a square.

When he takes the picture from me, I feel his hands trembling. He unfolds and smooths the paper. "I know. It's *Beauty*." He speaks in a whispered rush. "It goes with this poem about a girl who jumps off a cliff because—"

"I know why she jumps," I say, snatching the paper out of Fernando's grip.

He goes limp against the seat.

I cut my eyes at him and finger the drawing's creases, its yellowing reeds bent over in the wind looking like they are going to break. "You read the poem?"

"Unh-hunh," Fernando dreamily twirls his hair. "I liked it. It makes people happy."

"Are you talking about what I think you're not supposed to be talking about?"

Fernando reaches for the picture and nods as he folds it back up and into his pocket. "I heard some things."

"Are you nuts?"

"But even if you're not old enough to do a Happy Ending, you still have a chance. Because the dead are coming back for us. They'll take our lives for us. They'll kill us so we can find beauty. If we're worthy."

"Look," I poke his stomach, hard. "Cut it out with this. It's not true."

"Maybe it is." He pats his shirt where I poked him and turns away from me.

"Those Happy Endings people are a bunch of chickens who are just running away from their problems," I tell his back. I sound just like my mother. Taking a breath, I add, directly into his ear, "The Amazing Mister Fezundo doesn't need that Happy crap to find beauty."

The lights of the Identity Mall break onto his face and we disembark, avoiding the Blow Torchers tearing down pest strips and kicking the seats as they fight to be first out the door.

I steer Fernando toward At Last Music. He lets me guide him—I could push his face into the window of Merry's and he'd let me; when we pass the store, I almost feel like doing it. His sleeve is fuzzy beneath my fingers. What kind of a boy wears a fuzzy shirt?

"Sorry, Edie," he says.

"Are you?" I pull on his belt to make him stop walking. "You think you can come back from the dead and make everything beautiful." I reach up to pull him close by his collar so I can get my lips right next to his mutant eardrum again, "and then you would never do the wrong thing and everybody would be your friend. That's what you think, right?"

His skinny legs bend awkwardly and he ends up going down on one knee. Shoppers pass us, but I ignore their disapproving stares.

"Ow," he says, putting a hand up to his ear.

I snatch his fingers away. "Happy Endings is a big fat lie. When you die, that's it. Everything's over. You're out of the game."

He's motionless in his crouch, and I know that he's gone into one of his trances. If I walk away, he won't even notice. Eventually, he'll fall over and sleep.

Suddenly I ache to see the light of kinship in his gray irises, for him to do something, touch my hand or say I have international flair, give me that little piece of himself that he repeatedly gives and I repeatedly shake off. "Fernando?" I pull him up.

"What's up, doc?" He looks down at me, and I can tell that he appreciates all I've said. I start to tell him I'm sorry for yelling at him that day Lily Gates was on screen, but suddenly Dent's window display swims into focus, and I can see that it is crammed with cast-resin rabbits on Easter grass. A neon sign blinks on and off: COMMEMORATE NOW!

"No," I choke.

"What is it?" Fernando puts a finger on the glass.

Among the rabbits is a teenage girl mannequin filling out a blue-checked dress with adult curves. She's got her hand on one of the rabbits as though she is giving it a blessing, and she seems happy in her orange-brown mannequin skin with her clear blue eyes matching her dress; her even teeth radiate confidence and serenity. Nestled by one shiny blue pump is a live Dutch rabbit, a baby, who looks directly at us with its left eye.

"Shit, shit, shit." I cup my head in my hands. The resin rabbits are smoothly carved, clean, and ultrawhite. The real bunny looks nothing like them.

Fernando puts his hand on my back and pats it awkwardly, like he's just learned how to touch. I let him do it, instead of reaching around for his wrist and giving him a judo flip. I back away from the display. A woman with a double stroller swerves in front of me. "Watch where you're going. You nearly stepped on my kids!"

"I'm an epileptic," I tell her. "Show a little compassion." But she's already whizzing her babies past the Identity Mall nuclear fountain stocked with bloated, fluorescent fish. Several dead grasshoppers toss among the bubbles.

"Help me," I tell the fish. "Save the rabbits." I strain my ears to listen for fishy advice; the black and orange and green creatures crammed into the fountain's basin know how it is to be prisoners, dully awaiting the final fried nibble-nugget some shopper tosses in before the gastric overdose of Identity Mall fried treats causes them to croak. Why can't one of these fish rise above it all, evolve into a leader of fish and command all its sisters and brothers to refuse the shoppers' offerings, to grow legs or wings and escape the Identity Mall, hitch a ride to Hiawatha Lake or some nice pond in the country? Why can't one of the fish have something wise and magical to impart, like the fish in Indian legends or African folktales? Because they're stupid, that's why.

"I'll go inside and tell them to stop. We can stop it." Fernando's scooping out a grasshopper from the fountain onto the Identity Mall tile, and then, with a quickness I've never seen, he's pushing through Dent's revolving door. His long, skinny back disappears behind glass and I am left there in front of all the mortuary rabbits surrounding their doomed inspiration, the dead grasshopper glistening at my feet. There is too much light and sugary Identity Mall music and that pervasive Identity Mall smell of deep-fat frying. Heavily, I make my way to one of the polystroob benches under the topiary and sit, vaguely aware of an allergic reaction coming on and that I have nothing to wipe my nose.

A hand on my shoulder. Another tugs the opposite elbow. I swivel around but fail to see.

"All alone?"

The voice is tinny and mechanical, inhuman.

I sit very still, my nose plugged with mucus.

"Feeling sad? Bored? Sick of the same old Identity Mall

scene?" My guess is it's Ritchie or Daniel, wearing one of those voice scramblers. I focus my energy on willing Fernando to appear.

"Well, your troubles are over."

The other Blow Torcher chimes in. He too wears a voice scrambler. "Right. You just got lucky."

I am being lifted, or tugged, off the bench. My muscles don't seem to be working. Once I knew how to scream, but now I'm not certain I could form any sound as the two boys escort me out of the Identity Mall. They both wear welder's helmets and black gauntlet gloves, which look even blacker against the sleeves of my thin green shirt. The two colors remind me of something, very familiar. A grasshopper! I feel what might be a laugh at the back of my throat as I watch people maneuvering colored polystroob shopping bags toward their miniwagons.

I let myself be bundled into the far back of a miniwagon. This is where my mother puts groceries. There are no groceries now, just boxes of power tools; are we going to build something? Whose miniwagon is this? I can't see if there is anyone else inside. While they handcuff me, I look around for Fernando, but he's not in the parking lot. Ritchie and Daniel keep talking with their funny voices and I don't attempt to unscramble the words. My head is ringing.

They have handcuffed my wrists to something behind my back, and now they are handcuffing my ankles around a barbell. I am shoved flat, or as flat as possible with all the stuff back here. Someone honks and the door slams. The Blow Torchers don't get in the miniwagon, they just slap its side and run off as the someone honks again. I hear a man yell that we are parking in a handicapped space and he's a wheelchair person so are we leaving or not. A sleepy grumble is heard from the front of the miniwagon, "Fucking gimp," and my breath catches in my throat; I'm unable to sit up because of the cuffs.

Then the passenger door opens, bags rustle, and someone else says, "Now." We squeal out of the parking lot.

I know that voice. Ritchie and Daniel have positioned me so all I can see is the sky and the tops of telephone poles through the back window, but I know exactly what would be there if I could sit up and look at the front seat: the ratty ponytails of Alec Fogel and Judd DeMoan. In many ways, lying here with my spine crunched between boxes, metal-lyte poking my tailbone, is a big relief. Peace of mind can only happen when you get what you know you deserve, the smack you've been promised and been stuck cringing for has finally come to unstick you, knocking you down into relaxing surrender at last. Forget about losing points in Safety; once I'm mutilated I'll be officially disqualified. My prayers will be answered: Alice Jones will be spared. There is a God, and he or she or it is not as out of control as I have feared. I note the popcorn-shaped clouds framed by the window when we stop at traffic lights. How fluffy they are, a delight to behold. They interrupt the blue background like chubby smiles. I am suddenly, terribly happy.

"The clouds are pretty," I say. "Cumulus and altocumulus mostly. But I think that large mass might be a cumulonimbus. And it's possible that I saw an altostratus and a nimbostratus a ways back." Cheerful defiance creeps into my voice, so my words end up filling the miniwagon as a half yell.

"Shut up back there," Alec says. "We're not interested in hearing the freaking weather report."

"I just hope you brought some warm clothes," I call. "It may be tropical now, but those clouds spell s-n-o-w! Or at the very least icy precipitation!"

"Shut up!"

"Maybe hail! Yes, I predict hail!" My voice is consumed by the carpeted ceiling of the miniwagon. The air-conditioning is on, but now all the windows are being rolled down to let in the loud highway air. I have to scream to be heard. "Depending on the pressure system, of course!"

"Shut your fucking trap or I'll come back there and shut it for you!" Alec's voice declares supremacy over the racing wind.

"Since we have the time, I'd be happy to classify the types of snow crystals for you! First off, you've got your plate crystal, then there's the stellar crystal, my favorite because it's so starry, then come columns, needles, spatial dendrites—"

The miniwagon swerves hard onto the highway's shoulder. Gravel pings metal-lyte as we brake to a stop. Judd keeps the motor running.

"Listen, cunt. If you make one more sound, I'll slice your Jew dyke tongue right out of your throat."

Overhead, dense low-altitude rain clouds gather. My Jew dyke tongue is silent.

Rough gauntlet gloves shove me into the woods far beyond the Mohawk Canal park entrance, up behind the lean-to where Carolyn Dubois once saw a naked man twirling his penis. Fernando is probably looking for me now. He probably got thrown out of Dent's, or got spaced out just as he was going to tell someone off. Maybe he even forgot what he was doing and wandered over to the art supply section to check out the paint; he can stare at the colors shining in their see-through tubes for a long time. If he's in one of his "color trances," he'll forget all about me.

"Move it!" Alec pokes my calf with his Turbine Spike when I pause to scratch where the ankle cuff left a mark before Judd took it off. "This isn't one of your lazy-day nature hikes." At the lean-to, we stop and Alec lights a Skull as familiar voices wind through the trees. One of them is Rodney Spivey, the other sounds like Goetz Muller, who just moved here from Brickerton. I can't see the boys, but I hear their hard breath, hear their jackets working around their bodies, twigs and the husks of insects snapping under their feet.

"Man, she is one heavy mother!" Goetz's cracking voice.

"Don't drop her. Watch out for that branch."

Goetz pants, and there is a thud. Alec and Judd exchange glances. I'm really scared now. So this is what Alice Jones will be feeling, or would be feeling if she could have any idea of what is to come on the day of Pageant. And who is to say that she doesn't know? She's as eggheady as a professor, knows googols more than most people.

The pines are thick around us; no one would hear if I were to be an idiot and scream for help. The wind picks up and I smell the sour, boiled-pea water of the canal. Alec smokes while Judd holds my handcuffed arms, and Rodney and Goetz argue about whatever or whoever they have just dropped.

"Why'd you let go?"

"I was slipping, man. D'you want me to be all busted up, too?"

"They're coming back any minute. We don't have her set up like they said, and they'll be pissed. You don't know how pissed they can get."

Alec and Judd trade more looks as they listen to the other boys' conversation, then Alec flicks his Skull off into the woods.

Judd pushes me down into a crouch, my face against the lean-to. "Stay, dog."

A black-spotted bug crawls up on top of my Clickie and I focus on its tiny spots, will it to spread its wings and fly. The bug crawls around and around, aimless and purposeful all at once. If only my hands were free to help it.

"What's her problem?" Alec gives me another little kick, this time to my butt.

"She's a dog."

Both boys sigh.

Vibrations coming from the other side of the lean-to wall hit my forehead. The curses of Rodney and Goetz are somewhat subdued as they struggle to bring something onto the planked floor, and there's a lot of bumping and scraping noises. My tongue folds back on itself behind my teeth, its slightly grainy surface warm and comforting, like a little pet. My Jew dyke tongue. Touched by Lana's own. Lana, Lana. Where is she? How can I get out of here?

On either side of me: streams of pee. I smell it even before I realize that my head is flanked by Alec's and Judd's penises. Their piss foams darkly around my Clickies; thank God for platforms. I bend my head down to sink teeth into kneecap as the boys yuck it up with some spooky groaning noises. Above us, a weather-copter grinds through the sky, and I picture myself hopping up and down, waving and shouting, *Down here! I'm down here!*

"Hey, it's Fogel." Rodney's half-scared, half-delighted voice calls from within the lean-to. "What's up? You porkin' her?"

"No, moron. We're pissing her. Get back to work, we don't have all day."

They've built a hideous throne. It's painted black with tall metal-lyte spikes poking up from the backrest's edges and a saucer-sized hole painted to look like it's the pupil of a giant yellow eyeball, and I guess the metal-lyte spikes are supposed to be eyelashes. The seat itself is a lot bigger than a regular seat, almost a table, and each corner of it has a metal-lyte clasp of some sort. The throne's legs are painted a mournful red and when I see that red I start to cry. Rodney and Goetz stare, rumpled and sweaty, as Alec, with me pulled tight against his checked shirt, steps onto the gritty floor of the lean-to. *"Mi casa es su casa,"* he murmurs. Judd smiles lazily; the wooden walls of the lean-to smell like peanuts.

"Up your daisy," Alec kind of throws me at the contraption and starts pushing as I struggle to keep my footing. "Come on, I'm not going to do all the work. Get your ass up there."

I don't know what he wants. I'm facing the wrong way to sit down, but when I try to turn around, he yells at me in exasperation. Finally, he hoists my butt while I squirm my way up onto the tablelike seat, facing the eyeball. The other boys are still, like they're holding their breath. My sobs are the only sound.

Alec grabs my left ankle and clamps something down on top so I can't move it, and when he does the same to my other ankle, my knees slip and spread apart. If Judd weren't holding me up by the arms, my face would have crashed right into the yellow eyeball.

"Let go of one." The handcuffs are coming off and Alec clamps first my left wrist, then my right. The top half of the backrest is swung open and my head is shoved into the hole, then the top comes down and I hear the click of a lock around my neck.

"Please, n-no," I stammer. "L-leave me alone." The back wall of the lean-to looms in front of me, the whole free world is behind that wall; my wrists and ankles throb.

"Now." Crumbs of dirt fall off his demon rooster cap as Alec's face ducks down to meet mine. His perfect teeth flash, an inch away. "Comfy, Jew dyke?"

Rodney, or maybe Goetz, giggles. Alec's red-capped head bumps mine quick and hard, then he's gone, out of sight. Apprehension travels like a runaway shuttle through my veins. The vinyl-wood of the boys' contraption bites into my neck, but I don't have the muscle control now to lift my head even a quarter inch. I'm shaking hard enough to move the whole lean-to right down the trail and into the canal as the whole catalogue of Blow Torcher crimes runs through my mind.

Judd comes around the throne, giving me a view of watery blue eyes and his slumped shoulders. He looks at me with absentminded curiosity, like he can't remember how I got up here and why this particular event needs his attention. With great effort, his mouth opens in a yawn and I see a green candy on the back of his tongue. His whole tongue is dark green.

"You're ugly," he tells me, and licks the tip of my nose with his green tongue. Underneath the candy smell, there is a bitter, salami stink.

"Let's do this." Alec's tone is all business. His palm presses down hard against my ass, the younger boys mumble something, and Alec tells them to shut up. Something pointy, not a finger, traces down the crack of my ass through my pants and I hear the seam rip with a rush of cool air.

"Noo," I whimper.

Judd has the hiccups. I can see him off to the side of me, sucking on his candy and trying not to choke. Behind me, Rodney and Goetz say nothing while Alec slides something cold and hard underneath the elastic legband of my underpants.

"I'm not enjoying this, Frankenstein. You want to help a little?" His metal-lyte instrument pricks my butt cheek and I cry out.

"Not like that! Do it sexy." He pricks my butt cheek again. "Moan sexy, you dumb hedgehog."

I moan, tears falling onto the lean-to floor. "Stop. Please, stop—"

All the boys are breathing quickly. Alec slaps my ass in frustration. "Don't tell me to stop. Do it!"

I can only take shallow breaths, as if my lungs are broken. The sound of my crying hits the walls of the lean-to and comes back at me like quicksand, each ragged gasp piled up on top of the one before it; I am smothering myself with my own air. Again, in between sobs, I moan.

"God! What am I dealing with here?" Alec spits off to the side. "Do you have any idea what sexy is? How do you expect to get that robot's dick to rise with that pitiful act? You disgust me, Frankenstein." He pricks me again. "Now, moan!"

I moan and moan. Alice Jones's quivering nose appears on

the underside of my closed eyelids, the delicate nap of her fur is against my palms as I grasp the back of her neck with one hand, raise the knockout club with the other, and—

"Damn," Rodney's voice is awed.

"Shit, Fogel. You are mad." Judd chuckles.

Alec sighs with great effort. "Look. The sooner you do what I say, the sooner we can all go home."

My mouth is dry. The lean-to spins through my tears. Judd hiccups against the wall. Rodney and Goetz snicker. I moan, trying to believe that I willed this to happen to get out of Pageant and spare Alice Jones; I am capable of sacrificing my dignity if not possibly my life to save another.

I feel air on my butt as Alec passes. His Turbine Spike sport shoes boom along the lean-to floor. "What are you doing here?"

"I don't appreciate this, Alec." The words ring out like sacred chords. Lana! "You know I told you not to mess with her. You gave me your word."

"Cunt," Rodney growls.

"Can it, Spivey." Lana strides inside the lean-to and starts unstrapping me. Her face peers around the throne to give me a grave wink and send my heart squealing.

"We were just teasing her. It's not like we were going to do anything to hurt her," Alec whines. "When did you get back from Texas?"

"Just in time, obviously. What's this rip in her pants?"

Lana helps me off the throne, steadies my shakes.

"It was a joke! We were just playing around, for shit's sake." Alec tries to block our way as we move out of the lean-to. From the looks of things, cloudy, acid rain is about to explode from the now sunless sky.

"You gave your word," Lana shoves her chin at him and he backs out of our path. "I'm just sorry Edie had to find out how worthless it is. I apologize, Edie."

"It's okay," I breathe, still fighting tears.

"Wait a minute," Alec goes for her arm but she elbows him away.

"Get off me."

"Lana—"

"I said get off."

The first smelly raindrops fall.

"That's not what you said the other night."

"Get off me! How many times do I have to say it?" Her hands chop lines in the rainy air.

"I want to explain something to you. Can you just wait a minute?"

Rodney and Goetz shift nervously on the pine needles. Judd crinkles cellophane as he takes out another candy and pops it in his mouth. The rain hasn't reached full force but there's a steady wet stink falling, and this seems to please Judd enormously as he leans against a dead tree trunk, sucking his green candy, eyes half-closed.

"There isn't anything to explain. I've seen everything and it all makes sense."

"Damn, babe. Why are you being like this?"

I stare at the rain beading up on Alec's slick-haired skull. The skin on his face is pulled tight.

"We're out of here, Alec. I leave town for a few days and you can't even do this one thing."

"Look, *I love you*," he whispers hoarsely. "Why do you have to be such a bitch?"

"I told you to get your fucking hand off me." The leatherite fabric of Lana's blazer squeaks as Alec struggles to hold her wet sleeve.

"You're sick, you know that? It's not normal, what you do." Alec looks like he might even cry. His ponytail has come undone, and his hair swings around, sticking to his wet face. Tripping over a branch, he loses his grip but grabs for her wrist again and she doesn't struggle away, just calmly sticks her middle finger straight into his face, moving it up and down, slow.

"Is this what you want to see? Abnormal behavior?"

"I could hurt you." His face squashes in disgust and suddenly I am very afraid for her.

"Do it, I dare you," Lana croons, "go ahead, do it." Her long, beautiful finger waves in his face.

Rain pecks harder and harder at my cheeks. The drops come down on us like a judgment and nothing happens except Alec holding Lana's wrist until he snorts and drops it like he's sick to even look at any part of Lana ever again.

"Let's go," I whisper.

"In a minute." Lana stands with her hands on her hips now, chiding Alec like a mother, "Are you through?" and the disgusted look fades from his face, his posture crumples. "Alec? You want to say anything?"

Alec seems tranced, his head sort of bobs on his neck like he's trying to say yes but can't, the raindrops collecting in his empty palms.

That night I receive two phone calls: Lana from the emergency room where she is waiting to have her finger stitched up; Alec didn't bite off the whole thing, only down to the knuckle, also she got his word that none of the gang will report my incident to the Rules Committee; and Fernando from home, weird excitement in his voice as he tells of smashing all the cast-resin rabbits with a Kitty Scratch Pole snuck out of Dent's pet department—he got arrested, but his mom isn't mad.

11

I hear Hebrew. A prayer. My mother is down in the family nook on her knees behind a fence of candles, reading from a tattered black book, a can of Just Like Lemon Fresh Spray Wax and the Feminine Woman of Conscience Pageant Handbook at her side. I didn't even know she knew how to read Hebrew. When the Yiddish she picked up from Bubbeh involuntarily pops out, she'll be sure to punish herself for the slip, but now she enunciates each Semitic syllable with crisp politeness and a longing that makes me want to take her hand and look deep into her eyes.

In the kitchen, Bubbeh and my father discuss the need for an umbrella.

"There was thunder, Neil. Ten minutes ago the whole room lit up. You didn't see it?"

"I was in the bathroom. I didn't notice. We can drive the miniwagon, if you like." Back one day from his sales trip, he looks about our kitchen dazed, like Gulliver, washed up on a beach, surrounded by miniature people tying him down in the sand.

"What? Around the corner? Don't be silly. What's a little storm? We'll walk and get the exercise. *Mamaleh*, you want to come with?"

"Where?" I plant myself in the shade of her bosom, allow her arms to encircle my shoulders. I long to collapse into her; how good it would feel to just cry against her Indian-print blouse.

"The neighborhood association is having a crisis meeting. Those Insecticide Huts aren't working right."

My father speaks from inside the hall closet, "I can't find the umbrellas, Esther. Maybe we'd better take the miniwagon." A flash of lightning whitewashes the world outside our kitchen and loud thunder cracks.

"Nonsense, what's a little rain? Come on, *mamaleh*, we'll wear our raincoats and go see what all the fuss is about."

The air smells like rotten pears. As soon as we get halfway down the block, the sky lets loose.

"Bubbeh, look out!" I grab her hand and pull her aside as a squad of beefy grasshoppers leap down from the bare branches of a kangaroo topiary.

"My God! They *are* getting bigger!" My father bats at them with his wet hands, scattering them away from us and the tree. "Ruined," he says. "They've killed this one for sure. A young tree like this isn't going to come back. Look at the level of destruction on these branches."

"Come on, Neil. There's nothing we can do out here." Bubbeh tugs his arm gently as several more grasshoppers whiz by overhead.

By the time we are in the neighborhood association clubhouse, even my underwear is damp and reeking of the stinky rain. Somehow, Bubbeh's hair emerges dry from a protective bonnet, but my slicker hood kept slipping and my hair is stuck defeatedly against my head. I sneeze and Mrs. Popoff gives me some tissue towels from the kitchen to dry off with; the thin paper instantly comes apart. Bubbeh produces a dry muslin prayer shawl from her big purse and offers it to me, but I make her use it on her own legs and feet. My father just drips.

Fernando sidles up to me, a new pride in his voice. "My juvenile hearing is set for the second week of May. You wanna come?"

I never did thank him properly for his brave gesture. "Sure."

"My mom says I might have to do community service, maybe stand around the Identity Mall and wear a sign that says I'm sorry for vandalizing. That'll be deluxe, hunh?"

My Clickies squish out a grimy trail of rainwater as we walk toward the few remaining free seats in the back. "It's better than going to jail, I guess. Hey, what's that around your neck?"

"Wearable air purifier. It oxidizes toxic chemicals and fumes and viruses that cause allergic reactions. Our lawyer's going to try to get all the criminal charges dropped by saying I was having anaphylactic shock because of the Identity Mall air freshener and my brain went funny."

"Maybe that's what happened."

"Maybe. Anyway, I have to wear this now, to show that I'm taking responsibility."

As we sit, I give him a secret, slant-eyed look. It's true, he does look newly responsible, with his nose and chin and forehead all pointed straight ahead in such a definite way.

I hear the double rear exit doors swing open and turn to see a clique of Gentle Welcome nuns slip in and stand humbly at the back of the room just as Dr. Niblick strikes the gong. He looks pissed.

"I'd like to start the meeting," he barks into the microphone. The reverb is turned up and he sounds as if he is speaking from inside a space pod. Naturally, no one adjusts the sound. "The enemy has returned, people, and it is stronger and more resilient than ever. The Insecticide Huts are not cutting it, and our ancient battle resumes. This is war."

"Here, here!" Old Mr. Pullings claps. "I've been saying it all along—"

Dr. Niblick continues, louder. "I have spoken with the mayor today and we are working together to draw up a plan of action. Hopefully, this crisis will unite all of Deansville, and maybe the whole state. We need to put aside our petty, day-to-day bickering and unite to save the value of our property."

"Ditto!" Mrs. Pullings tugs at her husband's sleeve as he rises unsteadily to talk some more out of turn. Outside the clubhouse windows, lightning turns the golfer and tennis player topiary display silver, backlighting a busy group of hoppers jawing away at the leafy sportsmen. Fernando pokes me in the arm to point out a colossal pair of eyes at the opposite window, fixed hungrily on a small indoor topiary adorning an end table as if they've found the Hanging Gardens of Babylon. People shift tensely in their seats. The Gentle Welcome nuns clutch rosaries and hold hands.

Fernando taps the top of my head. "Look at them. They're at all the windows. It's that time."

"What time?" I look up and see them, too, their hard shell faces pressed against the glass.

"I've noticed that lately every day at this time, they go kind of crazy, like throw a fit or something. Sometimes they fight each other."

At the window nearest us, I see spindly black forelegs clawing at the glass, searching for an opening.

Grimly, Dr. Niblick calls the first speaker, Mrs. Hiller. She uses the first of her two minutes to complain about mud in the clubhouse foyer.

More neighbors take turns complaining at the microphone, a few offer feeble suggestions, and one of the Gentle Welcome nuns steps up to detail a regimen of prayer she believes will be helpful while Dr. Niblick stands by with his big thumb cocked over a stopwatch.

"They're right against the windowpanes," Mrs. Hiller calls out of turn. "It's the indoor topiary they're after. I warned Phyllis about putting live plants inside. Reglupolate topiary is a much more sensible option, and my husband would be happy to offer a sizable discount package with the mud mats . . ."

My poor father. He looks so pathetic, sitting there dripping and not sticking up for himself while Mrs. Hiller goes on and on about the benefits of reglupolate topiary versus the live stuff, all because her squeaky-voiced husband, Fred, is a reglupolate rep. I'd like to go up to the microphone and rally for my father and his live topiary, but my plans are interrupted by the sound of breaking glass.

"It used a rock," Fernando grabs my wrist. "It held a rock in its claw and used it as a tool."

And then the meeting is adjourned as grasshoppers pour in through the jagged hole and swoop down on the nearest topiary, Victorian tea settings for six.

"Tenderness, Neil. That's all I want. But for you it's only about things that don't live. Butterflies that don't fly. Moths pinned to paper." Since we returned from the meeting two hours ago, she's been fighting with him at a high-pitched frequency that signals something out of the ordinary may happen. Bubbeh is carving wiccan symbols into eggplants in the kitchen, but I am compelled to crack open the bedroom door and keep watch. "Even your trees aren't really allowed to live. Those trees have no freedom."

"Oh, God." My father stands with bent head, two fingers pressed into the bridge of his nose.

"I only want a marriage!" Her arms hug his thighs and she presses her face against his zipper, sobbing, her voice so broken it feels like a piece of my own throat has come loose. "Hold me, Neil, I'm dying."

"Stop. Don't do that." My father tries to push her off him, but she has already undone his pants, and the muscles in her arms are flexing against his hips to hold him as her expert mouth sets to work. I back off down the hall, slamming doors as I streak through the house, yanking the keys to the miniwagon off my mother's handcrafted, seashell-studded key rack. I know how to operate a vehicle.

Skeletons of topiary penguins and ballerinas shine in the streetlights on the chewed-up grass medians. I make the miniwagon roll through the nighttime neighborhood, steering with clenched fingers, aware of each wheel's position on the blacktop. This morning, during Electric Polyrubber Man, I did a pathetic imitation of my mother sucking the blow-up dummy's fingers and felt a storm of sorrow brew in my heart. During Freestyle Walking, she showed me a move she called the ankle-to-heel-to-ankle kiss, but no matter how many times we went over it, I looked like I was kicking myself. We are both only too aware of the fifty remaining days until Pageant.

The sound of crunching is unremitting. Throughout the neighborhood, what's left of the topiary rings with the munchings of grasshopper jaws and the volleys of gunshot, and I see small fires in the bushes. The mayor has requested that people stay patient and abstain from shooting or burning, at least until his plan is executed, but we're a democratic, free-thinking neighborhood. What the elements of this plan are is still a mystery, probably even to the mayor, but tonight his jolly, potato-nosed face appeared on screen in a special emergency broadcast. He appealed to people's good sense and need for order and announced that a more effective insecticide was currently being investigated, then he probably downed a couple of Hazamarco-fathogerol and went home to bed.

They slice the air overhead, a growly black sheet winging through the satellite receptors on our rooftops. No stars, no moon, no sky. Grasshoppers, some big as crows, land on topiary elves, mushrooms, fire hydrants, and pigs. With this early spring, there are more leaves, but not enough to satisfy the appetites of these corpulent pests. They stride across lawns, leap down sidewalks and streets in search of chlorophyll. The fields of Our Lady of Gentle Welcome are bald.

Circling back to our street, my right foot strains to reach the gas, hovers above the pedal when I want to slow; I'm too afraid to touch the brake, and to avoid running over the Hoyts' yapping fox terrier, Peepers, I plow into the sycamore at the edge of our driveway. Appalled, I turn off the engine without putting the gear in park. In the headlights, everything in the neighborhood looks tilted and huge, and once again the rain that has been bloating the sky plops out in a torrent. I lie down across the front seats and wait.

"What's gotten into you?" Under a golf umbrella, my mother's nervous face looms above me in the miniwagon's door frame. I can tell she's not sure how angry to be, and I feel a flutter of power. My lips are sealed.

"Have you been smoking drugs?"

I allow her to sniff me, open my mouth wide to exhale, and climb out of the miniwagon. "I *will* score high in Electric Polyrubber Man. You don't think I can do it, but you're wrong." My eyes hold hers for a long minute before I walk through the slashing rain up the driveway and into the house.

"I never said you couldn't do it," she calls after me. "I said it seems like you *don't want to.*"

I am the only child she will ever have; I am what she struggled with her body to sculpt. I'm still an unfinished product, but it already looks like I'm not going to be what she had in mind when I am done.

The front fender is dented, a headlight broken. A raw gash in the sycamore. She speaks in serious tones while I stand with my back against the kitchen wall; my father stands motionless in the doorway, his hands dangling, then he goes upstairs. When she is through explaining that she has the utmost faith in my abilities and that it's not going to make things easier if I start acting out instead of sitting down and processing my feelings, she goes up to her bedroom and shuts the door, and I hear the screen volume on high.

As I head up to my own room, my father comes hurtling down. I try to pass him, but we do that little dance where both people keep choosing the same side and nobody can get any-where. I long to lay my head against his chest and listen to the beat of his heart through his clean blue shirt, but instead I press myself flat against the banister. "Forgot to do the . . . thing," he mumbles as he passes. Before I can even consider what it is I want to say to him, he's gone, diving for cover in the basement to hunch over his workbench and dream of cumulus as he deli-cately sticks a pin into the thorax of another dead moth.

I follow him downstairs, but keep my distance in the unfin-ished part of the basement. It's primeval in those rooms, air musty with the stench of my father's dead Lepidoptera, laced with chemicals from our Little Miss Scientist Home Lab: just the kind of place where you can imagine getting your forearms peeled with a butter curler like Lucinda Freeman last summer on that dark afternoon during the solar eclipse. The lights here are just bulbs you have to turn on by pulling a string. At night it's too dark even to find the strings and you have to reach around until you feel one of them brush the back of your hand like a fingernail.

Tonight my father has turned the light on. Alice Jones is aloof in her cage, and I carefully avoid looking at her as I make my way to the workbench. Just yards away, the other man in the house, our blow-up dummy, does nothing on the family nook couch. Does my father ever sneak a comparative look at him? Has he ever touched the dummy? Is he curious about what his wife feels when she takes one of those polystroob balls in her mouth? Is he jealous? Or is the idea of his daughter having sex, even simulated sex, just too unwieldy for his mind to grasp? I slip past him, still unable to find the right thing to say.

I lift the lid of the sterilfrostitron. There isn't much inside: a few packages of Skippy Peas and a jumbo carton of Fruitberry ice milk dessert. Tomorrow, Grocery Town day, would usually see it crammed once more with frozen Just Like Gourmet dinners in sweating boxes, except with Bubbeh here, my mother forgoes them. Right now, I enjoy the near-empty coldness. I bend and stick my head way inside, drinking in the freon-scented frost, the slight wind and little cracking noises. I lean in like a diver, lost in the thick white hills until I'm nearly freezer-burned. After I graduate from submarine school, I'll request to be stationed in Antarctic waters. I'll torch any land or ice floes till they melt right into the frigid sea; I'd never have to go ashore then; there would be no shore.

Surrounded by the shimmering corpses of butterflies, my father tinkers with the Insecticide Hut's dials and tubing, his face looking worried enough to crack as he sorts through the multicolored wiring. He thinks that the system may have shorted out, or gotten plugged up somehow. His sports shirt has come untucked and shows pale love handles when he bends.

"How's it going, Dad? Find anything?" Does he hear the hopelessness in my voice? We are a household unfamiliar with success; even Bubbeh's witchcraft is not enough to fight this bare fact.

"Not yet. I'm still trying to figure out which tube is regulated by which switch. It's a lot more complicated than I thought it would be."

I peer into the innards of the Insecticide Hut. My nose starts to run, and the familiar itchy feeling begins in the corners of my eyes. I flick at the loose wire with my thumb. "This one looks like it's gotten disconnected."

"You're right. It doesn't seem to go anywhere." He pulls on the wire and out it comes. His forehead creases, but he tries to smile. "Pretty bad for business, this grasshopper situation."

"Are you going to be laid off?"

My father shrugs and fiddles with the Hut's dials. "Maybe a

miniature hacksaw would work. I've got one around here some-where." He straightens up, pauses as if he's just heard his name called over an intercom, then gives a small, familiar groan. I don't want to look, because the pain in his eyes chills me to the marrow. "Ohhh. Ooh. Edie—" The Insecticide Hut clatters to the floor and rolls under the workbench as he staggers over to a sawhorse, clutching his belly, his whole face grimacing. "The phone. Get me the—ooh—would you mind—ooh."

"What's wrong?"

"Tell Mom to, ooh, call the, the, ohh, Gastro—oh—enterol-ogy Salon, ooh." He is bent double over the sawhorse and his words are not all that audible. I stand there, sneezing, longing to do something, wishing please, please, not this, not now, please don't let him get so stressed out about the grasshoppers in his topiary or Electric Polyrubber Man that he gets sick. With great effort, he lifts his face. I sneeze and sneeze.

"Please, Edie. Ooh."

I almost touch his hand gripping the sawhorse, but when I see the tiny grasshopper crawl out of an Insecticide Hut tube, I decide against it. Instead, I reach for his antique phone and, shaking, dial the number myself.

"It's the answering service," I tell him in a whispery voice. "A recording."

Bubbeh drives him to General Memorial General; my mother stays home to calm me down. After a dose of Clorimioforbutal, I relax enough to go downstairs to his workbench, to sit on his stool and flick his butterfly net at the ceiling, catching the glow-ing lightbulb in its weave. The Insecticide Hut, fallen and use-less, is at my feet. I kick at its curved side, push it back and forth with my Clickies, trancing out to the rolling sound until the new sound of liquid being disturbed causes me to look: a chemical minipond grows from the Hut onto the floor, and if my senses weren't so dulled from the sedative, I would no doubt faint from the fumes. The tiny grasshopper I noticed before is now hopping sprightly around the edge of the puddle. Apparently, I am not the only one who is experiencing resistance to the insecticide's powers. This little bug seems only too happy to frolic in the poisonous soup, is in fact slurping the stuff with its flinty lips in a display of uninhibited greed.

I lower the net to my lap and quietly watch. More of them are coming, creeping out of the baseboard. They lick and suck and swill until the floor is dry.

To take our minds off my father under observation in his hospital bed at General Memorial General, Bubbeh and I ride the shuttle to Wong's; we're going to get takeout and have a picnic downtown in the municipal park. It's not the best day for it, the API is suffocatingly high, but Bubbeh thinks Wong's food is the best cure for anything. I'm sneezing like a madwoman even though I took my mother's offer of Pristodristonaifahgural. They make my stomach ache and my thoughts scatter like minnows facing a shark, but it's better than never breathing. The day is loaded down with haze and a bitter humidity from yesterday's storm. Everything looks like it's been punched a few times: homes sag, mall parking lots are nearly void of miniwagons even during lunch hour, topiary branches are mangled and stripped, and I'm unable to stop calculating blame ratios— grasshoppers vs. Electric Polyrubber Man—in relation to my father's attack. Only the grasshoppers are full of ferocious energy, zooming and limitless at every latitude as we pass through town: several mammoth brutes patrol the front door of Marnie's Beauty Parlor, a sinister team eyes the astroturf inside the Bargain Sports window, each traffic light, corner mailbox, porch railing, and decorative lawn ornament boasts at least one scarlet-eyed hopper flexing its wings.

Inside Wong's, reality is cheerfully denied. The downtown lunchers are here for their food, pleased to be sheltered from the bad air by Wong's magic red ceiling. He seems sincerely glad to see my grandmother, who's an excellent flirt. Busy as it is, he makes us special vegetarian woo-woo balls wrapped in lotus leaves tied with bright string.

"That hat for you look fine," Wong tells her, his baby hands gesturing ecstatically toward the chickens dancing on Bubbeh's rain bonnet. "Chicken one lucky bird. You make a good luck today with that hat."

As he hands her our bag, the nostrils of her dragon nose dilate in a grand sniff. "It's enough to make me leave home and move to Deansville for good. A person could get addicted to a smell like this." Even though I can't smell a thing, I know that everything smells like Five-Spice Chicken, even our vegetarian woo-woo balls smell of it, but Bubbeh's caps beam radiantly at nonvegetarian, chicken-killing Wong, and he takes her hand.

"You listen to the whisper of the wind. All secrets come home."

Bubbeh nods, and we head back into the oppressive air toward the park.

We settle on a damp iron bench in front of the broken fountain with the statue of the first Franklin Echo Sr., founder of Deansville. The park is not very well maintained.

Bubbeh pokes into her lotus leaf with a chopstick. "Wong's quite a cook. Too bad he's not Jewish." She winks at me with her wrinkled eye.

"Maybe he could convert."

"He's too old for a *bris*. And I don't like them uncircumsized." She giggles through a mouthful of Chinese food. I get busy untying the string from around my lotus leaf. This topic makes me queasy; Electric Polyrubber Man could go either way, although my mother thinks he'll be cut because it's more American. "Laugh with me, *mamaleh*. When I was your age, my girlfriends and I always laughed about boys' penises. It's easier that way."

I manage a weak smile.

"I know what you're thinking, darling. But that's what I want to talk to you about." A number of grasshoppers buzz overhead to crouch on the bare branches of the park's elms and oaks, eyeing our lotus leaves. I scoop out the filling from mine and put the leaf back in the bag. Bubbeh slaps them off as they invade (for all their newly aquired size and tool-wielding prowess, they've still got the same skittish bug brain), and I put her leaf in the bag, too.

"I'm not doing it for Lorraine, though," she says, chewing. "I want to do it for you, and not because it matters to me whether you win or not. I just want you to have what you want. And if I tell you what I'm going to tell you"—she pauses, and when she bends to poke her face closer to mine, I can smell Wong's potent woo-woo sauce on her breath—"you will win. You want to?"

I nod, reluctant and greedy.

"Then that's all I need to know."

Bubbeh looks away, waiting to hear something, and I keep quiet. Her voice is low and close to my ear as she at last begins to talk. "You know how your mother became Mulch Queen. You know how Zadeh Mort and I helped." She shakes her head. "I'm not saying it was the right thing, but she was so desperate to win some pageant, and I thought she might hurt herself. Anyway, all these pageants are fixed. And this one—it's all politics, there's nothing ethical or sportswomanlike about it." The hairs poking out of her star-shaped birthmark tremble.

"I don't get it."

"The Just Like That Conglomerate is the major Pageant donor. Franklin Echo holds a considerable amount of their stock. And they're going to be hit with the biggest class action suit this country has ever seen. People are poised to act."

"Who? What people?"

The lines around her lips pinch as she sweeps an arm before us. I'm supposed to understand, to see the people Bubbeh sees. I don't.

"Sometimes hard choices have to be made, but as a species, we're losing our grip. All those 'accidental' deaths! Everybody's breasts falling off from cancer! The Just Like That Conglomerate manufactures the insecticides and other chemicals that are causing breast cancer, and all the deaths from toxic exposure. They're also in control of all the manufacturers who make the medications used for treatment." Her canvas Chunkie Sports kick out from the bench at an invisible target, their jeweled flowers sending off sparks of colored light. "What is that Mystery Powders ca-ca? A big cute ad for chemicals. Electric Polyrubber Man? Throw in some sex and the whole country is cross-eyed, with their tongues hanging to their bunions. The Feminine Woman of Conscience queen tours small towns in a big-deal headdress, sheds a few tears over toxic exposure, and everybody's ruffled feathers are smoothed."

I stare down at what was once grass in shock. What is Bubbeh saying?

"Don't worry about the robot. It won't matter what you do, or how soft mister polyrubber's shlong is, let the other girls provide the show. I've got some dirt on Franklin Echo and I don't mind throwing it in his face to help my granddaughter be a queen. He thinks he's so smooth, sitting on the board of directors of the National Toxic Death Prevention Society. One hand writing letters to the president screaming for prevention, the other behind his back giving money to support the manufacture of poisons. How do you think that would look on the front page of the *Deansville Post*?"

"Blackmail?"

Bubbeh sniffs noisily in the damp air, looking like the world's shrewdest rogue.

"We can't—"

"Shh. Don't say 'can't.' " Her big hands massage my shoulders.

"No, Bubbeh. Thanks, but—no thanks."

Her hands slide off me with a final shiatsu and she unwraps a fortune cookie. I watch her crack it open with her teeth. Then she turns, her face singing with light, the fortune paper bright against her tongue. "It's okay. If you want to go through with it the regular way, that's fine with me. I just didn't want you should suffer."

I kiss her birthmarked cheek, amazed that she would go to such lengths for me. But doesn't she recognize that I still have a damned good chance of winning all on my own?

"I believe in Beauty." I read the statement as per the instructions on the orange card. A woman who identifies herself as Consoler Ann says she is glad that I called.

"In the beginning, there is beauty," her sweet voice continues. "The people returned and they made beauty and everything that was not beautiful was vaporized. How can I help you?"

"I'd just like to get some information." My body hunches over the phone as I crouch in the corner of my room. It's three o'clock in the morning and everyone in the house is asleep, but the boundaries of dreamers are vague and untrustworthy, especially with only a month to go before Pageant, so I must word things carefully. "I'm interested in the process."

"I see. Are you planning a Happy Ending?"

"No! I mean, it's more probable that a friend of mine is interested in comprehending the world's pain. They've got a fair amount of pain themselves, of course. Which is why I am making this call."

"So they are actively suffering?" Consoler Ann sounds like she might be about to kiss me right through the phone; I'm not sure if my face is hot from the danger of being discovered or her intimate crooning.

"Yes, my friend feels pretty terrible. She's been, er, beaten up and, ah, put into jail for something she didn't even do."

"I'm so sorry. Of course, being a victim of injustice and other external negative conditions will lead to what is erroneously considered a natural death. Happy Endophoresy believes that all medical, accidental, or criminal reasons for termination are simply false causes. A Happy Ending is the only true death, the only guaranteed chance of rebirth. Agreeing to a voluntary renunciation of all relationship to wickedness, otherwise known as agreeing to a Happy Ending, is the first step in the process. Has your friend taken this step?"

The velvety quality of her speech is very seductive. I picture her with blue eyes and a firm, tiny waist. "Unh-hunh. I would say that she has."

"Then the next step would be for your friend to involve herself in a charitable activity to become closer to other world sufferers. Has she done this?"

"I don't know. She may have."

Consoler Ann breathes into my ear through the wires. "Like most scientific processes, the steps can be rather complicated. Would you like me to send you some instructions? We don't have screen, though, so it will have to be through the postal service."

She sounds so knowledgeable, so comforting. Consoler Ann could tell me to eat shit on Crumpitz and I'd be glad to listen.

"Could you give them to me in person? My privacy at home is kind of compromised. I don't think I should receive any mail."

"That really won't be possible. I'm sorry."

"Maybe you could just drop them off in a prearranged place. I know someone who got instructions through a drop-off. She got the instructions for a Contacting."

"I'm sorry, honey. I can mail them to you at a different address, say a post office box, but we don't do drop-offs. I hate to say it, but I think the person who told you she got her instructions through a drop-off may have been confused."

Do I hear a judgmental note in Consoler Ann's enchanting voice? It occurs to me that her sudden opposition may indicate a hidden, difficult nature. "Are you calling my friend a liar?"

"Dear. Lies are a source of negativity and for me to acknowledge negativity at this stage of my process would be to negate the entire process."

"Well how about acknowledging that Contactings are bullshit? How about hearing the truth about Happy Endings at your stage of the process?" I'm aware that my voice is a little loud, but Consoler Ann seems to be drifting away from her end of the receiver; the titillating music of her vocal cords is rapidly turning sour.

"I'm going to hang up now, sweetheart. All is beauty. Believe in beauty."

"Wait a min—"

There is a series of clicks and then the dial tone's dirge.

"Damn." I fall sideways with one foot asleep, the receiver lifeless against my palm.

Four o'clock brings eight bars of "Taking a Chance on Love" and the screen's early edition conditional weather report of clear skies. How much of my life have I wasted? How little might possibly be left! How did I get to be so old? Fourteen years is more than a decade, just nine years away from a quarter century.

"I can't sleep," I say, clutching the phone to my head till it hurts.

"Hey, Chumly, is that crying I hear? Are you okay?"

"Not really."

I sneak out of the house in bare feet. For the past month, Lana has been in and out of town, and we've had no chance to be alone. When we are enclosed in the Grimaldi garage, our bodies curled deep into the bucket seats of her father's TR3, the tiny interior car light secretly warming the tops of our heads, she takes off the bandage and I feel my own fingers prickle. Lana puts her other hand on my shoulder as I look: what is left of her finger is a swollen, purple-black outrage. Her hand looks desperate, the magic is misshapen, and I love her so much right then all I want to do is kill something.

"Hey, easy there," she says, wrapping the finger back up in the lyccra-gauze, "it's only one out of ten." Then she unzips, tilts her hip to pull down the waistband of her pants and show me the almond-shaped scrape where they removed the skin for the graft. There's a sympathetic burning in my own hip and I yearn to cover her red wound with my tongue. She's surprisingly cool now about the loss. "He's deranged," she says, zipping her pants back up. "He could have done anything. I actually never thought he'd have the balls, but see, life does not cease to amaze."

When I ask her what she plans to do for revenge, she just lights a Bull's Eye cigar and raises her broken eyebrow. We inhale Easy-Go and Leatherize and the burning fruit smell of the smoke.

"So what's up? Worried about Pageant?" She flicks the headlights on and off a bunch of times, turns the ignition, and distractedly fiddles with the radio's buttons before settling on a talk show about mentals.

I look away, embarrassed at her mention of the topic. I shouldn't have come here. A public service announcement for No Happy Endings comes on and we both wince; Lana changes the channel.

"Are you coming to watch me win?"

Lana searches my face and I have to look at Mr. Grimaldi's

miniature polystroob Mussolini dashboard statue to deflect her intensity. In the white beam of the headlights, two rat-sized grasshoppers leap among the cleaning solvents and lawn chemicals stacked on metal-lyte shelving at the back of the garage. Lana watches the insects as she says, "You know how I feel about it." The grasshoppers spread their dark wings.

I flick at Mussolini's head with my thumb and forefinger; he doesn't move. Smarmy music fills the car. "But we're . . . friends."

"And?"

"I need you to be there," I blurt. "I can't do it without you."

"So drop out."

I punch the radio off button. Immediately, I am ready to fight. "Never mind. I don't need you. You just use people. Just because you think Pageant is for feebles doesn't mean you're better than everyone else."

Her lips purse and then relax in a sigh, and when she finally speaks her voice is soft, sadder than I've ever heard her. "Look, it's late and I'm pretty tired. Plus the painkillers I'm taking are knocking me out." She does yawn then, though of course you don't have to be a star actress to fake that. Her good hand switches off all the car lights and reaches over to unlatch the door.

I sit there in the dark, my hand on the passenger door handle, thinking of ten different points I could be making, aware that it will be a good long while before I seek out Lana Grimaldi's company again.

"Let's not fight anymore, okay?" She drops her cigar to the garage floor and stamps out the glow. Grasshoppers buzz above the Triumph's roof.

"Estrufeniberickosickal." My mother holds up an oval of silver foil embedded with meds that look nauseatingly familiar. "Just because I keep my door unlocked does not mean you have carte blanche to go through all my private things. What you would want with these pills at your age, I can't imagine anyway. I hope that you are not in trouble, because—"

"I told you I thought they were for headaches!" I scream again.

She sucks her cheek. Her pink lipstick looks very wet. She's got the kitchen door open to air out the house, and I can hear the Sweeneys' Weed Terminator growling louder and then fainter as it moves around their topiary. I should be lying in its path.

"And I told you that if you have a headache, you *ask* me for something if you can't find the Just Like Aspirin. And lower your voice, Bubbeh is napping." She articulates each phoneme. Between us, the silver foil flashes. "These are Estrufeniberick-osickal birth control pills which I take to keep my hormones balanced—and this is definitely not something a girl who has just started to menstruate wants to fool around with. Jesus! I am sick in my guts to think about it." Her face gleams over me like a large, cold pearl.

"Edie." She speaks quietly, and her eyelids droop. "This is very, very serious."

A heat is going through me, like the coils of a dual-control thermostatic diffuser, slowly getting hotter and brighter. If only I could dive into some water. But it's not the beach I want, too salty, I'm craving the chemical waters of a motel pool. I want to be sterilized.

"How many did you take? Both of them at once? Because they contain a very high dosage of estrogen. You know I'm going to have to call Dr. Kent."

"Why? So you can use them with *him*? For your *affair*?" I back away from my mother's raised hand, but she is light on her feet—two fingers latch onto my lips and pinch them together. "Shut up."

Even in panic, her battle strategy is a marvel. It is she who has something to hide; she is really taking the pills to prevent pregnancy, never mind her weeping and wailing about miscarriages and toxemia and an upside-down uterus. Supposedly, she and my father never have sex these days. So is it Dr. Kent? Braided Dr. Plow? *Wong?*

"What is all the yelling? I lie down for two minutes and there's already yelling. What is it, *mamaleh*? What's wrong?" Bubbeh comes into the kitchen, thick gray curls protected in one of her bonnets, this one patterned with snarling poodles.

"Freeze it right there, Ma." With the teakettle whistling alarm on the stove behind her, my mother is suddenly the security guard of our kitchen, pointing silver foil straight at my grandmother's heart. "Edie has taken some of my prescription hormone medication."

"What? What are you talking? Edie hasn't taken your pills. You're crazy. She wouldn't do that." My grandmother points a little silver foil of her own: strudel peers up at me from the sparkling nest in her palms. "Take. I just made them this morning."

Hesitating, I reach in. Strudel may not be the best thing during crisis.

"Excuse me, people. I'm only talking."

"Lorraine, have a piece. That diet of yours is making you too nervous. All the time with these stories." Bubbeh munches one of the pastries and pours us both a glass of milk. Her mouth is full, caps in great working order. "Delicious." A few crumbs settle on her lips as she talks. "Smell. Now *that's* aromatherapy." The teakettle continues to pierce the sound barrier.

"Ma, I do not appreciate your fatuous remarks. All my life I've tried to elicit a little support, just a word of comfort—" My mother's lips fold together and disappear into her mouth. It's one of her unattractive expressions and she only does it when she wants people to know that they are dealing with a woman who isn't afraid to look unattractive when she needs to make a point.

Bubbeh flexes a sagging muscle in one of her yogaerobics routines. Her voice is light. "Comfort? Who needs comfort? Not your own family. Not the family you didn't speak to for three years."

"Not three years. *Two* years."

"I don't think so."

"Exactly my point! Even Dr. Plow says that I have always been a victim of profound misunderstanding. Frankly, I'm getting damn sick of it."

Bubbeh rolls her head around on her wrinkly neck, and I turn away, glad that the focus is off my crime, but sorry that my mother has to suffer Bubbeh's abuse. "You were disrespectful. I was only trying to help you get what you wanted."

My mother opens a cupboard and stares at the contents, snarling. "I never asked you to sneak around behind my back."

"I was only thinking of you."

"That's exactly the kind of warped thinking that has me spending two hundred and fifty dollars an hour to lie on a couch twice a week!" My mother's espadrille kicks the cupboard shut and she storms out of the room. Bubbeh looks at me and shrugs as her daughter's voice assails us from the stairs. "When will you people get it?"

I shut my eyes and start counting.

"Extra Electric Polyrubber Man practice today in one hour, Edie. We've only got two weeks to whip you into shape for this, so be downstairs and be ready in one hour. *One!*"

Around us, molecules are swirling. My grandmother bats at the air in a jumpless jumping jack.

"Bubbeh, I— she—," I am on the verge of confession, but I've got a piece of walnut stuck in a tooth.

"She pushes you too hard." Bubbeh stops mid–deep knee bend and calmly plucks out more strudel from the foil to put in front of me, flaky dough scattering onto the table and the floor. Then she shuts off the burner and moves the shrieking teakettle to one of my mother's painted macaroni trivets. "So noisy. It's not right what she does."

Here's something else that is not right: me and this lousy blow-up dummy. Is it my fault I am not a good actress? I am not purposely trying to thwart my success, as she complains. If she would just clam up for a minute, I could get it right. To feel the hard gold band of the headdress circling my head, I can welcome the idea that Electric Polyrubber Man's pubes will leave scratches on my face, I can, I know I can. Last night, The Amazing Mister Fezundo willed an asteroid to crash into the ocean without harming any sea life. I am determined to win.

"*Eeeeeee,*" my mother gnashes her teeth. Her hands do a slow-motion dance of frustration. "If you cannot act as you are told—as I have bent over backwards to teach you—I cannot be held accountable." My neck prickles; she has been in her room for the last hour, and by the look in her eyes she hasn't been quietly reading how to create a bikini out of first-aid tape in *Mrs. Craft Magazine*. She's changed out of her espadrilles into her alligator-simskin mules, her ivory toenail polish slippery in the family nook light.

"I'm trying, Mom, please don't get mad." I force my tongue into the dummy's mouth with what I imagine is real sex appeal.

She warned me, but still I am not prepared when she whips the dummy off my face and flings it across the room. Thin bones pop up in the backs of her hands as she spreads them wide to squeeze and slap at her thighs. In her cage, Alice Jones thumps a back leg in fear, cedar chips go flying through the bars. Some part of me notes that Bubbeh is in the kitchen above us, knifing the skin and eyes from potatoes with her muscled hands. I can smell onions cooking in hot butter.

I retrieve the blow-up dummy from the corner of the room and sit back down on the couch. I can pretend not to see her eyes full of defeat. I can do this thing. I can prove to her that I'm not a thief or a liar or a girl who can't make out with a polystroob man.

Or a real man.

Dutifully, I pinch the blow-up dummy's nipples and employ great gentleness as I rub his penis with my instep. I stick my finger inside his butthole and wiggle it back and forth while I lick the underside of his earlobe.

"Don't you know anything?" My mother's voice is slurred. Her breasts heave toward me. I remove my finger from the dummy's anus and shrink back against the couch. Its eagle-print heritage fabric is rough on my skin. I glance up. There—a pearly pink submarine, a girl with a hatchet waves—this way, hurry! If only it were true. The blow-up dummy's polystroob squeaks and farts against my bare arms. His legs fly up toward the ceiling, his floppy penis whips from side to side. My mother and the blow-up dummy jockey for position.

"Mom, please," I pant. "You're going to pop him!"

"Let go then." My mother's nails are making a real impression in the blow-up dummy's quadricep.

"I just— Give me a chance." Ridiculously, I can't seem to give up my hold on the dummy's throat. "I know what I'm doing wrong now. Watch, I can do it right—"

"This is how it's done, you little—" Her torso flattens the dummy's chest and there is a soft, pleasant sound of rushing air. With a deft snap, she jerks my chin toward the floor and my lower jaw falls open. Her tongue, an energetic creature with its own secret life, sweeps across my tonsils like a comet.

One of life's truths: No matter how clearly you try to transmit information, some people can't receive it. Because they are defective. And these defective people are so excellent at being defective, they can flip you into being defective, too, using almost no effort. In just seconds—transmission whacked.

My crotch is a puddle of fire. I hear little pops. Airless polystroob limbs whiz by. My mother and I are joined at the nose, the blow-up dummy only a thin membrane between us. Her nostrils cover mine as her face presses down; I grow larger and larger with her air and there is no way for me to exhale—she is blowing me up like a dummy except my skin cannot hold all that she forces into me. Jittery currents travel down the back of my neck and spine, do a donut around my rectum and charge back up my stomach and chest. Any minute my intestines will pop out with a *boing*. The spaces between my teeth are flossed, uvula donged, palate excavated—wow—my mom can *kiss*.

"Are you *INSANE??!!*" I shove her from me and scramble off the cushions to a standing position. I plant my feet wide, my whole body shaking. The blow-up dummy drifts limply to the floor.

"Oh Edie," my mother backhands her lips to wipe. She raises her palms in the stop position. "You are so frustrating. For once, can't you simply get it?"

Alice Jones watches us attentively from behind the bars of her cage.

"No," I say finally. I am drenched with perspiration, embarrassed for my mouth to open when I talk. "I can't."

My mother is silent and furious.

Disregard transmission, I tell my brain, and hang my head.

Synthetic lemon vapors climb the walls, hang in clouds beneath the ceiling, swirl hotly around the bulb of the Li'l Stained Glass pansy light. The blow-up dummy has had his polystroob muscles restored to blow-up dummy tautness, but training has been abandoned. Ten days till show time. Hail strikes the house and I watch balls of ice bounce off the bare trees. My hands press against the windowpane, sensing rather than feeling the cold hits. In a minute, the sun shines and the sky blues, but our backyard and the surrounding landscape do not look genuinely bright. There is a beaten, mistrustful vibe in the streets. In the Sweeneys' yard, the Insecticide Hut deliveryman comes out from the shelter of the toolshed to continue refilling the Huts. Even from here, I can see the doubt in his eyes.

My mother tiptoes down hallways, trailing lemon, her peppery smell obliterated at last. This afternoon she's wearing a zippered housecoat I've never seen before and wraparound motorcycle sunglasses. Her hair is bunched up weirdly on one side, flaked with dandruff.

"I smell something funny," I say, meeting her in the hall. It's the first thing we've said to each other since she frenched me in the family nook five days ago.

"Really?" She pulls down her sunglasses and looks at me for

a full minute, as if she's checking for something lost. I look away first, feel the heat creeping under my arms. After a minute she says, "I'm sorry."

In the dimness, I cut my eyes at her—pieces seem to be floating away; when I turn my head I'm not sure if I'll see her whole. How sorry is she?

"I've started smoking again." She pulls a pack from her housecoat pocket and lights up. "I feel like I am being a terrible example to you. I'm so sorry."

"You're sorry because you're smoking? That's why you're sorry?"

The green of her eyes is a pale ring around her enlarged pupils. "I haven't been able to sleep lately. Too many dreams. Last night I dreamt your father was killed by the sterilfrostitron. It fell on him. Oh, God. It was awful."

I don't say anything and we stand there in her smoke. Another cigarette comes to life, and I notice she looks like she's lost several quarts of blood. I wait, watching her coral nails flash in what little brightness is left of the day as she taps another ash into her cupped palm.

"Don't smokers use ashtrays?" I let my voice drip with sarcasm.

"There isn't one. I'm going to quit just as soon as I get through this. Dr. Plow says I shouldn't pressure myself."

"It's getting dark." I jerk the switch and fill the hall with light.

"No." She turns the light back off. "You don't mind, do you? My eyes." She touches her sunglasses with her smoking hand.

"Sure." Even though I am using what she calls my pathologically flippant tone, she takes no notice, just continues to puff away, her free hand abstractedly pushing at her hair. She reaches back into her pocket, searching. "Baby. I'm not feeling so confident these days." She giggles a little, then honks into a tissue and is quiet. When she starts talking again, her voice is whispering, meek. "I'm so strung out. I took something I shouldn't have. It was an accident, I misread the label. You know, if I could just *count* on someone. On *anything*."

Suddenly she's too close, hugging me around my neck, teary, sunglassed face pressing into my shoulder. "Oh, Edie. That dream. It was horrid. He was pinned there. Just like one of his butterflies."

"Mom. Cut it out. Let go of me."

"Okay," she says in a small voice, but doesn't loosen her grip.

"Stop it." I manage to shake her off.

"Sorry. Did I hurt you?"

I flick the light back on, covering the switch with my hand so she can't get to it.

"Mother."

"Yes, honey?"

"What is that smell?"

"What smell?"

"I smell lemon. It's all over the house. I've been smelling it all day."

"I don't know, sweeties. I guess I spilled something when I was cleaning. Don't worry about it." Her beautiful knees are bent inward, as if they are sharing a secret; her slippered feet position themselves uncertainly on the carpet.

"Are you getting high with a spray can?"

"Edie. Please don't. Dr. Plow is this close to prescribing Tarvovivaverovinol and if I have to start taking that again, all hell is going to break loose in my system. You know what happened last time." She lets out a long breath. "I swear, sometimes I wonder if that man ever reads the contraindication and side effect inserts."

"You kissed me! You stuck your tongue down my throat!"

My mother's hand goes up, but she drops it. "Please. I was

just—I guess I shouldn't have. I guess I made a mistake, but I'm just doing the best I know how. I want to be a good mother to you, that's all I want."

"I don't believe it."

She rubs the bottom of her chin with two fingers and leans against the wall, slumping, just a small woman, and it occurs to me that she doesn't look like she's lost weight or even blood, it's as if she's lost pounds of something a lot more invaluable. "Edie, I am only trying to make something out of you. I want you to be a—"

"I'm not a craft."

"Of course not. Darling—"

"Keep your hands off me!" I push into her stomach, and she lets out a moan. When she takes off her sunglasses to wipe her eyes, I tell her, "I don't want you at Pageant. If you try to come with me, I'll tell everyone at the Virtue Club what you did—I'll—I'll drop out of Pageant because of you."

My mother looks up from her tissue. Without her sunglasses, her face looks weak, pupils so dilated now the green irises are nearly gone. Her voice is lonely, lost in her unfamiliar, weightless body, "Oh, honey. I really blew it this time, didn't I?"

Whistling, Bubbeh yanks out silver hairs and one by one they are lined up on a black velveteenite cloth in the guest bathroom. Dawn hasn't graced the sky yet, but, still in my pajamas and half asleep, I can see all of America's mothers' hands in their yawning daughters' hair, torturing the strands—curly, straight, moussed, gelled, relaxed, dyed, permed—into grand constructions. It's Pageant morning, and no doubt everyone has already downed their meds and crunched their Toast Flipz and sailed them into their colons with tumblers of Natural Prune-n-Low and several mugs of Expressora. My own mother snores gently in medicated slumber while Bubbeh weaves ninety-one of her hairs into my hair construction, improvising a design more deluxe than anything my mother had planned, as if she were channeling Hollywood hairdressers of yore. We're going for a regal, naval officer look for the opening parade, and with my crisp white blouse, long black real linen skirt, and imposing hair, I should be ready to captain an entire fleet of nuclear subs, but the real truth is that I am the joke at which no one laughs. It's Alice Jones's last day and Bubbeh's face looks troubled, and not just because we don't have any more of Alice Jones's favorite flavor of Bunny Bake-em's to bring along.

Before we leave, I run back upstairs and softly push open my mother's door. She lies in a starfish shape, my dear sweet stupid mother, flat on her back (appliquéd quilt tucked under chin, bat eyemask a contrast with her creamy brow) for hours more in artificial daytime sleep while I am toiling away in Franklin Echo's Dome. Her hair swirls out on the pillow in little question marks as I tiptoe, a little unsteady because of my towering hair construction, to kneel next to her and watch the hypnotic rise and fall of the bedding with her breath. She is alive. Her sleeping lips are pastel ghosts of her real mouth, that brazen lipsticked source of so much power. "A girl's tongue can never get tired," she has told me and told me. "It is her second most important muscle."

"Mommy." I shape the words, but take care not to make a sound. "I'm going now. I just want you to know—I won't disappoint you today." I stand and raise one finger over her and draw a line in the air down the length of her body. If she opened her eyes right now, I would tell her I love her and then run for it. Her empty bedside water pitcher has a lonesome sheen in the dim light; my last thought as I leave the room is how sad it will be if she wakes up and is thirsty.

Downstairs in the kitchen, Bubbeh is elegant in a beaded

suede gown, made especially for her by the Native American manager of Starz Crystals in Waterburgh. Alice Jones blinks out at me from her travel case on the counter.

"I can't decide whether or not to wear the mink," Bubbeh says, frowning over the coat.

Cautiously, so as not to mess my hair construction, I reach to give her an awkward hug.

She straightens, wiping the corners of her eyes with her farm woman's thumb. "Save it for later, *mamaleh*. I don't want you should wrinkle." She pets my arm. "I'm just a little emotional this morning, that's all. You're growing up, my little *mamaleh*, and I'm growing old."

"You're not old, you're in great shape. You're in better shape than—lots of people."

"I'm getting tired. This world is too full of nonsense. A young girl like you shouldn't be so worried all the time." She reaches to stroke the rose quartz crystal on the cord around her neck. "I know you're disappointed, but in the long run, it's a good thing she's staying home. She'd only make you nervous."

"Oh, Bubbeh." I try desperately to get close to her, but the need to keep from wrinkling or dismantling my hair construction keeps us apart. "It's not your fault she sucks those spray cans and—" Instantly, I cover my mouth with my hand.

Bubbeh's profile turns. "What?" She takes hold of my shoulders, letting the mink drop to the floor.

"Nothing. Forget it. It's only a figure of speech." What kind of a feeb rats on her mother to *her* mother? Wriggling away from her hands, I reach for the fur and start to sneeze.

"*Oy.* You see what it is to bring dead animals in the house? Don't touch it, Edie. Leave it on the floor, it's all right. I don't want you to get an allergic reaction."

My hair construction crumbles a little with my sneeze. There are wrinkles in my skirt near the knee. I have every intention of winning and no intention of leaving this kitchen. How could I be anyone but my mother's daughter?

There are noises in the basement. Bubbeh urges me to go downstairs to say good-bye to my father, fresh from another visit to the sterile sheets of General Memorial General. We bump into each other in the darkness outside the family nook.

"Oh! You're still here?"

Once again the fact of his unplayed drums lands on me like a beast. When Pageant is finally over, I'm going to ask him to teach me how to play, and I'll practice every day after school for three hours until my hands are tough as metal-lyte. Maybe we can give a concert for the Virtue Club or at one of his topiary salesmen luncheons. I could try again to learn the proper flick of a butterfly net and accompany him on his hunts. We'll pal around in matching pocket vests. "What are you doing down here in the dark?"

"What I should have done a long time ago—oof!" He brushes past me, and I follow to see him, blow-up dummy in hand, take the stairs two at a time. The dummy's hairy nakedness bumps against the walls of the stairwell.

In the kitchen, Bubbeh and I watch wide-eyed while, only half-dressed in boxers and a shirt with one of my mother's crocheted ties dangling loosely around his neck, my father slices down the center of the dummy's chest, chopping off each arm and leg with the electric carving knife, tossing its airless penis and balls onto the floor.

"Ow!" He cries out as if he were the one losing limbs and genitals.

"Where are your pants, Neil?" Bubbeh asks.

My hand trembles on the doorknob and I notice that Bubbeh's nose is getting red and quivery as my father throws down the vibrating knife and awkwardly hurls himself into a chair, tie sliding off his neck and onto his boxer shorts. The girlish lips twist to show his little mouse teeth as he grips the edge of the kitchen table, giving me a guilty look. "I never liked the idea. I should have said something." He leans toward me and I move away, irrationally glad of the pile of mink between us. The moles on my father's cheek have grown larger and darker, and there is pain in his small eyes.

"Ooh. I was hoping to be able to come and watch, but— ooh, it's starting up again," he says, gasping a little for breath. "It's not bad enough for me to go back to General Memorial General, but I think I'd better stay home and rest. So, I . . . wish you luck. I hope you do well. I—ooh—think you—ooh—look very nice."

"Really?"

There's a dot of Shaver's Helper left on his neck that I would like to wipe off. Instead, I straighten my skirt.

"Buck up, Dad," I say, moving backwards. "When I win the prize money, we can all take a vacation."

I stare at the blow-up dummy's dismembered torso and parts scattered over the heap of dead mink on our kitchen floor. The little Swiss boy pops out of our simfab Swiss chalet clock and dongs. Eight bars of "Taking a Chance on Love" are clearly audible through the open front door. Throughout Deansville, miniwagons full of mothers and daughters race through yellow lights on their way to the Franklin Echo Dome. Later on, the fathers will come to sit in the audience and try to stay awake. The Blow Torchers will be there, too, freshly scrubbed in ties and jackets as per the Rules, weapon-free (as per the weapon detectors and frisking stations) models of decorum—but during Electric Polyrubber Man, all the males in the audience will lean a little forward, even though they will keep their bodies clear of each other, focusing with lowered eyebrows and set jaws. As one supreme being, they will pass judgment on each girl, calculating and weighing statistics, paying special attention to proportion and girth, and no matter how perfect her technique, how naturally sensual and feminine she is to behold in her official cherry teddy and stilettos—she will never make those eyes and jaws relax. She will never score the full one hundred points, will always fall short of the ideal, will always cause the watchers to wonder if there aren't some better girls to watch in another Pageant somewhere else.

All except my father. True enough, he won't be there watching, but if he were, he alone would turn away. He wouldn't judge. He's a nice guy.

"Thanks, Dad," I say, carefully edging my hair construction out the door. "See you later."

A cold sun winks at us from between dirty clouds on the horizon as it struggles up into the colorless sky. Hard to tell if the mighty diseased rain will keep its daily routine or the big yellow Just Like Meat Planet tents will keep the picnickers outside the Franklin Echo Dome safe and dry. The parking lot is already three-quarters full when we pull in, and I catch sight of the enormous Feminine Woman of Conscience truffle float parked next to the dome, and next to it the Electric Polyrubber Man armored truck. The robot must be in the dome already, lying in his padlocked vault, circuits buzzing in anticipation. Security guards, on foot and in patrol carts, cruise among the arriving mothers and daughters loaded down with costumes, cosmetic lockers, and rabbit travel cases. In the space next to ours, the family of an Insecticide Hut deliveryman arrives in his truck; the daughter's hair construction boasts mirrored grasshoppers leaping out of a mobile planted in the center of her auburn bouffant.

"Watch your hair as you get out, *mamaleh*," Bubbeh says, patting my leg. Because of the height of my construction, I've had to ride with my head tipped backwards. "How's your neck feel? Not too cramped?"

"I'm okay." I slide myself out of the miniwagon with care and then open the back to get my bags. Thankfully, Bubbeh carries Alice Jones. In front of us, an actor in a Just Like Meat Planet astronaut suit drops his puffy wig in a puddle and scowls.

Members of Deansville's chapter of the Virtue Club huddle together with clipboards at the front entrance, wearing grim Virtue Club expressions. In the lobby, Bethany Prewitt sits swanlike with her legs tucked up under her on a cushioned window seat, black hair climbing off her face into a fascinating swoop, mother seated with her back bent forward to supply a desk so Bethany can fill out her registration forms. All the girls have brought their mothers—the vinyl-wood-paneled room is full of attractive women touching their daughters' hair constructions, adjusting collars, whispering words of encouragement under large framed oils of Deansville's citizens racing frogs at the Mohawk Canal and other scenes from long ago. Bubbeh looks both imposing and lost in her beaded gown. The action of her farm woman's body is all wrong under the fabric as she navigates us through the crowd. I walk a few paces behind her. If anyone asks me where my mother is, I am going to say she's being hermetically pressurized at the Cancer Salon.

At the registration table, under life-sized photographs of all the dark-suited Franklin Echoes past and present and one memorial photo of Mary Wendy Echo (one of the surgical casualties of Girl Scout Troop 76), like the other forty-nine contestants, I am loaded up by brisk attendants with a five-pound stack of registration forms and my official bar code: 9547833000896572187342. We each get a bag of complimentary treats: miniboxes of Snurps, travel-sized freshen-up kits, pharmaceutical samples for acne and disassociation, Just Like Meat Planet stickers, and one copy of the glossy official Pageant program, its cover photo boasting the famous headdress autographed by—who else?—Franklin Echo. Weigh-in with Nurse

Fogg takes place while we fill out the forms, and I try not to focus on each girl's feet showing under the curtain as she removes
her shoes and steps up on the scale. When it's my turn, I notice
that pounds are deducted for clothes and hairspray, and I pray
that the metal-lyte counter floats to the right place.

"One hundred even," declares Nurse Fogg. She looks at me
and shakes her head. "When this happens, I'm supposed to
reweigh you without your clothes, to double-check." Her
chapped hands give my biceps a quick feel. "Well, your muscle
tone seems normal to me. You're healthy, right? No problems
eating? Sleeping? Urinating? Breathing?"

With all the grandness I can muster, I shake my head and
make my eyes big to show how ridiculous it would be to have
problems like those. Nurse Fogg clamps her lips together significantly as she decides not to make me undress, then writes a few
notes on my health form before she struggles with the height
stick under my hair construction to find the top of my skull.

"Whoever thought up this hair construction idea is a real
joker. How am I supposed to check height?" Grunting, she gives
up with the height stick, and eyeballs me professionally. "You're
at least five foot one. Aren't you?"

"Five two, actually," I lie.

She writes it down on my form and rubber-stamps it with the
official Pageant health seal. "Done. Just pee in this cup and
leave it on the back of the toilet. Rest room's down the hall."

In the bathroom, Bethany slams into the stall next to mine.
She's smoking and I don't hear her urinating, and when I stand
on the toilet tank to get a peek at her, the last of her smoke is
curling upward as her Skull is drowned in the toilet water. I try
not to slip when I see her take a test tube out of her vagina and
pour the liquid from it into her pee cup. Her hair construction
tilts against the slick walls of the stall as she glances up to give
me a nasty smile. "Say one word to anyone and I'll hunt your
Jewish ass down with a surface-to-surface missile." I duck back

down and try to force a few drops of urine out, but nothing comes even after I hear her bang her way back out into the lobby. My body is locked, and it's clear that no matter how long I sit here, no liquid will exit. Leaving my stall with my unused pee cup hidden in a wad of toilet paper, I hang around next to the sinks until the other contestants leave. Then I sneak back into Bethany's stall and pour a little of her pee into my cup.

"Hurry, darling." In the corridor, Bubbeh strides toward me pushing a shopping cart full of our stuff, with Alice Jones riding on the bottom part usually reserved for the economy cases of Baby Yammies in Marshmallow Sauce that my mother likes to stash away for her diet cheats. "They want all the contestants in the dressing room for a talk."

We enter the gilded, curving doorway of Section F and head into the dome. The rows of folding chairs and bleachers rising two hundred feet up to disappear in the roof's steely beams are lit only by the red emergency exit lights while technicians on ladders continue to focus lights onstage. Banners proclaiming Pageant's sponsors—Just Like That, Virtue Club, Slerkimer County Insecticide Hut Delivery Service, Ronald Pritchert for Reelection—vie gaudily for attention, blasting out from around the stage whenever they are struck by light. As we push the shopping cart down the aisle, sections of the stage continue to flare up and go dark, and then, in a dramatic explosion of light, the gold headdress bursts into view atop its thirty-foot brass-ite pedestal. Bubbeh and I pause to stare.

"It's got your name on it." Bubbeh makes a fist and raises it in the air.

My jaw pops as I try to speak. Even from down here, the headdress's precious historic stones look imposing. It dawns on me that the headdress could be cursed; those ancient Egyptians were always running around putting the evil eye on things. Perhaps the headdress wasn't the source of Queen Ankameretikia's power, but instead the reason for her death. I make a mental note to ask Bubbeh for an antidote to hexes when I regain the power of speech, but right now, above the velvet curtains, the purple and gold Feminine Woman of Conscience computer billboard sparkles amid a recorded roar of drums. A man shoves past us down the aisle, shouting into his headset, "What the fuck do you think you're doing, Herb? Where are the dancing flags? For the last time, get those goddamn flags lit before you turn on the screen!" Technicians check and recheck fire and glitter machines, stack cans of decorative explosives in the wings.

Mrs. Horner, president of the Virtue Club, is chief stage manager. She is my height in her platform heels and wears a garland of simfab lilies on her stiff gray bob. What's left of her nose after a record number of operations is lost on her hectic face, everything about Mrs. Horner is jumping unless it has been surgically fixed down, and she burbles instructions like a cartoon bird. Only when she discusses the prizes with us does her manner calm into Virtue Club rectitude.

"The girl who is crowned queen today will receive a $500,000 scholarship, product sponsorship opportunities, and entrée into a world peopled with Hollywood celebrities, high-ranking politicians, and European counts." Mrs. Horner beams while mothers elbow daughters, then takes a moment to adjust her garland and consult her notes. "And, in a very recent development"—here her busy face pauses suspensefully—"the Virtue Club has just been informed that one of our major corporate donors will sponsor an entire summer at a special biochemical research camp in San Jose, California, for the top scorer in Mystery Powders." The skin at the back of my neck stiffens in a chill, but as I look around me, I see blankness in the eyes of the other contestants. Mrs. Horner continues brightly, "But we mustn't forget that the real winner has already been 'chosen,' and that decision is based on observing the attitude of love and generosity of spirit with which each contestant undertook her training. In this respect, even marriage to a European count cannot compare, because nothing supersedes inner rewards."

I sneak a look at Bethany near the back, silently moving her lips with her eyes shut. Next to her, Eileen Morton scrapes at her chin with a thumbnail until her mother gives her hand a slap.

"That scholarship would be such a help," a mother I don't recognize confides to Bubbeh.

"If higher education wasn't so ridiculously expensive, our girls wouldn't have to prostitute themselves to get the money to go," Bubbeh coos and the mother's face bubbles up with discomfort.

"That sort of negative attitude is a little out of place here," she says out of the side of her mouth, steering her daughter closer to the front.

Mrs. Horner continues, "Remember to keep your feet together, and maintain strength in your convictions. Express your opinions with clarity and show a sincere character at all times. Don't look too serious during Mystery Powders, and above all smile, smile, smile. Has everyone registered her rabbit for a mortuary statue? You'll find a discount coupon from Dent's in your complimentary shopping bag."

We are each assigned a semiprivate cubicle not quite tall enough to block out spies. Throughout the dressing room, hair constructions poke up over the cubicles' carpeted panels. Bethany, with her bladder still full of contaminated urine, is clear across the room.

"How you feeling? Okay?" Bubbeh asks from behind me, where she is affixing my parade cottontail to the back of my skirt. For the opening parade, all contestants have to wear the tails, as well as bunny noses, whiskers, and ears perched high atop our hair constructions. We'll promenade in formation around the outside of the dome with the Deansville militia marching band, pushing our rabbits in baby carriages for all the gawking picnickers, media, and experts; holding the hands of contestants' mothers will be the image specialists, color psychologists, total package coaches, and conniving Mrs. Vrick— all there with teeth on edge, glands pumping overtime.

"I'm okay." I stare down into the satiny depths of the baby carriage where Alice Jones crouches, her triangle nose sniffing this unfamiliar air. Her floppy ears twitch gently. I've practiced sewing muffs with the syntho-skins we got from Mrs. Vrick. I made sure to throw them in the trash-pulverizer after my mother gave them the thumbs-up. Okay, I can make one hell of a muff. But can I skin a real hide? The hide of a creature I have fed and petted, even snuggled with against my mother's injunction? My mother has also told me not to close my eyes when I deliver the deathblow; it's a sure way to lose points. Alice Jones's eyes are orbs of gentleness. During the parade, she will obey my command to stand on her hind legs and blow a kiss from the carriage just as we pass the mayor. Each contestant is allowed one improvised move, and this is my mother's genius. Is she dreaming of it now?

"Those chickens you, uh, killed back on the farm. Do you feel guilty about it?"

Bubbeh's touch is delicate as she pins one long white rabbit ear into my hair; it's a real ear, real fur, and the cottontail too; only the whiskers are polystroob. "You've thought about what you're going to do, right?" she says. "You've weighed the pros and cons, yes?"

"I guess."

"Then do what you think is right."

"What if I don't quite know?"

"It's a little late to figure this out, *mamaleh*." Bubbeh gives my whiskers a final tweak so they don't tickle my cheeks while I am marching. "You know you can always bow out gracefully. There's still time for that."

"I don't want to quit."

"If you want to leave right now, it's fine with me."

"I don't want to leave. I just wish I didn't have to kill Alice Jones."

"Edie." Bubbeh squats down so the bridge of her mythical nose is level with mine. "I'd like to tell you that what you're going to do is all right, but it's not. Not according to my beliefs. But I will tell you something else."

"What?" I ask, miserably scratching at my cottontail.

The warning bell for the parade dings in our ears. Bubbeh winks. "You're my *mamaleh*. And I don't care who or what you slice, strangle, poison, bomb, beat, or shoot with a thirty-gauge shotgun—for as long as my heart ticks, I'll stand behind you. I won't let you fall."

Outside, everyone in town is clapping and cheering; as I march left, right, left, turn, wave, knees high, and turn again under the iron-bright sky, people bump into my view: Fernando and both his parents, Ms. Cranston and the other out-of-work teachers, Dr. Kent, all the Blow Torchers, a gaggle of Gentle Welcome nuns, our entire neighborhood association, Mrs. Vrick, Wong. Only Lana is missing. And my parents.

A surge of snapping cameras and waving flags throughout the crowd produces a sudden decrease in the blood supply to my brain, but I manage to get through most of the formations without screwing up. Only once do I turn right instead of left, when I think I see Lana's red weatherbreaker whistling through the space between two miniwagons. My baby carriage slams into Serena Fairchild's, nearly jolting her Giant Angora out onto the pavement. She snarls something at me through her smile, but I can't hear what she says because of the gold-sashed, white-gloved trombone player sliding out his oompah-pahs an inch from my head. When I give Alice Jones the command for her mayoral kiss, she executes it with such dignity and humility, several mayoral attendants and one security guard have to blink back tears.

"Bubbeh, do you think I have time to go outside?" We're back in the dressing room, doing a little preliminary stretching, some of Bubbeh's yogaerobics.

"Did you forget something?"

"No. I just need to talk to a friend of mine. I thought I saw her in the parking lot during the parade."

Bubbeh flicks her wrist around to look at her watch and then consults our program. "I guess you have time. The emcee is going to make his opening remarks and then the former queens will perform their music and dance number." She smiles at me with adoring eyes. "Do whatever you need to do to feel comfortable."

I weave through the dressing room cubicles with a sense of purpose, avoiding the other contestants puking into polystroob bowls and breathing into brown paper bags. By the door next to the stacks of rabbits now stored once more in their travel cases, Mrs. Sweeney's niece Sarah Tetter scratches hives poorly covered up with a thick layer of liquid Sin Concealer. Alice Jones is somewhere in the middle row, but I make sure not to look in her direction.

The asses of all Slerkimer County's citizens cover every last seat in the auditorium, and even with their backs to me, I feel very conspicuous as I sidle along the back wall searching for Lana's red weatherbreaker. On stage, the Virtue Club's national ambassador, Ralph Slaughter, emcees with an amateur's inhibited gusto. "Today is a day when our community has the privilege to witness the personal development of its young women. The fifty contestants chosen to compete are Slerkimer County's cream of the crop and well on their way to becoming successful human beings. The girls you see here today may be the movie stars and researchers of tomorrow. Today, as the Virtue Club hosts the annual Feminine Woman of Conscience Pageant, we also give thanks to the leaders of our community, notably Mayor Ronald Pritchert, for his efforts to terminate the recent grasshopper plague. These are precarious times and I think I speak for all of Deansville when I say, thank you, Mayor Ronald Pritchert, for taking time out of your campaign to attend to this problem, and may the upcoming election be a landslide for you."

When everyone stands up to applaud, I creep toward the Section K exit. Avoiding collision with a Virtue Club usher carrying a tray of Snurps, I race out of the auditorium into the corridor, my hair construction wobbling alarmingly on my head. The ceiling loudspeakers resound with the opening synthesizer chords of Deansville's celebrated classically trained pianist, Joan DeMoan (mother of Judd, himself practically unrecognizable today in a plaid suit and a haircut), as she accompanies Ralph Slaughter singing his original composition "There She Went" while a group of former Feminine Women of Conscience prance around him in a feathered fan routine. I've seen them practice during rehearsals, and not once have they gotten it right.

Is Lana here? She could be in the parking lot, smoking and nursing her half a finger, undecided about whether to lend me her support inside the dome.

I feel a balloon of hope spiral inside my chest. She'll kiss me and everything will fall into place. Her kiss could do that, make all my doubts settle down into one solid answer. The parking lot is a landscape of colored metal-lyte, hulking shells of insects on wheels, rows and rows of them, quietly waiting to come to life. I zigzag through the slim aisles between miniwagons, sure that Lana's brooding face will be just around the next taillight. At the Insecticide Hut truck parked beside our miniwagon, I pause to catch my breath, leaning against the truck's lurid green and black lettering. Above my head, pings on metal-lyte: grasshoppers, leaping on the truck's roof, some crawling on the front windshield, scrabbling to get inside. I circle the truck, fascinated by the bugs' urgency. What could they want? I brush them off the back windows to peer inside but don't see anything out of the ordinary, just the usual group of refill canisters and tanks.

And then something jabs me in the solar plexus. I jump back, fanning at my blouse, expecting a grasshopper to fall away. But there is no pair of disgruntled wings, no spiny legs and devil eyes. It's a set of keys stuck in the door, forgotten in all the pre-Pageant excitement. Without thinking too much about it, I ease them out of the keyhole into my linen pocket and take one last look around the parking lot. No Lana.

Back inside the dome, Ralph Slaughter's baritone sings of the sweet and intangible enigma of a queen's personality and I know that this is right before the big chicken-feather snowfall finale. It'll take the stagehands a few minutes to sweep the stage afterwards, but I'm about to be late for Freestyle Walking.

We march up the aisle toward the Feminine Woman of Conscience computer billboard, electronically whetting the crowd's appetite with its tantalizing pre-Pageant animations: lindy-hopping Just Like Meat Planet astronauts, families hugging on lawns next to their mortuary rabbits, spinning, balletic configurations of Mystery Powder beakers, the Electric Polyrubber Man armored truck weaving in and out of traffic. Cameras flash and people shout encouragement for their favorite contestants. I focus on not tripping the girl in front of me. The Rules Committee is a dim clump of bodies behind their glassed-in private box and I wonder if Franklin Echo is there; he has a phobia about public appearances, is rumored to have had a vision of a sniper's bullet entering the base of his spine. When we are arranged on the stage risers in our pyramid shape, Ralph Slaughter has everyone in the audience get up to give us a standing ovation.

"Each one of these young ladies has worked her tail off to get here today. Each and every one of them is a winner!"

At the judges' table, no one stands or claps. The faces of the five judges show that they doubt very much our tails have been worked off. During our ovation, they sip from water glasses and tidy up their papers, and as I unsuccessfully seek out sympathetic eye contact with each one, willing them to gaze at the future queen, I get a big zero. Judge number one, Theodora Conrad, plucks deliberately at the gold chain holding her eyeglasses around her neck, pulling the chain out and then setting it back on her chest as if she is exercising. Judge number two, Martin Buckner, sniffs into a large violet handkerchief, which he then folds and folds and folds very precisely and tucks under his water glass. Hezikiah Miller, judge number three, clamps his puckered lips together over a white goatee and glares at Ralph Slaughter. Judges four and five, Mary Hammerson and Whitney Clemmersmith, both inspect their fingernails, she by holding her hand flat on the Rules Book in front of her and he by curling his fingertips over his palm and bringing them close to his nose. They are all wearing the gray-blue Virtue Club officer blazer that my mother says has the most unflattering cut she has ever seen. She once turned down a nomination for vice president just because of those blazers.

My face scalds under the lights, even though the air inside the dome is frosty. Freestyle Walking begins, and everything my mother has taught me is burned from memory. Ralph Slaughter reads into the microphone, "Our first contestant is Gretchen DuQuette. Gretchen is five foot nine inches tall and weighs one hundred and twenty pounds. She's a champion swimmer, speaks five languages, and works part-time as an intern at Len's Kidney Transplant Telemarketing Agency."

Gretchen's long, shapely calves in four-inch glitter heels draw whistles and applause from the audience as she navigates the spiked ramp, wheeling fire pits, and tight corners of the obstacle course. One fire pit wheels inches from her right knee just as Ralph reads the part in her bio about Gretchen watching her baby sister get run over by a narcoleptic bus driver and vowing to be a lobbyist for Hazer, the amphetamine manufacturers union, when she grows up. It's obvious that this is a painful memory for Gretchen, because the flames catch a bit of her nylon and she has to slap her leg fast to put it out. The audience moans in compassion, and all the judges make quick marks on their papers.

Bethany walks the course easy as a cat licking fish oil. Not one false move, and every time her feet execute a certain tricky little sidestep, some woman in the audience shouts, "Praise be!" Ralph Slaughter reads her bio in a hushed voice, working in a vibrato when he tells about Bethany's commitment to knowing herself through meditation and volunteering at the Birth Defects Salon twice a week after school. The judges' heads lean together as they confer, nodding while Bethany tiptoes through the last of the spikes and finales right next to Ralph at the podium. The stage lights glisten on her Just Like Eyebrow piercing. Ralph shakes her hand and smooths back his hair before beginning the get-to-know-you chat.

"So, Bethany, you've used visualization and meditation techniques to achieve a lot of success thus far in your life."

"That's right, Mr. Slaughter."

"Would you mind telling us how you do it?"

"Not at all." Bethany's hair construction rises above Ralph Slaughter's own thinning hair imperiously, and the approval in Ralph Slaughter's eyes is clear across the stage. "I like to wear loose, comfortable clothing and lie down in a dim room. Sometimes I light candles."

"Do you wear a shift type of thing? Or would you be wearing pants?"

"I guess I wear shorts mostly. But sometimes I do wear a loose dress."

"I see. And you lie on, what, a bed? The floor?"

"Oh, I have a special meditation mat."

"That you put on the floor."

"Yes." Bethany arches her neck and gives it a delicate scratch. Ralph Slaughter seems to note every ligament. "And then I close my eyes and relax all my muscles, one by one, starting with my toes and working my way up my body right to the top of my head."

"Heh, heh. You relax each toe, do you?"

"Yup. I sure do."

I can't listen anymore. Other girls near me let out sighs of frustration. Though the stage lights make it impossible to see the faces in the audience, I can sense the self-importance of Bethany's fans welling up, already hear the neighborly boasting—"Feminine Woman of Conscience lives right down the street from me! Her mother pots petunias for our garden club!" No question about it: Bethany's a fresh-faced miracle, confident and soul-searching underneath two feet of vibrant hair.

Still no hint of Lana, although she could be sneaking around somewhere. It's too bad if she's not here, because even though my mother's moves are but a distant dream, I pick my herky-jerky way through the cruising fire pits onto the spiked ramp, positive that the technician has increased the speed, yet always I (narrowly) manage to avoid getting burned. I can tell that the audience finds me exciting. At one point, I do a slapstick skid on the oiled polystroob tarp and the crowd makes pity sounds; probably they are sorry I didn't fall all the way down, but when I straighten and continue with a bold stride, not missing a beat, I know I've won them back. I throw in some fancy embellishments, too: raising one knee and kicking behind the other leg just before I shift weight to hop spikes; making circular motions with my big toe as I tilt gracefully to the side and skip around a large reglupolate bush with daggerlike leaves. When I finish, the applause is deafening, and both Bethany and Gretchen are several shades paler than normal.

Ralph Slaughter's face is a mask of amused tolerance as he questions me during our chat. "Your mother is the official craftswoman of the Virtue Club. Do you have any special arts and crafts interests?"

I'm supposed to say that I do. My mother has drilled me repeatedly on the steps for making log cabins out of Peanutty But'rs and rolled slices of Just Like Bread. I am also supposed to say that I enjoy making puppets of famous people from socks and styroplated craft balls. We are going for a folksy, innocent quality to balance my brainy look.

"Yes, Mr. Slaughter. I enjoy making puppets from Peanutty But'rs." Through the microphone, my voice sounds like several of these puppets might be perched on my tongue.

Ralph Slaughter looks impressed. "Sounds interesting. How do you get them to work exactly?"

My ankle is throbbing from that last near fall and I'm a bit distracted. "I don't know. I guess my idea is still a work-in-progress." That's a phrase my mother has said to use if I ever get stuck; she thinks it makes me sound extra conscientious.

"Good for you, Edie." Ralph's voice loses a little of his emcee luster. "Your father is a topiary salesman. I guess you know quite a lot about trees. Why don't you tell us what kind of tree you would be if you could be any tree in the world?"

I purposefully don't look at the judges. "I'd like to be a grasshopper-proof tree. The kind of tree immune to all pest attacks."

"What an idea! Any idea what kind of tree that would be?"

"No. That kind of tree doesn't exist. Although in my spare time I'm working on grafting together a special hybrid redwood-palm that I believe will be completely pest-resistant. One day." I look right at the judges then, zoom in on their arching eyebrows and pinched nostrils; certainly I've made a lasting impression with this zinger.

I ace Juggling, Large Number Estimation, and Needlework Odyssey, which more than compensates for my lackluster showing during Better Person Skills. Now even the judges are sneaking little looks my way when they think I'm not paying attention. The other girls are not so very practiced in their arts. Only Bethany seems to present any real competition, although in the lightning round of Drug-Addict Prevention Bee, she confuses the side effects of Jorzinuzinol with the contraindications of Jargonazerafol. Her face is a study as she tries to keep those dimples in her cheeks; I've noticed that Bethany's deep dimples don't appear naturally, that she has to arrange her face specially to create indentations.

The last event before intermission is Mystery Powders, and I am trembling when I put on my safety goggles. I wonder if my mother is awake yet, if she even knows what day it is. On the table in front of me, glass beakers and test tubes glow with hazardous substances, flasks bubble in their anodized-iron stands. My head reels from the acrid, sinus-scorching fumes while the judges pierce us with their focus, and I'm definitely not imagining that their eyes are mostly trained on me. The stage lights have been lowered to a reddish orange glow that flushes the skin of my fellow contestants, and, with their hair shooting out in spikes and plumes from their heads, and their eyes in a distorted bloat from the lenses of their protective goggles, they look as though they've just been cooking in a thermurderator. I snap on a pair of latex gloves and take each delicate beaker in hand, calling my findings into the microphone while Joan De-Moan plays a dignified march. At my table, Miranda Poehleer sneezes away a gloveful of banana-colored powder and then looks up in anguish; the judges make marks. Four tables away, I see Bethany's latexed fingers fumble with a Büchner funnel during her titration. All around me, pop-eyed girls struggle to adjust the traction and torque of their neutro-ventilators, gobs of petrolubie squirt uncontrollably into the air and onto the stage instead of carefully lubricating high-density binocoverto-scopes.

This is my event, my time to shine. Lana has said it, Bubbeh has said it, Mrs. Horner confirmed it, and the expressions on the judges' faces have sealed it with blood: Electric Polyrubber Man may be worth one hundred points, but the seventy-five points to be had in Mystery Powders are triple-dipped in significance. I look out into the audience and wonder where Mr. and Mrs. Gold, dead Benny Gold's parents, might be sitting and whether or not they are touching. As we girls distill and filter the dangerous particles and droplets, will Mr. Gold reach out and cover his wife's hand with his own? Will all the other relatives of the people who accidentally died from toxic exposure sit up a little straighter on their folding chairs and bleacher benches and cross their fingers in hope? Because up on this stage right now we are so much more than teenage girls competing to be Feminine Woman of Conscience. Every time our high, youthful voices correctly identify a Mystery Powder (or liquid), we are angels of God, imbued with the capacity to save souls, or at least to serve as an excellent distraction from the fact that more and more souls are kicking the bucket and there's nothing to be done about it. Or is there? Maybe it would be an honor to attend that research slave camp in San Jose, maybe as good as submarine school, maybe I could be helping people stay alive, restoring a balance between humanity and nature. Might be all the fumes, but suddenly I feel so good, I could almost tip over my table. Into the microphone, I announce my final substance, "Potassium bisulfate, a toxin and irritant," just before the last buzzer sounds and I ace the event.

During intermission, the dressing room is a busy scene of contestant seizures and self-mutilation and mothers jacking themselves up on more Expressora, then popping meds to calm down. Melissa Fowler, the only one who had the nerve to show up with braces on her teeth, is clawing her forearms, cheeks squished under tear-filled eyes. Jackie MerPelle has fainted and is lying like a crumpled sack on the floor outside her cubicle, and hairy Lois Darrah's mother furiously plucks at her eyebrows with a tweezer while Lois sits grasping a bloody tissue in her lap. The next event is part one of Sacrificial Rabbit Raising; part two, the actual sacrifice, will be the last event in Pageant, after Electric Polyrubber Man.

Where the hell is Lana? Up at the reservoir, communing with Domino, smoking a big fat Bull's Eye cigar? Has she been in the audience the whole time, witnessing my triumphs? How can I think with all this commotion? Maggie Birchener is making loud, jagged cries, and when she throws herself onto her mother's shoes, her mother bends down and plucks her up by the back of the dress, yelling that her hair construction is ruined. Bubbeh tells me to just keep breathing. I try to look interested in reading the Pageant program, but the picture of Bethany, with her superhuman bone structure, stings me. The quote under it reads, "I believe in magic." My picture shows me off as the girl whose mother almost didn't push hard enough to get her out of the uterus; it's the face of someone who doesn't know which way to go. Like the rest of my bio, the quote was written by my mother: "Victory is in the Lord."

Probably the audience is going for snacks: Snurps, Just Like Meat Planet shish kebabs, Cherry Butz. The Blow Torchers in their nice suits and slicked-down hair will be crunching and farting demurely, perhaps holding betting confabs in the men's room, licking Just Like Meat grease from their fingers as they count the bills. I could probably win my own pile just by wagering that not one of them has put any money on me. Maybe this will give me some satisfaction, maybe this will be the inspiration I need to get me through the end. Then, through the forest of hair constructions, I see Mrs. Vrick's werewolf sideburns and pale green scrub dress coming my way. She's got her green aviator glasses on, and when she stops to chat with Cara Gainey's plump mother who talks an inch from her face, she takes them off and sucks on the frame. Another mother joins them, making frantic gestures at the rows of rabbits in their travel cases. But Mrs. Vrick is glancing over at me the whole time she speaks with the others and I know that she is wondering where my mother is, and whether or not she'll get a bonus to her consultant's percentage when I win the headdress.

"Edie, I've been trying to find you." Mrs. Vrick swings into our cubicle, placing her thick-waisted torso between my body and Bubbeh's. "Where's your mother? I haven't seen her all day."

"She's really sick." I try to see Bubbeh from around Mrs. Vrick's scrub dress.

"Is there something I can do to help?" Bubbeh rises to her full height, an inch below Mrs. Vrick's head. "We're preparing for the next event."

"I know that." Mrs. Vrick speaks as though she is cutting off each word with a bayonet. "I'm Janet Vrick, the rabbit expert, and I have been advising Edie and Lorraine. We've worked out a special routine, and I just want to know if everything's going according to plan." She turns away from Bubbeh and back to me. "Is your mother in the audience? I looked in the parking lot, but she wasn't in the miniwagon. There's no answer at the house."

"She's coming now."

There's not enough room in the cubicle for the three of us. Bubbeh presses her own big body forward, forcing Mrs. Vrick to take a little step back into the carpeted partition. My aching foot in its T-strap pump lands in the center of our open cosmetic locker as I try to give them more room.

"My daughter will be arriving any moment. I'm sure she's got everything under control. She had a fever this morning, but when I phoned, she said that she felt much better and would be here for the second half."

Mrs. Vrick's long cheeks are sucked in as her nostrils wing out. Behind the green aviator glasses, her eyes are still full of distrust. "I'm just checking that everything is all right with my top pupil. You understand that I've worked very hard, too." Her movie star mouth attempts civility. "I'm a scientist, and although I care very much about Edie and wish her all the success in her own right, her performance will have certain effects for me as well." She pauses. "I've been taking a risk, focusing on you so much, Edie. We can't know whether or not any of the judges will succumb to any—er—personal prejudices."

"What sort of prejudices?" Bubbeh asks.

"I'm not saying that *I* feel this way, of course." Mrs. Vrick avoids Bubbeh's pointed gaze and trains her eyes on mine. "But there have been rumors regarding such things as—er—heritage. All I'm saying is that you need to be 150 percent together up there, Edie."

Squaring her shoulders, Bubbeh reaches around Mrs. Vrick to give me a small tap. "*Mamaleh*, why don't you go to the toilet now while there's still time?" She gives me a look that says Mrs. Vrick is about to whistle Dixie, roll over, and play dead. "I'll handle this."

Mrs. Vrick opens her mouth to protest, but Bubbeh's defiant nose comes all the way between us as I shake the cosmetics off my foot and escape.

The Feminine Woman of Conscience computer billboard blares out an advertisement for Dent's mortuary rabbits as we wheel our rabbit strollers onto the stage. Despite Bubbeh's efforts, my hair construction is seriously wilted. I can barely look at Alice Jones sitting so sweetly like the little rabbit princess that she is, with her velvety ears draped around her twitching nose. During the routines, I see that Bethany's rabbit is a Satin, black with the shiniest smooth lie-down fur. What a muff that bunny will make.

The stage is jumping: Harlequins, Checkered Giants, Flemish Giants, Silver Foxes, Dwarf Hotots—big-haired girls clap and whistle and stamp their feet as they attempt to get their rabbits to hop through the paces. All around me contestants are mugging for the judges as rabbits consistently fail to mind. Sarah Tetter's Checkered Giant chews at the monkey bars then poops while swinging midair, an instant and humiliating loss of thirty points. As Alice Jones proceeds to calmly sail through each trick, people in the audience are on their feet, cheering, and I begin to warm to the event. There's a tidy orderliness to our teamwork that I can appreciate: I command and Alice Jones obeys. It's fun. There's nothing cheap about training a pet to show off her intelligence and look cute, it's actually pretty wonderful. Just listen to the applause, even the judges begrudgingly express a little joy. Of course the other contestants shoot me assassinating looks, but I maintain a smooth tempo as I tie Alice Jones's apron around her furry middle at the start of Apple Pie Bake.

Miniature thermurderators sparkle. Alice Jones is a model of homemaking as she balances her just-baked minipie on the tip of her nose at the end of the routine.

The crowd goes wild.

"You did very well." Bubbeh's eyes are red-rimmed and worried when we return to our cubicle. She is barely helping me as I struggle into the official cherry teddy (my mother's genius was to order it two sizes too small to make me look as if I have a figure), and her fingers can't quite bobby-pin the white beanie onto my hair construction.

"I was the best! I rule! If what Mrs. Vrick says is true, it won't matter, I'm acing everything!"

"*Mamaleh. Oy,* this is all a mistake." Bubbeh pins and unpins the beanie from my hair. "This Pageant, I don't know what it's teaching you."

"What do you mean? I thought you said you'd stand behind me." I reach for the beanie but she won't let it go.

"Yes, yes. But seeing Alice Jones up there . . . I never knew that she could do karate or walk a tightrope. It's not natural, it's bad luck, I just have a feeling."

Mrs. Rounds, mother of the perfect-breasted Rachel, who almost didn't compete after a nasty incident with a frozen sea bass, pokes her eyes over the top of our cubicle; I lower my voice, still trying to wrestle the beanie out of Bubbeh's hand.

"I don't see it that way. I'm enjoying myself."

"That's what I'm afraid of." Bubbeh's nose quivers and the edges of her nostrils turn a deep, frightened pink. She clasps me to her, causing yet more erosion to my hair construction. "My girl, my best girl. What are they doing to you?"

"Stop, Bubbeh. My hair." Impatience tingles in my chest.

Mrs. Horner's garlanded head bursts into our cubicle. Frowning, she chirps at us, "Why aren't you ready? Get that beanie pinned on, you're holding up the line."

Bubbeh seems to be having a meltdown. I look at her questioningly, but then Mrs. Horner, seeing the beanie drooping in Bubbeh's fingers, grabs the bobby pins to jam it onto my head herself even though she's not tall enough to reach the top, and the beanie ends up plastered to the front of my hair like a bull's-eye. Her tiny child hand is surprisingly strong as she hauls me over to the other girls. Bubbeh doesn't follow, and the last glimpse I have as we leave to meet Electric Polyrubber Man is of her lifting her rose quartz crystal necklace from around her neck and holding it up in front of her as if it is full of germs.

"Like your beanie," Bethany whispers to me as we stand in the dim backstage listening to the end of Ralph Slaughter's song about beautiful caring hearts and willing helpful hands. "Good luck, queeeen."

I don't honor her with a response even though I can think of about forty-six smart things to say back. The Amazing Mister Fezundo has taught me about focus, and right now every last shred of tissue in my body is concentrating on giving Electric Polyrubber Man the rise of his life. I look at Bethany, her silver Just Like Eyebrow piercing glinting like a wishing star, and smile. On a submarine, confidence and doubt are bunkmates: your enemy is sure you have the ability and the intent to do something, but they don't know where or when. "Good luck to you," I say.

One long bass note sounds and a smatter of cameras flash throughout the vast auditorium as we girls march onstage into formation. The ancient Egyptian headdress is a marvelous sheen high above us on its brass-ite pedestal; surrounding it, the four red-sashed, gold-buttoned guards with their white gloves holding submachine guns keep all expressions locked off their faces. At the pinching elastic thigh of my teddy, ruffles scratch; my bare arms are pickled with gooseflesh; smoke machines pump a creeping mist across the stage; and Ralph Slaughter's pinky-ringed hands rise slowly as he gasps into the microphone: "Let us pray." Pageant is supposed to be nondenominational, like the Virtue Club itself, but they always include prayers at their meetings, nonreligious prayers that give thanks to, as Ralph Slaughter now says, ". . . you fill in the blank." The audience drones the copy on their handouts: "Thank (fill in the blank) for blessing this community with such dedicated, virtuous examples of femininity, and may this day be marked as one that celebrates the survival of the human species and our ability to love one another with gentleness and compassion, and let us honor the miracle of all that it means to be human in this great country of ours where the freedom to be an individual is taken so seriously. Amen."

The steel vault, large enough to house a family of rhinoceroses, glides out on silent tracks under a single follow spot. Next

to me, Karen Pederson is having an asthma attack into the puff-
n-suck inhaler she wears around her neck. Bethany stands a row
behind, chin lifted, wet pink tongue warming up for Electric
Polyrubber Man behind her Salvation-colored lips. I would
swear that a herd of beetles are boring directly through the
tendons in my knees, but I won't choke. I can do this. On a
submarine, there is no margin for error. A wrong move—for example, a single soup can falling against the hull during a large-
angle move—can mean detection, and then death. A leak can
make a sub a coffin.

Two of Deansville's militia, officers with a ton of gold braid
fussing at their shoulders, pull open the heavy doors of the vault
to the accompaniment of trumpets and drums. A tidal wave of
silence blows through the audience; then, as Electric Polyrubber
Man rolls from his vault belly first, there are shrieks from some
of the mothers. When I catch sight of him, I get sentimental for
my blow-up dummy on the family nook couch. How can I perform all the caresses and sucking moves my mother has taught
me on such a monster? The buds on my tongue have the flavor
of wet fur, of rust, of the fuchsia lipstick my mother wore the
day her own tongue went diving down into my throat. If she
were here now, she wouldn't be shrieking; her wide mouth
would twitch empathetically, her creamy biceps would tense to
enfold the robot as she would have me do, with a slow, deliberately increasing pressure of bosom on bosom. Even with
Electric Polyrubber Man's mighty chest before me, I can't help
wondering: in the stillness of her bedroom, what are her breasts
like right now? Soft and hanging heavier at the sides as she lies
roped down on the bed, nipples relaxed and gently bumped
around the center tips. Is my father up there now, touching
and licking them as she has instructed me to do with Electric
Polyrubber Man, as she has begged my father to do to her, as
she did to him before his libido went AWOL?

Electric Polyrubber Man is a honey-colored colossus. His genitals are in fact coated with Just Like Honey, which, Ralph Slaughter informs the whole dumbstruck bunch of us, is a special perk: the contestants will be able to perform their task with more enjoyment and, because Just Like Honey is sugar free, without fear of weight gain or tooth decay. "Of course, after each contestant," Ralph assures us, "the robot will be wiped down with Hygeehyde and then given a fresh coating." The face of Electric Polyrubber Man is familiar and unfamiliar at the same time, like a good friend who's changed hair color, or had minor cosmetic surgery, but it's not until Ralph Slaughter explains the Committee's decision to forgo the beard and the hat that I see the uncanny resemblance: Electric Polyrubber Man has the virtuous bone structure of none other than our own dear Franklin Echo. The robot's body is another story. No skinny billionaire dignity for him—this guy has pecs and abs that would make Mr. Universe look as tough as lettuce in a Shrimpeeze Salad. Each thick robotic finger probably weighs as much as a small dog. What will his rubbery flesh feel like under my tongue? Will his bushy pubic hair get caught in my teeth? "Franklin Echo will forever be known as a man of generosity and great moral vision," Ralph swoons. "Who better than Franklin as inspiration for our girls to become women who will do our country proud?"

The sight of the remote-controlled penis blocks my arteries. Each judge has his or her own remote, and only by total consensus will Electric Polyrubber Man get it up all the way. Judges push the rise and fall buttons to calibrate degrees of arousal as they evaluate contestants' techniques; the computer billboard will flash animation, statistics, and commentary: *Tumescence— 10.3 centimeters!* (Electric Polyrubber Man cartoon character grins.) *Getting there! Oops! Tumescence—9.5 centimeters!* (Electric Polyrubber Man cartoon character frowns.) *Maybe not! Uh-oh! Tumescence—2 centimeters!* (Electric Polyrubber Man cartoon character kicks girl cartoon character in the butt.) *This girl needs some help!*

My ears buzz shut as Ralph Slaughter shares the measurement of the robot's fully erect state, but they buzz unfortunately open to hear that the maximum volume and range of the nontoxic pseudoejaculate will be sixteen ounces and thirty meters, respectively. A little ball of depression rolls through me. Can I really get Electric Polyrubber Franklin Echo's penis to shoot the full sixteen ounces? Will his fluid geyser into the air thirty entire meters? Or will my ineptitude only inspire him to leak out a couple of drops?

". . . and Smardeelux, the manufacturer of Urophollogilazine, the choice for sexually challenged men, has generously underwritten the cost of Electric Polyrubber Man's genitals." Ralph's mouth opens to say more, but then he pauses, head cocked to the side as if listening to a distant siren, brow wrinkling in a very un-emcee-like expression of intuitiveness for a moment before he resumes cataloguing the four zillion and ninety-eight separate manufacturing processes involved in creating Electric Polyrubber Man.

Ralph should pay more attention to his intuition. But really, what can he do when the first cat-sized grasshopper swoops down from the dome's beams to whiz around the stage? A second titanic grasshopper flies in over the heads of the audience to greet its mate, and together the two hoppers fly a duet back and forth over the Franklin Echoey head of Electric Polyrubber Man. Deansville's militiamen tense, but no shots are fired. Janine Prendergast, first in this event, looks confused. Ralph looks blank. He's done with his speech, but he hasn't announced her, and I can see that she's wondering whether she should begin; we've been told that music is the cue to leave our spots and come forward when it's our turn. Janine looks at Joan DeMoan, in a position of shock with hands clawed and unmoving over her synthesizer, and then hesitates between the risers and the dais where Electric Polyrubber Man is waiting. Unable to connect with either Ralph or Joan for direction, her slightly bucked teeth digging into her lower lip, she starts her slow, gyrating approach, square, thin buttocks rocking from side to side as she wobbles forward in her heels. At the dais now, her white beanie jiggles dangerously atop her hair construction as she steps up on the platform and slides her arms around the robot's thick neck. With a look of mortified terror on her face, she gives each presidential cheek a chaste, preliminary peck. The grasshoppers carry on their monotonous flight.

At this point, Ralph Slaughter snaps out of his fog and reels away from the microphone in anger, gesturing upward and shouting to the technicians. Joan DeMoan begins to play as Janine proceeds to arouse the robot with overrehearsed technique; her mother steadfastly pantomimes each move from the wings stage right. The judges push buttons on their remotes. Franklin Echo's Electric Polyrubber Just Like Honey–coated penis droops.

Several contestants and a bucket of Hygeehyde later, the two grasshoppers briefly stop their disruptive flying to rest atop the edges of the glass box that holds the headdress. When it's my turn to please the robot, I approach stealthily, synchronizing each hip to Joan DeMoan's improvised bossa nova. Each contestant gets to choose her beat, and I chose the suave Latin rhythm because of a certain Mystic Fangs number that is Lana's favorite. Not that Joan DeMoan's antiseptic noodling recalls any sense of the great Mystic Fangs, but there is a sort of rinky-dink romance in the chords, and I let it seep into my limbs as I play a little footsie with Electric Polyrubber Man's well-shaped toes. More than a thousand eyes are processing my image, sifting it over in more than a thousand brains, installing it forever in more than a thousand memories, maybe feeling it take root between more than a thousand legs. Is Lana watching? Will this turn her on? Alec Fogel, Judd DeMoan, Rodney, and Goetz: they are all seeing me now, their hands in suit pockets, surreptitiously rubbing hard-ons. I look good and I know it. Not because I'm pretty. I look good because for once I am inspired.

Franklin Echo Electric Polyrubber Man is no longer before me. It is Lana's fingers I suck, deliberately going down on each knuckle, flicking my tongue on the pulse point of her wrist, up along the inside of her forearm to nibble on her inner elbow crease. Quicker than thought, my body dances around her, touching, kissing, rubbing here and there and there and there and there. I find places on her body not even she has found and give them the party of their cellular life. From the corner of my eye, I see her massive penis growing, jutting out from beneath her belly, but I am not ready to give it my full attention. There's way too much fun to be had elsewhere, her ears and neck alone could occupy me easily for the next seventy or eighty days.

But I am not that far gone. I hear the gentle warning beeps that tell me how much time I have left. I whisper to her that there will be more later, when we are alone, married, honeymooning through the rest of our lives. Her nipples tighten against my lips. My fingers are gluey from the bonbon of her crotch. Bossa nova and grasshopper jazz play around our heads and we are dizzy and euphoric with true love. When I bring her to climax, her sex sprays a jet stream, glitter machines pump gusts of colored tinsel, canned explosives are thunderous booms that shake the stage, and Joan DeMoan's elbows swoop like hawks as she pounds out a last, hysterical chord.

Ninety-three points. More than enough to make up for my worst event, Hair Construction, and even that not too shabby a showing at sixty out of a possible seventy-five. When it is over, too faint to return to formation, I amble instead into the wings, weak-kneed and sticky-chinned. Where am I? Bubbeh's arms are around me; the mothers of other contestants glare; a pale-faced woman in a Better Dress clasps her heart: Bethany's mom;

I think I hear someone spit. Nurse Fogg waves a container of sharp fumes beneath my nose, and after I puke I am helped onto a stretcher.

In the makeshift infirmary, Bubbeh's anxious face comes in and out of focus.

"Here. Drink some water."

Nurse Fogg gives me a professional look as I sip from Bubbeh's offered cup. "Too much excitement. Happens all the time." The back of her chapped hand presses my forehead. "She's not running a temperature, so if you're okay sitting with her, I'm going to get back and watch the rest of the event." At the doorway she pauses, almost smiling. "That was quite a discharge, missy."

"Are you all right?" Bubbeh lays a cool wet cloth on my forehead after Nurse Fogg is gone.

My head is whirling, but I shake off the cloth and sit up, considering the next event. "It looks like I'm going to win. Bethany Prewitt and I are tied for first place. And you know she can't even hold her knockout club without hypertensing."

"I'm worried about you, darling. You don't look right."

In the corridor, a line of grasshoppers move past the door. They are jumping in a strong, soldierly rhythm.

I take her hand, my mind made up. "It's okay, Bubbeh. I'm a realist, just like Mom says." If I quit now, I'll never be a Feminine Woman of Conscience queen. I'll never get to be a movie star or live in a castle in the south of Romania with a pack of servants calling me Countess Stein. I'll never get to go to the Mystery Powders research camp and discover a nontoxic substitute for Just Like Organochlorines. But I will be reborn: unsatisfactory daughter of Lorraine and Neil no longer, my genetic structure will morph into a new configuration, Tinkertoy shape will beef up into something like the interlocking gear teeth of a nuclear destroyer; I'll be the love child of Lily Gates and The Amazing Mister Fezundo: a magic-making radical honored by rabbits throughout the world. "I'm going to spare Alice Jones's life. But I feel bad about the other rabbits. It doesn't seem right to save her and let all the others die. Don't we have a responsibility to try and do something for them?"

Bubbeh's eyes brighten.

And then I remember the keys.

Unloading the canisters from the back of the truck, I catch Bubbeh's eye. "Are you scared?" If anything happens to her, I will throw myself headfirst into a public nuclear bomb precipitator.

"I know what to do if there's trouble, darling, don't worry about me." She chops the air in a yogaerobics move. "I watch screen, I've seen the crime shows."

"I can't promise that this is going to work, but if I'm right, this stuff is like vitamins to them now. Before, it used to kill them, or we *thought* it did, but actually they just changed shape, mutated, and now they've come back resistant to the poison."

"Edie! Man! Oh, man!" Fernando is breathing like a crazy person behind me, and as I turn to him, my nose bumps his bony chest.

"What are you doing out here?"

"I heard you and Bubbeh talking. What's up, doc?" The barracuda shape on his front teeth catches daylight, his gray eyes are changed, alert in a way that makes him seem capable of something worthwhile. All around us, sun flashes on miniwagon roofs, and the parking lot air has a briefly comforting smell of summertime asphalt.

"How'd you like to give us a hand?" I thrust a canister into his arms and for once he doesn't go limp.

We carry our subterfuge in polystroob bags, and while Bubbeh and Fernando cover the perimeter of the auditorium during the changeover between Electric Polyrubber Man and Sacrificial Rabbit, I heist a screwdriver, poke a hole in the bottom of my canister, and slip among the technicians checking equipment to drip out a tasty path at the circumference of the stage. I keep the bag low to the ground and walk around as if I'm exactly where I'm supposed to be. It's amazing how confident a person can feel when she acts on her beliefs.

I stash the used canister in a trash bin and meet Bubbeh back in the cubicle. She hands me my knockout club, sparkling importantly with my mother's glitter design.

"God help you," Bubbeh leans her face down to press her star-shaped birthmark against my own cheek. A tear rolls between our flesh.

The dressing room is emptying out, cubicles abandoned harum-scarum with Pageant clutter; our rabbits in their travel cases form rows of distressed noses next to the line of their future murderers. "I've got principles," I tell her, weight sinking firmly into the heels of my feet as we move to join the line.

She blows her nose into a rainbow-colored hankie. "You're my best girl." And when we near the stage the folds of her cheeks rise as she hisses, "Go kick ass."

The sacrifice is going to be very classy: Joan DeMoan playing the organ mode on her synthesizer and the stage all tender blue light. Once the rabbits are skinned, we're supposed to dip their hides in a special chemical bath to quick-process them, then stand at attention while fifty sewing machines are wheeled onstage for the grand finale muff-making race. As the first organ notes wail out from the speakers, we bow our heads. Ralph Slaughter leads us in another of the Virtue Club's nondenominational prayers.

I slant my eyes to the edges of the stage. Will they come? The two big grasshoppers that plagued us during Electric Polyrubber Man are no longer sitting up on the headdress's box, seem in fact to be absent from the whole stage area. I calm myself by counting, visualizing myself in a metallic sharkskin Amazing Mister Fezundo suit—this will be as grand a magic trick as any of his feats. At prayer's end, our bowed heads rise and we march to the sacrificial tables.

The other contestants have to use restraining hands, but Alice Jones is erect and motionless in front of me; she will move when I tell her to do so, and only then. With blue gels casting an eerie light on her brown fur, she almost looks like her own mortuary statue. How could I ever have even considered killing her? The knockout club sizzles in my hand. At a certain point in the music, we will begin taking turns in the deathblow rotation.

A hand up to shield my eyes, and the audience is visible, rippling uneasily. There are shouts. "They're coming!" More shouts. A few people are hurrying up aisles, small children in tow. Joan DeMoan hangs on a chord, vamping until the situation becomes clear. Obviously, she can see that something is awry. A fire? Death in the crowd? The pianist's eyes squint at the rapidly escalating confusion in the audience. Ralph Slaughter motions for her to continue.

Rabbits grow more restless. There is movement on the stage, a familiar crawling motion under the blue light, my heart pounds. Contestants poke each other, hands cover mouths, and eyes go big—"Look out!"—and Cara Gainy is the first to hit the floor, squashing her hair construction with protective hands. Her rabbit, a twenty-pound Flemish Giant, hops from the table and runs downstage to leap over footlights and off the stage. Other rabbits follow suit as grasshoppers cruise in from all angles, swoop down in schools from the beams, canter up the front of the stage, waddle in from stage left and stage right on pumped-up legs to dine at the creeks Fernando, Bubbeh, and I poured out from the Insecticide Hut refill canisters.

Alice Jones remains fixed to her spot until I grab her in my arms and duck under our table. Contestants are running every which way, a few stand dazed like cows in a rainstorm. Mothers and daughters weep as security guards, all yelling into pink security guard phones, swish everyone through the exits. The audience vaults over the backs of grasshoppers munching away at the chemicaled floor. People pour from the auditorium, even Alec Fogel and the Blow Torchers are leaving. I don't see Bubbeh or Fernando anywhere. I pray they are back out in the parking lot, ditching their canisters and warming up the miniwagon for our escape. At the microphone, Ralph Slaughter is telling everyone to calm down, to file out in an orderly fashion. In their spit-shined boots, Deansville's militiamen train their submachine gun sights on everything and anything, shooting nothing, while behind the glassed-in box, the Rules Committee is gone, whisked away to safety at the first hint of trouble. Hyperkinetic Mrs. Horner is a zipping dwarf across the stage, her fallen garland of simfab lilies crushed underfoot. Virtue Club attendants and judges bump into one another, water glasses and scorecards cascade to the ground.

The air is roiling with hoppers, their snarling bass line burrows under my breast and I feel wild, delirious with power. The entire dome fizzes and pops with the grasshoppers' music, or maybe it is the sound of my own triumphant nervous system that I am hearing, an unbelievably sweet group of sonar signals ringing in my ears. "See?" I tell Alice Jones. "I told you I'd save your ass." Well above our chaos, the headdress is fantastic and aloof. It would have been so deluxe to have its queenly horns and lotuses against my scalp. Too bad there's no headdress for a real feminine woman of conscience.

I should probably get out of here and meet up with Bubbeh and Fernando, but I'm still savoring the moment when bullhorned voices shout, "Happy Endings! Happy Endings!" over the commotion. I squeeze Alice Jones tighter in disbelief. In front of me, at what seems like supernatural height, the silhouette of a nun appears, backlit upon a table, arms defiantly akimbo.

I squint up at her, see her legs fly from under her sky blue habit to leap with a bang onto my table, then bound off again to the next, as she leaps her way across tabletops toward Ralph Slaughter's abandoned podium. I struggle up to a standing position, Alice Jones tight against the derailed bodice of my teddy.

"Freeze!" In the microphone, Lily Gates's voice is a little on the extraterrestrial side. She must be wearing a voice scrambler turned to low, and under her pointy nun hat, her face is entirely covered by a bright orange ski mask. So this is Lily Gates. She's not exactly what I'd expected, but I can't say why.

Right between the judges' box and the stage, the Happy Endings people are there, in view at last, people I recognize yelling into bullhorns—Dr. Kent, members of our neighborhood association, Virtue Club attendants, Gentle Welcome nuns—look at them!

"Pageant is an antibeauty experience!" a man I don't know shouts into his bullhorn. "We protest the misuse of beauty!"

The straps of my pumps bite into my ankles as I move toward the podium where Lily Gates is holding up a blinking silver box in her gloved hand.

"I am Lily Gates," she yells into the microphone, as Deansville's militiamen close in around her. "And I have a bomb. So nobody move."

I don't move. Not even to put a hand up to shield my eyes from the stage lights so I can see if the security guards are also following her orders and not calling for help on their phones. I do see that the militiamen are not inching back their trigger fingers as Lily Gates shakes a yellow knapsack off her shoulders and whistles a command.

Of course. This is the missing piece, all those phone calls and trips out of town, her evasive responses. Who else but Lana Grimaldi could pull off the stunt of being a firebombing nun and get away clear? But right now another stunt is being pulled, as Domino the wild rabbit climbs the brass-ite pedestal, her brown fur burning like a white-hot flame under the headdress's spotlight, climbing up and up and up and then pushing with her hind legs to leap onto the edge of the glass box that holds the headdress. It's definitely a stunt when she balances there on the thin corner, gripping the glass with her toes, and leans down into the box.

The grasshoppers keep coming, the crowd grazing the insecticide trails is jostled by new arrivals, fights break out in explosions of wings all around the dome. The only people left to see it are the militiamen, security guards, and the crew of Happy Endings, but they are mostly watching Lily Gates, her half-finger poised in its glove over the detonator's big red button, stunned that they will be blown up and have to lose their big chance at a real Happy Ending. Meanwhile, cottontail aimed at the ceiling, Domino makes several attempts to reach the headdress, and just when it looks as if she might be slipping, she snags ancient Egyptian filigree in her teeth, swings back around, and leaps fearlessly down into Lily's habit, now stretched out like a net. It all happens lightning fast: shots crack the air, the Happy Endings hit the decks in fear, security guards catch stray militia bullets and yowl. Lily backs away with Domino and the headdress, brandishing the detonator like a shield.

"Cease fire! Anyone continues to shoot, I push the button and we all bite the big one." Her voice is free of panic, steady, and I can see that the gunmen are taking her seriously. She beckons me with a jerk of her pointed head. "You."

I do as I am told and load the headdress into her knapsack. Lily Gates threatens anyone who moves with the detonator. Then, with great deliberation, she puts a glove on my bare arm and leans close enough for me to see those familiar eggplant eyes behind the mask. "I get like this sometimes," she says in her scrambled voice. "Capeesh?"

"Yeah. Nice work."

She fits Domino into my arms next to Alice Jones and whispers, "Go out the back door and get in the TR3." She walks us backwards toward the exit, making sure no one moves to follow. "I've got some things to take care of here. I'll meet you later."

Mrs. Grimaldi is at the wheel with the top down, trying to give me a timid smile from under her gingham kerchief. We've never actually had a conversation. I climb in and put the headdress in the space at my feet. The two rabbits huddle on my lap. It feels awkward to be sitting in the Triumph with Lana's mother beside me; on top of everything that has happened, this is maybe the weirdest thing of all. Once upon a time, Lana lived inside this woman. This ordinary, gray-haired woman wearing white athletic socks and a dress my mother would use as a polishing rag is the person who first caused Lana's heart to beat. I'm amazed.

Involuntarily, I compare Mrs. Grimaldi with my mother's loveliness. My mother: once I bobbed inside her satin belly. Will I ever again look at those old pictures of her, dewy and flushed as she held me—the one fetus that didn't die from her poisonous blood, her long-awaited little bean?

Mrs. Grimaldi's no driver, and the Triumph dies and dies as she hesitates at the clutch. Every time the car jerks forward and halts, Mrs. Grimaldi says something in Italian and tightens her kerchief before trying again. I don't know where we're supposed to go to meet Lana, but I do know if we don't get out of here soon, I'll be knitting therapeutic tea cozies at Springfield and who knows where Mrs. Grimaldi will end up.

"Ease off the pedal as you gently press down on the gas, like you're dancing," I finally work up the nerve to say. I haven't done it myself, but I've seen Lana rehearse it enough times. "Maybe it would help if I gave you a beat." It starts off awkwardly, and the sound of it is peculiar and fake in my ears, but suddenly I'm humming a boroonga and Mrs. Grimaldi has got us in gear.

I hum the boroonga all the way downtown, and it's as if Mrs. Grimaldi and I are really dancing together, an odd, touchless partner dance with me sensing just when to slow a phrase, she matching the motion of her feet to follow my voice. We never actually go faster than second, and getting through the stoplights gives both of us a workout—her weathered, restaurant-slave hand gripping the wheel as though it might fly off while she tugs wildly at the gearshift, my voice climbing unsteadily to hum in the upper register as I wonder: How did this woman end up with a daughter who wins trophies in tumbling, lives after being buried alive, and sets off firebombs in rooms filled with synthetic meat? I hum louder. Mrs. Grimaldi doesn't seem to mind that Lana is so different from her, and she doesn't notice the glitch in my voice as we pull into Wong's parking lot with a surprisingly smooth stop.

"*Grazie.*" She gives my forearm a small pat.

"No problem." When we go to put the headdress in the trunk, I see their suitcases, and I know that this is it, Lana is finally taking her mother away for good. Together, we raise the convertible's top to lock the rabbits in the car, and then I follow Mrs. Grimaldi over to the entrance of Wong's, miserably aware of my destroyed hair construction and too-tight teddy. How can I get her to take me with them? Lana is Lily Gates, and I saved the rabbits, she can't possibly leave Deansville without me.

Mrs. Grimaldi knocks without success on the glass door with its big Closed sign, and so I bang on it until a short Chinese lady pops into view and looks at us without letting us in. We all stand there looking at each other through the glass, with the woman seeming as if she is about to smile, as if maybe she is always about to smile but forgot how.

"Excuse me." I push my mouth close to the door. "We're supposed to meet someone here." The door stays closed. It's

ridiculous that after all I've been through, this tiny person who
has lost the ability to smile is standing on the side of the door
where I am supposed to be, and I am outside with Lana's
mother. Suddenly I am woozy, squirrels running around in my
bowels. I pound on the glass, harder than before. "Let us in!
You have to open this door, do you understand?" The little
woman opens her mouth in a frightened oh, and I bang my fists
against the door, kick at the vinyl-wood frame and slap it. From
the corner of my eye, I see Mrs. Grimaldi backing away against
the neostucco, cowering next to a potted fern. The Chinese
woman is still there behind the door, hugging her chest as I
curse and yell at her, "Open this motherfucking door! Do you
understand English? Open up!" How can there be so many feebles living in one town? I called the grasshoppers and they
came. I saved the rabbits and forfeited Pageant. I ditched my
Bubbeh and my best friend to be here. Every kick feels justified,
every vinyl-wood splinter that breaks off from the frame brings
a new rush, my aortic wall pulsating a superfast boroonga
rhythm with the mad beat of my heart, the bodice of my cherry
teddy threatening to pop right off my chest—a roar escapes: I
am savage, a primordial being, the pest of all pests if you will,
and I am fighting to survive. I take off my high-heeled pump
and smash it into the Closed sign until, failing to break through
with one shoe, I take off the other one and bash them both repeatedly into the sign, stopping only when I hear the satisfying
and humiliating sound of total destruction.

A bumpy, blistering red rash has developed on my arms, neck,
chest, and from the itch of it, my stomach as well. My hands are
cut. Not too deep, but they hurt, and Lana's face when she
wraps the wounds in lyccra-gauze is unhappy.

"What happened, Edie?"

I shrug, mortified about the rash, the metal-lyte stool in

Wong's kitchen cold under my skimpily clad butt. Wong, luminous and chubby in his kitchen whites, serves Mrs. Grimaldi tea while the little Chinese woman slurps glossy green noodles from a bowl, her eyes never leaving my face.

"Better not to try on empty stomach," Wong tells me, offering noodles. I don't have the heart to tell him I'm not hungry.

"We were just coming in. Little Pear wasn't supposed to open the door until we let her know it was all right." Lana finishes wrapping my cuts with a flourish. "You really freaked. And that rash looks pretty bad. How did it happen?"

Again, I lift and lower my shoulders, the only form of communication I have left.

"I saw you with the Insecticide Hut canister. I know what you did." She smiles then for the first time, her eyes registering respect. "I was going to wait until after the winner was announced, you know, to be fair. I never wanted to take away anyone's title." Gently, she touches my rash. "I bet you're reacting to all those Just Like Organochlorines."

It's an allergic reaction all right, but not to any external toxin, it's organic, this rash, a response to the internal toxins that have broken free of their membranes and raged throughout my system. These pink, pus-filled bumps have been germinating ever since I gave Fernando his first judo flip, they began soaking up enough raw energy to sprout when I dealt the facsimile rabbit that perfect deathblow, finally getting the juice they needed to break through my skin as I battered down Wong's front door. I saved the rabbits, but my heart is still shadowed, corrupt, and irredeemable. How could Lana ever truly love a person with such a bad heart?

Wong offers me a tea towel steaming with some grayish poultice and tells me it will "make red spots nice skin again." It smells otherworldly and unpleasant and yet I do as he says, even though this rash is very possibly permanent.

"There isn't a lot of time now." Lana turns to her mother

and starts a conversation in Italian during which her mother's replies are long, worried, and completely unintelligible. Lana's Italian is slow, and her soothing tone sounds as though she is trying to convince Mrs. Grimaldi of something. Now Wong brings over a huge bowl of fortune cookies and sets them in front of me, smiling, his tiny hands beating like the wings of hummingbirds around his face as he invites me to "eat much luck."

When at last the Grimaldis finish talking and both look satisfied, I let the poulticed tea towel drop to the floor and say, "I can't stay here. Please take me with you. I won't freak out anymore if I can go with you." My heartbeat echoes in my head, an uneven, insubstantial sound. If I stay here in Deansville, I will become as bad as any Blow Torcher, or worse. Winning wouldn't have made me superior, it would have made me the worst kind of feeble, the kind that *think* they know better, that *think* they are freer and smarter than everybody else but in reality are an exact carbon copy of any of the multitudes of feebles they feel such disdain for. How can I make Lana need me now? My love for her doesn't belong in Deansville, and I don't want to be saved from it, I want to fall, deeper and deeper, in love with Lana's bumpy nose like the prow of a sub, her broken eyebrow, her elegant, mutilated hand. "I love you," I whisper frantically. "I know it sounds corny but it's absolutely uncorny. We're like two anglerfish, they join their blood vessels together for the female to feed the male to give him the strength to mate with her and make more anglerfish so the species can survive. It's the deepest kind of love; even though the fish are really vicious-looking with huge teeth, they need each other." As I talk, I plunge both hands into the bowl of fortune cookies and accidentally break a bunch and grind them into crumbs, more than a few unread fortune strips leap out onto the floor. My hands hurt because of the cuts, but there's one unbroken fortune cookie left and I manage to offer it to Lana without showing pain. "Open it. Let's do whatever it says."

Her face serious, she takes the cookie and sets it gently on the counter, watches me for a long minute, then glances at her mother now quietly sipping from a flowered cup. "Chumly," she says and lays her head on my shoulder, and the weight of her head melts my nerves, everything will be all right, she does love me despite my weak, violent tendencies. But her head pops off my shoulder too quickly, and her eyes fill with irony as they hold mine again. The kitchen is silent except for the sound of Little Pear's slurps and something bubbling over a gas flame. My life is over. I will return home to my mother and suffer the greatest punishment she can devise, unknowable in its ability to torment; probably she has refueled with a jug of Expressora and is on the phone devising it with Mrs. Vrick right this second.

And then, even as it's happening, even as she gives me my answer (because she is after all still that beautiful princess from the Bronx who has the power to give fate the raspberry), even as I'm lit with shivers of gladness, a flicker of insecurity still wiggles inside me, and so I hear but do not completely believe her when she drawls out the magic phrase, "How could I ever let the ears of a sonar operator stay here and grow wax?"

Well, it's a little cramped, and Wong's donated kitchen whites are too big for me, but I am in the Triumph on the road with my girl. And her mother. And our two rabbits, who Lana promises will soon find liberty at the next state park.

And we have the headdress.

It's like winning, even my mother would have to recognize that I am victorious, maybe not exactly as she envisioned it, but weren't all her efforts riding on the one great hope that I would end up somewhere better, rise up from what has always appeared to be a disappointment to become the woman my mother could never be no matter how many Virtue Club meetings she attended or which meds she slid down her throat? I'm already miles past the Slerkimer County limits, so in a sense I have not failed her, I have not, as she unfortunately will be too pissed to see, disobeyed or dishonored her, not really. Anyone would affirm that I should be angry with her—a mother's tongue has no business probing a daughter's throat—but I'm not. I'm looking forward to loving her again, I really am—out of reach, out of range of her peppery smell.

It's snowing now, great messy flakes, but we have to ride with the top down so I can fit in the car. Lana steers with her knee and shifts gears with her left hand while her mother holds safe the bandaged finger on her right. Except for the weather, the whole situation is under control, Lana tells us, a paint job and new license plates for the car, a buyer for the headdress, her father's away on a gambling trip in Atlantic City and won't find out we're gone and pitch his fit until next week. I consider my father, and wonder what he'll do when he finds me missing; his passionate destruction of the dummy brought out a new side I'd be interested in seeing again. Still, I am here in her car, I'm the person that is here watching while she navigates, feeling the tickle of her hair on my face as it blows into the backseat, or at least the place where there would be a backseat if this was a bigger car.

She is Lily Gates, destroyer of Just Like Meat Planets, making her own law while all of Deansville continues to drive their miniwagons, faces fixed in smug, automated ignorance, erranding back and forth to the polystroob halls of Grocery Town and the Cheese-n-Fun.

"We can make a lean-to out of a poncho, hide out in the woods until they've stopped looking for us." I speak at the side of her head, not in her ear exactly, but close enough. "We can eat wild plants. I know how to test them for poison by doing the Universal Edibility Test. I can make a water filter out of a pant leg. If we get wounded, we can do the maggot cure. It's gross, and a little dangerous, but it might save our lives."

"Great, Edie," she says. "That's great."

Nightfall brings a balmy blanket full of tropical secrets as we drive west, the air rolling over us to dry our snow-wet clothes. Hanging on the big sky, the Pleiades are a group of friends chatting while Mrs. Grimaldi snores with brief, nasal hiccups, her head tipped to the side. Lana and I are going to bring her someplace safe, after which, Lana says, we'll have to move on for a while to make it harder for the authorities to track us. She knows people all over the country, part of a huge underground political network that is fighting to bring down the Just Like That Conglomerate, and they will help us. The Happy Endings people are part of it, but we say it aloud at the same time: we're not going to participate in Happy Endophoresy. "I'm sick of suicides," Lana says, breaking off her father's dashboard Mussolini statue with a snap. She chucks it over her shoulder, out of the car. "Happy endings are indecorous."

I agree. I want to live to see how things turn out. In fact, listening to her talk about all her plans for remodeling the world has a surprising effect on me: I feel the urge to put my stamp on things, too, to talk my way into early admission to the sonar operator training program in submarine school, for example, and listen for things no one else has ever heard, has ever even thought of listening for. Who knows what discoveries are out there for me to make, and if all I do is tag along with Lana's sleeve in hand, I will never know what they are. It hadn't really sunk in until now that she would keep going after we got her mother to safety. I suppose I never really considered what would happen. Then again, she *is* Lana Grimaldi, even if she thinks she's Lily Gates, and maybe I can persuade her to do something else, something important of course, something that will give me a chance to show her the real Edie Stein.

Overhead more stars keep popping into view as the clouds dissolve. Lana keeps the radio low. Sometime around midnight, we set Domino and Alice Jones free among the chirpings and buzzings of a pine forest. The dark needles softly brush our heads. My rash is starting to fade. In the morning, we drop Mrs. Grimaldi off at her sister's house in Muncie and wave good-bye.

We stop to pee at a truckstop. While Lana goes to the rest room, I borrow her phone to have a private conversation with my mother. Googols of stars sugar the sky.

"We're going to find something new and transform," I say into the mouthpiece. "At least, I hope we can." It might be my lack of sleep, but seeing Lana's tears as she carried her mother's luggage across the threshold of her Aunt Connie's house may have caused question marks to dizzily circle my head, bleaching out my present reality, leaving me minus a dimension, a cartoon Edie doing a stop-action walk through a series of cartoon panels, the last panel missing, the punch line lost. As I watched Lana and her mother in their good-bye embrace, my mother's arms curved invisibly around my waist, pressing me against her silky dress, and her voice murmured phrases of comfort, hinting at the laughter and the zany Candy dances we would share in a more settled future. Even early admission to submarine school would not feel as nice as that. Of course I had to phone her.

"So you're calling to tell me that you're running away?" She sounds different, defeated and ashamed.

I hesitate, fiddling with the phone's antenna. "I suppose I am."

"Okay."

"That's all you're going to say? You're not going to yell at me or try to track me down?"

"Of course I'm going to try to track you down. I'm your

mother, you're my daughter, that's what happens. This is the law of families, Edie, I'm not making it up."

"I see. And if I tell you that your efforts will be futile?"

"I'll still try."

"You will."

"Yes. I may not be very good at showing it, but the fact is that no matter what you do, I love you. I will always love you."

Mile-long semis pull into the parking lot, their headlights flashing on my squirming kitchen whites, making me a glowing albino worm along the great highway darkness. Lana comes out of the rest room and gets back in the Triumph. Parked beneath the bright and towering Just Like Meat Planet sign with its galaxy of sausages orbiting a big hungry astronaut, she sips Mondo Surge and waits for me to finish talking. I watch her bandaged hand push hair away from her face and from here she looks small and fatigued, as unlike a revolutionary bomber as a grasshopper.

My mother loves me, will always love me, and even through the tiny polystroob receiver I can hear that those words of hers will be a priceless sound for as long as I live. "I wanted to be a queen. I really wanted to walk down that aisle wearing the headdress in front of the whole Slerkimer County." There's silence on the other end of the phone. "I was this close. That headdress was as good as mine, but I sabotaged my own win. After all your hard work, I made the grasshoppers come into the dome and ruin Pageant for everyone."

"You did what you felt in your heart was right. I'm proud of you for that."

The relief that courses through me relaxes me so much I lose some muscle control and drop to my knees. She is proud of me. I did the exact opposite of what she wanted and she is proud of me. "Ouch," I say, feeling parking lot stones bite into my kneecaps.

"What happened? Are you hurt?"

"No." I manage to stand, and flick a few stuck stones off my pants. A little circle of blood shows on the white fabric, and there's a stinging in my leg, but it feels nice, like someone's given it a hard kiss. "I'm okay, I just walked into something by accident."

"Oh." Her voice still has an odd tone, the tone of someone who is uncertain what sound will come out when she opens her mouth, the tone of someone who desperately wants to say one perfect word. "Well, be careful . . ."

"Yeah. I will." My free right hand dangles alone and I raise it with its dirty lyccra-gauze bandages, palm up, then curl it into a fist and hold my thumb.

I can't know what my mother is holding with her free right hand. But our left hands hold our respective phones up to our ears, our mouths placed against the miniature and powerful microphones, and we spend a little more of the night listening to each other breathe.

I never do get to pee, but the first trucker who sees my thumb just happens to be going all the way to Deansville.

Exhausted, I curl my legs under me in the cab of the truck and as I am falling asleep I think of the people back home who are waiting, imagine how relieved they will feel knowing that their love for me will not end up in a void; it's an awful act—sacrilegious even—to reject love, because what does it really cost a person to let it in? Love can't harm you, it's not a poison. Even too much of it will only give you a little temporary queasiness. There is no wrong kind of love, I know that now, no matter how damaging, it's just—as the dictionary says—an out-of-control feeling. You can't blame people for their choices. Or their methods. It's annoying as hell, but as much of a fact as a torpedo blasting its target. I can make things better with my mother, with my father, and Fernando, too. And it gives me great peace of mind to know that I am not abandoning Bubbeh.

The truck's many wheels roll grandly up the exit ramp to catch the eastern route leading back to my people, and I dream of two girls in a car on screen. The driver has her restless hands relaxed and whole once more, the passenger is rashless, free of blame. Long shot of the two roaring up some country road going anywhere with the top down on their TR3, the driver's long, earth-colored hair fighting raucously with the wind. Close-up on the passenger turning to look at the driver's capable profile, then leaning over to whisper a kiss. The driver grins and the passenger is happy, happier than she has ever remembered being, especially to see how the driver works the wheel of that Triumph, spinning the wheel from one side of the highway to the other, hands symmetrical and complete, her fingers tapping along with the radio as if the place that is left behind and all that is sour there is just a bug squashed irrelevantly against her windshield.

I want to thank my wonderful agent, Jane Gelfman, for her unswerving belief, and my brilliant and meticulous editor, Becky Saletan, who is blessed with the gift of incomparable clarity. Further gratitude goes to the readers who offered opinions and support along the way: Nina Aledort, Marina Budhos, Audrey Ferber, Sheri Holman, Gary Morris, Deborah Schupack, Chris Tokar, and Katrin Wilde. Special thanks to Alan Burdick and Lynne Tillman for their key suggestions. To Nicky Allen, Benjamin Bossi, June Edelstein, and Susan Ito, I owe an indescribable debt for insight, encouragement, and love. To Dana Matthews, many kisses for her cabin, her camera, and herself. To the Harmon Lake Gang—Karen Margolis, Rob Simonds, Liana and Jonah Simonds—the deepest thanks for giving me shelter and a beautiful place to canoe. To Christopher McVey, abundant love for all the sweetness, stability, and humor he brings to every writing day. Big thanks to Brian Ableman, Christian Brachvogel, Meyer Braiterman, Laurel Carpenter, Ellie Covan of Dixon Place, Orlando Frizado, Deborah Glazer, Joy Katz, Karen Kraig, Jonathan McVey, Jenna Spevack, Ginger Strand, Wintry Sylvan, and Rae C. Wright, all of whom provided plenty to keep me alive and well during this long and bumpy journey. I also gratefully acknowledge Blue Mountain Center, the Mac-Dowell Colony, and the Writers Room for time, space, and sustenance during the writing of this book.